FREDERIKA BRADFORD & CL MARIE

ISBN-13: 979-8-9859331-0-9 (paperback)

ISBN-13: 979-8-9859331-1-6 (eBook)

Library of Congress Control Number: 2022904864

Cover designed by MiblArt

Edited by Frederika Bradford & Jessica Flaherty

Publisher: Frederika Bradford

www.frederikabradford.com

Max Bet

Frederika Bradford

& CL Marie

Chapter One

♣

Sneakers slapped pavement as Grayson Lee enjoyed a morning run along the seaside. Half the shops along the boardwalk were open, early rising tourists snapping photos across the Atlantic, setting up camp in the sand, or stumbling from a casino. His playlist switched tracks to a slower, more purposeful beat with roots in '90s dance music. He grinned to himself, but it wasn't over the newest song.

Grayson's pace slowed to meet the change in tempo. His attention rested squarely on the nicely rounded backside of a waitress as she wiped down a tabletop just outside open cafe doors. He slowed to a walk, eyes lowering along the length of her only to finish the return trip to meet her unamused stare.

Tugging the headphones from his ears, Grayson asked amidst a few lungfuls of air. "What're you…a size six?"

Catching a sigh before it could leave her lips, the young woman balled up a damp rag and brushed a loose tendril of caramel blond hair from her cheek with the back of her wrist. Sometimes, it was difficult to maintain a modicum of professionalism. It was also a struggle to land a job on the infamous island during the busy summer tourist season, and she was walking a thin line keeping herself employed as it was. The last thing Laurel Price wanted, or needed, was to get another warning from her boss regarding her inability to accept a bit of unsolicited male attention. It was part of the job, and part of the Atlantic City lifestyle, he'd said, as if she hadn't been born and raised there.

"Are you looking for a table, sir?" Laurel asked with a tight smile, ignoring his question. She gestured toward the table she'd just cleared. "Coffee, maybe?"

"Sounds good, but no." Holding an earbud, he gestured towards her. "You been waitressing long?"

As a bike whizzed past, he took another step closer and glanced to the canopy above the restaurant to note the name, Coastal Cafe.

"A while," Laurel confirmed, maintaining her pleasant expression as she moved to step around him. "Well, if you'll excuse me..."

Grayson blocked her path easily. "Hold up a sec." His dark brown eyes roamed her face at the new, closer proximity before he asked, "You good at it?"

"Why don't you have a seat, order something, and find out?" she recommended tightly.

Laurel held his gaze despite the uncharacteristic warmth pooling in her cheeks. She'd dealt with attractive men before, but his overconfident personality had her frustration defensively rising in equal measures.

"Espresso?" she pressed, keeping her blue eyes on his handsome, chiseled features. She silently begged him to stop looking her over, hating the smirk as it rose to his lips. "And how about a croissant with that?"

Grayson's grin grew. "Another time." Catching on that she was in no mood to humor his line of questioning, he extracted his cell phone from his pocket and produced a business card from a magnetic case. "I need an experienced waitress for seven to midnight tomorrow. Size six."

Laurel couldn't help her surprise at the job offer. She reached for the offered card and took a moment to skim the embossed black type. Nothing more than a name and a phone number.

"Grayson Lee," she read aloud. "Is this a business event?"

His hand teetered in the air, rolling one way and then the other at the wrist to suggest it wasn't exactly as she said. "It's legit," he assured simply, starting to back up. "At Borgata's."

Laurel considered the offer, unsure. A gig at Borgata Hotel & Casino sounded like good work, but they had staff for their events. However, money was money, and she was still a few thousand away from her ultimate savings goal.

"I can't be the only size six, experienced waitress you've come across," she challenged skeptically, holding up his card as he tucked his earbuds back into place.

Giving a casual shrug, Grayson turned to go. After a few strides, he turned back to add, "It's two hundred, plus tips," leaving her gawking after him.

At the end of the boardwalk, he sent the good news to a friend.

Grayson: You owe me — might have found a replacement for Cindy
Alaric: Forgive me for not thanking you, considering it was your fault she quit.
Grayson: You're welcome, bro

Chapter Two

♦

"What the hell are you scowling over?" Parker Campbell accused, raking a hand back through his mussed brown hair. Across from him, his long-time friend, practically his brother, looked murderous. Not that that was anything new.

Parker nodded toward the phone in his friend's hand. "Al, who was that?"

"Gray," came the reply through a low grunt. "Making sure to piss me off before my morning shit," he explained and finished off the last of his coffee before standing.

Parker leaned his chair back onto its two hind legs. His eyes crinkled with mirth behind a pair of Ray-Ban aviators. "Ah. Of course." Grayson was always stirring up trouble, fulfilling a sort of younger brother role despite no blood relation.

The trio came in and out of one another's lives, traveling as work required, but they'd grown into a chosen family of sorts over the years. Of the three, Alaric Nacario had always maintained the position of older brother, with the weight of the world on his shoulders. He was the most reliable, the hardest worker, and was the most in need of a vacation.

A spread of half-empty plates and various forms of glassware were still laid out on the tabletop between them, the evidence of an expensive breakfast. As an operations manager at Borgata Hotel & Casino, these sorts of meals were the norm for Alaric. As a businessman and casual high-stakes gambler, they were normal for Parker Campbell, too.

"Gray does have that habit, doesn't he?" Parker grinned, the faintest trace of an Australian accent in his voice. "He on his way back?"

Alaric swiped his wallet and cell from the table. "Do I look like his mother?"

Parker was unphased. Since grad school, Alaric had had a hot button temper.

Alaric rolled his head on his neck, the tension easing slightly. "Stop by the event later," he suggested to his friend. "Bring the home-wrecker if you catch up with him."

♥ ♠ ♦ ♣

"Can I get a smile with my service, please?"

Sadie Bache watched the familiar blonde behind the pastry case as her Danish was retrieved, the smirk on her lips conveying the humor behind her words. "Care to share, hon?"

Laurel's lips lifted into a tired smile. "Oh, hey."

"Take a break?" Sadie suggested. Over the past couple of weeks, she had regularly made it to Coastal Cafe, and they had become easy acquaintances.

"You know, I'm still not quite sure what keeps you coming back to this place," Laurel confessed as she bagged Sadie's order. A glance at the few occupied tables confirmed the other patrons looked content enough that she could spare a few minutes.

"Weird morning," Laurel confessed as she poured herself a cup of coffee and joined Sadie at one of the bistro tables.

Sadie sipped her macchiato with a content hum. "Okay, caffeine ingested. Now define 'weird,'" she prompted and swept her unruly mass of long, dark waves off her shoulders.

Laurel experienced a short moment of intense envy. Sadie was not only beautiful, but she also carried herself with confidence and was extremely charismatic. She dressed immaculately, was successful, and oozed sex appeal. If Laurel was being honest with herself, she probably had something of a girl crush on the woman.

Laurel took a deep breath and reached into the front pouch of her waist apron. She set Grayson Lee's business card on the glass tabletop and slid it over.

"This guy was out running the boardwalk this morning and asked if I'd wait tables at some private event," she explained. "At Borgata's."

After a pause of interest, Sadie lifted the card. "Grayson Lee," she read. She turned over the card a couple of times, underwhelmed. "It's just a name and number," she observed.

"Yeah," Laurel confirmed, her suspicions high.

Joining the wait staff of Borgata's sounded like a great opportunity, but Sadie was reading from Laurel that there was more to it. Grinning, she asked, "Was this private event in his hotel room, by any chance?"

Laurel couldn't help the laugh that bubbled up as she took back the card. "God, probably," she muttered, running a thumb along the embossed lettering.

"I'm not even considering it, really, but he said it was two hundred. Plus tips."

After a pause, Laurel confessed, "Okay, maybe I'm considering it."

Sadie's brows lifted, revealing even more of her dark green eyes. "Sounds a little too good to be true. Because this," Sadie paused to extend a manicured finger to flick the offending card, "is shady."

Laurel deflated. She couldn't help it, she wanted it to be legit. Sadie seemed older, early thirties to Laurel's upper twenties, and she was inclined to trust her friend's instincts.

However, Sadie surprised her by offering, "You know, I'm staying at Borgata's. Need a wingwoman?"

Laurel chewed at the corner of her lip to curb a smile. Two hundred dollars was two hundred dollars, no two ways about it. She was nodding before she'd decided to accept.

"I guess I'll be giving Mr. Grayson Lee," she emphasized in an amused tone, "a call then."

Chapter Three

♠

After a shower, breakfast, and a leisurely perusal of the local paper, Grayson found himself wholly bored. It was a common side effect of his lifestyle and one he suffered from quite frequently.

For a professional gambler like Grayson Lee, casinos were his office, not a fun-filled escape. The amenities were nice enough; great view, minibar, pool, spa, and room service, but they had lost most of the glitz and glam over the six years he'd been playing. When he'd started, at twenty-six, he'd loved the lifestyle. At thirty-two, he rarely felt excitement in his day-to-day.

When his phone rang, he hopped up to answer it. "Parker," he sighed in relief. "Save me you big, handsome wallaby."

A genuine laugh was the half-Australian's reply. Although he'd spent less than a third of his early life down under, Parker's native-Australian mother had influenced his intonation and vocabulary just as much as his American father. The accent came and went, but alcohol and shameless flirting almost always made it more prominent.

"Sounds like someone got an early start today," Parker noted, checking his designer wristwatch as he navigated the hallways of Borgata Hotel. "Only you could manage to piss Al off before eleven AM."

"Come on, Park, you know I'm an overachiever." Grayson was already heading for the door. "Which bar can I find you at?"

"Funny," Parker smirked. "Meet me in the lobby."

Grayson was thankful for the rescue. The life of a professional gambler brought him to Atlantic City often, and Alaric could usually only handle him for short periods of time.

Just outside Borgata's entrance, Parker lit a quick cigarette. His plan was to rope Grayson into a short shopping excursion to The Walk, a cluster of nearby retail stores. While he waited for his ride, he observed an Escalade limousine emptying a string of young women in skintight outfits, clustered around a man that looked twice Parker's thirty-two years of age. He observed with an amused smile, catching the eye of more than one of the young women.

Parker gave a start when Grayson clapped him on the back.

"I'm yours until nightfall," Grayson announced.

"Oh, goodie," Parker replied dryly, disposing of his barely touched cigarette.

Towards the manicured landscaping, a town car pulled through the valet area. Parker led the way, approaching their ride for the day. However, as he pulled open the back door, he was greeted by a pair of long, attractive, unexpected legs.

Apparently, this was not their ride.

Parker's sunglass-shaded gray eyes trailed upward to see a manicured hand extended, awaiting assistance. He paused to take in the green eyes, the dark silken curls, and the smirk that formed on painted lips.

"Are we helping or are we staring?" she prompted.

Parker's brows popped and he offered a lopsided smile, along with his hand. "Sorry, doll. Thought this was my car."

Sadie Bache's eyes sparkled with amusement as she realized the handsome stranger was not a valet, but a guest of the hotel and casino. She tucked a clutch beneath an arm, a loose camel colored coat draped over a flattering burgundy dress. Sadie stepped from the vehicle onto velvet pumps, pausing to give him a proper once-over. His suit was pressed, his hair lightly styled, and his accent wasn't lost on her, either.

He kept a hand in hers, removing his sunglasses with the other. It wasn't often someone caught Parker Campbell's interest so effortlessly.

Behind the pair, Grayson assessed the town car. "Not ours, then?"

Keeping his attention on the vision in front of him, Parker replied, "Can't say I'm disappointed."

With a light laugh, Sadie pulled her hand free and retrieved a pair of sunglasses from her hair. "Well, I don't like to share," she said, managing a wink before her green eyes were hidden by dark glass. "If you'll excuse me."

A member of hotel management was quick to materialize beside her. "Ms. Bache, lovely to have you again. I apologize I wasn't on-site last week to welcome you."

Parker stared after the woman as she went, his smile broad.

Grayson pulled on his arm, a playful whine in his voice. He knew he stood a good chance of losing his friend to this mystery woman. "Hey. No. We have plans, Park. Focus."

Parker's grin was a fixed accessory on his face. Apparently, if he'd heard correctly, this woman was Ms. Bache. Not Mrs. Bache. *Miss* Bache. Unmarried didn't necessarily mean available, but it was enough to give Parker hope.

"That ours?" Grayson asked, pulling Parker's attention to an identical town car rolling up the drive.

The pair of friends slid into the correct vehicle and Parker gave the driver information on where they were headed.

"Shopping?" Grayson asked, shocked. "We're not even drunk yet."

"I need new dress shirts," Parker laughed. "We can get drunk after. You said you were bored." Even as they pulled away, he couldn't help but watch as Ms. Bache disappeared through the front doors of the hotel.

As if the reminder of his boredom brought about a wave of sadness, Grayson slumped. "I'm expecting a tournament invitation out west, but the wait is brutal, bro."

Parker nodded in understanding. His lifestyle had low points, too. "The old man wants me to report back to the Manhattan office in a couple of days," Parker explained. "He needs me involved in shareholder meetings for Q2 results."

The business world was not one Grayson understood, but he respected both Alaric and Parker's chosen professions. Alaric Nacario had worked his way up to a senior level role at Borgata Hotel & Casino, and Parker Campbell had managed to walk a line between helping with the family business and striking out on his own. They both worked harder than Grayson did, and Grayson knew it.

"Think you'll be back this way after that?"

"Maybe."

Parker was used to a balanced life of leisure. When he was asked to consult or support the investment firm the previous generations of Campbells had built, he did what he could. He was lucky he wasn't pressured into a nine-to-five situation, and he balanced that work with his interest in professional gambling. It afforded him the finances to fund a lifestyle many desired.

Grayson ran a hand through his head of light brown hair and offered, "If you can push your trip a week out, I'll bet Al could line up a game uptown."

"Wish I could," Parker sighed. "I'm not the one calling the shots."

"Well, I'll see what he can do anyway. If you're still out there in a week or two, we'll save you a seat."

Parker nodded, already looking forward to the idea. "So, what happened this morning, anyway?" he asked, his attention on Grayson. "Al didn't say."

Looking somewhat guilty, Grayson launched into an explanation. "Alaric might have lost a waitress and it might have been my fault."

The car filled with laughter.

"Seriously, mate. You just can't keep your hands out of the cookie jar."

Grayson was quick to add, "In my defense, she never said she had a fiancé."

"As if you would have asked," Parker smirked.

Parker had him there. Grayson couldn't help himself.

"So how are you fixing this mess?" the older man asked.

Although his mystery, size-six waitress had yet to formally accept his proposal, Grayson was confident she would come around to his inflated offer.

"I've got a line out on a replacement."

Chapter Four

♥

Laurel slipped through the back door of the cafe on her mid-afternoon break. The business card she'd been given earlier that morning was burning a hole through her pocket. Was she making a mistake in accepting the too-good-to-be-true offer? Maybe. Was it worth the risk? Also, maybe. Those odds were good enough for her. Deciding to carpe diem and all that, Laurel carefully keyed in the number. She trusted her senses enough to know that she would jump ship if necessary.

"You've got Grayson."

Laurel froze at the sound of his voice, her gaze out over the ocean as her jaw worked. Hearing his arrogance, even in his simple introduction, had her irritation rising.

Grayson was glad for the distraction from the task at hand: picking out tie and shirt combinations for Parker.

"I'll do it for three hundred," Laurel blurted out, surprising herself with a counteroffer to his original job opportunity. "Plus tips, of course."

After a beat, Grayson replied with humored interest, "That's fabulous, darling. Now, before you slap me for assuming what you're referring to, mind filling me in?"

Laurel's eyes fell shut in a mixture of frustration and embarrassment. Warmth crept up her neck and her eyes reopened to glare out at the rolling surf.

"I guess you solicit women for more than just waitressing gigs. Interesting."

A slow grin tugged at Grayson's lips. He'd had a hunch, but now it was clear that this was the attractive woman from the boardwalk that morning.

"I'm wounded," he replied. "But the rate is two, like I said."

"Plus tips, of course," he belatedly echoed.

"Two-fifty," she countered, "For travel expenses."

Parker arched a brow at the laugh his friend barked out behind him. He gave him a curious look, and Grayson mouthed, "the replacement."

To Laurel, he replied, "Sweetie. The gig was one-fifty, but I offered two due to the last-minute nature of this job. You want to haggle? Go to a yard sale."

It took considerable effort for Laurel to school her reaction to the condescending nickname and tone. She'd known this man a collective five minutes and already he was insufferable. Fortunately, Laurel had the good sense to pick her battles.

"I suppose that's fair," she said in a sugary sweet tone, perfected by years of working in the service industry.

"Fantastic," Grayson replied, giving Parker a thumbs up over the color combo he was currently considering. "Seven o'clock tomorrow at Borgata's. Room eleven-seventy-two. Black stockings, black heels, hair in a bun."

She supposed that was all she needed and welcomed the opportunity to end the call. "See you then."

When the line went dead, Grayson stared down at the phone in his hand, his grin practically splitting his face.

"Replacement, huh?" Parker mused as he handed over a black American Express card to a saleswoman. "Cute, I hope."

"Size six," Grayson grinned. "Just my type."

♥ ♠ ♦ ♣

The next day, an hour before her mysterious catering gig, Laurel stepped into Borgata Hotel's lobby. She'd arranged to meet with Sadie in her suite prior to the job, to change her outfit and game plan an exit strategy. She adjusted the duffel bag on her shoulder, which carried her makeup and clothing.

Laurel had only set foot inside the high-end hotel once or twice, though never to gamble; thankfully, she hadn't inherited that trait. Still, she couldn't help but envy the luxury around her. Laurel knew it paled in comparison to Las Vegas, or at least that's what she'd been told, but Borgata Hotel & Casino was the most popular spot in Atlantic City. There were suites that cost thousands and restaurants and spa services that cost hundreds. It was a lifestyle she would never understand; Laurel still lived with her alcoholic mother and was known to stretch groceries past their 'best by' date.

Locating the bank of elevators, Laurel shared a ride with a handsy couple up to the twenty-third floor. As she approached Sadie's suite, she realized there were a lot fewer doors on this level.

Sadie greeted her with an exuberant smile. "Hey, hot stuff."

"Hi," Laurel laughed, following her inside to witness the grandeur of a Borgata

Hotel suite first-hand. Dropping her bag to a chaise lounge, she muttered, "God, I want your life."

"It has its moments," Sadie smiled, moving over to the wet bar to pour them each a glass of wine. "So, tonight's the big night. Are you nervous?"

Distracted by the expansive accommodations, Laurel paced the room. The suite was about the size of her mother's entire house. It seemed to have all the comforts of home, and through an open door she spied a jacuzzi big enough for at least two.

"Well," Laurel began, regaining her bearings, "Considering the guy who gave me the job is an absolute charmer…" she muttered, sarcasm thick.

Sadie handed off a glass and led them out to a private balcony, where they took up residence on a pair of cushioned wicker chairs. "Cheers. To a potentially dangerous, but lucrative evening."

Laurel tapped their glasses together, immensely grateful for the alcohol. It would help take the edge off, at least.

Sadie sipped and swirled. "Tell me more about Mr. Charming."

"Ugh," Laurel groaned. "He's one of those self-important, overly confident, turns-everything-into-a-joke types. He definitely believes every woman on the planet wants to sleep with him."

Sadie's brows lifted curiously. "Maybe they do."

Laurel glared at Sadie's growing smile. "No."

"No?"

"No. I don't go for guys who notice my dress size *and comment on it*," Laurel laughed.

Sadie only shrugged as if it wasn't the worst thing she'd heard.

"And he called me sweetie. Like he was talking to a child," Laurel added for good measure. "Extremely condescending."

Sadie continued to say nothing, allowing Laurel the space to get it all out.

"No," Laurel repeated, firmly. "I don't care how good-looking he is."

Feeling accomplished, Sadie smirked. Laurel's rant had supplied Sadie with more than sufficient evidence. "He's good-looking, huh?"

Before Laurel could argue, Sadie playfully added, "Maybe you *are* hoping this private event is just the two of you."

Defeated, Laurel gave into her new friend's teasing with a laugh. "Not for only two hundred dollars, I'm not."

♥ ♠ ♦ ♣

In suite 1172, Grayson arrived to find his best friend and organizer for the evening, Alaric Nacario, already ready to pick a fight.

"You're lucky I invited you tonight, Gray."

"Still sore about that, are you?" Grayson mused, sweeping the suite to take in its modified appearance. The typical living room furniture had been removed and instead there was a card table circled by five high-backed chairs. "Let it go, already. I got you the replacement."

"Your girl's a no-show," Alaric informed. "I've got one fucking waitress for tonight," he said, gesturing to an adjoining bedroom where Grayson assumed said waitress was changing. Normally, one waitress would have been fine for this sized get-together, but he had one of his high, high rollers attending that he needed to impress.

Tiredly, Grayson dropped his eyes to his heavy timepiece. "Al. It's not even seven."

In the empty hallway, Laurel steadied her breathing and smoothed down the front of her fitted skirt. Sadie had helped Laurel achieve a flawless, neutral look with a satiny red lip. Her hair, stockings, and heels were all to Grayson's specifications and she played it safe with a plain white, tailored Oxford.

As the doorbell chimed, Alaric opened the door to reveal the young woman. He breathed something of a relieved sigh and muttered, "Well, thank God." He stepped back to give her room and instructed, "Bedroom's on the left. You can change in there."

Laurel's steps didn't falter, but she was confused. What exactly was she expected to change into? She gave Alaric a small smile, following his gesture towards the bedroom. She felt relief as she spied a couple of people scattered throughout the hotel room and took comfort in the fact that this seemed to be a genuine job opportunity after all.

Grayson's gaze fell on the back of their newest arrival as she crossed the suite. She had yet to spot him, and he grinned as Alaric rejoined his side.

"Told you so."

Within the bedroom, Laurel was greeted by a young woman around her own age.

"Oh, hey," she said, gesturing to the remaining outfit laid out on the bed. "That's yours, I guess. I'm Stacy."

They shook hands before Stacy pointed towards the main area. "I should start serving."

Laurel nodded, her attention lingering on the remaining black cocktail dress. It was a bit shorter than her current skirt, but all things considered it wasn't terrible. Holding up the tasteful yet revealing dress at arm's length, Laurel let a dry laugh slip at the glaring "6" printed on the tag. Thankfully, for both her and Mr. Grayson Lee, it fit perfectly. The plunging neckline was sure to score her some healthy tips, too. She checked her reflection in the full-length mirror, gathered her mental strength, and ventured back out to the sitting area. By then, all the players had arrived and taken their seats.

Laurel made a beeline for the bar in the corner of the room to see how she could best help Stacy. She still hadn't been given any specifics, but it was clear she was meant to be a cocktail waitress for the evening.

"Gentlemen," Alaric began, resting his hands on the backs of Grayson's and another player's chairs. These were well-known, familiar players that required no introductions amongst them. "Our game tonight is seven-card stud."

Alaric commenced with simple house rules, including a declaration of a five hundred dollar buy-in. Once the formalities were out of the way, he managed a small smile. "Now, let's make some change."

A metal briefcase was set on a nearby surface and Alaric entered a combination on the handle. It opened to reveal orderly rows of chips in various denominations. "Grayson?" Alaric prompted.

At the bar, Laurel's head whipped around. She hadn't checked to see if he was in attendance. In all honesty, once a different man had opened the door, she wondered if Grayson Lee would even be present that evening.

Grayson's attention was trained on the wait staff, and he grinned when Laurel finally took note of him. He took in her appearance, pleased to see she cleaned up extraordinarily well.

"Grayson."

Turning back to Alaric, Grayson produced a handful of large bills and exchanged them for chips. Once he was set, he requested, "How about we get that liquor flowing?"

Alaric looked up to see Stacy pouring martinis. He asked of Grayson, "What's your girl's name?"

After a beat of hesitation, Grayson grinned.

"Six."

Without even questioning it, Alaric called over, "Six, please get Mr. Lee something to drink."

At first, Laurel didn't react. However, she noticed that Stacy wasn't reacting, either. Jaw tensing, realization dawned on Laurel.

"Oh, no he didn't..." she grumbled to herself.

Taking a slow breath to keep calm, Laurel turned to offer a smile of acknowledgement. There was no doubt that the nickname had been Grayson's handiwork. Grayson, who hadn't bothered with proper introductions when they'd first met.

"Of course," she replied as she crossed towards them. She had seen the cash buy-in these men were so casually exchanging for chips; it would be in her and her wallet's best interest to be sweet no matter how it grated on her every nerve.

Laurel approached the chair Grayson was seated in and, performing the part perfectly, held his gaze and asked, "What can I get for you, Mr. Lee?"

Grayson cracked his knuckles, smiling in amusement at her act. "What do you recommend, Six?"

"Something on the rocks?" she suggested, but then shook her head with a decisive smile as if reading him more accurately. "A bourbon Manhattan. Let me take care of that for you."

As she stepped away to fix him the drink, she let her hand trail subtly across his shoulders.

Grayson chuckled, keeping his eyes on her the entire time she fixed his beverage and started the return trip. He was enjoying her attitude very much, and was both interested in, and amused by, the sassy young woman.

Laurel set the drink down on a square napkin, turning to the man seated on Grayson's right. "Can I get you something to drink?"

The blond-haired man barely looked in her direction, rattling off a simple order. Before she left the table again, however, her attention flashed back to Grayson to note the amusement there.

At the small makeshift bar area, Laurel caught Stacy's attention with a whisper, "Do you regularly work these things?"

Stacy nodded. "Anytime I can," she confirmed, finishing off an extra dirty martini. "It's great. Real easy money." She slipped away to deliver the drink, and Laurel watched as she was tugged off her feet and into the lap of a man possibly twice her age.

Laurel couldn't help the way her eyes narrowed at the display.

When Stacy passed Laurel again, she offered an exaggerated eye-roll. "I know, I know, but I made six hundred in tips once. I mean, there were twice as many players, but I can't even make that much in a full shift at my other job, and I'm topless half the time."

CHAPTER FIVE

♣

Laurel wasn't so naive as to believe high rollers would be perfect gentlemen. She could handle a little objectification if she walked away with the sort of money Stacy had mentioned receiving for a few hours' worth of work. As the night progressed, and hand after hand moved chips around the board, quite a few in Grayson's direction, Alaric approached his newest hire.

"Six."

Laurel had caught onto the fact that this was the man in charge. After observing his interactions with the card players, she found him vastly more intimidating than any of the others present. Still, she wore a smile when she crossed to meet him.

"Yes?"

His assessment of her was brief and candid. She looked good, had a good attitude, and had gotten right to work.

"I might have more opportunities for you."

He handed over his business card. Unlike Grayson's, Alaric Nacario's was standard issue from Borgata Hotel & Casino. "Liquor them up, flirt, and keep them smiling," he requested.

Laurel had a feeling there was a compliment lost in there, somewhere. Although she hadn't gone looking for this job, Stacy hadn't been lying; it seemed like easy money. She even had a few chips stashed at the bar already to show for it.

Graciously, Laurel accepted the card. "Of course. Thank you." She noted his empty hands and offered, "Can I get you anything?"

"No," he replied, gesturing for her to head back to his players.

An hour or so later, Grayson realized he'd been ordering a few more drinks than normal to get the attention of a certain someone. The last few hands proved that he could stand to take a break.

"I fold," Grayson announced, pushing back from the table though he kept his seat.

"Really, Gray?" one of the players teased. "You're making this easy. That's not your style."

Grayson shrugged, catching Laurel's wrist as she passed behind him. "C'mere," he encouraged, drumming his fingers on his thigh.

Were it not for Alaric's mention of keeping her in mind for future work, Laurel might have rolled her eyes and walked right past. However, she wanted those future opportunities. Plus, Grayson hadn't contributed to her tips just yet.

Laurel didn't miss a beat as she carefully set herself onto his thigh with one arm draped loosely across his shoulders. "Bad luck tonight?" she asked, nodding toward the table. She could certainly pretend to like Grayson Lee, just for one night.

"No such thing," Grayson replied confidently. He held her gaze for a long moment, one hand around her back, the other settled on her knee. "You fit right in here," he told her. "I'm impressed."

She offered a demure smile, about to lean in and offer a cheeky retort. However, she was struck by the scent of his cologne, mingling with the scent of the bourbon she'd been serving him. It wasn't exactly a turn-off, and it was enough to cause her to quietly clear her throat. She decided she needed some space before she went along a little too well with the charade.

Noting his empty glass, she offered, "Would you like another Manhattan?"

"Get Stacy to make it," he requested, unwilling to give up his company just yet.

Laurel cleared her throat. Gently, her fingers skirted the nape of his neck as she replied, "She can't make them like I can." Without waiting for a response, she lifted her weight from his lap. "Sit tight." She praised herself on her flawless performance and willed the start of a blush to fade.

Grayson groaned, earning a few chuckles from the other members at the table.

When she returned and handed over a refill, Laurel escaped his attempt to pull her back into his lap by offering her attention in another way. She stepped behind Grayson's chair and slid her hands onto his shoulders. Gently, she began to work her hands against his neck in a slow massage.

"Oh, now wait just a second..." another player laughed, tossing his cards face-down onto the table. "I fold too, pretty lady." He slid a green chip from his pile and held it up knowingly. "Come on over here."

If Grayson planned to keep her attention, he was going to have to compete for it. Slow steps carried Laurel to the other side of the table, and she positioned herself behind the other player instead. As her hands began to move, she couldn't help but meet Grayson's stare for just a moment.

"Stacy," Laurel called as her partner for the evening began to collect some empty glasses. "Would you please get this gentleman another martini?"

The man laughed, reaching up to put his hand atop one of Laurel's long enough to say, "It's Jack, sweetheart. Call me Jack."

"Jack*ass*," Grayson corrected.

"Fuck off," Jack laughed. "Don't be jealous, Gray."

Laurel drew in her lips to keep from smiling too widely. "Jack," she repeated, as if committing the name to memory. "Looks like you're doing well tonight." Again, her gaze flickered to Grayson. She couldn't seem to help herself.

Grayson smirked to himself as he pushed a purple chip to the center of the table to buy into the next hand. Jack was too cocky for his own good. With such high stakes, it was anyone's night this early on.

Throughout the evening, the flirtatious nature between Grayson and Laurel, who was still known to Alaric only as 'Six,' wasn't lost on him. Alaric waited until an opportune moment to pull her aside, when all glasses were full, and the players were engrossed in a hand with a particularly large pot.

"I have one rule," Alaric informed, battling frustration that he had to formalize such a thing. "And it's non-negotiable."

"All right," Laurel replied carefully. She wasn't sure where Alaric was going with this, but she could sense it was important.

He held her gaze for a long moment before nodding towards the card table. "If you want to work for me, Grayson's off limits."

Laurel's lips began to pull upward into a laugh, but she quickly schooled it. He wasn't kidding.

"I— yeah, of course," Laurel found herself stammering. "I'm just keeping everyone happy. Like you said," she assured.

Alaric gave her another scrutinizing look, which she sustained.

"Okay," he finally said. "So long as we're clear." His good friend had a track record of screwing his staff. Alaric saw the appeal; Grayson was rich, attractive, and fun-loving, but his friend could also be an asshole. Alaric was nearly his opposite, almost too devoted to his work. Try as he might, he couldn't help but be envious of his fun-loving friend. The fact that Grayson could gain the attention of any woman he wanted seemed like a gross miscarriage of justice.

Laurel nodded to confirm. "It won't be a problem."

"Helloooo," Jack called over in Laurel's direction, waving another green chip.

Laurel flashed him a smile and then looked to Alaric, waiting for confirmation that the embarrassing conversation was over.

♥ ♠ ♦ ♣

The hours passed, the chips moved, and soon Jack's cocky grin faded to a nasty snarl. He had stopped trying to win Laurel's attention and was instead focused on winning back what he'd lost. What was worse, he was taking his frustration out on her. Long gone were the smiles and generous tips. Now, he waved her away and grunted his discontent at the time it took her to refill his glass.

Grayson, on the other hand, kept his cool all night whether he was up or down.

By the final hand, however, Laurel noticed that Grayson hadn't tipped her or Stacy all evening. She hoped he was planning to do so before he left the room, or her opinion of him would become even worse.

"Last hand, gentlemen," Alaric announced.

Laurel took a moment to congratulate herself on making it through an interesting evening. She'd made a good first impression on Alaric Nacario, the evening's host, and had quite a few chips to cash in. Hopefully, Grayson would sweeten that deal, she'd get her pay, and go home richer than she would have for working a full weekend shift at the cafe. All in all, not a bad night.

She jumped at a particularly loud bark of laughter, turning to see Grayson clapping for himself.

"That's a wrap," the dealer proclaimed, gesturing to Grayson's hand to call the win.

The final game had a richer pot than most that evening; a desperate attempt for some to reclaim their losses. Chairs moved, the players began to cash out, and Laurel mimicked Stacy's pleasant smile as she lingered for any final tips.

"Thanks, ladies," one of the players said, tossing a black one-hundred-dollar chip to each of the waitresses.

Another did the same, though Laurel spied his hand lingering on Stacy's hip as the pair said good night. She wondered if they knew one another; from what she could see, Stacy didn't seem to mind the attention.

As the suite emptied, Alaric counted out three hundred dollars in cash and split it between the two women. Laurel lingered, recounting her share to find it short of what she expected. Unsure of what had been agreed upon with the other waitress, Laurel waited until Stacy went to change before speaking up. "Excuse me, Alaric? I was told tonight would pay two hundred."

Alaric paused in locking the briefcase containing the chips and cash from the evening. He said nothing for a moment before turning to Grayson.

"You promise her two hundred?"

"Yep."

"You know you're making up that extra fifty, right?"

"Yep."

Alaric turned back to her. "Well, there you go."

Laurel watched as Alaric moved to leave, suddenly nervous at the realization that she would be left alone with Grayson if she didn't hurry. However, Laurel sure as hell wasn't leaving without the rest of her earnings.

She stepped over to Grayson, arching her brows with an open palm. "I have an early shift at the cafe tomorrow," she excused her impatience, all pretense gone. She was no longer batting her lashes for him; the evening was over, as far as she was concerned.

Grayson gave her outstretched hand a short slap, grinning. "Nice work, Six," he praised. "You sure know how to make a guy feel special."

As she inhaled a breath and prepared to let him have it, Grayson pressed a chip into her still-extended palm. "Go on," he laughed. "Get out of here."

Laurel's fingers closed around the coin, forcing herself to swallow any retort. "Goodnight, Grayson."

Passing Stacy on her way to change with an exchange of goodbyes, Laurel tucked her handful of chips into her purse to cash out at the casino downstairs. It was only when she was buttoning up her Oxford that she thought to count her tips. She had two black chips, one hundred dollars each, and a handful of green chips, twenty-five each. Grayson had owed her fifty dollars, but she saw no light blue chip. Instead, there was one purple chip. She gasped when she read its printed monetary value.

Quickly, Laurel gathered the rest of her things and hurried back out to the sitting area, but the suite was empty; Grayson was long gone. She couldn't help the nervous excitement she felt as she rode the elevator down to the casino below. Thanks to Grayson's contribution of five hundred, Laurel was going home with just shy of a thousand dollars that night.

CHAPTER SIX

♦

The following morning, Grayson was once again on the boardwalk. This time, however, he was at Coastal Cafe even before his workout began. He caught Laurel's attention as he sauntered over, and she stood from wiping down a bistro table, looking less than pleased to see him. Grayson was mildly surprised to see hostility in her eyes.

He approached cautiously, laughing. "What?"

Laurel was quick to launch into an accusation. "Just what exactly were you trying to pull last night?" she asked, hand on her hip.

The expression he offered made him seem almost innocent, but Laurel wasn't buying it. "You owed me fifty last night," she reminded.

Grayson gave a slow nod, as if not comprehending her frustration. "And I paid you."

Lowering her voice so as not to be overheard, she stated, "You gave me *five hundred*, Grayson."

Not that she was planning to give him the chip back, of course. She'd already cashed it and deposited the money in her bank account that very morning. But still, she felt compelled to call him out.

After a beat, in an overly exaggerated movement, Grayson stumbled back with a hand to his head. "Oh, my God," he proclaimed. "I must be color blind."

Laurel stared at him, completely unaffected by his early morning humor.

"Hilarious," she deadpanned.

He waggled his eyebrows at her. "I thought so."

They now had the attention of the only occupied table in the cafe, and Laurel took Grayson's arm to pull him aside, closer to the boardwalk rail and the lapping water below.

"You tipped me four hundred fifty dollars," she explained unnecessarily.

"You're good at math," he observed.

"Oh my God, Grayson," she whined. "That's more than four times what anyone else tipped me."

"They're cheap. Look, Six, did you see how much I won last night?" he questioned. He had raked in a lot of purple chips, and he didn't look the least bit put out by the idea of over-tipping her.

She ignored the nickname, a small smile finally curving her lips. "You always get your way, don't you?" It had to have something to do with that grin of his. How many women had he been able to charm that way in the past?

"It's Laurel, by the way," she added.

He donned that shit-eating grin of his and repeated her name. "Gotta say, I kind of like Six better."

From across the boardwalk, a man barked her name, raising his hands in frustration.

"Sorry, Sam!" Laurel called over, giving Grayson a stern look. "Can you go, please? You're going to get me fired."

Grayson's amusement faded as he looked in the direction of the kitchen and the man watching them.

"Did you like working for Alaric last night?" he asked.

Laurel started walking backwards, shrugging. "Easy money," she offered, echoing Stacy's sentiments.

"Good." He gave a nod and started to walk in the opposite direction, casting another glance towards the kitchen on his way. "Same deal tonight at five."

Laurel's steps slowed. "T—tonight? I—" She couldn't quite get the words out, but Grayson was nearly out of earshot. She lifted a hand in defeat, giving him a thumbs up to confirm.

Laurel watched as Grayson replaced his earbuds and started jogging off down the boardwalk, her eyes trailing lower than she'd meant them to.

"Off limits, off limits," she muttered to herself, turning on her heels.

♥ ♠ ♦ ♣

That evening, Laurel arrived at Borgata Hotel & Casino a little closer to the actual call time. Now that she knew what to expect, and that it was indeed legit, Laurel felt more comfortable. She'd dressed casually and had packed a quick make-up kit and any hair products she'd need, assuming she'd once again be asked to slip into a cocktail dress.

She headed straight for the room to get ready, wanting her new employer to see that she took the job seriously. If she could be to Alaric Nacario what Stacy was, another on-call waitress, she could fulfill her savings goals and get the hell out of Dodge quicker than she'd ever thought possible.

As she rode the elevator, she sent a quick text off to Sadie:

Laurel: working another private event tonight. Same deal, same room. Can I maybe crash on your couch if it runs too late?

Laurel wasn't sure if she'd be able to keep her eyes open long enough to make it back home that night. The past twenty-four hours had taken a lot out of her, mentally and emotionally.

She arrived at room 1172 and knocked twice. Rather than Alaric this time, Grayson opened the door, all charm. "Good evening," he greeted, stepping back to allow her entry.

A few steps in, Laurel noticed that the room had been arranged back into its standard appearance, the card table removed. "Is tonight a different type of event?" she asked, also noting with growing suspicion that they were the only two present.

It had been underhanded, but Grayson had doubted that Laurel would have accepted the offer of a date. He had done the only thing he knew to guarantee her presence, which was to lie. Rather than admit that off-the-bat, Grayson tucked his hands into his pockets and gave a guilty smile.

"Grayson?" she pressed, alarm bells going off in her mind.

Slowly, he stepped closer, placing himself between her and the door, "So, funny thing…"

Laurel's hand immediately shot out, as if to ward him off or keep him back, her head quickly shaking. "Explain yourself. Right now."

Grayson had the good sense to look concerned at her reaction, taking his hands from his pockets to hold them up. He backed off and gave an uncomfortable laugh. "Wow. Sorry. I kind of saw this going another way."

"Another—?" she tried, exasperated. Was he serious? She huffed out a laugh, dropped her duffle, and gestured around the empty suite in disbelief.

"Don't freak," he replied, his hands still raised. "There's no game," he quickly offered up the truth. "I'm taking you out for Chinese."

Laurel's pulse was racing, but she did a quick assessment of the situation and decided that Grayson Lee was truly just a very idiotic, very immature man. She lifted her eyes toward the paneled ceiling, doing her best to subdue her rising anger.

"Let me get this straight. You lured me to a room under false pretenses to take me out to dinner. Do I have that right?" she squinted.

Grayson looked mildly ashamed, his brown eyes assessing her. "Well, when you say it like that…"

She gave a frustrated laugh. "Jesus Christ, you are insane."

The room was silent for a few moments, during which Grayson rightly kept the distance between them and didn't try to offer further excuses. Finally, he broke the silence by complimenting her appearance. "You look nice."

That seemed to break the spell she was under. The disbelieving, appalled spell that had rendered her speechless. "Grayson," she groaned. "You cannot *lure women…*" She became enraged that she even had to teach him this lesson, but after a long minute she seemed to deflate. It wasn't her problem that Grayson didn't know what proper behavior was or wasn't.

"You know what, I'm flattered. Really," she attempted, remaining where she stood. "But if there's no game, I shouldn't be here."

Grayson's eyes dropped to her hand, a quick confirmation that he hadn't overlooked a wedding band or engagement ring. While it wasn't unheard of for waitresses to remove their rings to increase tips, he hadn't noticed one at the cafe, either.

"Are you taken or something?"

Laurel rolled her eyes, but the hint of a smile pulled at the corner of her lips. She hated herself for it.

"A girl can't just be uninterested?" she challenged.

Grayson smirked, and she hated him even more, because his grin was becoming her weakness. Of course, he thought himself irresistible.

He reached back to open the door for them. "Come on, Six. We've got reservations."

Laurel reasoned, to herself, that she followed him only to escape the confines of the hotel suite, but the promise of a free dinner had her stomach rumbling hopefully. Alaric's only rule echoed in her head. In the elevator, she decided to draw the line. "This stops at dinner," she told him. "I'm serious."

"It's a little early to put the brakes on," he pointed out playfully.

"Don't get your hopes up," she added, crossing her arms. Her duffle bag was left in the suite, and though she didn't want to drag it along to dinner, she realized it was a mistake to leave it behind. It meant a guaranteed return trip to the room later. Laurel glared over at him, thinking that had probably been part of his plan.

As she stared, she realized then what he wore, and had a moment of feeling underdressed. It was ridiculous, considering she was on a date she hadn't agreed to in the first place, but a feeling she couldn't help. Grayson donned a blazer atop a dark gray t-shirt and jeans, and he somehow managed to look better than the many stiff suits occupying the restaurant when they arrived.

"Mr. Lee," the hostess greeted warmly. She ran a hand down her long blond braid while smiling his way. "You're early."

Grayson looked at Laurel beside him with an innocent smile. "Her fault."

Laurel muttered, "I can't believe you," over her shoulder as they were led to their table. She was feeling more and more inadequately dressed with each table they passed, and she tugged discreetly at the hem of her casual dress.

"Um, hi."

Halfway to their seats, Laurel turned to see a woman's hand on her elbow, and then Sadie's voice registered. She was smiling, looking mildly confused.

"I just got your text," Sadie said.

Relief flashed in Laurel's blue eyes as she welcomed Sadie's familiar face. "He ambushed me. There's no event tonight," she explained, uncaring that Grayson was standing directly beside her and hearing every word. "He doesn't seem to comprehend my lack of interest and wouldn't accept no for an answer."

Grayson's brows lifted in mild surprise at her boldness at having this conversation in front of him, and he turned his attention to Sadie to introduce himself. "Grayson Lee."

Sadie licked her lips, taking a moment to decide if she admired the guy or felt sorry for him. "Sadie Bache." Her brow wrinkled, as if just putting the name and face together, and she felt an inkling of recognition. "You're a card player."

Grayson nodded, giving her a similar assessing look. He recognized her name. "As are you."

They shook hands and Sadie began nodding, looking back to Laurel with a look of despair. "Best of luck with this one, hon."

Laurel's response was a simple, flat glare.

"Text me if you still want to crash later," Sadie offered, laughing as Laurel began steering Grayson in the direction the hostess had gone.

"But I completely understand if you have other plans!" Sadie shouted after them, unembarrassed.

Laurel, on the other hand, was turning a lovely shade of pink. "Shut up," she told Grayson before he could utter a word.

They settled down in a booth and Laurel spent a moment blanching over the menu. She would have never been able to afford this place for a casual dinner, and she was suddenly looking forward to spending some of Grayson's money. "Let's get a bottle of wine," she teased.

"Now you're speaking my language," he replied easily.

Laurel's attempt at a joke clearly backfired, and Grayson had the server recommending options before she could clarify.

Once their orders had been taken, Laurel found herself searching for something to discuss; something other than how full of himself Grayson was, or how he'd roped her into this evening. Thankfully, Grayson filled the silence first.

"You always live here? Atlantic City?"

"My whole life."

Her body language spoke volumes and Grayson deduced that she was less than thrilled with that fact.

"Can't wait to get out of here," she added.

That didn't surprise him. Unless you were addicted to gambling or the lifestyle fast money could afford, it wasn't a desired locale. "This date or this city?" he teased, his brown eyes alight.

She smirked. "Both. Bet you love it here, though. Seems like you do all right for yourself."

"Sometimes," Grayson replied truthfully. Gambling had its moments, but it was a lonely lifestyle all the same. "When you 'get out of here,' where are you headed?"

Without an ounce of hesitation, Laurel replied, "Manhattan."

"Typical," Grayson sighed. "Everyone always wants to go to the big city. I'm telling you, you'll be disappointed."

Undeterred, Laurel took a sip of water. "My mom never made it there, but I will."

Grayson sensed there was a lengthy backstory there, but he kept things light. "I've no doubt you will, Six."

"As soon as I've got enough money saved, I'm gone."

The mention of money being a motivating factor wasn't lost on Grayson.

The waiter appeared and showed off the wine label before uncorking the bottle, pouring them each a glass and leaving the bottle nestled in a bucket of ice.

Once they were alone again, Grayson inquired, "What if I were to bet you'd be in New York next week?"

Laurel's brows rose and she scoffed. "I would say you'd lose."

"Not permanently," he amended, waving off her skepticism. "Humor me. If you end up in New York next week, what would I win?"

Laurel considered it, trying to read beyond his expression. If he was planning something, like an invitation to New York for a weekend, Laurel knew she'd have a hard time refusing. It was the one place she'd always wanted to go, and where she ultimately wanted to live. An all-expenses-paid trip was something she could only dream of. Still, she was reminded of two important factors. First, Alaric had been very clear with her that she was not to get romantically involved with Grayson. Second, she wouldn't accept a trip out of the state with someone she barely knew and could barely stand to be around.

For now, she was happy lying to herself about that second factor.

Resolved that she wouldn't accept an invitation if he offered one, Laurel saw no way she could possibly end up in The Big Apple.

"That would be your call," she replied, referring to the 'prize.'

"Excellent answer," Grayson grinned.

CHAPTER SEVEN

♠

"So, I've never gambled before," Laurel announced midway through their meal.

Grayson pivoted his plate, pointing to his Szechuan chili chicken for her to try. "You're shitting me. How is that even possible?"

"Nope, not even a slot machine." Her laughter was genuine as she helped herself to his dinner. "My God, this is delicious."

"I vote we pop that cherry after dinner," Grayson announced, choking suddenly on a laugh as the waiter materialized to switch out their empty glasses.

"Definitely not," Laurel insisted, despite her smile. There was a very good reason she didn't gamble, and that reason was her roommate, her mother. "Besides," she reminded, "I told you this stops at dinner."

Grayson offered a groan in response. "You can't be serious."

Laurel set her cheek against her palm, watching him with a smug lift of her brows. "I said just dinner, Grayson."

"First off, Chinese food gets everyone in the mood. Second, you can use my money for your first gambling attempt," he added for good measure.

She scoffed aloud, shaking her head. "I can say with absolute certainty I have never been horny after Chinese."

As he grinned, mulling over her comment, Laurel debated the offer. It was an interesting idea, betting Grayson's money and watching it drain away. It would almost serve him right.

Laurel spun her wine glass by its base, considering. "Just one machine?"

"Or table," he offered.

Laurel weighed the possibility of getting addicted to gambling after trying a single game and found the odds low. Even if she won, she wouldn't be taking any of the money home.

"Or table," she agreed.

Grayson nodded, clearly pleased that he'd negotiated for more than just dinner. "Not the most exciting evening on record, but it'll do," he declared.

He settled the bill by charging it to his room and politely pulled out her chair. "Let's see what you're into."

Laurel smoothed the front of her jersey dress and laughed at his constant double entendres. She took a moment to find her balance, realizing it required a bit more concentration than expected. It was her own fault for suggesting they order a bottle of wine, but Grayson's fault for ordering Manhattans to see if they were subpar to Laurel's bartending skills.

He offered his arm, and she took it reluctantly, shooting him a playful glare. "Shut up."

They made their way to the casino floor where over three thousand machines and two hundred fifty tables created a tingling roar of excitement via melodic bells and whistles. The laughter and care-free nature of casinos was what had lured Grayson into card playing, initially. That and the money, of course. These days, he was less glamoured by the ever-flowing alcohol, extraordinary sums of money, or the travel. Now, it was just a job.

As they perused the tables, Grayson pointed out each game. "Don't rush into it," he advised, keeping Laurel's hand on his arm as they wove through the crowds. "This is a big decision."

"Please," she laughed, dryly. "They're all equally fixed so that the house wins."

He gave her a look. "Is that a direct quote from *Oceans Eleven*?"

Laurel ignored him. She stood by what she said, casinos were a form of entertainment that you paid to enjoy. They were not meant to be fair opportunities. Her mother had been playing for thirty years and no matter how many times she was up, she was down more than twice as often.

A particular cluster of machines caught Laurel's attention. There were diamonds glittering across an LED screen that stood five feet taller than the digital slots themselves. The flashing marquee's jackpot was just over four hundred thousand dollars. With a widening smile, she began to pull Grayson toward it.

"Oh, hell no," he laughed, pulling back against her hold. "No way."

Laurel turned those blue eyes of hers on him, looking hopeful. She didn't even need to utter a single word.

Grayson muttered his reluctance as he allowed her to pull him along, criticizing her choice. He reached into his jacket for his Borgata player's card, still hesitating. "You're sure about this?"

Seated on the cushioned stool, Laurel swiveled at her hips a few times. "I'm sure," she confirmed. It was a one-dollar slot machine, which she figured was a safe way to ease her into gambling.

"Amateur," he teased.

With some small amount of pain, Grayson placed his player's card into her palm. He showed her what to do and then gestured to the lit-up button declaring Max Bet. "Hit that first and then let 'er rip." For good measure he placed both his hands on her shoulders, leaning close. "Luck be a lady tonight."

Laughing, Laurel slapped the button and watched, overwhelmed, as the digital tumblers spun, chiming and pinging. She knew what slot machines did from plenty of movies, but it was different experiencing it in person. The roar of the casino floor, the smell of smoke in the air, and the feel of Grayson's warm palms on her shoulders all made an impression.

One at a time, the tumblers slowed to a stop, and a dozen digital-colored lines zigzagged across the screen in odd patterns. "Is that good?" she asked, looking back at him. It looked and sounded like she'd won something, at least.

"I'm no expert," Grayson grinned, leaning forward to point to the message display, "But I think you won four dollars."

Laurel's brows perked. "Four dollars? How much did I bet?"

"Good question," he praised, pointing out the Max Bet information in the instructions above her head. "Twenty-five dollars."

She swiveled, hand going to her mouth. "I'm— I'm so sorry," she quickly offered, gesturing to the two-foot-high dollar symbol above their heads. "This is supposed to be a dollar!"

He laughed, his tone reassuring. "It's fine. Max Bet increases your chances." He placed his hands back on her shoulders and turned her forward. "Come on, go again."

Looking much more hesitant than before, Laurel squirmed. Twenty-five dollars per bet? If she placed even a few more bets she would lose as much money as she'd earned at the cafe during her last shift.

Grayson sensed her unease and leaned forward to press the button himself. "The casinos pre-load my player card. It's fine, Six."

His words helped. She knew that high rollers were given benefits, and she took a deep breath as she attempted to read the zigzags herself this time. "What does any of this even mean?"

"No one knows," he reassured. "Just keep playing."

"Well, for twenty-five dollars a pop, I'd like to know what I'm doing," she contested, trying not to notice how good his hands felt.

Playfully, Grayson talked her through it. "You press this button over and over and hope you don't lose all your money."

Laurel smirked, but then after a particularly loud and long trill of alarms, she gasped and pointed at the credit meter. "Holy shit, holy shit!"

He hated to burst her bubble, but explained, "Sorry, but no. That's the number of credits on my card, not your winnings."

She calmed then but squinted at the display. "It says twelve thousand."

Grayson said nothing.

"Twelve thousand credits?" she practically shouted. "On a dollar slot machine, that's—!"

Grayson smirked. "You really are good at math."

"Okay, we're done here," Laurel told him, beginning to rise. There was no way the casino pre-loaded his card with twelve thousand dollars. That was his hard-earned money, and a lot more than she had in her bank account at the moment.

Grayson's hands remained firm, keeping her seated. "Have I told you the best part about gambling?" Grayson asked, hoping to smooth things over with a change of subject.

"Is it the twelve thousand dollars on your card?" she hissed.

Shaking his head, Grayson turned and greeted a cocktail waitress sporting a tray and a cup overflowing with tips. "Get you two some drinks?" she offered.

"Yes, thank you. A Manhattan and a dry martini with a twist."

"You got it," she winked, scribbling on a notepad as she continued down the row of slot machines.

"Grayson," Laurel whined, defeated at his confidence. "I told you, we're done. We had dinner and played a slot machine. The night's over."

Grayson leaned closer, combing his fingers through her hair as he reminded, "You have to have at least one free drink. It's a slot machine rite of passage."

She'd heard that the alcohol was free, to keep patrons liquored up and spending, but it was kind of neat to experience it.

"One drink," she stated firmly, pointing at him for good measure.

"On my honor," he agreed, swiveling her back to face the slot machine. "Just while we wait," he reasoned further.

With a sigh, Laurel dismissed the nagging discomfort with how freely Grayson spent his money. She spun thrice more, yielding a pathetic return each time, and shook her head in disbelief. "I just lost what I made last week at the cafe," she announced, leaning back against Grayson behind her. "Please. Take pity," she laughed, though made no move to slip from the stool.

"Wimp." Grayson leaned over Laurel's shoulder and punched Max Bet with the side of a closed fist. No dice. He did it again twice more in rapid succession and then the machine began to sing as the display tallied a sixty-two-dollar win.

Laurel looked thrilled, which inflated Grayson's ego quite nicely. "It's all in the wrist," he smirked.

"Sure," she humored. As if to prove him wrong, she mimicked his barbaric fist-punch to the machine. She sat in defeat as forty dollars in winnings was displayed. "You're unbelievable," she laughed, shoving him to rid him of a pleased smirk. "This is all based on probability and random odds."

"Wow, you sure know how to have a good time," he commented, raking back his light brown hair. He rotated her chair until she faced him, and just before he could say anything more, their drinks appeared.

She accepted hers, noting with some surprise that Grayson added a twenty dollar bill to the woman's tip glass.

"You know," Laurel told him when they were alone once more. "It defeats the purpose of 'free' if you pay more than the drinks are worth."

"But she'll remember us, and come by more frequently," he countered.

Laurel smiled, enjoying a few sips of her drink as she scanned their surroundings. There were women and men, all varying ages, all experiencing varying emotions. Overall, the room was vibrant with excitement and laughter. Even those who were yelling at the machine seemed to be doing so with playful exuberance. However, it wasn't always like this. Laurel knew that if she were here on a weekday afternoon the mood would be different. Desperate. And that sobered her.

"I should probably get going."

Although he expected it, her decision to depart was disappointing. "I'll walk you up," he agreed.

Laurel was thankful he didn't argue further and accepted the offer. Yet as they crossed towards the elevators, she noticed Grayson's steps slowing beside a green felted table. She knew enough to know what roulette was, though she'd never played.

"Grayson…" she warned.

"Literally two minutes," he told her, reaching into his jacket for his wallet. "We place one bet, win or lose."

She was starting to panic. He must have already spent close to six hundred dollars that evening between dinner and gambling. "Come on, I really don't want to keep blowing your money," she pleaded.

Grayson peeled off a hundred-dollar bill and exchanged it for chips at the table. "Live a little, Six."

Grinning, he reached out as bets were being placed and set down all four chips. One, he placed directly on the number six, others on the corners above and below, and the last on that row. He had a hundred dollars riding on the number six, in the most ways possible.

"Let's see if I'm getting lucky tonight," he grinned.

Laurel wasn't sure why some chips were off-center and others weren't, but she caught the gist that he was betting on the number that had become her nickname. She shoved him gently, her blue eyes tracking the glossy white marble as it skipped and stuttered over the slowing wheel. For a heart-stopping moment, Laurel honestly thought their luck had been miraculous.

"Nine," the dealer announced.

Laurel realized how close they'd come and laughed in disbelief. She watched as chips were slid across to Grayson and her brow dipped. "You won something?"

"I split six and nine," he informed, grinning. "Odds were seventeen-to-one."

His math was faster than hers. He leaned down to whisper beside her ear, "Four twenty-five."

Laurel was left dumbstruck. In literally two minutes Grayson had taken a hundred dollars and more than quadrupled it.

"You're drooling," he teased, sliding a warm hand around the curve of her side. "Let's cash out."

An unexpected shiver danced along Laurel's spine at his touch, and she was nodding before she caught herself. His arm stayed firmly around her while they stood in line together. Grayson's lips appeared to be permanently affixed beside her ear. "Do you get the hype now?" he asked curiously.

Honestly, she did. Those moments while she waited for the wheel to stop spinning had been drenched in anticipation, and the excitement of finding out Grayson had not only won, but won a good amount, per her standards, had left an impression. Unfortunately for her, it wasn't necessarily a good one. She felt like she understood her mother more, and she pitied her.

"Next, please," the clerk called.

The pair stepped forward and Grayson set the chips on the counter. "Large bills, please."

Suddenly, Laurel was aware of how low his hand had slipped against her back. She hated how easily his touch commanded her attention. As the cashier counted out bills, Laurel disengaged herself from Grayson's side. "I'll meet you at the elevator," she said, slipping away before he could question it.

She decided to go the long way through the lobby to clear her head. Despite the cool air conditioning being pumped throughout the hotel and casino, her skin felt warm and flushed.

"Six."

She turned at the sound of her name, dismayed to see the one person she had been hoping to avoid.

CHAPTER EIGHT

♥

Alaric stood with an iPad resting in his open palm, distracted. He'd spied Laurel and approached but thought nothing of her presence at Borgata Hotel. "Good running into you," he said. "I've got something in the mix for Monday. How does a lunch shift sound?"

Laurel glanced behind her, praying Grayson wasn't on her heels. "Yeah, sure. I can do that, I think." She tried her best to sound as calm and professional as her currently tipsy state would allow.

Alaric glanced up, brow tense. "A yes or a no, if you don't mind."

Laurel cleared her throat. "Sorry, yes. Definitely. Thank you for the opportunity."

Alaric's eyes lingered on her for a long moment. "You're welcome," he finally replied. She looked jumpy, but he didn't think to pry. "I'll need your number."

"My number," she repeated dumbly, nodding. "Of course."

As she fumbled for her phone, her mind began to race, formulating plausible excuses if Grayson came wandering over with his foot in his mouth. She couldn't lose this job opportunity with Alaric. It was more money than she could possibly earn while clothed.

"Your number," he repeated.

Laurel looked up to find he was poised to take her number on his tablet, and she laughed, nodding. "Right, sorry." She rattled it off, stealing another momentary glance around for any sign of her unbidden date.

"It's not a game, just lunch," Alaric explained.

"Sure," she replied, taking a hopeful step towards the elevators. "I'll just wait to hear from you then?" she asked.

Ignoring the social cue for ending their conversation, Alaric checked the time and asked, "Have you eaten?"

For a fraction of a second, Laurel was flattered. Was he about to suggest they get dinner together? She hadn't seen that coming a mile away.

"I just did, actually," she explained, looking somewhat apologetic.

Alaric cleared his throat and nodded, but before he could complete the turn, Grayson was there.

"Hey, Al," Grayson grinned, clamping a hand on his friend's shoulder. His attention shifted to Laurel conspiratorially before back to his friend. "I just cleaned you out, I'm afraid," he teased, gesturing over his shoulder in the direction of the casino.

Laurel was quick to spin her own narrative for the evening. "Mr. Lee, right?" she asked, acting surprised to cross paths with the off-limits card player in front of her new boss.

Grayson's expression turned wry, but he played along. "That's right."

Ignoring the awkwardness, Alaric eyed his friend. "Blackjack?" he guessed.

"Nah," Grayson replied, still keeping an eye on Laurel. "Roulette."

"Couldn't have been that much, then," Alaric commented, eyes back on his screen as a notification drew his attention downward.

Grayson used the opportunity to shoot Laurel a short curious look.

"I've actually got to head up to a friend's room," Laurel excused with a smile, stepping away. "I'll see you, Mr. Nacario."

Distracted by his device, Alaric failed to reply.

"I'll see you," Grayson echoed to Alaric, excusing himself as well. He received the same disinterested silence and jogged to ensure he caught the elevator with Laurel.

"Start talking," Grayson instructed, amused.

Laurel shook her head, saying nothing until they were behind closed elevator doors. She glanced at the other occupant and lowered her voice, embarrassed. "He asked me to follow one rule if I want to keep working for him."

It wasn't hard to guess what Alaric had required, but Grayson was going to enjoy forcing her to say it. Grinning, he guessed, "You have to pretend you keep forgetting my name?"

She glared. "I have to pretend we didn't just have dinner together."

Grayson offered an overdramatic sigh. It was clear that Alaric had made Laurel promise to keep away from him, and that news only made him more pleased with the fact that he'd managed to take her out that night. Grayson pressed a closed fist to the mirrored wall of the elevator behind her, leaning closer. "And yet here you are."

There was a quiet chime as the elevator came to a stop on the eighth floor, letting off the last remaining occupant. The doors slid shut and Laurel scooted out from beneath Grayson's weight.

"Don't remind me," she muttered, brushing her fingers through her blond hair.

His knuckles slid from the cool glass, and he pocketed his hands, stepping up beside her so their hips touched. “You do realize it’s not even eight o’clock.”

With no windows in the casino, that fact hadn’t registered. Either way, it didn’t matter to Laurel. “And you remember I said this stops at dinner,” she reminded pointedly.

They reached their desired floor and Laurel stepped off first, ignoring how flushed she felt in response to his idle flirtations.

In the hallway, trailing just behind, Grayson confessed, “You know, I would be completely okay with just going down on you.”

Laurel’s steps faltered and she reached out to steady herself on the wall, turning to stare back at him in disbelief. Had he seriously just made that statement aloud? Despite her best efforts, Laurel couldn’t control the pitch of her next breath or the way her throat suddenly seemed too dry to speak. She watched him close the distance, felt his hands settle just above her hips.

Staring up at him, Laurel began to slowly shake her head. “You’re off-limits, Grayson,” she managed in a wavering voice.

He tipped his head forward, lips against her cheek. “That’s what makes it so exciting,” he breathed.

They were steps away from their destination, room 1172, and Laurel’s breath began to grow heavy with the consideration of his offer.

Reading her hesitation, Grayson slipped his hand into Laurel’s and guided her the few final doors down the hall. Laurel was silent as she followed, swallowing a whimper as he passed the room key over the keypad to gain entry. Once inside, Laurel kept walking, straight towards her duffle bag.

“Six...” he chastised, shaking his head with an ever-present grin. “Do you honestly think you’re leaving?”

She turned to find him blocking the door and bit her tongue. “If I want to leave, I’m leaving,” she told him, but her resolve was shaky at best. She wanted to demand that he stop looking at her like that, but she couldn’t form the words.

Grayson stepped closer. “I’m not going to stop you,” he assured, reminded of how poorly she’d responded to being lured under false pretenses. “I just want you to consider letting me have what I want.”

She laughed at that, outraged. “You’ve been getting what you want all night, Grayson!”

“And you’ve been having a good time,” he countered.

Laurel looked away. He wasn’t wrong, and he had to know the effect he was having on her. If he didn’t, he would have given up by now.

Grayson sensed her hesitation and took advantage of it. “Am I wrong?”

Her breath was getting harder to catch by the moment. “No, but I told you. Alaric said—”

Her excuse was bullshit, and his expression conveyed his feelings on the matter. “Unless you tell him, Al won’t find out,” he assured, brows lifting as if to await her next excuse.

Thankfully, there was none. Laurel licked her lips, eyes roaming his cocky features, weighing the pros and cons of the situation.

Considering there were none, he didn't wait long.

"Ready to say yes?"

Laurel bit back the urge to argue once more. What was wrong with taking the pleasure he was so willing to offer, and she was so clearly interested in receiving? If there was no fear of Alaric finding out, there was no valid excuse. She didn't have to like the guy to be attracted to him, or hook up with him, and he wasn't even asking that much of her.

Laurel perceptively relaxed, her hands curling around Grayson's biceps. She found her gaze pulled in by the curve of his mouth, as always.

"We're not having sex," she managed, hoping it sounded non-negotiable.

Clearly pleased by her acceptance, but unwilling to help a retort, he asked, "What are we, fifteen?" His tone was light and amused, his lips dipping closer to brush against hers.

Weakening, Laurel slowly returned the soft nudges of his lips. It was almost too easy to sink forward, letting him continue to have his way.

As he engaged her in a slow kiss, Grayson's fingertips gathered around her soft sundress, and he began to bunch the jersey material upwards. He found the elastic across her hips and toyed with the stretched material.

Laurel's lips parted against his, her next breath drawn sharp as she felt his fingers graze the feverish skin beneath her dress. As badly as she'd hoped to deny Grayson's playful advances, her body was not planning to cooperate.

"Just touch me already," she begged pathetically against his mouth.

Grayson's next exhale was mingled with deep laughter and he claimed Laurel's mouth with his own, feverishly. Fingers pushed and then dove. Soon, he granted her request, his hand tucked snugly between her thighs.

"Back up," he mumbled against her lips, starting to nudge her towards the couch.

His touch sent a burning shiver up her spine, and Laurel belatedly began to stumble and follow his advances. As she fell to sit on the small sofa, she tugged Grayson with her to keep him from losing his grip on her.

The pair fell lengthwise across the cushions. Laurel attempted to say something but seemed to think better of it and drew him back to her lips instead. She ignored any potential embarrassment over her rising desperation and closed her hands into fists in his jacket, pushing it free of his shoulders.

A quiet groan left Grayson as he knelt up, retracting from her body to rid himself of the burden of his blazer. He stared down at her, taking in the flush across her neck, and the way her dress had hiked upwards around her waist.

"Christ, you're beautiful."

Laurel exhaled in something like a breathy laugh, and he was on her again, tucking his fingers against her within the cocoon of her satin underwear. Her lips lost some momentum against his as a quiet moan leaked from her throat in response, hips arching up toward his touch.

To Grayson's delight he found she was damp already, and his fingers slid along the folds of her body as he coaxed her to a gasp. Their mouths met over and over, a dam broken, and Grayson pressed his tongue to hers, groaning.

Laurel's hands fisted in his shirt at his sides, whimpering as his fingertip grazed her clit. He was moving after only a minute, kneeling once again to peel her underwear free of her legs and drop them somewhere off to the side. Grayson ran his hands up along her smooth, tanned legs, feeling them quiver beneath his touch as he lowered his head to kiss a path up her inner thigh.

Laurel lay boneless, watching his ascent with heavy-lidded eyes. She realized with some satisfaction that the entire night had acted like foreplay. Grayson had worked her up to a fever pitch without her even realizing. Her eyes followed his mouth as it slipped higher, and she held her breath when his eyes met hers.

Grayson offered only an amused smirk before he closed the distance and, with a heated exhale, opened his mouth to her.

Her body went tight as a bowstring for a moment, a warm shudder engulfing her. One of her hands reached back for the arm of the couch, the other delving into Grayson's hair with a soft moan of pleasure at the heat of his mouth. "Fuck, yes."

Encouraged by her outburst and her touch, Grayson delved deeper, straining his tongue to slip inside her warmth. Her slickness and heat were no less intense than his mind had envisioned. With a groan, he focused wholly on tonguing the bundle of nerves sending shocks through her system.

Laurel's hips rolled upwards from the couch on instinct, her head spinning over the building pleasure she felt from his efforts. She whimpered his name, her fingertips scraping over the back of his neck, and she forced her eyes to open to fix on his face. When his heated eyes met hers, he drew his tongue against her in a long, intimate stroke, and she felt her features flush a deeper shade.

Grayson was quick to build her pleasure with constant nudges, expert concentration, and just the right speed. With a frantic yet subtle nod, she began to fall over the edge. She was mildly ashamed of herself for not holding on longer, but pleasure was pleasure.

Grayson growled in satisfaction as she came. The way Laurel's body began shivering was incredibly sexy. He moved his lips and tongue slower, helping her ride out her orgasm. His grin was smug as he sat back, rubbing his jaw.

"You're welcome," he said simply.

Laurel's breathing was ragged, as if she'd been sprinting. She ran a hand over her own chest, letting it linger at the bunched fabric around her midsection. With a soft laugh, she pushed her dress down to cover herself and began to sit up. She was forced to press a palm to his chest, pushing him back a few feet along the couch. "You..." she breathed, patting him in affectionate praise, "are very good at that."

Ego sufficiently inflated, Grayson watched her with a grin. He tangled a hand in his light brown hair, leaning against the back of the couch. "I appreciate your appreciation."

They sat there for a couple of minutes, just calming their breathing, before Grayson reached out to smooth her hair against the side of her head.

"Wait here a sec," he requested. "I'll walk you out."

She watched him head for the bathroom, shocked beyond belief that he was planning to honor his initial offer. The longer she sat alone, the longer she had to stew in her resurfacing frustration. She hadn't wanted to go to dinner, yet she'd gone. She hadn't wanted to gamble, yet she had. She'd wanted to stay uninvolved with Grayson, yet he'd just had his mouth in very involved places. In the end, she was torn between worshiping him for his talents and hating him for his ability to manipulate her.

Once Laurel was in a Lyft, courtesy of her unsolicited date, she checked her notifications.

Alaric: Monday. Noon. White oxford shirt, black miniskirt, black heels. Poolside cabana Aruba. $100+tips. Confirm.
Alaric: Please confirm.
Laurel: I'll be there. Thanks again.

Laurel sighed in relief at the businesslike messages from her new employer. It didn't seem like he'd caught wind of anything amiss between herself and Grayson.

There was one more text awaiting her.

Sadie: I guess you're having fun with Mr. Charming. Good for you.
Laurel: I'll be around the resort Monday. Can you do a late lunch? Have a story for you...

Laurel stared out the window at the passing cars and scenery as she was taken further away from the action of the city. It was a sobering reminder that she had a very different life and lifestyle than Grayson. She was typically 'the help' at fancy dinners, taking orders or slinging cocktails. Somehow, Grayson had managed to make her forget that fact.

She smiled to herself, deciding to just look back at the night for what it was: fun.

Laurel slipped her phone back into her bag, frowning as her knuckles grazed a wad of unfamiliar bills. She stared down at the stack, eyes quickly going to the taxi driver and then back down again, keeping them hidden as she quickly counted. Four hundred twenty-five dollars. There was no question in her mind where it had come from, and she sat there for a long minute in utter disbelief.

Shakily, she typed out a message in as thankful a manner as she could manage, considering her conflicting feelings on the fact that Grayson would let her keep the winnings.

Laurel: If you keep giving me money, I'm going to start thinking I owe you something.

Not that the implication was something she terribly minded after their encounter in the suite that evening. Still, the charitable aspect had her battling feelings of unworthiness. His actions showed a general flippancy toward money. Laurel, on the other hand, lived by the value of a dollar; she worked hard and kept her and her mother afloat. Laurel wanted to be accepting and thankful, but she envied the way Grayson could so easily tip her five hundred dollars, have twelve thousand credits on his players' card, or slip over four hundred dollars into her purse.

Grayson: I'm alright with that

Chapter Nine

♣

The following week, Parker was enjoying his final night in Atlantic City in the most clichéd manner possible. He was making his rounds on the casino floor along the invisible divide between slots and tables, a whiskey in hand. Grayson was MIA, or deliberately lying low, and Alaric was undoubtedly indulging himself in yet more work.

Parker slowed to a stop, considering one of the blackjack tables to his right, as a flash of green caught his eye. For a few seconds he allowed himself to admire the exposed slope of a woman's back, veiled by loose, dark waves. She was perched on a cushioned stool at the left-most table, and he noted the affectionate way a man to her right was tracing her spine. His brows lifted subtly as she turned her face, revealing the profile of the elusive Ms. Bache whom he'd met briefly, in a happy accident.

He supposed he shouldn't be surprised to see her on the arm of someone; she was stunning, and the green dress hugging her perfectly curved figure was the stuff of Parker Campbell's dreams.

Where most men would have enjoyed the sight and moved along, Parker had a knack for tempting fate. He casually joined the table, slipping onto the unoccupied stool to the woman's left. He set down his drink and a few large bills, signaling a buy-in to the dealer. Parker hadn't earned Ms. Bache's attention just yet, and so he greeted her with a compliment.

"Green is definitely your color, doll."

Sadie paused as the compliment registered and she turned, curious if she was imagining the slight accent. Recognition flashed in her eyes, followed by amusement. Before words were exchanged, Parker noted her nearly empty glass, a martini from the looks of it, and turned to catch a passing waitress's attention for a refill. He paid virtually no mind to the perplexed-looking man he'd presumed to be Ms. Bache's date.

"Small world," Sadie greeted, offering him her full attention. She gave him a proper assessment in the bright casino, liking what she saw.

"So it is," Parker replied, accepting the denomination of chips supplied by the dealer.

Feeling a hand settle against her exposed back, Sadie offered the faintest roll of her eyes. The move was meant to stake a claim, her date clearly threatened by Parker's presence, and Sadie all but wrote him off at that moment; she didn't do well with clingy or insecure men.

"Ante up," the dealer called.

Sadie placed a chip in the center of the white circle in front of her. "Joining us for a few hands?" she asked their new player.

"Why not," Parker replied, his eyes never leaving her face. As usual, the combination of whiskey and unapologetic flirtation was stressing his ordinarily subtle accent. He flashed her a wider smile as he added a chip to the pot. "Got all night."

The waitress returned and replaced Sadie's empty glass with the new beverage. Before Sadie could thank her, Parker added a generous chip to the server's tip glass and Sadie nodded her thanks.

The cards were dealt, and Sadie leaned aside to whisper something to her date who, shortly after, removed his arm from around her.

With manicured fingers, Sadie slid another chip towards her cards, splitting her eights.

Parker watched with interest. He tapped the table and was dealt another card, waving to stand.

The dealer split Sadie's eights and dealt additional cards. After doubling down on an eleven, it paid off as she was left with hands of twenty and eighteen.

Parker's smile broadened at her good fortune, or strategy. He noticed she was finishing off her drink, almost too quickly, and he looked over to spy her date splitting tens, no doubt a failed attempt at impressing her.

"Your boyfriend might not have wanted to do that," Parker mumbled, leaning towards her.

She was polite enough to hold her tongue, but her amusement was clear. She leaned an inch in his direction, clarifying for him in the quietest of voices, "My date is an imbecile."

"Dealer has eighteen."

Sadie looked back to hear "push" as her bets were matched. She raked her nails across the green surface, collecting her chips.

Parker ordered himself and Sadie another beverage and repeated his bet, unable to help his drifting attention. His eyes were continuously drawn to the profile beside him; everything from the curve of her small nose to the graceful slope of her neck set his skin on fire.

Sadie and her date beat the dealer that round, which seemed to fluff up the man's undue confidence. He finally sensed he should check on his date's glass, and Parker offered a wink when the man realized Parker had never let her be without.

"Should we find another table?" he asked, hand returning to Sadie's spine.

"Why, Stew?" she asked calmly, facing him. "Can't take the competition?"

Even the dealer had to conceal a smile at that remark.

Sadie saved him further embarrassment by patting his arm. "Why don't you put our name down at the restaurant?" she offered. "I'll play a few more rounds. Hurry back."

He was left little room for negotiation and stood, buttoning his suit jacket. "Alright," he replied, leaning in to brush his lips against her cheek, which she allowed.

As soon as she was no longer supervised, Parker turned to her in amusement. "I'm wildly interested in learning how you came to meet Stew."

Sadie crossed her legs towards Parker, angling herself the slightest bit more in his direction as they opted out of the next hand dealt.

"No, you're not," she said.

"You're right, I'm not," he conceded, his gray eyes sweeping over her appreciatively. "Though I can't understand it."

"He's very sweet," Sadie defended, but her grin was knowing. She was not nearly as invested in him as he was in her.

"Is he now?" he humored her, lifting his glass to drain it. "Sweet's your type, then?"

Her low laugh preceded a nonchalant shrug. "Not particularly."

Parker lowered his glass and set his arm on the tabletop, across from hers. He let his fingers overlap her arm and went for broke. "I'm sure you're used to this, but you are the single most beautiful woman I have ever laid eyes on."

The blatant statement earned him a pleased smile and Sadie found his mixture of confidence and frustration to be rather endearing. She studied him for a long minute, turning her arm to draw a finger along his skin flirtatiously.

"That so?" she fished.

His grin conveyed the fact that they both knew what was happening here, and it was only a matter of time before she ditched her date on a whim. Sadie retracted her hand and brushed her dark hair off her shoulders.

She weighed her options; spend the rest of the evening with the sweet gentleman she had met at the hotel earlier that week or explore a possible night of mind-numbing passion with this Australian mystery man. The choice was easy.

Sadie rose to her feet and signaled to the dealer that she'd like larger chips for ease of cashing out.

"Are you going to just sit there?" she urged her companion. "I'd rather not have to explain myself," she added, waving her hand towards the empty seat to her right.

Parker was quick to follow, leaving a chip on the table for the dealer.

"Thanks for the game, mate."

There was no dancing around things after that, and the two departed the casino in favor of a quieter place. As Sadie passed her new company into his hotel suite, she finally asked, "So what's your name, handsome?"

"Parker," he smiled, a dimple carved into his cheek. His eyes followed her every move. "Yours, darling?"

"Sadie." She caught his intense stare and laughed in a low, teasing way. "You'd better be worth it," she mumbled. "My expectations are high."

He was all too eager to accept her challenge.

They closed the distance and Parker eagerly got his hands on her, at last. He leaned in, all confidence. "I never disappoint." His lips pressed to the hollow behind her ear and grinned as the scent of her perfume grew stronger.

"I'll be the judge of that," she mused.

Sadie prided herself on being an excellent judge of character; it was necessary in her line of work. Although she knew practically nothing about Parker last-name-unknown, Sadie deduced key character traits from their two run-ins, which had led to her decision to throw caution to the wind and follow him back to his room.

Firstly, aside from her requesting assistance out of her town car and the light touch to her arm a few minutes ago, Parker had kept his hands to himself. Secondly, his confidence was not arrogance. Thirdly, Parker had not been in the company of other dates either time she'd seen him.

She couldn't say the same for herself, of course.

Regardless, those factors made Parker a decent guy, in her opinion. Decent enough to sleep with, at least. It didn't hurt that since running into the foreigner in the hotel carport, she'd fantasized about what would have happened had she stayed and offered to share her mode of transportation.

Parker's hands roamed, just enjoying the feel of her and the silken material moving against her curves. His lips left a charged wake, ultimately finding her mouth. Between slow, deep kisses, he requested, "Tell me what you're into. We've established you're not particularly into 'sweet.'"

Sadie hummed, leaning into him for a lengthier kiss, her curtain of hair sweeping along his forearms. "No," she mused, catching his lip with her teeth. "I'm not."

Growling, Parker untied the thin string behind her neck to loosen the front panels of her dress, letting them slip downwards between their bodies.

"Humor me," he pressed, withdrawing his touch just long enough to shrug his suit jacket off and drop it to the floor.

Stepping back, Sadie kept a teasing distance between them, unphased that she was topless. Her eyelids grew heavy as she watched him unbutton his shirt, slowly advancing on her. She confessed, "Haven't found much I'm *not* into."

His eyes were drawn to her full breasts, licking his lips at the surprise he saw just beneath them. Ink, drawn beneath the swell of each breast, rising in the center. He'd never seen a woman with a sternum tattoo before, and he stood marveling at the lace style design that only seemed to make her even more exotic. The sight of her, paired with her confession moments ago, had his pants pulling taught.

Sadie backed towards the bedroom door as her fingers moved to the zipper running along her hip. She slowly eased it downward, the fabric whispering off her skin to the floor. She stepped out of the circle of her dress in only a nude lace thong, climbing onto the king-sized bed.

The playfulness was adding to the lust Parker felt taking firm control. "Tell me what you want," he insisted as he unbuckled his belt and pulled it free.

Sadie took great pleasure in observing him, propping herself up on her elbows as she tossed her hair back behind her. "First," she began, wetting her lips. "I want you right here." Her legs parted on the bed, inviting.

Parker realized very quickly that Sadie was just his speed. He groaned, dropping his knees to the edge of the bed as he undid the button and zipper of his jeans. He left them in place, crawling towards her.

Sadie gasped when Parker buried his face between her thighs, against the thin strip of fabric there. He inhaled deeply, groaning, and then began to tease her with his mouth.

"God," she breathed, both her hands fisting in his brown hair. "You cocky son of a—"

Parker looked up, tsking as he withdrew his mouth. "What was that, darling?"

Using the grip in his hair, Sadie pushed him back down. "Nothing."

He gave a satisfied smirk and returned to the apex of her thighs, a finger easily drawing the fabric aside to give him direct access to her heat.

It wasn't that Sadie didn't enjoy this particular act, she was enjoying it a hell of a lot at that moment, but she wanted something more.

"Come up here and fuck me," she breathed, desperate.

Parker was all too happy to oblige, and he crawled up her body, pushing his clothing down to free himself.

"Hang on," he said, moving aside to reach for the hotel nightstand.

Sadie let out a quiet whimper of protest as his attention moved elsewhere. "Parker," she complained.

"Just a sec," he laughed, breathless. "Let me get a damn condom."

"Skip it," she begged, pulling at his arm to bring him back to her. It was a bold request, but she was lost to her pleasure.

Parker paused; brow furrowed. "That's…unexpected." He'd never been with a woman who had refused protection.

Sadie held his eyes for a long moment before she stated, "I'm clean and I can't have kids."

Parker shifted in thought, returning above Sadie.

"IUD?" he asked. The way she'd worded her confession had him feeling the need to clarify.

Sadie shook her head, repeating herself. "Can't have kids."

Parker ran his fingers along her cheek and swept a dark curl of her hair away. For a few seconds, he said nothing. Ultimately, he weighed any potential consequences to her request and then dismissed them.

"Put your arms around my neck," he instructed.

Sadie didn't normally go around sharing her medical history, but it was her truth. With nothing more than a satisfied hum, she complied. Accepting Parker's offer of a guaranteed night of passion had clearly been the right move.

Parker groaned at the image of her naked body wrapped around him and he, with his pants still low on his hips, slid into her welcoming heat easily.

Sadie tipped her head back, eyes sliding shut at the satisfying feeling of him filling her.

He reached down to hike one of her legs up at his hip, moving against her in a firm, pleasurable rhythm. It was a rare treat for Parker to find himself without need for a condom. His movements were sharp, but his thrusts were deep, as he listened to her moans and gasps, repeating what seemed to bring her the most pleasure. He could tell from her faster, harder breathing that the angle at which their hips connected was causing extra sensitivity. He couldn't help but reach between them and slip his thumb against the bundle of nerves between her slick folds.

Sadie's next breath was shaky, a tremble causing her frame to shudder against him. Somewhere in the fog of pleasure and inebriation, Sadie's hand curled beneath Parker's chin and directed his lips back to hers. Her tongue pressed feverishly to his, encouraging him with nails drawing down his bare arm.

In the final moments leading up to her climax, Sadie's lips fell still, and she focused her concentration on clenching and unclenching around him, until she came with a fierce shudder.

Parker slid one arm around her lower back to draw her up into an arch as he railed her for the final few minutes. She shuddered against him a second time as he finally erupted with pleasure.

In the silence that stretched, their echoing breaths the only sound filling the spacious bedroom, Sadie declared, "You'll be pleased to know," she swallowed, "That you did not disappoint."

Parker rolled onto his back, laughing happily. "I'm glad."

He was still grinning as he commented, "Stew's probably still looking for you."

Sadie laughed, though she had the sense to feel mildly guilty about how she'd handled the situation downstairs. Still, she had to confess, "He never stood a chance."

"I know," Parker winked.

A short while later, after cleaning up and donning a Borgata Hotel robe, Sadie found Parker enjoying a cigarette on the balcony. He wore his pants and nothing more, and she leaned back against the railing to face him, watching him curiously. "Didn't peg you for a smoker."

He turned away as he exhaled, nodding. "Nasty habit."

They stood in companionable silence until Parker asked, "So how long are you in town?"

"I come and go."

In the short time she'd been in his suite, she'd noticed that Parker wasn't living out of a suitcase. "You?"

He squinted, lifting a wrist to check the time. "For another eight hours or so. City bound in the morning. New York."

"New York?" she echoed, looking surprised. "With that accent, I figured somewhere abroad."

Parker nodded, combing back his brown hair. "Mum's Australian, father's American." His expression turned curious, and he asked, "What about you, Sadie Bache?"

"Well," she began, pausing momentarily to wonder when she'd shared her last name. "I have roots in Santa Monica, but I travel more than I don't."

"Amazing we managed to cross paths, considering the odds," Parker pointed out. Between Australia, California, New York, and sporadic work schedules, it was funny that they'd met in New Jersey.

"Not exactly," she countered, waving around them. "Casinos are sort of my office."

Now, she had his attention. "How so?"

"I'm a professional card player," she confessed, curious how he'd take the news. She'd experienced the full gambit of reactions to her profession, from admiration to disgust.

Parker's smile doubled. "You don't say…"

Sadie couldn't quite decipher his reaction. "What's that smile about?"

"I dabble."

"You dabble?"

"In cards, doll. I play my fair share."

Sadie beamed at that, looking positively tickled at the idea. "You don't say."

By the time they were dressed once more, Parker escorted Sadie from his suite to hers.

"Such a gentleman," she praised, looking through her purse. She withdrew her key card and a business card, holding out the latter in his direction. "In case our paths magically cross again."

Parker accepted the card happily. The promise of another night was an exciting prospect. "Here's to hoping."

CHAPTER TEN

Come Monday afternoon, Laurel found that Alaric's lunch function was equally easy money, but the tips weren't comparable to the previous week. Still, she was glad to be picking up another gig and was hopeful to keep the offers coming. The only barrier to that was Grayson, and she felt certain she could keep what had happened between her legs between the two of them.

Laurel stood at a small private bar that had been outfitted especially for Alaric's private lunch, putting liquor bottles back in order as she wrapped up her shift. Her smile grew as she caught sight of Sadie, waving on her approach.

"Wow, you look amazing," Laurel praised, taking in the sight of the older woman in a sheer white sarong wrapped around an equally brilliant bikini beneath.

"And you owe me details from the other night," Sadie replied with a grin, adjusting her oversized sunglasses. "Lots and lots of details."

Laughing, Laurel shook her head. "Not here," she said. Alaric was still lingering, and she turned to gesture over her shoulder. "The boss."

Sadie looked behind Laurel, studying the back of a very familiar man. "Alaric?" she asked.

As his name was spoken, he turned, and Alaric gave a professional smile of recognition as his gaze fixed on Sadie. "Hello there, Sadie," he greeted, joining the pair.

"You two know one another?" Laurel was surprised, but she supposed it made sense. They were both at Borgata's on business, after all.

Alaric gave Laurel a curious look, but he didn't bother inquiring after their friendship. "All finished?" he asked.

Laurel sighed. "Just about." She shot Sadie an apologetic look before turning back to finish clearing the tables.

To Sadie, Alaric said, "I'm arranging a game tonight, actually. I was hoping you'd join us."

"Delightful," she replied, patting his arm affectionately. "I was starting to think I was wasting my time here. Text me the details."

As Laurel finished cleaning, untying the half apron from around her hips, she nearly collided directly with a hotel guest who had been enjoying the pool.

"You work here, right?" the young woman asked, a light sweatshirt hanging open to reveal a swimsuit beneath. "Can we get a round of margaritas?" She gestured to a small group of girls crowded around a few lounge chairs.

Laurel gave an apologetic shake of her head. "I was handling a private lunch event," she explained, sweeping the area to locate the pool bar several yards away. "They can help you over there, though."

The young woman squinted across the pool to spot the bar, yet before she could offer a choice word or two, another young woman spoke up from behind her.

"Ash, come on," she called, having clearly overheard their exchange. "I want to go look at the menu, anyway."

As Laurel turned away, she found herself almost bowled over yet again. This time, however, Grayson stood at her back wearing his trademark grin.

"You—" she started, whipping around to look for Alaric. "What are you doing here?" she accused.

"Calm down, he's busy," Grayson assured. "I waited until he was distracted."

He closed a hand around the apron she held to draw her forward. "I want more than a taste," Grayson confessed. "You free tonight?"

Laurel's mouth hung open, heat pooling in her face, and she scoffed. "Did you seriously just say that? No, I—"

Grayson lifted his stare behind her, and his face fell. "Shit, Al's coming back," he said, impatient. "Tonight?"

Laurel attempted to turn, but Grayson pulled on the apron to keep her attention. "Please don't," she argued pathetically. "I need this job."

Grayson attempted to move closer, and Laurel panicked at the idea of being seen in a compromising situation.

"Fine!" she blurted. He clearly wasn't going to leave until he had the answer he wanted, anyway.

Grayson's demeanor noticeably relaxed and he winked.

"Great. I'll text you."

Laurel turned then, quickly scanning their surroundings. When she spotted Alaric seated at an empty cabana, his attention completely absorbed in his task at hand, she glared. Grayson had used her fear to motivate her to agree to another date.

"That goddamned jackass."

Taking a deep, calming breath, Laurel told herself to drop it and collect her wages. She approached Alaric, leaning into his field of vision.

"Hey, sorry to bother you. I'm all finished."

Alaric glanced up from the vendor contract he was reviewing, nodding. "Good work today." He flipped through his binder and pulled cash from an envelope, counting out a small pile of twenties. "I'll walk you out."

Laurel accepted the cash with thanks, palming the bills. "You know you really don't have to," she offered, watching as he rose to his feet. She gestured towards the hotel doors to assure him she could see herself out. "I know you have better things to do," she added.

"Oh?"

Laurel watched him curiously. Was it just her, or had he sounded insulted?

"Yeah, it's fine," she assured as she turned to walk backwards and put space between them, even as he hefted his binder and began to approach. "Call me anytime. I'll take any gigs you've got."

Alaric slowed a couple of feet from her, watching curiously. Was it just him, or did she suddenly seem nervous? Dismissing it but keeping a watchful eye on his newest part-time employee, he moved to head in the opposite direction.

In that moment, as Laurel watched Alaric turn, she realized with alarm that he failed to realize how close to the pool's edge he'd gotten.

"Alaric!" she gasped.

He turned forward sharply at the warning, managing to only wobble before he reached for purchase. He grabbed for the closest support, a passing waitress, and steadied himself on her arm.

Although neither of them went down, her tray of drinks took a dive. Three bottles of beer slid and fell, crashing around the cement where one young woman had been sitting with her legs in the pool.

With barely enough time to react, much less get herself out of harm's way, the seated brunette instinctively wrapped her arms over her head. She felt the splash of pool water, beer, and a sharp sting against her thigh.

Alaric went directly into management mode. As a chorus of gasps, complaints, laughter, and clapping surrounded them, Alaric quickly snapped a mutter of 'plastic cups only at the pool' to the unfamiliar waitress. She seemed close to tears at her mistake, and he groaned at the fact that she was probably new and hadn't been trained properly. He at least had the sense to ensure the waitress was unharmed and sent her off to retrieve maintenance.

A twenty-foot arc around the accident had cleared, and a handful of young women were shouting in their direction.

"Gem, are you alright?"

The young woman seated at the pool's edge assessed her leg, calling back, "Yeah, I think so."

A piece of broken glass had ricocheted, leaving a paper-thin trail of blood trickling down her thigh. She made a move to lift her leg from the pool so as not to contaminate the water.

"Don't move."

Gemma froze, turning her head up to the man towering above her. "I'm bleeding, though."

Alaric set his binder on the edge of the closest lounge chair and carefully knelt beside her, holding out a hand to convey she should stay put. On inspection, it seemed shallow, purely superficial. He relaxed, but only slightly.

He turned to see Laurel still frozen and directed, "Six, get some clean towels and a first aid kit."

Laurel gestured behind her, unsure. "I mean, I can tell a staff member…"

Alaric addressed the small cluster of people still watching them. "Very sorry for the interruption, everyone." He gestured to the other end of the grotto and instructed, "For your safety, please enjoy another pool until the glass is cleared."

Realizing she wouldn't receive a further response, Laurel sighed and went in search of assistance.

Gemma shifted uncomfortably, cupping a hand around the line of blood to ensure it didn't drip into the pool. She hated the attention this accident was affording her.

Alaric returned his attention to the young woman beside him. He lightly set a hand on her back beneath the band of her bathing suit top. "Don't try to get up just yet. Please."

Annoyed sighs and mutters surrounded them as the pool slowly emptied, but a cluster of young women still lingered from a safe distance away.

"Is it bad?" one called over.

Another gasped, "Oh my God, is that blood?"

"Smile!" one called, snapping photos.

"Guys, stop," the brunette complained through an uncomfortable laugh, waving them off. "It's fine. Seriously."

Alaric remained perched at her side, waiting on Laurel's return. Frustration pulled at the edges of his calm composure. He couldn't wait to see those photos all over social media later, tagging Borgata Hotel & Casino. He lifted a hand to her friends, politely acknowledging them in the hopes that they'd feel that their friend was in good hands.

"Here for the weekend?" Alaric asked, filling the time.

Gemma Blake turned back to face him, studying his profile as he scanned their surroundings. She felt heat rising in her cheeks, noticing just how handsome he was, and that he kept a hand at her back.

"A week, actually," she replied, tucking damp hair behind her ear. "Bachelorette party, for my friend." She noticed the perpetual knot between his brows and offered, "I really am all right."

Alaric noticed her friends had yet to disperse. "If you'd like to visit the bar, I'll see that your group's drinks are covered today."

His generosity had the desired effect and they scattered, headed directly for the closest pool bar.

When Alaric returned his stare to the young woman beside him, he startled at the smile she offered.

"Thank you," she said. "That was very nice of you."

Words died on his lips as Alaric finally stopped staring at the girl's thigh long enough to take in her appearance. She was being a good sport about the accident, attempting to laugh it off rather than sue, and he found her demeanor to be both appreciated and adorable.

Laurel returned then, looking winded but triumphant with a first aid kit. "Got it." Two additional staff trailed her, with a broom and rolling garbage can.

"Do you mind if I pick you up?" Alaric asked, regarding the broken glass littering the pool deck.

"Oh." She was clearly surprised by the question. "That's fine, but I don't want to make a mess of your clothes." Between the beer, pool water, and the thin trail of blood on her leg, she was sure to transfer something to his nice suit.

"We dry clean on-site."

It was meant to be a joke, but Alaric lacked any visual indicator for humor or sarcasm. There was a beat of silence before she burst out laughing. Laurel looked on in confusion.

Alaric managed a weak smile and stood, removing his sport coat. He rolled his sleeves to the elbows, partially revealing tattoo sleeves.

"You'll have to fight the urge to put your feet on the ground when I lift you," he said.

Distracted by the dark ink, Gemma nodded.

Alaric swept some of the visible glass aside with his shoe and carefully eased closer. He gingerly scooped her into his arms. "Can you wrap your—? Thank you."

Her weight appeared to have little effect on him, and as he carried her clear of the mess, Gemma found herself grinning, childishly. "Are you always this clumsy?" she teased.

With a bit of surprised embarrassment, Alaric shook his head. "The opposite."

He gave a few instructions to the cleaning crew and then deposited the half-naked young woman on the futon in an empty cabana. Laurel followed close behind, arms burdened with towels, the first aid kit, and Alaric's jacket and binder.

"Your name's Gem?" Alaric asked.

"Gemma," she clarified, settling onto the soft mattress.

Alaric fanned out one of the towels around her shoulders, earning another blush and thank you from Gemma. He pulled over a piece of modular furniture and sat, rummaging through the kit.

"I'm Alaric," he introduced, opening an alcohol wipe.

Laurel was at a loss for words at the scene unfolding. Alaric seemed genuinely embarrassed; the typically imposing and impatient hard-ass was gone.

"What do you do here at the hotel, Alaric?" Gemma asked conversationally, watching his hands as he treated her wound.

"Senior Operations Manager," he offered. "How many people are you traveling with?"

"There are six of us, total."

He smoothed a waterproof butterfly closure across the cut and announced, "I'll comp you and your friends some tickets to a show. Was there anything specific you wanted to see?"

"Oh no, you really don't have to do that," Gemma was quick to assure. "Covering our drinks is more than enough."

Alaric turned to spot Laurel trying to get his attention, gesturing that she had to leave. "Don't pack up," he replied. "Need you a little longer."

Giving her no time to respond, Alaric returned his attention to Gemma. "It's done," he assured her, regarding the free tickets. "Have your friends choose a show."

Alaric was so serious; Gemma couldn't help but smile again. "I think I'm going to pull through," she assured him, looking at her injury. "I had a very good surgeon," she praised.

That earned a small lift of his lips.

"Are you always this serious, too?" Gemma asked, nudging his calf with her bare foot.

Alaric paused in packing up the first aid kit, glancing almost self-consciously behind him where Laurel tried to look busy on her phone. Slowly, he began to relax.

"Mostly," he confessed.

"I can tell," Gemma whispered conspiratorially.

He offered a more good-natured smile. "Well, your injury happened at my place of work because I wasn't paying attention," he reasoned.

Gemma shook her head. "It's just a scratch—"

"This cabana's open for the rest of today," he informed. "Six can stay on and you and your friends are welcome to use it."

Laurel's brows went up as Alaric committed her to tending to them, biting her tongue at the fact that she had a conflicting shift at the cafe.

Gemma blanched. Drinks, tickets, and a cabana?

"I didn't lose my leg, you know," she joked. "Seriously, you've already done plenty."

Alaric placed a hand on her shoulder as he rose, watching her. "I know," he replied. "But I can offer it, and your friends would love it."

He wasn't wrong about that, and Gemma was glad to see he finally wore something akin to an easygoing smile. Her gaze drifted over to the woman he'd referred to as Six before nodding. "Okay. Thank you."

Before departing, Alaric offered Gemma a business card. "Call," he encouraged, "When your friends choose a show. I'll take care of it."

Gemma ran her thumb over the embossed lettering of Alaric's business card and thanked him again.

As he stepped away, Laurel was right on his heels. "I'm really sorry, but I can't stay," she told him.

The cafe was a pathetic job in comparison, but it was reliable. She had yet to establish any sort of routine work agreement with Alaric to justify risking it.

"There are plenty of servers around, I'm sure someone else can cover the cabana," she insisted.

Alaric folded his jacket over an arm, his shirt damp from carrying Gemma. He seemed unphased by Laurel's plea. He tucked his binder under an arm and gave her an assessing look.

"I've got an important game in New York on Friday. I usually bring my own team. I'm willing to take you along, but I need you here. Now."

Laurel's expression morphed into one of disbelief, and she stood in shocked silence for a long beat.

"New York?" she echoed.

"Upper east side," Alaric replied.

Laurel bit her lips, nodding quickly; it was all she could do to contain her excitement. The prospect of getting paid to visit New York for the first time in her life was far too great an opportunity to pass up.

"I'll stay," she assured. "I'll stay today, and I'll take the New York offer, too."

Alaric nodded. He couldn't help his attention as it drifted back to Gemma. She was waving across the pool at her friends, beckoning them to join her.

"I'll make sure they're taken care of here,"' Laurel reassured. "Don't worry about a thing."

Laurel tied her apron back around her hips and fished out her phone. She dreaded breaking the news to Sam, her boss at Coastal Cafe. He was a jerk, and she knew he wouldn't accept that she had a conflict with her second job. In fact, he was still sore over the two times she had been forced to call out sick to take care of her mother.

She probably should have leaned on the family emergency excuse once more, but he had held it over her head and used it as the reason she hadn't gotten a wage increase in the past six months. In the end, she went with the truth. Her wage at the cafe was crap, and she couldn't pass up Alaric's offer in favor of waiting tables.

Laurel: I'm sorry, I can't come in today. I picked up another PT job and I have a conflict between shifts. It's money I can't afford to lose. Can I switch with Beth and take tomorrow morning?
Sam: Don't bother.
Sam: I'll mail your last check.

She glared at the screen, more annoyed with Sam than with the fact that he'd just fired her. She might have been more upset, if it wasn't for the promise of a trip to New York later that week. However, for Alaric to fulfill that promise, and for her to remain employed, she knew she needed to go above and beyond for this group of young women.

She sent off one more text before getting to work.

Laurel: Alaric needs me to stay indefinitely. PR issue with a guest.
Grayson: K text when you're done

♥ ♠ ♦ ♣

"I just wanted to say thank you."

Laurel looked up from where she was stacking empty snack baskets to see Gemma, looking apologetic. The group of young women that Alaric had asked her to wait on had been occupying the cabana for almost five full hours, the sun now starting to set.

Gemma gestured over her shoulder. "They're all pretty wasted now so I'm going to try dragging them back to our rooms."

She looked uncomfortable as she held out a handful of bills. "I know it's not what you'd normally make."

Laurel hadn't expected these girls to tip like Alaric's high rollers, and Gemma's offer was extremely kind. "Thank you. And don't worry about it," she assured, accepting the tip graciously. "Alaric just wanted to make things right."

Gemma's fingertips traced the bandage on her thigh idly. "I tried to refuse, you know," she smiled. "He's a tough guy to say no to."

Laurel sighed. "You're not wrong about that."

Chapter Eleven

♠

"I'm heading into the meeting as we speak," Parker said into his cell phone. He was back in New York, at his father's midtown office. He strode down the opulent hallway towards one of the board rooms, the clicking of heels trailing him.

He ended the call at the door and turned to find his father's assistant waiting. "Hannah," Parker greeted, his smile tight.

"Your father?" she guessed with a sympathetic smile, handing over the folders she carried.

He confirmed her suspicion with whom he was speaking and accepted the short stack. "Thanks. Is lunch already ordered for everyone?"

"Of course," Hannah replied.

"Too late to add one of those juice drinks?" he winked.

"I'll handle it," she assured, waving him to go inside. "All the partners have already arrived."

"Thanks, doll."

She turned to go, and Parker had a brief flashback to Sadie Bache, her green silk dress sliding down and away from the curves of his body.

"Not the time," Parker grumbled to himself, pushing through the glass doors.

♥ ♠ ♦ ♣

That evening, Grayson sauntered into a suite dedicated to one of Alaric's private card games.

"Thanks for throwing me some last-minute action," Grayson said, noting that aside from Alaric, the dealer, and Stacy, the room was otherwise empty.

"Where is everyone?"

He still planned on making it to the boardwalk to meet Laurel, so the sooner the game started the better.

"They'll be here."

"A beer, Mr. Lee?" Stacy offered.

"Please," he nodded, pointing out a Guinness in the ice-filled galvanized tub.

Behind him, Grayson heard the footfalls of another arrival. He turned to follow a pair of heels upwards to reveal a dazzling smile, and a familiar face wearing it.

"Sadie," Alaric greeted with a kiss on her cheek. "Thanks for making the time."

"That's why I'm in town," she replied.

Grayson's grin grew as he approached, waiting for the woman to recognize him as Laurel's date from the previous week. He couldn't come right out and say it, seeing as how Alaric was present, but it seemed he didn't need to.

"You," Sadie laughed, regarding him.

"Me," he confirmed. "Nice to see you again."

"You as well. Is…" She seemed to think better of asking and instead did a quick sweep of the room to confirm that Laurel was not in attendance.

"Would you like a drink?" he offered, skirting the topic. He inclined his head to the corner of the room where Stacy was mixing martinis. With a bit more privacy, he offered, "I'll be seeing our mutual friend a bit later on tonight."

"Is that so?" she mused, requesting a glass of wine for herself.

The door opened and the rest of their party arrived, followed by a round of introductions for those who needed them. Once all players had a drink in hand, they congregated around the table for some good old-fashioned Texas hold'em.

As cards were dealt, Sadie began to compose a quick text message to Laurel regarding the coincidental meeting, but she was interrupted by a hand on her shoulder. "Cards are hot. No phones, please."

Sadie tucked her cell phone back into her clutch.

"If I haven't learned how to count cards by now, I'm certainly not going to pick it up with a Google search."

Contradictory to his own words, Alaric stepped aside as his phone vibrated. 'Six' flashed on screen and he quickly accepted it.

"What's wrong?"

"Alaric, hey. Everything's fine. The bachelorette party finished up. Was there anything else you needed before I headed home?"

He relaxed a fraction at her response.

"No, thank you. Come up to fifteen-eleven and I'll pay you for the day."

Alaric pocketed his phone and moved to the back windows that overlooked the grotto. Far below he could see plenty of people enjoying the pool, but from the fifteenth floor it was hard to distinguish if any of the clusters of women included Gemma and her friends.

When Laurel arrived, Stacy greeted her at the door. "Are you working this one, too?" Laurel still wore her outfit and apron from waiting on the poolside group.

"No, I just finished. Need to check in with Alaric," she excused, slipping inside.

Laurel glimpsed the players seated around the table and did a double take when she realized she knew not one, but two of the participants. Sadie and Grayson sat across from one another, both absorbed in their game.

Laurel's eyes went wide at the sight, but she forced herself to reign in any reaction when she spotted Alaric who was stepping into the adjoining bedroom with his cell phone. He left the door open, so she felt it would be fine to pop her head in and let him see that she had arrived.

As Laurel skirted the table, Grayson's gaze lifted, a mixture of surprise and curiosity crossing his face. Sadie wasn't far behind, looking mischievously between her and Grayson.

Face hot, Laurel rolled her eyes and opted to ignore them both.

In the adjacent room, Alaric's call-waiting tone beeped through his current conversation.

"Greg, I have to cut this short," he apologized, "We can finalize the rest over email." After an exchange of goodbyes, Alaric accepted the waiting call and lowered himself to sit on the edge of the bed. He'd been going since six that morning and it was now creeping close to fourteen hours later.

"This is Alaric," he answered.

"Hi," replied a female voice. "It's Gemma Blake. From the pool?" She sounded unsure, worried she may have interrupted him. "Is this a bad time?"

At the doorway, he saw Laurel move into view and he held up a finger, giving the international sign for "hang on." Then, he pointed to the door, signaling for her to close it. Alaric felt a bit more comfortable with the added privacy.

"Hello," he replied a little stiffly. "Is everything all right?"

Gemma sighed. "Turns out, they had to amputate."

When he didn't respond right away, Gemma filled the space with a quiet laugh. "Too soon?"

Alaric cracked a smile, rolling his head on his neck in a stretch. "Very funny," he chided.

"Is everything alright with you?" she asked in return. "You sound busy. Or annoyed. Or both."

"I'm alright. Better now."

They were both quiet for a moment.

Alaric rubbed his face with a hand, clarifying, "I just mean now that most of my day is over."

Something about Gemma had him smiling, uncharacteristically. She was sweet and adorable, and he was surprised by how nice it felt to hear from her. It was throwing him for a loop, and he inwardly groaned at how poorly he was navigating the phone call.

"And I'm glad you called," he rushed to add, belatedly wondering if it had been too forward.

Gemma had holed up in the bathroom to place this call, and she was suddenly glad for the privacy.

"Oh," she replied simply.

Her friends were expecting her to request the tickets he'd promised, but she suddenly felt as though it would be a mistake to mention the reason she'd called. She felt the tips of her ears warming as she mustered the nerve to ask with a cautious smile, "I was wondering what kind of hours a senior operations manager works."

Gemma covered her face with a hand, waiting in the tense silence for his response or rejection. If she was going to humiliate herself with a lame attempt at flirting, at least he couldn't witness her embarrassment firsthand.

Alaric was rendered speechless for a long moment, during which time he reached up to undo a shirt button at the base of his throat.

"It varies," he answered honestly.

He wasn't trying to discourage her; he just couldn't give as simple an answer as nine-to-five.

Gemma's hand slowly fell from her face, and she stared at her reflection in the mirror, wondering, "Are you still working now?"

He was and wasn't. These organized games were part of his job, but he wasn't technically required to oversee them start to finish.

"I can talk," he offered. He suddenly felt very juvenile and hoped to distract her with concern for the earlier accident, "I was worried about you. Your leg, I mean."

Gemma blushed at his response. "I'm fine, really."

The silence stretched.

With great regret, she admitted, "I can't stay on the phone. My friends and I are headed to dinner at that Mexican place downstairs. I just wanted to thank you again."

"Did you ask about the tickets yet?"

Gemma cringed at the sound of her loud-mouthed friend, Ashlee, yelling through the door. There was no way Alaric hadn't overheard.

"Gemma?" Alaric asked, but there was a smile in his voice. "Have your friends picked a show?"

"God, I'm so sorry," she breathed. "They want to go to a comedy show tomorrow night, but I really, really didn't call just because of that."

Alaric was nodding faintly to himself, amused by her embarrassment. "It's okay. I know the show you're talking about. I'll take care of it."

Once they'd ended their conversation, Alaric returned to find Laurel lingering by the bar. "Sorry about that," he excused.

Laurel's brows went up. "You're in a good mood."

That seemed to bring his demeanor right back down to all business all the time and Laurel dismissed it with a shake of her head.

"We were going to settle up for today?"

Alaric nodded and produced an envelope from his jacket pocket. "And we should talk about New York."

She accepted the cash, looking surprised. "Sure. Now?"

He checked his watch, considering. "Let's have breakfast at seven."

Laurel hesitated, but only briefly. She would have to be up at five-thirty in the morning to make that timetable. Defeated, she gave a nod of acceptance. Sleep be damned, she was going to New York.

Chapter Twelve

♥

Laurel spied Grayson where they had agreed to meet, at the bench nearest to the boardwalk clocktower.

"I hope you know," she announced by way of greeting, "I have even more incentive to stay away from you now than I did before."

At Grayson's questioning look, she informed, "Alaric is officially my only source of income."

He gave her a once-over and then set a hand on her hip when she was close enough, leaning in to greet her with a brief kiss. "Hi to you, too."

She allowed the show of affection but offered a roll of her eyes. "Did you win your game?"

"Always," he nodded, leaning back against the railing.

"I won our game, too," he added. "Our bet."

Laurel eyed him, curious about the smug satisfaction emanating from him. It was more than usual.

"Our bet?" she echoed.

"New York," he clarified. "Don't tell me you forgot."

In all honesty, Laurel had been waiting for him to find out. She wondered if it might not come up between him and Alaric, and if she could be the one to break the news.

"Okay, first of all," she prefaced. "That was a hypothetical bet. It didn't count."

"Oh, this is good," Grayson laughed, nodding for her to go on. "And second of all?"

Laurel glared, shoving his shoulder. "Second of all, you're a jackass."

"There was nothing hypothetical about it," he assured, drawing her closer. "You wanted to go to New York, and I helped."

Alaric had made the offer sound casual, but she wondered if Grayson had played a part in the deal. She wasn't sure how, considering Alaric wanted them to stay away from one another.

"So, what you're saying is, you *fixed* the bet," she corrected. "I'd say that nullifies your win."

Grayson rolled his eyes.

Now curious, she asked, "Wait, are you going, too?"

She wasn't too keen on admitting it, but it was nice to think she'd have a friendly face accompanying her on the trip. If Grayson was participating in the game she was working, maybe the other player she knew was, too.

"Sadie?" she asked.

"I'm going to pretend you didn't look more excited when you asked about Sadie," Grayson mumbled, releasing her to start walking. "I'm going," he confirmed. "I've got no idea about your friend."

She followed, digging her phone out of her pocket to ask Sadie directly.

"You can text her later," Grayson interrupted, grabbing the device. "We're busy." He jammed it into his pocket and captured her hand.

Laurel allowed it, telling herself that it was more exhausting to fight with him than not.

"So, what's this about Alaric being your only source of income?" he pressed.

"Lost my other job."

"At the cafe?"

She nodded.

"Are you alright with that?"

Laurel gave him a lopsided smile. "I mean, it's not ideal, but so long as Alaric keeps booking me, I'll be doing better than I was before."

He gave her hand a comforting squeeze.

"By the way," he said, returning to their earlier discussion. "You said it would be my call on what I won," he reminded. "When New York happened."

"You're not serious," Laurel accused.

"Why would I not be serious?" he laughed, his dark brown eyes sparkling with amusement. "You wanted to go to New York. It's happening. I won."

Rather than argue, she eyed him curiously, swinging their clasped hands. "Just what exactly do you want?"

Grayson's grin doubled in width. "Easy. We share a room in New York."

Honestly, Laurel thought it was almost too simple a request. He could have asked for anything, and he was choosing to spend more time with her. Almost as soon as she'd had the thought, she shook her head; he was manipulating her. Either way, she couldn't accept his terms. This was a work trip. Plus, she wasn't planning on letting him see how easy it would have been to say yes.

"No can do. There's the Alaric factor, remember?"

"Al will never know," he countered easily. "It's not like he's going to check on us. He's too busy for that."

"Grayson, no," she argued, slowing to a stop on the boardwalk. She tipped her head back, threading her fingers into her hair. "I shouldn't even be here right now." She was refusing his offer to room together but was still meeting up with him to spend time together. If anyone was responsible for mixed signals, it was her.

Laurel took a deep breath, about to tell him all the reasons he needed to accept that she was leaving, accept that she was declining his offer, and to pursue someone else. However, when she finally looked back at him, a soft smile was in place of his typical grin.

"Don't go," he requested.

Laurel groaned pathetically at how easily she caved. She barely knew Grayson, yet his upbeat attitude and playfulness was something she'd been missing in her life recently. Her own circumstances were grim, and she longed for the carefree attitude Grayson seemed to offer.

"Laurel," he stressed, finally using her real name. "Please."

It was the first time she'd ever seen him look genuine, be sincere, and act polite. It was almost strange. Feeling as though it was her turn to lighten the mood, she grumbled, "I'm starting to notice you can't ever take no for an answer."

He seemed to follow her lead, returning to his default attitude. "Not in my vocabulary."

The conversation trailed off as the two picked up walking side-by-side again, Grayson reaching for Laurel's hand. Once more, she allowed it. More than allow it, she was starting to enjoy it. Grayson's efforts seemed to be winning her over, but she still had that nagging voice in the back of her head that warned her she was playing with fire.

Alaric and his offer of work was her ticket out of Atlantic City. She needed money to pay off the last of her mom's overdue bills and build up enough for first and last month's rent at a new place. A new place in New York.

"You mentioned working early tomorrow," Grayson prompted.

Laurel nodded. "Alaric wants to meet for breakfast."

He gave her a curious look, teasing, "You two-timing me, Six?"

She shoved his shoulder with her own. "That would require us actually dating and no, he wants to talk about logistics for New York."

Though Grayson could have stressed that they were literally on a date at that moment, he could sense it was a fact best left unsaid.

When Laurel came to realize exactly where Grayson was leading them, her eyes widened. "You're not serious."

Grayson approached the motorcycle with confidence, pulling keys from his pocket. "Where's your sense of adventure?" he chastised, handing her his helmet.

Laurel knew next to nothing about motorcycles. Despite her concern about Grayson's driving capabilities, she was surprised to find she was excited at the opportunity to ride one.

"Come back to the hotel with me," he offered, aware he might be pushing his luck.

"That's a bad idea," she replied, suddenly fascinated with the helmet's straps as she adjusted them.

Grayson's silence prompted her to continue.

"You know as well as I do that there's only one reason for me to go back with you."

Grayson tugged Laurel closer then, adjusting the straps beneath her chin. "So, you can sleep in?" he offered, clearly pleased with himself. "So, you can use tiny bottles of shampoo? So, you don't have to make the—"

"I get it!" she laughed, shoving him off her. "Keep your distance, smartass. I'm not compromising New York."

"I'm the reason you're going!" he laughed, incredulous. He seemed to get an idea then and added, "I can take it away, you know."

"You could, but you won't," she replied, taking it upon herself to slide her hand back into his.

She was right, of course.

"Come back with me," he repeated. "Not for sex."

She looked dubious.

"You can sleep, roll out of bed, take a hot shower, and eat breakfast," he explained, as if it were the simplest thing in the world. "I promise I won't hog the covers."

Laurel glared. Of course, he would want them to sleep in the same bed, even if this was just an offer of convenience. He was not making it easy to avoid the temptation he offered, and she almost hated letting him have his way, but it was an alluring offer.

Laurel watched Grayson mount the bike and she took a deep breath before declaring, "There will be a pillow wall."

Chapter Thirteen

♣

There was no pillow wall.

They'd managed about ten minutes in the confines of Grayson's room before they were on one another.

"Don't let me regret this," she mumbled against his mouth.

"Never," he breathed, hands roaming her body. He stripped off each article of clothing, leaving a trail in their wake. They were both desperate for one another, despite Laurel's reservations.

Naked, they stumbled together towards the bedroom. Grayson was attempting to walk, kiss her, and fish a condom out of his wallet all at the same time. He was failing.

"Just give it," Laurel groaned, pulling his wallet out of his grasp. Since it was clear where things were headed and Laurel had clearly given in, she seemed to be on a mission. Laurel pulled the foil package free, ditched the wallet over her shoulder, and tore it open.

"Now that's what I'm talking about," Grayson chuckled, leaning in to catch her lips once more.

She tipped her head back out of reach, her hands sliding down between them to find him already fully hard. She worked the condom onto him, watching his hooded eyes as he gave her room to sheath his erection.

"It's been a little while, by the way," she confessed.

He lifted a knee onto the edge of the bed, crawling over her as she eased back. "How long's a little while?"

A shaky laugh left her, and she pulled his mouth down to her own. "None of your business."

When Laurel had first met Grayson outside the cafe, she'd never imagined she'd be in bed with him several days later. She normally wouldn't have given him the time of day, which was her usual response to any flirtatious interest. It wasn't that she was averse to dating, or to hooking up. She'd had her fair share of male attention, but, as she'd said, it had been a while. She kept up with her birth control well enough, just in case.

Things at home had been increasingly draining, and she hadn't been in the headspace to enjoy casual things like dating.

However, Grayson hadn't given in to her attempts at pulling away. He'd lured her in with the promise of a job and kept her interest with his playful mannerisms. Each time she gave an excuse as to why they should stop, he easily poked holes in her reasoning. He constantly reminded her that things weren't all that serious and had goaded her into letting her guard down.

As Grayson parted her thighs with his knees and slid into her, Laurel let out a soft breath of pleasure. He was watching her, his usual mischievous grin replaced by something entirely new. She swallowed under the weight of his stare, returning his gaze.

"Christ, you're beautiful."

He'd said those exact words before, the last time he'd been between her thighs.

"You're not so bad yourself," she replied, breath catching as he shifted.

Grayson wasted no time in rocking against her, setting a pace of slow, deep thrusts. She yielded around him, body pliant and warm beneath him.

Tucking his head down, Grayson captured the peak of her breast with his lips. He was rewarded with another breathy moan and took her nipple into his mouth.

Laurel watched him with half-lidded eyes, lips parted to accommodate her heavy breathing as he sank back into her again and again. Slowly, almost contemplating the gesture before acting on it, her arms wound around his neck to hold him close. She whimpered a broken curse as a warm shiver rushed up her spine.

His voice was low, breath hot on her neck. "I've got you."

All things considered, it was a relatively vanilla coupling, and yet Laurel felt electricity in her veins as Grayson increased his thrusts. The wave of pleasure rolled up from her toes and she let out a pitched shout of pleasure as it barreled over her.

Her orgasm was sudden, rippling through her in several intense shudders. She was only half aware of Grayson's heavy grunt, his loss of tempo as he rode out his own release.

Lying supine beneath him, Laurel blinked up at the ceiling.

"That was…"

"Amazing?" Grayson offered, his laughter low and breathy as he leaned down to kiss her.

"I was going to say fast," she confessed.

Grayson's head shot up, his look one of sheer disbelief. "Did you just—?"

"I meant me," she laughed, shoving at his chest to push him aside.

Complying, Grayson shifted from her and disposed of the condom. "I honestly can't tell if you're insulting or praising me," he confessed, but laughed regardless.

"For my ego's sake I'll assume I hit all the right buttons faster than most."

Rolling her eyes, Laurel slipped from the bed and headed for the adjoining bathroom.

"Sure. Go ahead and think that, hot shot."

"Same room in New York!" Grayson called after her, grinning once more.

Smiling to herself, Laurel shut the door and met her reflection in the mirror. She looked well and thoroughly flushed, hair mussed, and lips swollen. Although sleeping with Grayson had been satisfying, it jeopardized her one and only job. She had told herself that she was drawing a line, that she would follow the only rule given to her to dig herself out of her current situation faster. Apparently, she couldn't. A fact which disappointed her.

After a leisurely shower, Laurel returned to find Grayson had hardly moved aside from getting under the covers. His breathing was deep and even, and she was silently grateful for the ability to escape any sort of post-coital conversation. She set an alarm for six-fifteen and found a charging cord on Grayson's side of the bed. As she stood there, her eyes landed on the illuminated screen of his phone, the preview of a text message visible.

Nikki: I want to see you again before you leave for NY. Tomorrow night? xo

For a moment, Laurel felt nothing, and then the wave of jealousy struck hard. First, she hadn't meant to invade his privacy; she would never have looked at his messages purposefully. Second, Laurel hated that she felt anything in response to what she was seeing; Grayson wasn't supposed to mean anything to her. Last, she was risking everything by sleeping with him, and he had no cards on the table.

The unfairness of it infuriated her. She had half a mind to pack up and leave, but the amount of time, not to mention money, it would take for her to go all the way home only to come back a few hours later to meet with Alaric had her fatigued.

Laurel glanced over at Grayson where he slept, oblivious. She calmed as she reminded herself that there was nothing wrong with any of this. If Grayson was seeing or sleeping with someone else, that was his right. Unless she asked him not to, or at least admitted they were dating, he was free to do whatever he wanted. So, why did she care?

Chapter Fourteen

♦

Alaric returned to his room after the card game concluded. After a shower, he found himself antsy. He was exhausted, but he also knew that Gemma was just downstairs at one of Borgata's restaurants. It was only about an hour and a half since they'd spoken; there was a good chance she'd still be eating considering they had a large party.

Amazed that he found the energy, Alaric rode the elevator downstairs in a fresh suit, leaving his jacket upstairs.

"If she's there, I'll confirm her tickets. If she's not, I'll text her tomorrow," he muttered to himself.

Sure enough, Alaric spotted the group towards the front of the restaurant, toasting with a round of shots. As he approached, Gemma wasn't the first to spot him.

A petite brunette abruptly straightened and started talking, gesticulating to Gemma. He couldn't make out her words just yet, but the intention was clear. Six pairs of eyes landed on him.

"Alaric," Gemma acknowledged, not bothering to hide her surprise. "Um. Hi."

A blonde to her right was grinning so hard it had to hurt, but she was very clearly drunk.

"Ladies," he greeted them. There were a few snorts and some laughter, but Alaric wasn't dissuaded.

"Did you want to take a shot with us?" the blonde offered.

"Oh my God, Hailey, shut up," another laughed.

"Not tonight," he politely declined.

He ignored the teasing for the sake of watching Gemma, appreciating the low neckline of the silver and taupe dress she wore.

"Can I steal you?"

The words were out of his mouth before he could think of a better way to ask for a few moments alone.

Before she could answer, there were hands shoving at her and Gemma could only laugh at how embarrassing the situation had become.

"Sure," she mumbled, shooting her friends a glare. "I'll be right back."

"No hurry," Hailey smirked.

Alaric turned, nodding for them to head across the lobby together. "You're a wild bunch," he teased regarding the shots he'd witnessed.

"You alright in those heels?"

"I'll manage," she assured, tucking her curls behind her ear.

She felt more comfortable once they'd put distance between themselves and her friends, but then a new kind of nervousness took root.

"Where are we going?" she asked. For all she knew, he was leading her to his hotel room, if he even had a hotel room. She wondered if he lived on-site or if he had a house nearby. He seemed a bit older than her twenty-four years.

"The box office," he replied, stepping closer as a couple passed them in the opposite direction. "If that's all right."

She had to admit, she was disappointed. Not that she would have willingly gone home with him, but she was hoping his presence was related to more than just the free tickets he'd promised.

"Probably shouldn't have had that last tequila shot," Gemma joked.

Alaric cleared his throat. Was she fishing, or was she honestly this cute? He offered his arm, nodding to it until she clasped a hand around his bicep.

Gemma let out a quiet laugh at his chivalry, shaking her head to clear her blush. "Thanks."

Their steps were unhurried, and Alaric found himself enjoying the rare company at his side. They wove through the casino floor, excited cheers and whistles surrounding them. "Gemma," he said, catching her attention once more. "Where are you from?"

Gemma smiled up at him. "I'm from New York. What about you?"

Alaric had to admit, he was pleased by the news. It wasn't as if he expected her to be from the west coast; they would have chosen Vegas over Atlantic City in a heartbeat for a bachelorette. However, New York wasn't terribly far. And just why was he concerned about how far away she was, anyway?

Clearly distracted, he failed to respond to her question.

Gemma gave him an uncertain look. "Is that classified information?" she joked. "Where you're from?"

"Oh," he cracked a smile, looking caught. "No. Sorry, it's not. I'm from Iowa."

"Iowa?" she repeated, surprised. "Well, that's far. What brought you to Jersey?"

Unlike most of the locals, he hadn't grown up in the area or been sucked into the gambling lifestyle. "I went to grad school in New York," he explained. "Took this job shortly after."

Gemma considered that. If he'd already gone through graduate school and been working here a while, he was definitely older.

"Well, you're very good at it," she praised playfully, squeezing his arm.

He smirked, closing his free hand over her fingers where they lay. "Don't be cute."

Gemma felt a flutter in her stomach, but she couldn't tell if it was triggered by excitement or anxiety. This was flirting. He was flirting.

As they arrived at a bank of elevators, Gemma glanced over her shoulder towards the wall of cashiers and other services.

"Isn't the box office that way?"

Alaric hoped she didn't mind a detour. "A quick stop upstairs first."

As Gemma pulled back slightly to regard him, Alaric was quick to realize how that may have sounded.

"The Roof," he quickly assured. "I was just going to show you something."

Reassured, but only slightly, Gemma nodded. Her phone chimed in her purse, but there was no way she was letting go of Alaric's arm to check the message.

"Boyfriend checking up on you?" he asked, voice curious.

"No," Gemma reassured, and then laughed. "No, there's no boyfriend. That was probably one of my friends teasing me."

There was no need to ask what about, since it was obvious Alaric's presence had caused quite a stir.

"I hope they're not too hard on you," he offered.

They stepped into the elevator with a small family and Gemma released Alaric's arm, moving to stand at his front. She could practically feel his warmth behind her, and she stared ahead at their reflections in the mirrored panels. She felt his hand at her neck and gasped quietly, listening to his low chuckle as he drew a few strands of hair off her shoulder.

"Sorry," he offered quietly, amused by her reaction.

"No, it's…it's fine," she assured. As if to convey just how clearly fine it was, she reached back to find and clasp his fingers lightly.

Alaric lowered his attention to watch, turning his hand to take hers in his own. She really was ridiculously sweet. It was a small gesture, but it seemed to speak volumes.

The family departed, but they had only a few moments alone again before they reached the roof. Alaric led her straight into the night air, along a covered walkway.

Gemma hadn't realized his intention at first, but The Roof was Borgata Hotel & Casino's most exclusive nightclub. The music was pumping and a line of waiting guests stretched back to the elevators.

Slipping around a velvet rope, Alaric held it for her. "Perks of working here," he said.

Hand-in-hand, Alaric guided Gemma around the perimeter of the large clusters of people, catching a staff member for a quick minute. He was given a bottle of water and a rolled Borgata towel before they began walking again.

"Where are we going?" Gemma asked, leaning closer to be heard over the music.

He squeezed her hand in response and soon, they slipped along the side of a concrete building used for furniture storage during storm season. He slowed when they reached a long, empty stretch between the building and the thick glass railing enclosing the rooftop deck. There was only about two feet of space, but it was quieter and private.

He set the towel on the lip of a wide concrete planter and gestured for her to take a seat.

She sat gingerly, accepting the bottle of water as well. "This is nice," she complimented, but it was accusatory. "Do you bring all the girls you perform surgery on up here?"

Alaric leaned against the glass partition, facing her. "Cute."

Gemma looked out across the night's sky; the sun mostly set but still casting a warm glow over the ocean. It was otherworldly, really. She could scarcely believe she'd abandoned her friends to flirt with a total stranger, letting him pull her away to a private spot at some nightclub. It was the most excitement she'd had in a long time.

"How's your leg?" Alaric asked after the reminder of what had happened earlier.

"Fine," Gemma assured, quickly changing the topic to a much more interesting subject. "Can I see your tattoo?" She'd only caught a glimpse beneath his rolled sleeves by the pool and was itching to see more.

Alaric rubbed his jaw in thought, controlling a grin.

"Please?" she pressed.

Without a word, he began to unbutton the cuffs of his sleeves. He watched her watching him, encouraged by the blush staining her cheeks.

Beneath his shirt he wore a black tee, and he pulled at the material with a questioning look. He would have to remove it if she wanted to see the entire design.

Gemma nodded wordlessly.

Alaric reached back, pulling the fabric over his head to reveal toned abs and a myriad of images etched in dark ink. "It's still a work in progress."

Gemma had expected the sleeves, but she hadn't expected that his entire shoulders and upper chest would be covered as well. Her lips parted in silent surprise as she drank in the painstakingly inked skin and the ripples of muscle. Whatever mildly thrilling feeling she'd been experiencing easily kicked up several notches.

"Oh."

Alaric laughed, encouraged further by her reaction. "Just oh?" he asked, stepping closer until they were toe to toe.

From where she sat, Gemma stared up at him, gulping.

"They're beautiful," she offered honestly.

Alaric draped his shirts gently across her lap, freeing his hands. He raked them into her hair on either side of her neck and bent closer.

"You're beautiful," he countered.

Both alarmed and thrilled by his closeness, she whispered, "Thank you."

Alaric laughed, tipping forward to brush his lips to her forehead in an affectionate gesture. He drew back and reached for his shirts, but Gemma quickly took hold of the fabric, refusing to release them.

He gave her a curious look as she challenged, "You call that a kiss?"

The playful growl Alaric offered had Gemma's pulse kicking into overdrive.

"I suppose not," Alaric muttered, wrapping a large hand around Gemma's elbow to lift her to her feet. She stood at least a head shorter than him, staring upwards as he cupped the side of her face. His bare chest was warm and so close, and she couldn't help setting her hand lightly against his skin, over one of the more intricate designs.

"What's this—?" Before the words fully left her, Alaric had captured her lips with his own, throwing caution to the wind. There wasn't exactly a rule against fraternizing with guests, they were adults after all, but it was risky to be making out with someone at your place of work, in a blocked off area, shirtless.

The kiss lasted a good few minutes, during which time Gemma found herself leaning more and more against Alaric's sturdy frame.

When he lifted his head and broke the kiss, he was practically holding her up.

"You alright there, sweetheart?"

Gemma quietly cleared her throat, straightening herself. "Yes; thank you."

"Did you just…did you just thank me for kissing you?"

"No," she replied quickly, pushing his shirts into his chest. "Put your shirt back on."

He would have much rather evened the score by removing her dress, but he kept that thought to himself. Donning the black t-shirt, Alaric watched as Gemma seemed to wriggle with poorly contained glee in front of him.

"So, about those tickets," he began, playfully returning to the matter at hand. "The box office has them at will-call."

Gemma looked crestfallen at the sudden topic shift, but then Alaric added, "Though I was hoping you might come to dinner with me while your friends attend the performance."

Gemma's smile returned. "Comedy shows aren't really my thing anyway," she replied.

"So, that's a yes?" he clarified with a raised brow.

"That's a yes," she echoed.

He draped his long-sleeved shirt over an arm and then held out a hand for

Gemma. She was loath to put an end to this moment alone, but a dinner date was something she could look forward to. She lingered to look out at the city once more, taking a deep breath.

"It really is amazing up here. It's too bad we're only around for four more days."

Alaric said nothing, though he processed the information. The idea of Gemma no longer being around had him feeling surprisingly disappointed. Alaric was a hard worker, committed and loyal. He went above and beyond, took every opportunity afforded to him to better his career, and what did he have to show for it? He lived on-site at the hotel, worked most hours most days, and got to see his two closest friends only when they passed through town. That was the life he'd created for himself. And suddenly, it wasn't enough.

"But the wedding should be fun," Gemma went on. "My friend Kayla's getting married to her girlfriend, Jess. My ex is her brother and we set them up in the first place."

Alaric just stared back at her, thinking how unfair it was that the people he met never stayed long. He would probably never again meet someone like Gemma, living the way that he did.

Gemma belatedly realized that mentioning her ex may have been a mistake. "Sorry," she offered. "I have no idea why I brought that up."

Pulling on her hand, Alaric started to lead her back towards the elevator. "We've all got exes," he assured.

"I guess," Gemma agreed. She only had one major ex, and it was about time she got over him.

Slowing, Gemma dug her heels in so that Alaric was forced to turn.

Mustering up all the courage she could find, she asked, "Is there somewhere we can go that's more private?"

After a beat, Alaric smiled.

"My room or yours?"

Chapter Fifteen

♠

Alaric's exhaustion took a quick backseat to hope as Gemma agreed to head back to his room. He wasn't going to assume, but he'd be surprised if she'd turn him down after all the flirting they'd done. Plus, it had been her idea to relocate.

He let them into his hotel room and set his unworn button-down on the back of a chair. He went about his usual routine, emptying his pockets and stepping out of his shoes. It felt odd having someone with him, which didn't happen often. He was no saint, he partook in the occasional hookup, but they were few and far between.

Alaric had known from those early moments of meeting Gemma that he wanted to be around her again. Her smile was infectious, and though he liked to say he didn't have a type, he did.

He was grateful they weren't wasting any time, especially knowing she was going to be gone in only four short days.

Gemma set her purse beside his things, leaving her heels behind as well.

"I wasn't sure you lived here," she confessed.

"I do," he confirmed, gesturing around. It was no more furnished than a normal hotel room, which seemed a little sad to Gemma.

Alaric's heated gaze landed on her, waiting to follow her lead.

His stare was doing strange things to Gemma. She'd heard of lust at first sight, but she'd never felt it firsthand before.

Although Alaric knew very little about her beyond her name, she didn't mind in the slightest. He was kind of funny, extremely attractive, and had been sweet to her all day. If she was going to hook up with someone, he was pretty much the ideal candidate.

Summoning all the confidence she had, Gemma drew her brown hair forward over one shoulder and reached back for the zipper of her dress. The bodice sagged and she slipped her arms from the sleeves to let the weighty garment fall, her gaze never leaving Alaric's.

His hazel eyes took a lingering trip along her body as he reached for her. His palms cupped the sides of her jaw, and he lowered his lips to gently press to hers.

Gemma didn't have the words adequate to describe how it felt the moment their mouths came together again. She hadn't felt this level of attraction or desire towards another person before. Not even with her ex.

The pads of her fingers slipped beneath the hem of his shirt, climbing upwards and raising the fabric with her forearms' ascent.

"I want you," she whispered against his lips, ignoring the heat in her cheeks from her confession.

Alaric pulled her tighter to him, feeling the press of her curves down his front. Gemma seemed to take the words right out of his mouth. He moved, sweeping Gemma in a half circle as he lifted her from the ground. Much like he'd carried her from the poolside to the cabana earlier, he transported her to his bedroom.

Need flooded him. Desire, he expected, but need wasn't typically the winning emotion for Alaric in any situation. As soon as he set her down, he began to disrobe.

Gemma watched, transfixed at the raw desire she saw in his gaze. There was no questioning that he wanted this just as badly as she did. That fact calmed her somewhat, knowing she wasn't alone. She drank in the sight of his tattoos as they were once again revealed to her, noting the individual components and their detailed shading, and finding herself wondering just how long all that artwork had taken.

Once his shirt was gone and his pants were opened, Gemma pounced. Kneeling at the edge of the bed, she slipped her hands down the front of his loose pants and into his boxer briefs. It was the most brazen thing she'd ever done in her life, and she realized she was near to laughing in disbelief at her own actions.

Alaric rocked forward a bit, reaching out to steady himself with a hand on her arm. "Jesus," he breathed. "Warn a guy next time."

Gemma blinked up at him. Alaric's teasing comment was astonishing to witness, and she suddenly wanted more.

Biting her lower lip, Gemma cupped his length. She had to confess; she was startled by his size. He was both larger and older than both the young men she'd slept with before.

The warmth of her hand had Alaric's full attention. He remained still aside from his hand at her shoulder. Catching the strap of her bra, Alaric drew it down her pale skin. His other hand lifted, and he reached over to repeat the action. Then, he drew it lower to ease the cups from her breasts and bare them to him.

Gemma would have been self-conscious if it weren't for the way Alaric was responding to her touch. His erection hardened in her hand, and she moved her palm against him, watching his heavy gaze linger on her chest.

The silence between them continued as she slowly shifted her hand, stretching up to catch the back of his neck. Alaric tipped down, helping her reach him, and met her lips in a firm kiss. His hands cupped her small breasts, thumbs brushing across pert nipples.

They touched one another for a few long minutes, but Alaric was the first to withdraw. "If you keep that up, sweetheart," he mumbled, "I won't last another five minutes."

Gemma retracted her hand with a blush, making room to accommodate him as he climbed onto the bed. He detoured to retrieve a condom and Gemma nodded, thankful.

"On your back," he said, which had butterflies taking wing in her stomach.

Alaric hooked his fingertips into the sides of her underwear and drew them down her legs, drinking in her body as she was exposed to him. Her thighs opened, almost embarrassingly quick, and Alaric eagerly covered her. Gemma felt his fingers caress the slick heat between her legs and moaned softly.

He lowered his head to kiss her neck, rubbing his fingertips against her body.

There was no good reason why fingering Gemma would make Alaric think of New York, but he suddenly realized something ironic. Gemma was from New York and would be in Jersey for four more days. Alaric, on the other hand, lived in Jersey, but was going to New York in two days' time.

Thankfully, Gemma's next gasp drew his attention back to the moment and he decided to return to that line of thinking later. Deeming her more than ready, Alaric grasped his shaft and guided it into the tight heat of her body.

Gemma took a deep breath at the sensation, wrapping her ankles around his calves as she felt him wedge snuggly inside. She was thankful to find not much discomfort, the pressure of his size only making her more sensitive to even the slightest movement he made.

"Okay?" he breathed beside her ear.

Weakly, she nodded, turning her face to catch his lips.

Running on only four hours of sleep and a 14-hour workday, Alaric was practically delirious. Delirious, and smitten. When he'd met Gemma earlier, she'd been adorable and sweet, reassuring and kind. He never would have imagined her interested in sleeping with him at all, let alone so quickly. He wondered, briefly, if he was having a very lucid wet dream.

She groaned his name quietly and he cursed, rolling with her suddenly until she lay above him, her thighs splayed at his hips.

Gemma gasped at the sudden change in position and lifted herself weakly onto outstretched arms, hands pressing into the mattress just above his inked shoulders. Her bra was still stretched across her chest, bunched beneath her breasts and the straps looped at her elbows. Still, she tossed her dark hair over one shoulder, barely missing a beat as her hips lifted and lowered. She was too turned on by the sight of him beneath her to be embarrassed. A pink flush spotted her skin, but she shut her eyes, giving herself over to the pleasure building between them.

A few more rotations of her hips, a few thrusts upwards from below, and the pair were falling over into bliss one right after the other.

Alaric first, his fingers digging into her hips as he bowed up from the bed.

Gemma soon after, a quiet cry escaping her as she tensed and then gave a long, drawn-out shudder.

Gemma's brows wrinkled lightly as he rolled them again, his body remaining tight to hers. A mild aftershock rippled through her in response, and she gave a quick, obedient nod, her cheek pressed to his.

Alaric disengaged from her body, catching her lips in a slow kiss before he pulled away. As he padded to the bathroom, Gemma peeled the covers back to slip beneath, feeling shy in the dimly lit room.

"You would look unbelievable with a tattoo," he offered upon his return.

Of all the things Alaric could have said, his suggestion was unexpected. She wriggled out of her bra finally, leaving her naked beneath his sheets.

"Really?"

He dropped to lie alongside her. He drew the covers back, his fingertips grazing the skin of her arm, then her breast.

"Absolutely."

Goosebumps rose on her skin as she allowed him to touch her as he wished.

"I kind of always wanted one," she confessed, breath hitching as his lips replaced the path of his fingertips.

Pushing the covers away, Alaric pressed his bare body along hers, devouring her.

"Stay the night," he requested, to which Gemma easily agreed.

Chapter Sixteen

♥

It was completely unlike Alaric to oversleep, but he and Gemma had had quite the night. As a result, he'd left his phone outside of the bedroom, and hadn't heard his usual alarm.

When he finally awoke, more than an hour late to breakfast with Laurel, he cursed. He found his cell riddled with emails and messages; the top two texts being from Laurel and Parker.

Parker: Can't make Friday's game. Dealing with a work crisis. Sorry, mate.

Laurel: I'm sure you're busy. Just wanted to let you know I'm in the lobby.

Alaric cursed again on both accounts.

Gemma awoke shortly after, finding herself alone in bed. She tugged the sheet free and draped it around herself, peering out the door. She spotted Alaric in the kitchenette but frowned at the obviously tense expression he wore. He sat hunched over his computer and she was suddenly nervous all over again. Sure, last night was wonderful. Amazing, even. But he had to return to work, and she was probably overstaying her welcome.

"I'm sure my friends are probably wondering where I am," she said, announcing herself. She crossed his living area and scooped up her dress where they'd left it the night before.

Alaric watched her for a long moment, his posture noticeably relaxing. His response, however, had him bracing for the worst. "I have to go to New York tomorrow."

Surprised, Gemma stared back at him. The disappointment she felt was instantaneous and embarrassing. She thought she'd have four days of this: four days of more time alone, more flirting, more sex. She was finally being spontaneous, something her ex had told her she was incapable of.

"Okay," she replied, understanding. Still, she couldn't help but feel sad that their time together was now further limited.

Alaric looked between his computer screen and Gemma. She stood a dozen feet away, naked save for a sheet, her dress clutched in her hand. He had a startling realization that he was an absolute idiot. Who would walk away from this?

"Would you like me to stay?" he asked.

Gemma was thrown. She wasn't sure what it was that he had to do in New York, but why would it matter what she wanted? Obviously, if she had the choice between one more day with Alaric and three, she was going to want three.

"Is that a trick question?" she offered with a pathetic smile.

Alaric came around the small island to take her dress out of her hands.

"I don't actually want to go," he explained, hands going to her sheet-covered sides.

"Then don't?" she smiled, going up on her toes to meet his lips.

Lifting Gemma from the ground, Alaric grinned and carried her back to bed.

♥ ♠ ♦ ♣

URGENT: NYC Private Poker Game Tomorrow. Limited Availability.

Sadie,
I've been given the opportunity to arrange a last-minute high-stakes poker game in Manhattan. If your schedule permits, you would depart tomorrow, Friday, at 3:00pm and return Saturday evening by 7:00pm. All transportation, lodging, and meals will be covered. Borgata Hotel & Casino will also supply you with $1,000 to be used on-site at the game.

Participation in this game is first-come first-served. Although we'd love to guarantee you a spot, space is limited. If you are available to join, please reply ASAP and hopefully we can still extend the offer.

Alaric Nacario
Senior Operations Manager
Borgata Hotel, Casino & Spa

Sadie read through Alaric's email with interest. "Looks like I'm joining you," she told Laurel while they grabbed a late breakfast together.

Alaric had been a no-show and Laurel could have killed him. She had only agreed to stay with Grayson in his hotel room because of the breakfast meeting Alaric had insisted upon. Laurel had waited for over an hour, only to be greeted by a terse text of the logistical details. He hadn't even had the decency to properly cancel or apologize.

Alaric: Limo leaves tomorrow at 3 from Borgata entrance. Room reservation is under my name @ Ritz-Carlton Central Park. $500 + tips, hotel. Classy cocktail attire. Pls confirm.

Laurel: Got it.

As Sadie typed out a reply accepting the emailed offer, she continued, "Alaric needs another player in New York."

Laurel accepted another mimosa from their waitress as her smile grew.

"New York, where Mr. Great Sex lives?" she prompted.

The pair had just finished rehashing their latest escapades, including Sadie's newest admirer.

"I never called him that," Sadie admonished. "I called him Mr. Not My Town Car."

"Right," Laurel replied, laughing, "But he's obviously a man of many hats."

"As is Mr. Charming, apparently," Sadie tossed back at her, setting her phone down. She felt compelled to message Parker her latest travel plans but didn't want to come off as desperate.

Laurel groaned, cupping both hands over her face. "I regret telling you," she whined.

Sadie waved off her embarrassment.

"Oh, please. You're both obviously hot for one another. It was going to happen eventually, and it sounds to me like you needed it."

She wasn't wrong. Laurel hadn't had sex in a little over a year before Grayson, and he'd knocked her expectations out of the park. Her body seemed to thrum around him, which complicated matters.

"I may have seen a text on his phone from some other woman," Laurel confessed, but was quick to add, "I wasn't snooping. I was just standing there, using his charger, and it popped up."

"And you read it," Sadie concluded.

"Well, yeah."

"And what did it say?"

"I want to see you before you leave for New York," she sighed. "And then it suggested getting together tonight."

After a beat, Laurel accused, "Don't look at me like that."

Sadie laughed. "Well, you know what you have to do, right? You have to ask him out tonight and see who he chooses."

♥ ♠ ♦ ♣

"Kayla, come look!"

In the bachelorette's suite, half the young women were clustered at the door to receive a delivery.

"This is so sweet," Ashlee said, carrying a colorful floral arrangement to Kayla where she sat painting her nails.

"Jess is seriously the cutest," Hailey complimented, praising Kayla's intended.

Kayla leaned forward to smell the picture-perfect bouquet, beaming.

"Oh my God, these are so nice," she gushed, pointing to the card tucked between the stems. "Can someone read that?" she requested, fanning her wet nails.

Hailey plucked a small orange card from the arrangement that complemented the orchids. She opened her mouth as if to read a sonnet professing undying love. Instead, all that came out was, "Alaric Nacario?"

Gemma startled at the sound of Alaric's name, gasping as she quickly realized the flowers were not from Kayla's fiancé.

Gemma slowly stood up from her seat on the couch, trying to ignore the looks of sheer disbelief her friends offered as she gently extracted the card from Hailey's hold.

"I think these are for me," she confessed.

"Holy shit!" some of the girls exclaimed in near unison.

Hailey, at least, had the good sense to shoot Kayla an apologetic look. "Sorry. You know Jess loves you."

Kayla rolled her eyes. "I know, I know. It was my idea to do separate bachelorette parties," she sighed. "She's giving me space." She rounded on Gemma, looking devious. "But this is an interesting development. Those don't exactly scream 'thanks for the one-night stand.'"

A tall blonde fell to the sofa with a smirk. "Geez, Gem, what did you do for the guy?"

"You clearly left quite the impression," Kayla added.

"When are you seeing him again?" they prodded.

After a guilty pause, Gemma confessed, "Tonight, I think?"

"But we have the comedy—" Realization dawned on Ashlee's face. "Oh my God, you ho. You're ditching the show to go out with him again, aren't you?"

Gemma groaned and quickly spun to Kayla. "This is your weekend, Kayla. You know I'll go to the show if you want me there."

"You're uninvited," Kayla declared diplomatically. "I hereby ban you from the comedy show and our hotel room. You'll have to fend for yourself."

Gemma couldn't stop a pathetic smile from pulling at her lips. "You are literally the best."

Chapter Seventeen

♣

Alaric: I'm skipping NY. Need you to handle my usual intros/elbow rubbing. Limo leaves tomorrow at 3. Room under your name @ Ritz-Carlton Central Park.
Grayson: You owe me
Alaric: I never ask you for anything.
Grayson: Not my problem. You owe meeeeeeeeeee
Alaric: Pls be more professional in NY.
Grayson: You're the one who decided to put me in charge
Alaric: I'm regretting it already.

♥ ♠ ♦ ♣

At just past eight o'clock, Gemma stood by the elevators in the main lobby where Alaric had suggested they meet that night. Before her friends had left for the comedy show, they had insisted on helping her get ready for her date. Gemma was coerced into borrowing one of Ashlee's dresses; a short red cocktail dress she found herself pulling down every few minutes.

As the elevator doors slid open to reveal her date, she smiled.

Even if it hadn't been Gemma, Alaric was sure he still would have been caught staring, just like every other guy that was passing by; Gemma's dress was just a little too low at the top and a little too short at the bottom.

Heat flared behind his ears and Alaric stepped forward to greet her. He cleared his throat and offered in a playfully strained voice, "Are you kidding me with that dress?"

Gemma's skin flushed and she glanced down at herself, biting her lip playfully. "You like it?"

Alaric reached down to casually adjust his belt as he stepped around her. He liked it a little too much, apparently.

"Are you hungry?" he offered, sliding an arm around her back. They hadn't exactly made plans; they both knew how the night would end.

Gemma glanced around the lobby, towards the restaurants and the casino. When she spoke again, her blush deepened. "I heard room service here is actually pretty good."

Without missing a beat, Alaric used the arm around her back to turn her towards the elevators and proceed back the way he'd just come.

Laughing, Gemma covered her face in embarrassment. Were they really that bad? Skipping any sort of pretense and getting straight to the sex?

Gemma was grateful to have an elevator to themselves. As Alaric punched the button for his floor, she slid her arms around his waist and leaned into him, taking in the scent of his cologne. She felt a tug at the hem of her dress and looked down to see Alaric trying to conceal at least a little of her exposed thighs.

She looked up in time to see a young man practically gawking before the elevator doors slid shut. Groaning, Gemma turned her face into Alaric's chest, smiling as his arm came around her.

"You probably made his night," he teased.

Tipping her head back, Gemma stared up at Alaric as he watched her, leaning up to kiss him in the privacy of the elevator. "He's not the one I'm trying to impress."

"Consider your mission successful, sweetheart."

A beat later, she asked, "What if I said I wanted to get a tattoo before I leave?"

Surprise crossed Alaric's features. Gemma had admitted to having considered getting a tattoo before, but it still caught him off guard.

"I could call my guy," he offered, fingers skimming her arm affectionately. "See if he can squeeze you in."

Gemma shivered from his touch. "You'll go with me?"

Alaric nodded, leaning down to press their lips together as the elevator slowed. He'd spent the entire day thinking about her, their night together, and the fact that he'd rearranged his plans just to spend another few days in her company.

The New York game had only come about because Parker had been interested, so Alaric had set it up at Grayson's urging, but then Parker had backed out. This time, Alaric was doing something for himself.

Once they were inside his suite, Gemma kicked off her heels and reached back for the zipper to her dress.

Behind her, Alaric stated, "The bruschetta burger is pretty good, actually."

Gemma's hand stilled and she turned, mortified, only to find Alaric laughing at her. She clearly had very little interest in eating, and Alaric couldn't help but tease her.

Setting her hands on her hips, no longer trying to get out of her clothing, Gemma faced him expectantly.

"You think you're funny?"

Alaric grinned as he opened a drawer and pulled out the standard-issue room service menu.

"I feel like I should feed you," he explained, his gaze hot as it roamed down her body. "If we don't eat first, we might not get around to it."

Gemma licked her lips, hands slipping to hang at her sides. She took a step closer, reaching for his suit jacket. "After," she requested, voice quiet.

Alaric groaned as if he were put out, but it faded into one of need as Gemma pressed herself against him. He caught the back of her neck and kissed her, brushing his tongue against the seam of her lips.

She opened to him, moaning softly as his hands crept up along her bare thighs to grasp her hips. The dress fabric folded and pleated around her middle, and Alaric wasted no time in peeling her thong down her legs. As it slipped to the floor, so did Alaric and he knelt before her, leaning in to taste her.

The genuine gasp that leaked from Gemma was loud in the hotel room, and she grasped his shoulders as she felt the heat of his tongue on her most sensitive parts.

"Oh, my motherfucking biscuits and gravy," she exhaled in a rush.

Highly amused, Alaric leaned back to grin up at her. "What was that?" he asked.

"I— nothing," she assured, licking her lips. "I just usually…" She was losing any possibility of forming coherent thoughts as Alaric's mouth returned between her thighs. "It's usually just sex," she explained finally.

Alaric leaned back again, staring up at her for a long moment. "Am I—?" he began to ask, but he couldn't fathom the idea. "Am I the first one to do this for you?"

Gemma cleared her throat, brushing back her hair as she seemed to consider the question.

"Jesus Christ," he muttered, "If you have to think about…" Before he could finish that thought he was back at the junction between her legs, grasping her thighs to hold her close as he licked and stroked.

A low, quivering moan leaked from Gemma's throat, her head rolling forward. She was left panting in no time, shivering with each touch to her swollen clit. She staggered backwards as Alaric finally moved, and realized he was guiding her towards the couch. Once she'd sat, his hands were beneath her thighs, pulling her to the edge as he leaned back in.

Dazed and shivering in anticipation, Gemma slumped heavily into the couch. Her hands went into the neck of his sport coat, gripping the collar of his shirt beneath as she began to near a peak of pleasure she was desperate to crest.

Encouraged, Alaric reached between them, his fingers joining the efforts of his mouth. As his tongue focused on the button of nerves, he slid two thick fingers into her body, the ample wetness making it easy.

Gemma gasped and held tight, tensing up for a few long seconds before she let out a quiet cry of accomplishment as an orgasm wracked her lithe frame.

Rather pleased with himself for his performance, Alaric sat back on his heels. Gemma barely registered the fact that he was stripping; his sport coat slid to the floor, and his t-shirt sailed over his head.

When his tattooed chest and arms swam into view, Gemma moaned. Thanks to a little pregaming in the bachelorette suite, she felt warm and flushed, and thought him to be the most perfect specimen of a man she'd ever seen.

Alaric wiped his face clean with his shirt and then made short work of the rest of his clothes, standing once he was nude. Gemma's eyes roamed his skin, sliding up along his build and then back down to what was now at eye-level. He had apparently gotten worked up by going down on her, and she licked her lips as he stepped closer.

It was obvious what he was wondering, and she was very much willing. Sitting up on the coach, Gemma reached for his hips to pull him closer. He stared down through half-lidded eyes, determining that, unlike receiving oral sex, giving it was not as rare for her.

Gemma wrapped her hand around his thick shaft, leaning forward to caress the plump tip with the flat of her tongue. Alaric's groan was taken as helpful encouragement, and she turned her face to lick along his full length.

Watching her, Alaric was transfixed. He combed back her hair, letting his hand linger loosely behind her neck. His increasingly heavy breaths and the way his fingers tangled in her hair emboldened Gemma further. She took his erection into her mouth, working him with her hand and tongue.

His hands fell to her shoulders, and she managed a glance upwards, watching his expression contort. She had a feeling he was trying to prolong his release. With a final soft nudge of her lips to the underside of his shaft, she mumbled, "Condom?"

It took him a few seconds to convince himself to move, but Alaric eventually stepped back to retrieve one from his wallet in the pile of clothes at his feet. Once sheathed, Alaric pulled Gemma up from the couch and turned her around.

She was momentarily confused until he bent her forward and she grasped the back of the couch with a quiet, "Oh."

He encouraged her to set a knee against the couch cushions and then was lining up their bodies, pushing in from behind.

Gemma gasped, her arms tensing as her body rocked forward from his thrust. She still wore the red dress, and she had a vision of what they must look like at that moment, with Gemma braced against the couch and Alaric naked and bucking against her.

His hands tightened on her hips to keep her still and Gemma moaned, her head tipping forward weakly.

"I'm so close," she breathed.

Alaric's grunt of agreement was right beside her ear, and she knew he'd bowed over her, his breath hot on her neck. After another few minutes they both erupted in pleasure.

In the aftermath, as they enjoyed their room service dinner, Alaric's hand slipped into the gaping neck of Gemma's robe and drew downward to part the fabric.

"Right here," he said, tracing his fingers over the curve of her hip. "That's where you should get the tattoo."

Gemma laughed, pulling away at the ticklish sensation. She closed her robe and glared at him, pointing on the outside of the fleece. "Here?"

He nodded, leaning forward to steal a few sweet potato fries. Alaric wore a pair of sweatpants while Gemma wore his robe. Not a Borgata-issued robe, but his personal one. He liked the way she swam in the fabric.

"That could work," she considered. "You know," she added as she leaned back on the couch and pulled her legs up. "Before, when you asked about being the first to do that for me?"

Alaric gave a cautious smile. "Yes?"

"Well, I think you guessed that I'm not super experienced. I actually haven't been with a lot of people."

The way she'd offered the information had Alaric wondering if he should or shouldn't ask for clarification. Ultimately, he settled for simple acceptance of her shared history.

"Okay."

Gemma watched him, chewing her lip. "Like, only three. Including you."

Alaric gave a soft laugh of uncertainty. Was he supposed to be flattered? He wasn't entirely sure why she was sharing, and he felt trapped in how he was meant to respond. If he acted shocked, would she feel bad about herself? If he pretended not to care, would she think him insincere?

"I'm honored," he replied, carefully neutral.

"I'm twenty-four," Gemma blurted.

Alaric laughed, rolling his eyes as he wiped his hands on a cloth napkin. His flippant reaction conveyed that he wasn't taking her seriously, and that surprised her.

"I'm twenty-four," she repeated.

Doubt clouded Alaric's features as he stared back at her. "You're twenty-four," he repeated, licking his lips uncomfortably.

Gemma had suspected he was older from the beginning, but his reaction had her suddenly worried.

"I'm guessing you didn't realize," she offered, feeling her face warm. "Are you a lot older?"

Alaric nodded slowly, confirming. "Thirty-three," he confessed, curious to her reaction.

It was Gemma's turn to appear surprised, and they both regarded each other for a long minute. Neither of them seemed deterred, just thoughtful.

"Does it bother you?" she asked, hoping that he'd keep it to himself if it did. She was suddenly panicked that she'd ruined their fun-filled days together by revealing their age gap.

"Does it bother *you*?" he echoed.

Gemma considered the question. She'd only ever been with guys her own age and she personally found it flattering than a man as mature as Alaric had found her captivating. Personally, she found his age advantage on her to be unexpectedly appealing.

"No," she admitted.

Alaric took a deep breath, processing the new information. Gemma was young, but not underaged.

"Me neither," he replied.

The age gap was unexpected, but it would take a lot more than that to change Alaric's developing feelings.

CHAPTER EIGHTEEN

♦

That Friday, Laurel stood outside Borgata's entrance at three o'clock sharp, awaiting transport to New York. Combating the Jersey summer heat, she wore a cotton sundress with her hair swept up in a loose knot at the nape of her neck.

Arms wrapped around her from behind and a low voice murmured in her ear, "Hey, sexy."

Laurel was quick to wriggle out of his hold. "Hey," she greeted, doing a quick sweep for Alaric. "You're really bad at this whole discretion thing," she reminded him yet again.

Although Alaric wouldn't be traveling with them, Laurel wouldn't put it past him to arrive to see them off. She couldn't take any chances with public displays of affection with Grayson, despite the growing closeness between them.

Grayson obediently kept his hands to himself, though he looked less than thrilled. At least in New York there would be no one to supervise, and she would have no valid excuse to push him away.

An SUV limousine pulled into the carport and Grayson hefted his and Laurel's overnight bags.

Behind Laurel, Sadie announced, "I'm here, I'm here."

Laurel turned to greet her friend, the older woman's smile catching.

"What do you look so happy about?" Laurel accused as they crossed to the SUV.

"I am most definitely going to get me some in New York," she declared.

Smirking, Grayson mumbled, "Me, too."

Glaring at him as he helped load Sadie's bags into the truck, Laurel replied,

"Not if you keep this up."

"Are you over Mr. Great Sex?" Laurel asked Sadie as they took their seats.

"I'm planning to *surprise* Mr. Great Sex," Sadie clarified with delight, pushing her sunglasses into her hair.

Laurel looked impressed. "Any chance you've got a picture?"

Sadie considered it. While she didn't have any personal photos, a quick Google search confirmed that he was listed on the Campbell Holdings' website. She turned her phone for Laurel to see, grinning.

Laurel's jaw unhinged. "Are you serious?" she laughed. "He's drop-dead gorgeous. How did you ever let him out of your bedroom?"

Grayson's brows narrowed and he reached for the phone, but Laurel was quick to darken the screen and pass it back.

Sadie hummed in approval. "I know, right? I kind of can't stop thinking about him."

♥ ♠ ♦ ♣

Dressed to kill, Sadie entered the midtown Campbell Holdings' building with a plan and her famous poker face. If she was going to succeed in surprising Parker, that meant no calling ahead about her visit.

She sweet-talked her way into a visitor's pass and rode the elevators up, praying that he was in the office that day. She didn't know much about Parker's day-to-day life, but he seemed to split his time between gambling and helping with the family business. As it neared five-thirty that evening, she only hoped she could still catch him. She knew showing up unannounced was a roll of the dice, but that was what she did best.

The elevator opened to a set of glass doors, frost-etched with the Campbell Holdings' logo. The company's suite comprised the entire floor and was outfitted wall-to-wall with stainless steel, glass, and dark mahogany wood accents. She was greeted by a woman behind the reception desk.

"Good afternoon. How can I help you?"

Sadie moved her handbag from one elbow to the other, smoothing her long waves. "I have an appointment with Parker," she replied simply.

Plan A: Appear disinterested and overly confident.

"Of course," the young woman replied with well-practiced patience. She opened Parker's calendar on her computer screen and asked, "Your name, please?"

Looking insulted, Sadie guffawed. "Are you joking? Is he not expecting me?"

Hannah gave a polite smile and offered the universal sign for "just a minute." She pressed a button on her headset and waited.

"Parker, sorry to bother you. I don't see anything in your calendar, but there's a woman here to see you."

Parker turned away from the pile of paperwork on his desk to rub his eyes. He could only imagine that it was something his father had confirmed, a VIP client or the lead of an acquisition team. He replied into the intercom, "Okay. Thanks, Hannah. Send her in."

To Sadie, she offered a smile and stood to escort her. "Right this way."

Thrilled to hear that her ploy had worked, and Parker was present, Sadie followed suit. She smoothed a hand down her form fitting dress as she followed, straightening her posture. This was either going to go very well, or very poorly. If Parker didn't enjoy being surprised at his place of work, Sadie needed to ensure she remained unaffected. She planned to act calm and casual, no matter what.

Hannah led Sadie to a large boardroom, gesturing for her to go ahead. "Please have a seat. He'll be right with you."

Too nervous to sit, Sadie set her bag down and stepped over to the floor-to-ceiling windows to enjoy the view a lot of money could buy. No more than three minutes passed before Parker arrived, looking pristine in a tailored suit.

"I apologize for the wait," he offered, closing the door behind him.

Sadie gave a low laugh of amusement, turning to face him. "You need to step up your security, Parker. They'll let any pretty face in here."

Parker froze, astounded. He gave Sadie a lengthy once-over, lips parting. He had never been stunned speechless by any woman before. Sadie Bache, the woman who had been plaguing his thoughts since he'd first laid eyes on her in Atlantic City, was standing in his office. Unsurprisingly, she was just as glamorous as he'd remembered.

Somehow, Parker managed to recover from his shock with a soft clearing of his throat.

"Well," he said, stepping forward. "I've never had a stalker before."

Sadie smiled. This was going well so far, and she breathed a quiet breath of relief at the fact that he was taking her sudden appearance in stride. She approached to meet him in the center of the room, shrugging.

"Consider this your lucky day, then."

Shaking his head, Parker regarded her in awe. His accent was thickening, and he realized he was getting aroused just at the sight of her.

"I can't quite believe you're here, doll."

"Just for the night," she confessed. "I've got a game this evening."

His gray eyes lingered on her lips. He wasn't sure why he hadn't kissed her yet, but he worried if he did, he wouldn't be able to stop. "When does it end?"

"Couldn't say," she admitted. "Give me your number," she offered. "That, I couldn't find."

He laughed at the fact that she had managed to learn where to find him, but not locate his phone number. "All right," he agreed. He watched her extract her phone from her purse and dictated his number. How in the hell was he supposed to go back to work after this entertaining interruption?

In a rare quiet moment that followed, Sadie asked, "You don't mind my showing up unannounced?"

He could recognize the caution in her voice, but he was quick to shake his head and reassure, "This is a very welcome surprise."

Parker was no romantic, but when a woman like Sadie came calling you did not, under any circumstances, let her slip away.

With their brief exchange done, Sadie stepped around him and dragged a hand down his arm as she went. "I'll see you tonight, sugar daddy."

Parker's lips parted again, laughing at the term of endearment she'd chosen. It was ironic, given her own wealthy status, but he enjoyed the teasing. He refrained from reaching for her and instead accompanied Sadie at a close distance. His eyes roamed her figure, appreciating her curves and the sway of her hips.

He pressed the elevator call button, wishing with every fiber of his being that he could follow.

Sadie gave him a heated look as she stepped inside and winked, just as the doors slid closed.

Chapter Nineteen

♠

"Checking in?"

Grayson and Laurel stepped up to the hotel counter together. Laurel was buzzing with excitement, so much so that she failed to care that she was hanging on Grayson's arm. All thought of the text message she'd seen on Grayson's phone was out of her mind, or at least crammed as far back as possible, to make room for genuine delight at finally making it to The Big Apple. Testing his loyalty hadn't seemed fair when they were sneaking around to see one another.

She had finally reached New York. Even though it was a quick trip, she was elated. This was a first step in the direction of the new life she wanted for herself. She'd been glued to the window the entire drive in and couldn't stop marveling at the various aspects of their surroundings.

"Two rooms under Alaric Nacario and Grayson Lee," Grayson said at the check-in counter.

Although Grayson and Laurel were shacking up together in secret, the suite under Alaric's name was where the card game would take place.

They were given two keycards to each room and Grayson split both sets between him and Laurel.

"Grayson Lee," said an amused, deep voice from further back in the lobby line.

Grayson and Laurel stepped away from the front desk and Grayson smirked when he spied a familiar face of another card player.

"Roman Hill," Grayson greeted, shaking hands.

"Haven't seen your sorry face since the Denver tournament last year," Roman said by way of greeting, his attention lingering on Laurel. "And who's this?"

"This is Six." Being mindful of her desire to remain professional, Grayson offered, "She's a good friend of mine and an employee of Alaric's."

That scored him some points, and Laurel cast him an appreciative smile. She shook Roman's hand when he offered it. "Nice to meet you." He looked a bit older, maybe in his mid-forties, and she noted that his eyes seemed unable to remain above her shoulders.

"Lucky us," Roman grinned, his grasp lingering. "Six, was it? That's unique."

Laurel shrugged, offering an "it is what it is" sort of laugh. If Roman was going to be participating in Alaric's game that evening, she knew she stood to make some good tips from him if she kept him smiling.

Roman leaned closer as if sharing a secret and said, "It's nice to see Alaric's standards for employment have gone up."

Grayson extracted Laurel's hand from Roman's, giving him a mild glare. "Okay, Romeo. We'll see you later."

"You'd better be ready," Roman told him, smirking. "Payback's a bitch."

Putting a hand at Laurel's lower back, Grayson began to lead her towards the elevators, both their bags in his other hand.

"What was that about?" she asked.

"Nothing, he's just a sore loser. I cleaned him out last time I saw him."

Laurel glanced back as they waited for the elevator and gave a tight smile when she noticed Roman's stare had yet to leave her.

♥ ♠ ♦ ♣

Laurel: Did you find him?
Sadie: I blew his mind.
Sadie: Not literally. Yet.
Laurel: Ha
Laurel: Do you know a guy named Roman? Older? Saw him at the hotel. He's playing with you guys tonight. Good tipper?
Sadie: Hill? Total sleazeball. On my way back. Free for a drink?
Laurel: Yes! Lobby in 20

Taking up a pair of stools at a bar a few blocks down from the hotel, the women got right down to business discussing Sadie's visit to Parker's workplace.

"Considering how much fun we had last time, I'm not confident I'll make our drive back tomorrow," Sadie grinned.

"Wow," Laurel laughed, impressed.

Sadie was confident in herself and what she wanted, and Laurel envied her. Laurel knew she wanted a better life, but that didn't make her confident. She knew she wanted to relocate to New York, but that was about it. As for Grayson, she couldn't deny she liked him, but she wasn't stalking him or gushing about how he made her knees weak the way Sadie went on about Parker. Still, she thought that what they had going on behind closed doors was pretty good.

"Seems like you really like this guy," Laurel observed.

"I like his stamina," Sadie confirmed, accepting her martini with a wink. "Among other things."

Taking a deep breath, Laurel regarded the people and commotion around her. She was in a bar in the heart of New York's upper east side. It felt like a monumental accomplishment, but there wouldn't be many more of these feelings this trip. They had only an hour or so before the game was due to start.

"Are you planning to pull an all-nighter and go down to Times Square later?" Sadie ventured.

Suddenly, that sounded like the best idea Laurel had ever heard. What reason did she have to sleep that night? Absolutely none.

"One hundred percent," she decided, lifting her drink to toast her friend. "Win fast tonight so I can get a head start."

Sadie laughed, clinking glasses. "I promise to do my best."

♥ ♠ ♦ ♣

At five to seven, Grayson was lounging on the couch, on the phone with Alaric. "That's a lot of bullshit you're asking me to memorize," he complained.

"No, it's really not," Alaric replied tersely. "You've seen me do it a hundred times. The dealer will handle everything else."

"Jesus, you're so bossy." Grayson had to remove the phone from his ear due to the volume of Alaric's reply.

Laurel wasn't surprised to find Grayson giving Alaric a hard time. Ordinarily, his obstinance was part of his charm, not that she'd tell him that.

As the fourth and final player arrived, Laurel greeted him and offered to make him a drink. Mr. Maddox Harper was already acquainted with Roman, Sadie, and Grayson, so the usual pregame chit chat was brief. Laurel served drinks from the prearranged beverage cart and the players mingled on the balcony.

"We meet again, Six," Roman greeted. "Although now you look quite ravishing."

With a sweet smile, Laurel inquired as to what drink he'd prefer. She ignored his comment, wondering if he even realized his words registered as an insult to her earlier appearance. Regardless, he had the power to tip well enough to move up her New York timeline, so she made sure to be nothing but smiles in his presence.

Roman followed her back inside, lingering close as she prepared his cocktail. "Where did Alaric find you? If you don't mind me asking."

"I live there, in Atlantic City," she replied. She wasn't planning on giving him her whole life's story, nor how Grayson had connected her to Alaric in the first place. "I worked at a cafe."

"Well, that must have been exciting," he said. "Getting to leave that behind and come hang with the big boys."

Laurel almost failed in controlling her expression. Was he serious? It wasn't as if Alaric, or Grayson for that matter, had saved her from being destitute. She also didn't respect these gamblers much more than she did her old boss Sam, or any other coworker she'd had. Still, she had to keep her cool or risk going home short-changed.

"It's definitely been something," she acquiesced.

From the balcony, Laurel overheard Grayson's voice.

"Shall we get down to business, gentlemen?"

As the quad took their seats around the card table, Grayson detoured to where Laurel was refreshing Sadie's glass.

"Cool it with Roman," he requested.

Idle flirtation he could handle, but Roman was grating on his nerves. He didn't doubt the older man was leaning into Laurel specifically to upset him due to the outcome of their previous tournament. "He's not worth it."

Laurel gave him a tired sigh. "It's fine. I can handle myself."

She knew a lot better than Grayson did about what was and was not 'worth it.' Laurel wouldn't have been surprised if she learned Grayson had never had to worry about money a day in his life. Letting Roman flirt with her, if it ended in a hefty tip at the end of the night, was definitely 'worth it.'

As if to drive the point home to Grayson that he should let her do her job, she said, "Of course, Mr. Lee. Have a seat and I'll bring that drink right over for you."

Grayson wasn't pleased that she was clearly dismissing him, but he had a job to do that night, too.

"As you can all see, our host isn't with us," he announced to their small gathering. "But I'm sure you each received a five-page email about that."

A chuckle arose from the group, the mood light.

"So, let's be civilized, follow the rules Al usually gives us, and may our losers be graceful." Grayson's gaze fixed on Roman as he took his seat.

The dark-haired man's grin faded at the jab, and he lifted his glass to drain it, holding it up. "Six, would you mind?"

Laurel set a bourbon Manhattan at Grayson's elbow and skirted the table. "Of course, Roman. Would you like to try something else? I make a mean martini."

Pleased at the attention, Roman exchanged cash for chips with the dealer as he accepted her offer. "Extra dirty," he winked.

As Laurel prepared drinks, her mind began to wander to Grayson's behavior. Not here tonight, but his behavior at his other games. Before she started working for Alaric, did Grayson act the way Roman and the others did towards the hired help? She didn't think Grayson would be as derogatory towards women, but a flirtatious nature was synonymous with high rollers; they expected to be admired and get whatever they wanted. After all, Laurel had said no to Grayson a dozen times, and he almost always got his way.

Laurel hated to admit that she was still thinking about that text message she'd inadvertently seen. How had Grayson spent his last night in Atlantic City? She hadn't been able to do as Sadie suggested and offer to spend it together, as a test. It felt wrong, and she was a little worried he might decline. If he'd said he had other plans, she wasn't sure how she'd handle coming to New York with him. In the end, she'd chickened out.

The pair hadn't spoken from the time she'd left his suite earlier in the week until their departure earlier that afternoon. After seeing him almost daily, it felt like a lot of time apart. She also hated that she had noticed any of this; she didn't want to be as interested in him as she was. She was frustrated and irritated, with herself more so than with him.

"Six?"

Laurel realized she was being summoned on Roman's third attempt and she quickly shook off her thoughts. As she approached, Roman's hand subtly grazed her outer thigh and she couldn't help a quick glimpse over at Grayson, glad he seemed otherwise occupied.

One by one, bets were placed and raised. The foursome was head-to-head until a time came when both Sadie and Maddox folded. Grayson wasn't backing down, and he and Roman were at their first stand-off of the evening.

Roman's hand was suddenly on the small of Laurel's back and he told her, "Watch me win this hand, gorgeous."

After a moment of hesitation, Laurel perched herself on the armrest of his high-backed chair. She didn't necessarily want to encourage his behavior, nor did she want to see Grayson lose, but tips were tips.

Try as he might to focus, Grayson was frustrated. He was heated by Roman's behavior and pissed off by Laurel's. She was tempting the wrong guy, but he knew if he were to bring it up again, he'd risk instigating a fight that would ruin their remaining time in New York.

Grayson lost that hand, and then another. After the fourth, he called for a break.

"Hey, don't kill the flow," Sadie complained. Unlike Grayson, she was up.

"Another drink?" Laurel offered as the group dispersed, noticing Sadie checking her watch. "I'm sure he'll wait for you," she added with a knowing smile.

On the balcony, Grayson dug out his phone.

Grayson: Your game fucking blows
Alaric: You're losing, I take it.
Grayson: Roman's here
Alaric: Yes, I know. I invited him.

Grayson: Why???
Alaric: Because that is literally my job, Gray.

By eleven forty-five, the final hand of the night was in play. It took considerable effort for Laurel not to cheer for her friend as Sadie swept the pot.

"A deserved win," Roman commended, pushing back his chair.

The dealer began to cash out each player and Laurel noticed that Grayson was pocketing less than the others. She supposed that he, like everyone else, had good and bad days at his job. Laurel perked up as Maddox approached, slipping her two folded bills with a wink, which was a pleasant surprise considering he'd been so quiet all evening.

"Thank you," she said, recovering gracefully.

Major loss as the evening was, Grayson still handed Laurel a pair of fifties. "Wait for me," he told her, detouring to the balcony to phone Alaric and rehash the outcome of the night.

Sadie pressed a pair of hundreds into Laurel's palm.

"For Times Square," she winked. "Let's both enjoy ourselves tonight."

Laurel felt a little strange accepting money from her friend, but she couldn't deny how grateful she was for her generosity.

"Thank you. Now go, I know you're dying to get out of here."

The dealer bid Laurel goodnight and she gave him a smile of acknowledgement as she crossed to the bedroom. She was excited to switch out her heels for sneakers and make the most of her first night in New York. When the door clicked shut behind her, Laurel began to speak before turning.

"Do you want to go downtown with me tonight?"

"I'd love to."

She registered that the voice wasn't Grayson's and turned, surprised. "Oh, sorry. I didn't mean…I thought you left."

Roman held up cash in hand. "Just wanted to thank you for your services."

Pushing down her discomfort, Laurel approached and accepted the folded bills. It seemed to be at least a hundred. "I appreciate your generosity."

Roman brushed the curtain of her hair off her shoulder, stepping closer. "I can be very generous," he confirmed.

Laurel jerked back, trying to recover as she gave him a teasing smile. "I bet, but I really should be going."

Laurel hoped he would accept her polite rejection, seeing as his forwardness was borderline inappropriate. She glanced towards the closed bedroom door, silently cursing the fact that she was out of Grayson's line of sight.

Roman followed and slide a hand behind her neck to pull her forward. "Don't play dumb," he laughed, moving to kiss her.

She knew she'd served him quite a bit of alcohol that evening, but there was no excuse for his behavior.

"Stop," she said, jerking back to prevent him from his goal. Any flirtatious pretense was long gone. "Roman, stop," she repeated, feeling his other arm wind tighter around her back. He was a lot stronger than she'd thought.

"I don't think so," he grinned, running his hand down to her ass to give her backside a squeeze. "You don't get to tease me all night and then walk away."

"Get off of me!" she demanded, shoving. The cash fell to the floor and Laurel pushed again, bringing up her elbow to dislodge one of his arms. To hell with his money.

Her heart clenched as she recalled Grayson's warning and she felt a wave of humiliation. She gasped as Roman's hand tangled in her hair, tugging roughly to cease her struggles.

Desperate, Laurel screamed.

Chapter Twenty

♥

A wave of panic washed over Grayson at the sound of Laurel's cry. He tripped on the hotel carpet as he sprinted, his phone skittering across the room as he scrambled for the bedroom.

He found the door unlocked and swung it open, growing utterly still at the scene inside.

Roman turned at the interruption, sneering.

Laurel was panting, one of her hands in her hair atop Roman's, her head craned backwards. Roman was practically wrapped around her, his other hand somewhere beneath her dress that Grayson couldn't see.

"I'm going to fucking kill you," Grayson breathed before lunging.

Sensing the tables were turning, Roman released Laurel with a grunt of disgust. He managed to spit out, "Fucking tease," just before Grayson was on him.

Laurel staggered back, pressing herself to the wall and fighting a surge of nausea as the pair drunkenly grappled with one another.

Grayson managed a solid jab that had Roman's teeth clattering, but it wasn't nearly enough for him to feel satisfied. He was murderous, and intoxicated, but his reaction seemed to fan the flames of Roman's anger, too. With as much strength as he could muster, Roman slammed his fist into Grayson's abdomen in retaliation.

To Roman's credit, Grayson could feel that the older man had put all his weight behind the punch, but he was too slow. His fist managed to graze Grayson's side, earning a grunt from him, but it had missed its mark. Grayson returned the punch, landing it straight in Roman's gut.

Roman crumpled as his breath left him, grabbing the edge of the bed as he went down, clutching his stomach. Grayson tugged at Roman until the man's shirt ripped, and then threw him back to the ground.

"You piece of shit!" he yelled, shoving his shoe into Roman's back. His actions were uncoordinated, but effective.

Prioritizing his own personal safety over getting handsy with the cocktail waitress, Roman held out a hand to stop him.

"I— I got it," he wheezed.

Breathing hard, Grayson stared down at the older man. He was tempted to haul him to his feet and throw him over the balcony railing for touching Laurel against her will. He was surprised he was keeping a level head, considering how the room was repeatedly tipping from all the drinks he'd consumed.

Grayson's gaze whipped over to Laurel then, quickly assessing her. She seemed whole, but clearly shaken. When his eyes met hers, Laurel's trance appeared to break. She stumbled from the room into the adjoining bathroom, slamming the door.

Grayson's eyes fell shut for a moment, filled with too many emotions to handle. He felt sad for her, guilty that he hadn't prevented this, and angry; so very angry.

"Get the fuck out," Grayson slurred, his tone sharp. The adrenaline had spurred him into action, but he was nowhere near sober.

Roman got to his feet, leveling a glare on Grayson. "Listen..." he began, as if about to lecture him in a drunken stupor, but Grayson was in no mood to hear another word from the filth standing before him.

"One more word," he said, "and I will seriously fuck you up."

The room was silent aside from Roman's labored breathing as he picked himself up and limped unsteadily out of the suite.

Grayson ran his hands back through his hair, trying to put himself back together. He pulled off his suit jacket and threw it on the bed, sweaty and irritated. Finally, he approached the bathroom door. He stood outside of it, unsure.

"Laurel?"

Laurel pressed the palms of her hands to her eyes, hating how the sound of his voice made the tears flow harder. The fact that he'd used her real name made the situation even more serious.

"Can I come in?" he muttered.

She sniffled, pushing loose tendrils of her hair back. "Please don't," she called, voice breaking.

Grayson closed his hands into fists, exhaling heavily. "Did I not tell you to stay the fuck away from him?"

He knew it was a mistake the moment the words left his mouth. He was too angry to discuss what had just transpired. He knew it wasn't her fault that Roman had crossed a line; he was just upset that it had happened on his watch.

Laurel's posture went rigid as the reprimand hit her, and she turned to stare at the closed bathroom door in shock. She couldn't believe what she was hearing.

"Go to hell!" she yelled back, shooting to her feet. She was seething now, her embarrassment morphing quickly to rage. "You're such a fucking asshole!"

Tipping forward, Grayson pressed his forehead to the cool door. "I know," he sighed.

Laurel seemed to have no answer to that, and the two remained silent for a few long minutes.

Washing her face and drying her tears, Laurel gathered herself. She knew she couldn't stay in the bathroom forever. Grayson was quiet as he listened to the sounds on the other side of the door.

"I just want to make sure you're okay," he confessed. "Please—"

The door opened and Grayson's forehead slipped. He staggered forward, catching himself on the door jam. Laurel stared back at him as he righted himself, giving him a pathetic shake of her head.

"Move," she told him, slipping around.

Grayson turned to follow her with his gaze, rubbing the back of his neck.

She wasn't proud of it, and it pained her to do so, but Laurel picked up the money strewn across the floor. She added the bills to her purse, stepped out of her heels, and reached back to unzip her dress.

All the while, Grayson watched quietly.

"Can you bring my bag?" Laurel requested.

Both their belongings were in Grayson's suite, and he knew then that she was implying she would be staying in Alaric's room for the night. It pained him to think that he'd upset her that badly.

"Please," he begged, stepping closer. "I'm sorry."

Laurel's dress loosened around her, but she froze. He sounded honestly genuine, and she wasn't sure what to do with that. Glancing over at him, she observed, "You're drunk, Grayson."

He sensed it would be a mistake to touch her, so he stepped up beside her and leaned against the credenza. "Drunk and sorry," he confirmed. "Roman…he's a piece of shit, baby."

The affection in his voice, paired with his sweet talk, had the start of a tired smile lifting her lips.

"Come here," he requested, opening his arms.

Laurel tried to fight the comfort of his embrace. She thought it would serve him right to be left standing there, unable to have what he wanted for once. However, she wanted it just as much and it would be more of a denial to herself than to him. She tipped into his arms and they went around her quickly, enveloping her in his warmth.

"I've got you," he breathed, gently smoothing her hair down.

Curling her hands in his shirt, Laurel held herself to him and let his presence further calm her.

"I'm an idiot," she whispered.

"A sexy idiot," he mumbled in return, which had her laughing pathetically. He counted that as a win.

Laurel eased her arms around his middle and stood with him for a few long minutes in comfortable silence. When Grayson finally broke it, it was to state: "Your suite's bigger than mine."

His comment drew another weak laugh from Laurel. He had the unique ability to always keep things lighthearted and it seemed to break any lingering tension over what had just occurred.

Grayson's hands settled on her hips, and he eased back to look at her.

"Are you hurt?"

"No," she answered easily, shaking her head as she returned the assessment. "Did he land anything?"

Grayson scoffed. "He hits like a girl."

Laurel's eyes narrowed. "Would you like me to hit you so you can compare?"

Lips ticking up into a smile, Grayson amended, "He's not as strong as I am, Six. I'm fine."

Hearing her old nickname again made her relax even further. She patted his chest, placating him.

Grayson's hands played at the back of her unzippered dress, caressing her exposed skin. "Can I help you out of this?" he offered.

She suddenly needed to know something, something that would either make or break their night together.

"Are you sleeping with anyone else?"

Grayson looked wildly confused by the question. "How did we go from—"

"Who's Nikki?"

Totally lost, Grayson began to shake his head. "What—"

"What did you do last night?" she pressed.

He was either too drunk to follow their conversation, or she was coming out of left field with some hefty accusations.

The previous evening, Laurel hadn't invited Grayson out to see if he would choose her over the woman who had texted him. She regretted it now because there was no way to know aside from this confrontation.

"I ordered room service and watched Netflix," he replied carefully, his voice even. "Where are you going with this?"

Her stare dropped from his face, guilt rising. "Alone?"

Laurel had never envisioned herself being a jealous, suspicious girlfriend. Then again, she wasn't his girlfriend.

At Grayson's silence, she confessed, "I saw a message on your phone."

Before he had a chance to react, she was quick to add, "You're the kind of guy who gets who and what he wants, Grayson. I know I'm just your most recent conquest, but it'd be nice to know even a little about you sometimes."

Grayson's forehead furrowed as he tried to sober up for this conversation. As far as he was concerned, he'd done nothing to earn her distrust.

"If you saw something on my phone, you misunderstood it," he countered.

It was Laurel's turn to be silent.

"Nikki works at the hotel, in hospitality," he offered. Grayson tucked a knuckle beneath Laurel's chin to bring her attention back to his face. "I'm not sleeping with her. Or anyone else."

What surprised Laurel more than anything was that she automatically believed him. She felt relief as her questions were answered and she obtained the responses she'd been hoping to hear.

"Are you—" he began to ask in turn, but Laurel quickly cut him off with a shake of her head. "Just you."

Slowly, realization dawned on Grayson and his megawatt grin made Laurel groan in embarrassment.

"You were jealous," he declared happily.

Groaning, Laurel pushed at him. "Forget it," she grumbled.

Undeterred, Grayson tugged her closer into a tight hug, his hands slipping into the parted panels of her dress against her back.

"You like me," Grayson mumbled into her neck, swaying back and forth.

"What are you, five?" Laurel muttered, poking him in the ribs.

Hissing, he retracted his arms.

"Grayson?" she asked, concerned.

Untucking and pushing up his shirt, Laurel revealed an angry red stain across his abs. "Shit, we need to put ice on this."

They gathered their things, zipped Laurel back into her dress, and relocated to Grayson's suite. After a brief stop at the ice machine, Laurel had Grayson lying on the bed with a washcloth of ice pressed lightly to the forming bruise. She wore one of the hotel robes, seated beside him.

Grayson's chilled fingertips slipped beneath the terrycloth and Laurel playfully swatted his hand away.

"Thank you," she said finally. "For dealing with Roman. That was very 'big brother' of you."

Grayson gave a low snort. "I think defending your honor is more of a romantic notion, no?"

Laurel hummed in consideration. "Maybe. I wouldn't know."

Gathering that meant that Laurel had no brothers, he asked, "Sisters?"

Shaking her head in response, Laurel sighed, "It's always just been me and my mom. What about you?"

"A sister," he confirmed, brushing his fingers across her skin lightly, comfortingly. "We're not that close."

"Is she still living where you're originally from, or…"

He grinned at her sudden interest in him. "Well, I'm from Tennessee and she lives here in New York."

"Tennessee?" She was clearly surprised by the news. "You don't have an accent."

"Didn't stay in one place for very long," he explained. "Military school in

Connecticut and backpacking in Europe instead of college, then a few years in North Carolina where I've got a place. Plus, I get around playing cards."

Laurel's eyes widened as he shared. She had the good sense to question whether he was being honest. "Is all of that true?"

He chuckled, squeezing her thigh. "It was a suitcase, not a backpack, but yes."

She shoved his hand from her leg. "And the military school part?"

"It was more of a reform school," he admitted, shrugging casually. "It was just for a year." Grayson gave her thigh another playful squeeze. "You good?"

Laurel smiled, but it was tight. "It's just that I haven't really done anything like that. I haven't traveled. Until now, I've never even left Jersey."

"Does it matter?" he posed.

"It does to me," she answered honestly. The only thing he'd mentioned that Laurel could relate to was skipping college. It also surprised her to hear he had a residence in another state.

"Would you like to go somewhere? With me?"

Her smile was instant, and she suddenly felt shy, fixing the ice pack against his side. "Maybe."

"Maybe, my ass," he laughed.

"And what about you and me?" he prompted, picking up where they'd left off earlier. "Are we officially a thing now? Exclusive and all that?"

Laurel knew there would be consequences, and she wasn't sure how long they'd be able to hide it from Alaric, but she knew it was time to stop fighting her feelings.

"Yes," she confirmed, leaning down to press her lips to his. "We're exclusive."

Grayson's hand slid into her hair, keeping her close as he deepened the kiss with a quiet groan. Finally, he'd gotten her to confess that she wanted to be with him. The delayed gratification of hearing her agree she wanted a relationship was well worth the wait.

Laurel's fingertips ran down his bare chest until they found his half-unfastened belt and made quick work of finishing the task for him. She wanted him, and she was willing to be extra careful not to injure him further.

Grayson groaned as Laurel slid down his body, her lips descending over the defined muscles of his stomach. Reaching behind her neck, Laurel pulled her hair free, letting her caramel tresses tumble forward over her shoulders and tickle his bare skin.

She gently worked his cock free and took him into her mouth, tongue stroking the underside. Encouraged by his shaky exhale, Laurel took her time, head bobbing slowly in his lap. She welcomed him deeply down her throat again and again, moaning quietly to add the pleasurable effect of vibrations along his shaft.

In minutes, Grayson felt the tell-tale tightening sensation in his lower abdomen. He winced faintly at how it aggravated his fresh injury, but he was more than willing to bear it. However, if he didn't say something soon, she was going to be disappointed later.

"It's this..." he panted, his heavy-lidded stare watching her every move. "Or that."

Laurel lifted her head, licking her lips in thought. She could either continue and give him the pleasure he was building towards, or they could switch to sex.

"What do you want?" she asked huskily, leaning down to brush her tongue against the plump tip of his erection. "You decide."

He nodded towards her without delay, signaling her mouth. "This."

Laurel's lips curved and she took him back past her lips, tongue flicking and sliding against the sensitive underside. It wasn't long before she felt him twitching in her grasp and his hips arch faintly from the bed. Her lips withdrew to the head and her hand worked over him, encouraging him through his climax.

With a low groan of satisfaction, Grayson gave in and caved to his orgasm. His hand tensed in her hair, and he shuddered, releasing into her mouth.

When she finally sat back on her heels, she teased, "Feeling better?"

With a devilish grin, he stretched, his wince minor. "Good as new."

As Laurel headed for the bathroom, he called after her, "Hey, why don't we stay a few more days? I'll show you around the city."

Laurel reappeared in the doorway, clearly surprised.

"Really?"

Grayson grinned, his heart squeezing at just how happy these simple things could make her, and the fact that he could offer them.

"Yes, really."

She had no reason to decline, but she also had a very limited budget. "How much is that going to cost?"

Grayson smirked. "Many more sexual favors."

CHAPTER TWENTY-ONE

♣

Parker stood on the balcony of his penthouse apartment as he enjoyed a cigarette and tried not to check his phone for the umpteenth time that night. It was nearing midnight, and there had been no word from Sadie since he had sent his address earlier. He knew she was tied up at her game, but he was antsy.

Sadie tipped the cab driver generously and approached the uniformed doorman outside of Parker's building.

"Good evening," the man greeted. "Visiting?" He knew every face that came and went, and Sadie was new.

"Parker Campbell is expecting me," she replied as he held the door for her.

"I'll let him know you've arrived, ma'am."

Parker all but jogged back inside when he heard the chime of his intercom signaling a call from the building staff. Depressing the communication button, Parker replied, "Yes, go ahead."

"Sorry to bother you, Mr. Campbell. Your guest has arrived. A lovely young woman."

Parker's grin grew as the familiar voice of the doorman announced his waiting company. Of course, a woman like Sadie would just show up when it suited her, with no warning. He chuckled. "That's fine, Frank, thank you."

When Sadie arrived on his floor, Parker was waiting in the perpendicular hallway that led to his front door. He leaned casually against the frame; arms crossed. The moment she came into view, his smile split his face. "You sure took your time."

Sadie gave him an innocent look, gesturing back over her shoulder as she approached. "I can leave."

"Oh, no you don't," Parker laughed, making a grab for her. He took her oversized handbag and set it in the entryway, helping her out of her coat.

Sadie took a moment to appreciate what she could see thus far of his home. She expected to be impressed and she wasn't disappointed. He also looked positively perfect in a casual pair of joggers and a t-shirt.

She stepped out of her heels and dropped a good three to four inches, which she noticed made Parker's smile widen. Her hands hit the wall of his chest to slide upwards and she began to back him further inside.

"Hi," she greeted, grinning.

Parker laughed, his hands sliding around her sides. "Hi there, doll."

Wasting very little time, Sadie reached up to clasp her hands behind his neck and draw him into a kiss.

Groaning, Parker confessed against her lips, "You have no idea the things I want to do to you."

"Tell me," she breathed.

Parker briefly wondered if he'd fallen asleep while waiting for her, and if this was some sort of fantasy. However, when Sadie's teeth caught his lower lip and pinched, he knew he was just the luckiest man on Earth.

"You'll see," he growled.

The pair slowed to a stop in the center of his sitting area, caught up in a feverish kiss. Sadie worked Parker's shirt off quickly, her hands going to the invisible zipper along her hip. Once he helped her out of her dress, she was quick to tug his shirt free and toss it aside.

"You smell incredible," he groaned.

"That's the scent of victory," she laughed, her voice breathy. "Pulled in over thirty grand tonight."

Parker could appreciate how impressive that sort of single-night haul was. "You want to be my sugar mama?"

Sadie wasn't naive enough to think that their financial situations were equal, as Parker was clearly better off, but her situation typically intimidated men. Though Parker was only teasing, it was nice to be with a man unthreatened by her success.

"Only if you'll be my sugar daddy," she countered, pushing him back to step out of the last of his clothes.

Parker was used to gold diggers and charity cases and had been unfortunately involved in his fair share of those situations throughout his dating life. Sadie seemed a gift from the gods; gorgeous, confident, and wealthy.

"Are we doing this here?" Sadie asked, pushing her loose waves back and reaching for the clasp of her bra.

Shaking his head in amusement at her directness, Parker gave her the choice. "Anywhere." And then he added, "Everywhere."

Her eyes warmed, dropping her bra to the floor between them. Parker's eyes honed in on the ink between and beneath her breasts, repeatedly amazed by everything about her.

"Pick a wall," she said.

Parker had finally met his match, it seemed.

"A wall?" he groaned, raking his hands through his hair to show just how much she affected him.

"Christ, that one," he answered, gesturing as he began to back her up in the direction of smooth stone.

Sadie's back hit the cool slab of concrete and she gasped. "Interesting choice," she mused, turning her head to eye the dark gray slab behind her.

Leaning against the wall with one hand, Parker used his other to draw her underwear down. He grabbed her thigh and hiked it over his bare hip to spread her, but she gave a slow shake of her head and pushed him back.

Parker watched Sadie rotate to face the wall and he suffered a moment of agony at the fact that she was only in town for a single night. Since her visit to his office, he'd thought of nothing else, completing half the work he'd meant to, and he would have worried for his future if she was easily accessible. Still, a guy could dream.

Parker stepped up behind her and gripped Sadie's hips, leaning his weight against her. "You're incredible," he whispered, his breath hot on her neck. He kissed a path across her shoulder blades, sweeping her hair out of the way.

"You're not so bad your—"

Gasping, Sadie's words ended abruptly as Parker's fingers slipped between her thighs from behind. She moaned as he brushed them through her damp folds.

"I'm ready," she promised through a whimper. "Just fuck me."

In no position to deny her, Parker gave his length a quick few pumps before feeding it into her heat. Sadie's forehead dropped to the concrete, and she pressed her palms to it, using the leverage to rock back against him.

"Fuck, yes," Parker exhaled, setting a quick pace as he rocked. His thrusts were smooth and sharp, and each time he felt their bodies connect with a quiet slap, her muscles clenched in turn.

Stretching an arm behind her, Sadie grasped for him. "Don't hold back."

A strained sound escaped Parker's throat at her instruction. He used his hold to draw her hips with him as he took a couple of steps backwards, bending her further before he continued thrusting. The new position earned him a quiet cry from Sadie, and he held her hips tight, pistoning against her until they were both breathless.

When she fell apart first, Parker silently congratulated himself. Right behind her in his orgasm, he tensed and gave into the shudder-inducing pleasure rippling through him.

"You," he said pointedly, trying to catch his breath as he kissed her back adoringly, "are going to be the death of me, doll."

She hummed her approval over his worship, sluggishly lingering against the wall as she recovered.

"And here I was thinking how alive I feel," she teased.

As they cleaned up, Parker had a moment of clarity. He didn't want Sadie to leave.

"Stay," he requested.

Sadie paused in pulling a change of clothes from her bag. "Stay the night?" In these sorts of situations, clarification was key.

"A few nights," he countered. "Don't rush off."

Sadie was shaking her head, but Parker advanced with a playful warning. "Don't make me tie you up."

Smirking, Sadie replied, "Promises, promises."

"Okay, now you have to stay," he laughed.

CHAPTER TWENTY-TWO

♦

"Say that again?"

Gemma shifted under the weight of her friends' stares, trying to act casual about the fact that she'd just told them she was getting a tattoo.

"I have an appointment to get a tattoo later," she repeated, rolling her eyes.

The girls were packing early, planning on tying one on and sleeping in late for the final twenty-four hours of the bachelorette party.

"Gem," Kayla laughed, eyeing her friend knowingly. "This wouldn't have anything to do with a tall, dark, and handsome hotel manager, would it?"

"Operations manager," she corrected through a guilty mumble. "And I always wanted one, but he mentioned he's got a guy."

"Oh my God, girls. Did you hear that? He's got a guy!" Kayla exclaimed sarcastically.

Gemma glared and thanked Hailey when she swung a pillow into the bride-to-be's face.

"Can you just drop it?" Gemma requested, fixing her hair in the mirror. She'd worn a dress, per Alaric's recommendation, for ease of tattooing and comfort afterwards.

"It's permanent," they reminded.

If Gemma were being honest with herself, that was exactly what she liked about it. The tattoo would be a permanent memory of her trip to Atlantic City, her ability to be spontaneous, and her enjoyment of an amazing few nights with an amazing man. She might have had to leave the following day, but she wanted something to remember him by.

♥ ♠ ♦ ♣

Alaric: Where are you? The driver says no one's arrived yet to head back.
Grayson: Going to see Parker — count me out
Alaric: Where is everyone else?
Grayson: You paying me to babysit?
Alaric: GRAY. The girls didn't show. Find them.
Grayson: They're both staying
Alaric: Was that so fucking hard?
Grayson: Define 'so fucking hard'

♥ ♠ ♦ ♣

It came as no surprise to Alaric when Roman Hill called to check in about the previous evening's card game. It was typical to exchange pleasantries, congratulate winners, and soothe the ego of those less fortunate. However, when Roman called that morning, it wasn't to shoot the shit.

"Roman, hi," Alaric greeted, reclining in his office chair. "I heard Sadie made out like a bandit last night."

Having had a night to nurse his wounds and let his hatred for Grayson Lee fester, Roman was in no mood for idle banter. He launched into an attack almost instantly, though he kept his voice even. "What sort of scam are you trying to pull, putting that arrogant little shit in charge?"

Faltering at the unexpected tone on the other line, Alaric paused. "Roman, you appear to have me at a disadvantage."

"This isn't the first time I've seen a host and the hired help trying to fix a game."

Indignation replaced concern and Alaric rose to his feet, trying to remain calm despite the accusation. "I think there's been some sort of misunderstanding." He attempted to lead with facts and reminded, "Grayson was in the red, too, as far as I heard."

"You're a smart man, Alaric," Roman seethed. "I've always accepted your offers and brought you players. But he and that girl of yours were signaling all night. I don't take that shit lightly, and I'm just about ready to tell you to fuck off."

For once, Alaric wasn't sure what to say. Grayson was one of his closest friends, and for the past six years that they'd known one another they'd been as close as brothers. They butted heads often and Grayson was known to grate on Alaric's every nerve, but Grayson would never take advantage of him. Alaric didn't entertain Roman's accusations for a moment. Still, he had to be diplomatic and show that he planned to investigate.

"Roman," he said seriously. "I will speak to everyone who was present. There's never been an incident like this at any of my games."

"That you're *at*," Roman spat.

Alaric shut his eyes for a moment, fighting the guilt that followed. He'd chosen to miss one single game, and this was the result. This is what he'd always been worried about and why he'd always put the work first.

"At the very least," Roman continued. "You should hire waitresses that asshole isn't presently fucking."

Gritting his teeth, Alaric's fist clenched against his desk. This part, at least, was all too familiar. Although he didn't suspect his friend of cheating, he wouldn't put it past him to be sleeping with another one of his employees behind his back. Plus, Grayson and Laurel had both opted to extend their stay in New York. It was glaringly obvious that they were spending it together.

Biting back a shout of frustration, Alaric replied, "Roman. I will personally handle whatever inappropriate behavior you witnessed. I'll call you tomorrow." With that, he ended the call and slammed his phone down onto his desk.

After a few long minutes of deep breathing, Alaric placed a phone call. When he couldn't reach his intended target, he dialed another.

"You've got a lot of fucking nerve," he stated when Laurel answered.

Laurel's steps slowed at the entrance to Central Park, a lump lodging in her throat. She watched Grayson's back where he stood a dozen feet away at a street vendor.

Carefully, she replied, "Alaric? Is something wrong?"

"Put Grayson on. Now."

"I'm not with Grayson," she attempted.

"Bullshit," he snapped. "Roman just called."

Laurel's stomach knotted. Alaric had spoken to Roman. She found it highly improbable that Roman would have confessed to the events of the previous evening. Alaric's temper pointed to a more likely fact that he'd shifted blame onto Grayson.

Quick to change her tone, Laurel accused, "Oh yeah? And what exactly did he tell you?"

"That you're out of a job," he snapped. "I told you to steer clear of Gray. This is why. We get accused of rigging games."

Laurel's jaw clenched. She ignored the comment about her job for the moment. She could understand how fraternizing could lead to those sorts of possibilities, but she also knew Grayson well enough to know that he would never do such a thing, and she was shocked that Alaric seemed intent on confronting him. Shaking her head, Laurel launched into her own angry rant.

"Did he fucking mention how he tried to force himself on me?" she shouted, uncaring of the few stares she received on the sidewalk. "Grayson is the only reason I managed to walk out of that hotel room last night!"

Alaric was silent. He didn't know Laurel well enough to gauge whether she would lie about something this serious. Roman Hill had a reputation, but Alaric had never witnessed anything personally. Plus, Laurel had been nothing but professional with him. His mention of firing her could have forced her hand, but deep down he knew it was unlikely.

Calmer, Alaric requested, "Can you please put Grayson on the phone?"

Laurel shoved the phone at Grayson just as he returned. "For you," she muttered, trading him for the oversized pretzel and walking away to cool down.

Confused, Grayson looked down at the screen to see a call in progress with Alaric. He suffered a moment of panic on Laurel's behalf and then put the phone to his ear, wincing as he answered, "Al? That you?"

"Roman called me."

Instantly, Grayson's attitude darkened. "He's lucky I didn't kill him, Al. You've got to ditch him. I'm not kidding. If I ever see him again, I'm not going to be held responsible—"

"Alright," Alaric cut him off. He had his confirmation; Laurel was telling the truth.

"I told her to keep her distance from you, you know," Alaric added, meaning Laurel. "You got a magic dick or something?"

Thankful that Alaric wasn't going to chew him out for yet another 'infraction,' Grayson chuckled. "Or something."

"Well, you know I can't risk it, Gray. I've got to let her go. Roman claims you two were cheating."

"We—"

"I know, he's full of shit. But that's how it is. So, you two either quit it, or she can go elsewhere."

Grayson watched Laurel where she was pacing up and down the block, tearing apart her snack angrily. A weak smile played at his lips. "I really like her, Al. Don't punish her because of me."

"It's not a punishment," he replied calmly. "It's a policy, and I won't change it."

After a long stretch of silence, Grayson attempted the only compromise he could think of. "What if I don't play the games she works?" he offered. "Book her for whatever you can and replace me."

"That won't be good for you," Alaric argued.

"She needs the job."

Another long silence lapsed before Alaric heaved a sigh. "Suit yourself, Gray."

Relieved, Grayson broke into a genuine smile. Laurel keeping this job was much more important. He could find other games, in other cities, though it would take him away.

"And Roman's out," Grayson added more seriously.

"Obviously."

CHAPTER TWENTY-THREE

As Gemma and Alaric caught a ride towards the tattoo parlor, Gemma couldn't help but notice his tense expression. She was nervous for her appointment, but nothing could distract her from just how much he was brooding.

"Is it salvageable?" Gemma inquired at his side in the backseat, earning his attention. "Whatever issue you're brooding over," she explained, squeezing his hand.

He reached up to pinch the bridge of his nose, letting his actions speak for themselves.

"Is anyone dead?" she asked.

Alaric shook his head.

"Is anyone suing you?"

He cracked a smile, shaking his head once more.

"Is it the end of the world?"

"I get it, sweetheart," he laughed.

Leaning closer, Gemma pressed her lips to his in a brief kiss. "Better?"

"A little," he replied, squeezing her hand affectionately. "You know what would fix everything, though?"

Gemma's brows lifted curiously.

"You, not leaving tomorrow."

Gemma offered a sad smile. She would have liked that, too.

Alaric reached out to brush her cheek with a thumb, trying to convey his sincerity. "Is that an option?"

Surprised, Gemma's pulse quickened. It was one thing to joke around, but

Alaric seemed serious. He wanted her to stay longer, to let her friends return home while she lingered. She would have loved to accept his offer without a second thought, but she knew that she would have to leave eventually. Did she want to fall even further before ripping the band aid off, or was it better to keep to her original departure date? There was no denying that she was having an amazing time with Alaric, but was it extra special because their time was limited? Was she throwing herself into this fun break from reality because it helped her forget her recent past?

"I have to tell you something," Gemma stated, taking a deep breath. "I was engaged."

Alaric listened carefully, trying not to jump to conclusions.

The last thing Gemma wanted to do was sour things between them on their final day together, but Alaric might understand her better if he knew more about her history.

"I broke it off a few months ago. We were together for six years."

Gemma had already shared her limited sexual experience, but Alaric hadn't realized the reason for it was because she had been in a committed relationship since she was nineteen. She had been off the market, planning to marry someone. Alaric was surprised at how much that news unnerved him. He just couldn't picture it.

"Okay," he replied, trying to be accepting and supportive, but he had a feeling he knew where this was going, and he wasn't sure he could bear it. "Are you trying to tell me I'm just the rebound?"

Gemma's eyes went wide, and she quickly realized how he'd drawn that conclusion.

"No, I wasn't trying to say that at all," she rushed to assure, squeezing his hand. "I'm just having so much fun with you, I wouldn't want to ruin it."

After a moment of attempting to understand and failing, Alaric asked, "You wouldn't want to ruin it…by having more fun and staying longer?" he parroted back.

Gemma's brow wrinkled, realizing she wasn't quite able to convey her concern correctly. "That's not what I mean."

Alaric took a breath, glancing out the window. Things had taken a turn and he was wishing they could rewind five minutes or pretend he hadn't asked her to extend her trip in the first place.

Deflating beside him, Gemma realized she had made a horrible mistake by mentioning her ex again.

Doing his best not to shut down or press the issue, Alaric shrugged. It was tense, but he tried to look unaffected. On the inside, he felt like she'd thrown cold water on him. He thought Gemma was amazing and he wanted to do everything possible to spend even one or two more days with her. Meanwhile, she was trying to appreciate what they'd had and then return to her life in New York.

"I was just hoping you'd stay another day or two," Alaric told her, trying to keep things light.

Gemma watched the side of his face, giving it some real consideration. Logistically, at least.

"I'm not really prepared," she confessed. "I'd have to get a new flight, and I'm kind of already over my budget."

Alaric appreciated that she hadn't given him a definite no, but he felt it coming. He attempted to alleviate her concerns. "I can take care of all of that. My meals are free, and I have plenty of airline points."

Gemma bit her lip, wondering if she could accept that from him. It seemed so easy, and she wondered if it was meant to be.

"And I'll stay with you?" she hedged.

Alaric's laughter eased the tension. "You'd better."

Gemma dropped her head to his shoulder, blushing. "Okay," she caved. "Only until Monday."

Heaving a relieved sigh, Alaric kissed the top of Gemma's head. "Your friends will probably give you shit."

"Oh, they most definitely will," she laughed, turning Alaric's hand over to run her fingers across his palm. "I told them we'd meet up with them tonight. You can explain it to them."

"Great," he sighed. He couldn't wait to see the looks on their faces when Gemma told them she was going to remain behind with a virtual stranger.

At the tattoo parlor, Roses and Regrets, Alaric introduced Gemma to the acquaintance who would be tattooing her that afternoon.

"Well, well, well."

Shawn Malone spun his low stool to face the doorway as it was filled by the couple. "Too busy to get your outline filled, but not too busy to bring a friend by?" he accused.

Gemma couldn't help but admire the tattoo artist. He looked like a strait-laced gentleman from the chin up, but the endless dark ink swirling around his neck and leading beneath his shirt indicated there was a lot more to see.

"My shit takes hours," Alaric reasoned.

"I think your man's hit his quota," Shawn told Gemma. "What are we up to, Al? Thirty hours?"

Her embarrassment over Shawn assuming they were dating was replaced with awe at the count of hours Alaric had been under the needle.

"So, what brings you in today?" Shawn asked.

Gemma pointed over her shoulder towards the front waiting area and the mounted artwork. "I really like the black feather."

"Excellent taste," he praised. "Designed that one myself. Whereabouts?"

"She was thinking about her hip," Alaric replied. "But I know that's a rough spot."

"It is," Shawn nodded, waving for them to join him in his office. "But if you wanted a massage, you'd be at the fucking spa."

Laughing, Gemma assured, "It's okay. I've made up my mind."

"Okay, how big are we going?" he asked, gesturing for her to show him.

Gemma splayed her hand to its full length, setting her thumb at the curve of her waist and the tip of her middle finger just below where her underwear reached. She looked to Alaric to confirm.

"It's your body," he smiled. "But I agree."

Shawn clapped his hands together. "Got it. I'll draw it up. Meanwhile, time for you to get naked."

Alaric's unamused glare reassured Gemma that Shawn was only kidding, thankfully.

"Fine, fine. Keep the dress on, but I'll need your whole hip exposed so I'll give you a modesty sheet," Shawn relented.

Flushing, she nodded.

"Back in a bit," he said, closing the curtain behind him.

Alaric helped Gemma to lie on her side, laughing as she removed her underwear and gave them to him for safekeeping.

Alaric pulled out a folding chair and took a seat. "Nervous?" he asked.

"On a scale of one to ten, I'm a twelve," she admitted.

"Both in looks and nerves," he teased back.

"Don't be cute."

"This is a big deal, sweetheart. I can have my outline filled in if you change your mind, it won't be a wasted trip."

Shaking her head, Gemma met his gaze. "I'm not second guessing it."

When Shawn returned and applied the transfer tape, Gemma felt even more certain with her decision.

"Placement okay?" Shawn asked.

"It's perfect," she confirmed. "How long do you think it'll take?"

"Do you want a piece of shit on your body, or a piece of art?" he replied, but he was smiling.

Alaric clarified for her, "No more than two hours."

When they were ready to begin, Shawn put the buzzing needle to her skin and announced, "Here we go."

She held her breath and waited, brows wrinkled in anticipation. The first thought she had was that the pain was nowhere near as bad as she'd feared. It was a dull, burning sensation, but tolerable.

However, by the end of the first hour she understood how sitting for a longer session could be excruciating. The finished product was done in about ninety minutes and was well worth the time spent. Shawn sat back, wiping away the excess ink and setting the gun down on the nearby tray.

"That's it, my dear."

As the work had begun to wind down, Alaric had stood against the wall, watching the tattoo come to life. He helped Gemma to stand, nodding for Shawn to take a hike as the sheet fell away. As he went, Alaric pressed a few folded hundreds into Shawn's hand on a shake. "It's great, man."

Together, Alaric and Gemma admired the tattoo in Shawn's full-length mirror.

Gemma knew the instant she saw the feather etched into her skin that she regretted nothing. The ink and redness were vibrant against the backdrop of her pale complexion. Despite the lingering pain and the ache in her hips, she was smiling from ear to ear.

"Very sexy," Alaric praised, kissing the top of her head. "Happy?"

"Beyond," she confirmed. She couldn't stop staring at her reflection; it was a struggle to return to the table so Shawn could bandage her properly.

Once they were free to go, Gemma slowed at the front counter to check-out. Alaric's fingers clasped hers and nodded for her to follow him out.

"I still haven't paid," she reminded him.

"I took care of it," Alaric assured, holding the door for her. "Let's get something to eat."

Gemma stared, touched once again by his generosity. "Alaric…"

"Just say thank you and let's get dinner. What are you in the mood for?"

Gemma joked lamely, "A bottle of Advil?"

Alaric pulled up a rideshare app, but Gemma was still staring at him in disbelief for how casually he'd just gifted her the new artwork she proudly wore.

"Thank you," she told him genuinely. She knew that tattoos were expensive, and she'd had every intention of paying for her own.

Easing her closer, Alaric leaned down to place his lips to her forehead. "You're very welcome."

♥ ♠ ♦ ♣

When Gemma and Alaric regrouped with her friends that evening, Ashlee cornered him alone at the bar. She held up her empty glass to signal she was getting a refill, glancing over her shoulder to see Gemma and her friends sufficiently distracted.

"Whiskey sour?" Alaric asked, confirming what she'd been drinking that evening.

"Yeah, thanks."

As they waited to get a bartender's attention, Ashlee filled the silence. "That was really cool of you to comp us that cabana and those tickets."

"My pleasure."

Ashlee pursed her lips, trying to feel him out. What on Earth did Gemma, the sweetest and most fun-loving person Ashlee had ever known, manage to talk about with this stoic, brick wall of a man? She couldn't imagine what common ground existed between them.

"Gemma is seriously the last person I thought would ever get a tattoo," Ashlee confessed.

"Or be engaged," Alaric replied.

He was surprised by his own response. Sure, he'd been thinking about what Gemma had told him, but he hadn't had any intention of bringing it up.

"She told you about Ev?" Ashlee asked, her surprise genuine.

Alaric committed the name to memory.

"It was just…logical," Ashlee offered. "They were high school sweethearts."

Alaric was given an opportunity to order, and he was glad for the interruption. Ashlee, however, picked up the conversation as soon as he finished.

"Gemma still feels bad about breaking it off," she admitted. "I mean, I still consider him abusive, but she doesn't see it that way."

Alaric went rigid at this new piece of information and Ashlee rushed to add, "Controlling."

He turned to look over at Gemma with her friends, glad to see her laughing and relaxed.

"That's eighteen."

Alaric turned back to the bartender and paid, passing one of the drinks off to Ashlee.

"He's out of her life?" he asked, needing to confirm that Gemma was free of the abuse.

Ashlee hesitated. "They're not together anymore, but he's Jess's brother."

At the blank look Alaric gave her, she clarified with a gesture over her shoulder, "One of the brides' brothers."

"So, he'll be at the wedding," Alaric realized.

"He's *in* the wedding," she corrected. "He's paired up with her for all the escorting. Kayla offered to move things around, but Gemma insisted it was fine."

Unsure what to think, Alaric decided to share their latest news with her friend.

"Gemma's staying a few more days," he told Ashlee. "Here, with me."

Ashlee froze, her blond brows pulling together. "She never said anything about that to us."

"I just invited her," he explained. "She was going to tell you all tonight."

"Listen," Ashlee sighed, revving herself up for the 'if you hurt my friend, I'll hurt you' talk. "I think it's great Gem's been letting her hair down with you, but she doesn't know how to have a one-night stand."

"It's not," Alaric replied automatically.

Unsure, Ashlee asked, "It's not what?"

"A one-night stand," he clarified.

Ashlee rolled her eyes. She knew they'd seen each other for the last four days. "I didn't mean literally."

"No, it's not—"

Alaric wasn't sure what he was trying to say. That he genuinely liked her? That if it were up to him, they'd run with this thing they had? If he was going to confess any of that, it was going to be to Gemma and not to one of her friends.

"I'll drive her back myself," he decided.

Ashlee laughed until she realized he was serious. "Drive her back?" she questioned, confused. "Drive her home?"

"To the city," Alaric confirmed. "When she's ready to leave, I'll take her back."

"You do realize that's almost a five-hour drive," Ashlee offered.

Alaric's confusion was obvious, and Ashlee gave him a pitying look as she realized his mistake.

"We're from *upstate* New York, Alaric."

CHAPTER TWENTY-FOUR

♥

On the second of two additional days in New York, Sadie decided to plan an outing. She was due to depart early the following morning and wanted to thank Parker for his hospitality. Staying with him had been easier than she'd imagined. Parker had made time for her, seemed to appreciate that she made time for him, and treated her well.

Sadie cautioned herself not to get too comfortable; she'd be gone soon enough, and there was no guarantee they'd cross paths again. She knew that this could very well be the final day they spent together.

Calling his office, where Parker had made a brief appearance, Sadie caught him between meetings. "I'm taking you out tonight. I'll meet you at the office. What time's best?"

Parker chuckled. "We should be wrapping up around six. Do I get a hint?"

"No chance." For purely selfish reasons she wanted to witness his reaction in person.

Early that evening, Sadie hoisted her packed bag and gave herself a final once-over. She'd had to go shopping to prepare as she owned nothing suitable for their intended destination. Adjusting the cap on her head, she grinned. If she was right about this, Parker was going to be thrilled.

When she arrived, Sadie found Parker standing on the sidewalk just outside his building, finishing off a cigarette. It amused her to no end that he didn't notice her at first in her skinny jeans, sneakers, and raglan t-shirt. She was certainly presenting a different look, today.

"Bum a smoke?" she asked, sidling up beside him.

Parker turned and swept her from head to toe, his smile wide as his attention lingered on her Yankees hat. "You have never, ever looked sexier." He tossed aside the last of his cigarette and reached for her, drawing her in by her waist.

"You smell like smoke," she laughed, leaning away. Sadie handed off her oversized bag, gesturing for him to head back into the office. "Go get changed."

Parker noticed his worn jersey alongside some other clothes and sneakers. "Did you go through my things, darling?" he playfully accused.

"I was bored," she defended, pushing at him. "Now, hurry up. Game starts in an hour, and I want peanuts and crackerjack or whatever."

"Five minutes," he grinned, kissing her cheek.

It was a perfect afternoon with clear skies and a warm breeze. There was no better possibility for game days and as Sadie and Parker settled into their 'best available' seats, Parker slid his arm around her shoulders. "I'm impressed," he admitted.

Pleased beyond reason at his simple compliment, Sadie found the outing more than worth spending her day arranging it. "I have my moments."

"Is this your first game?"

"Here, yes," she confirmed. "First game on the east coast, but I sometimes go back home."

Mention of home seemed to sour the mood. She was only visiting, her time with Parker short. Hoping to keep things light, she leaned closer to whisper, "Don't tell anyone, but I'm an Angels fan."

Laughing, Parker nodded. "Your secret's safe with me."

They fell into companionable silence, Parker's hand relocating to Sadie's thigh. Her hand fell atop his in return, and she did her best to focus on the pre-game warm-ups happening on the field; anything other than her imminent departure.

After a few minutes of enjoying the atmosphere as the crowd grew, Sadie watched as Parker turned and caught the attention of someone seated behind them.

"Excuse me. Would you mind taking a picture of us? It's her first Yankees game."

The man looked between them, his eyes lingering on Sadie as she turned around in surprise. "Yeah, no problem," he replied, accepting Parker's phone.

Sadie's cheeks warmed at Parker's sudden request, and she laughed as they settled into a posed position. It wasn't hard to smile; in fact, it was hard to stop. Documented proof of their time together was something Sadie was looking forward to cherishing when she moved on.

As the man passed the phone back, Sadie reached for it. After confirming it had been a good likeness of them, she texted a copy to herself.

Parker flagged down a passing vendor and paid for two overpriced pints of beer.

"So, where to next?" he asked casually.

Accepting the drink, Sadie replied, "Connecticut."

"For how long?"

Sadie's green eyes lowered to her drink, contemplating. "I'm honestly not sure."

CHAPTER TWENTY-FIVE

♣

Laurel and Grayson had checked off a good deal of New York's finest tourist attractions. At the tail end of their second day exploring, they'd ended up at a club.

"Have you been here before?" Laurel asked as they flashed their IDs at the door.

"Once or twice," he confirmed. "My friend's going to meet us."

Laurel was tempted to ask if that friend was female but kept the jab to herself. He wouldn't introduce her to a former female companion unless he wanted a matching bruise on his other side. That, and he'd earned some major brownie points for smoothing things over with Alaric. She still had her job, so she'd decided to cut him some slack, at least until he made her angry again.

Grayson scanned the crowd and wove them through the bodies swaying to the loud music. At the bar he hugged someone, and Laurel stepped forward as Grayson made introductions.

"Park, this is Laurel."

Momentarily surprised at the fact that he'd used her real name, Laurel almost failed to realize she recognized the handsome man.

"Good to meet you, doll," he smiled. "What are you two drinking?"

Laurel's brows dipped as she studied him, confused. "Do I know you?"

Grayson's brows rose to his hairline and Parker reached out to pat his friend's chest. "No, I don't think so," he assured, winking. "I'm sure I'd remember."

"No, I'm sure I—" Laurel gasped suddenly, eyes going wide. "You're Mr. Great Sex!"

That seemed to render everyone speechless, and the trio stared at one another for a long minute.

"Sorry," Laurel blurted, flushing in embarrassment. Was she supposed to confess that she knew of him from Sadie, and explain how her friend had shown her a photo? Laurel wasn't sure Sadie wanted him to know how much she spoke about him to her friends.

"So help me God if you—" Grayson began, looking murderous as he turned to Parker.

Parker's hands went up in defense. "I've never seen her before, mate. I swear."

"You'd better not have," Grayson grumbled.

Clearly tongue-tied, Laurel shook her head and tried to quickly dismiss her outburst. "You just…you look like someone," she attempted weakly.

Grayson, unconvinced, eased an arm around her waist to stake a claim. He wasn't sure why she was acting star struck, but his ego was less than thrilled by this sudden development.

"My reputation precedes me," Parker laughed, dismissing the awkward situation good naturedly. "It's nice to meet you, Laurel."

"You, too," she smiled.

Hoping to further distract them from her blunder, Laurel inquired about the guys' history.

"So, how do you two know each other?" she asked, gesturing between them as they waited on a bartender.

Parker and Grayson exchanged glances and Grayson gestured for Parker to start.

"Well, I went to grad school here in the city with our friend Alaric," he volunteered.

"She knows Al," Grayson clarified. "She works for him."

Parker's brows lifted and he seemed to hesitate.

"He knows," Grayson assured. "He's fine with it."

"Somehow I doubt that," Parker laughed but waved it off. Grayson was going to be Grayson. "Eventually, Alaric invited me to a game with this fuckwit."

"I think I took you for twenty thou. that night," Grayson grinned, looking rather pleased with himself.

"Twenty-eight."

Laurel's eyes went wide as she looked between the two men laughing. The way they so casually threw around enormous sums of money was a completely foreign concept to her.

When the bartender appeared, Parker turned away to order them drinks and Laurel dug out her phone.

Laurel: Don't know if you're still in NY but MR GREAT SEX is here at a club with Grayson! Pictures do NOT do the man justice!
Sadie: Too funny. I left this morning.
Laurel: I didn't tell him that I know you.

Sadie: NBD

A short while later, Laurel managed to pull Grayson out onto the dance floor. He was a decent dancer; Laurel was pleased to find. She plucked his beer from his hand and tipped it to her lips. Her other slid around him to his back pocket, slipping inside with a grin.

"Should have taken you dancing sooner," Grayson smirked, arms going around her. His lips lowered to her neck, and he kissed her heated skin, tongue dragging over her pulse. In his ear, Laurel moaned quietly, just loud enough to be heard over the music.

"I haven't thanked you," Grayson said suddenly, lips beside her ear.

Laurel eased back to eye him, curious.

"For giving me a chance," he clarified. Grayson knew it had been difficult for Laurel to let her guard down. She'd also had a very legitimate reason to stay away: her livelihood. Especially since losing her job at the cafe, Alaric and his policies had been her only source of income.

Laurel stared at him quietly, their bodies moving together amidst the sea of club-goers.

"I guess I know when to fold," she smiled, sincere.

♥ ♠ ♦ ♣

A couple of hours later, Parker was half-carrying a blonde leech that had attached herself to him the moment she'd heard his accent.

"I'm calling it a night!" Parker called to Grayson and Laurel who were dancing on the outskirts of the floor.

Grayson removed a hand from Laurel's backside to raise it in farewell. Laurel's head swam at the amount of alcohol she'd consumed, but her gaze zeroed in on Parker and the woman draped against him. She eased back from Grayson to pull out her phone. If she hadn't been as drunk as she was, she might have realized she was stirring up trouble.

Laurel: Great sex lft bar with blonde whore. Dont know ur arrangement but thought u should know
Sadie: No arrangement, hon. Thanks for looking out for me. xo

When the taxi pulled up at the blonde's home, Parker helped his companion out of the backseat. "You smell amazing..." she purred as they crossed to the entrance of her building.

"Do you have your key?" Parker asked, waiting until she had her footing before he eased her weight from his side.

She nodded in confirmation, rummaging through her purse. She lifted her keychain triumphantly and grinned. "I'm about to rock your world, baby."

He highly doubted that, but he found her alcohol-induced confidence amusing. "I think you need some water and a good night's sleep," he observed.

She stared back at him, processing his words, and her expression turned insulted. "Excuse me?"

Parker gestured over his shoulder to the idling taxi, starting to back towards it. "We were just sharing a ride, doll."

He'd considered her offer but had steadily lost interest since setting foot outside the club.

The woman stared after him in shock, watching as the cab pulled away from the curb.

Chapter Twenty-Six

♦

Gemma leaned out of the bathroom, toothbrush hanging from her mouth. "What do you want to do today?"

"Same thing we did yesterday?" Alaric ventured.

She rinsed her mouth and hopped back into bed. "We spent yesterday in this bed," she reminded him.

Alaric grinned, tucking a hand behind his head as he stared up at her. "Exactly."

Cashing in on a rare couple of days off, Alaric had been more than happy to stay in and order room service with Gemma. It had been a perfect way to spend their extra time together.

He trailed his fingers along her leg, pinching gently. "Actually, we need to talk."

"Uh oh," she mumbled, playful. "That is usually the start to very bad conversations."

"You're adorable," he complimented, letting his fingertips dip below the hem of his t-shirt, which hung from her frame. "And beautiful. And funny."

Gemma felt her cheeks warming and she braced herself, unsure where he was planning to take this conversation. His words were sweet, but he seemed to want to discuss something serious.

Alaric continued, "And if you think you're never hearing from me again, you're also crazy."

Laughing in surprise, Gemma shoved at him. The idea of staying in touch with Alaric filled her with excitement, but it was too much to hope for.

"Yeah, okay."

Alaric pushed himself up, leaning back against the headboard. "Gemma, I'm serious. You're not disappearing on me."

"It's not that I'm disappearing," she insisted, "I live—"

Alaric took her hands, making a valiant effort at showing that he'd thought all of this through. "I've got vacation time. Have you ever done long-distance?" He knew it was a dumb question; she'd been in a relationship for six years with her high school sweetheart. Still, he wanted her to consider it.

"It's not impossible," he said finally.

Gemma drew in a shaky laugh, squeezing his hands. "I still live with my parents."

"Okay."

"And I'm still trying to figure out what to do with my life."

"Okay."

"And I can't afford to come visit you…"

"Gemma," he said, drawing her out of her spiral of excuses. "Would you like to try?"

With a lengthy exhale, Gemma collected herself. There was no doubt that she wanted to keep what they had going, she just wished it were more convenient. If they lived in the same town, or even the same state, it would make more sense. She was used to having her boyfriend as close as a classroom or few blocks over. Long-distance dating was brand new territory for her.

"I want to, yeah," she admitted.

Alaric smiled, brushing her hair off her face. "Then why do you look so sad?"

"Because either way, I still have to leave."

"Temporarily," he assured. He knew she would have a hard time adjusting to the idea, so he added, "We can talk every day."

Tipping forward, Gemma fell into him with a pathetic whimper. "Okay." It was the best she was going to get, after all.

"And maybe," Alaric added, rubbing her back. "Don't mention my age to your parents."

Gemma laughed, quick to agree. "We'll leave that part unsaid."

As it finally hit her, Gemma's smile was blinding. "We're really doing this?"

Alaric leaned down to kiss her, mumbling, "It's done."

Lifting, Gemma straddled his thighs and returned the kiss eagerly. She was going to try long-distance dating Alaric. Officially. It blew her mind.

"I love your tattoos," she breathed, tipping her head down to break the kiss. Slowly, she traced her fingertips along the ink, something she'd been doing often.

Alaric's hands slid up along her back beneath his shirt, smiling. "You may have mentioned that."

As Gemma continued to study him, Alaric couldn't help but grow aroused under her scrutinizing gaze.

"If you don't stop that," he chided. "We won't leave the room again."

Gemma bit her lip, clearly suggesting she didn't mind.

Sitting forward, Alaric nipped at her lips with a groan. "Turn around, then."

Gemma inched from his lap and turned, settling on her knees. "Like this?" she asked, watching him over her shoulder.

"Like that," he confirmed, climbing out from under the covers. He was naked and knelt behind Gemma to peel away her clothing. He watched as she shook out her hair and looked back to watch him.

Splaying a warm hand against her back, Alaric guided Gemma to lean forward until she caught her weight with her hands on the bed. He reached for a condom on the nightstand and rolled it into place, returning behind her to curl his hands around the fronts of her thighs.

Familiar with the position, but only just, Gemma licked her lips and waited, her breath heavy.

Without a word, Alaric guided his shaft between the slick folds at the apex of her thighs.

With a whimper of pleasure, Gemma's head dropped forward. Her hands pressed to the mattress, and she couldn't stop herself from rocking back against him to meet his first thrusts.

For minutes, there was no sound save for the rhythmic slapping of Alaric's body up against Gemma's while they lost themselves to the pleasure of it. Again and again, he moved, staring down through hooded eyes at her bouncing figure and her recently inked skin. In no time he was breathing hard, his back caving as he bucked against her more rapidly.

She whimpered at his faster pace, moaning his name a second later as she felt her pleasure quickly nearing its peak. Arms buckling, Gemma fell forward and caught herself on her forearms instead, gasping. The new angle of her hips had her grasping at the bed covers.

"You—" Alaric attempted to ask.

"Yeah," Gemma assured, breathless. "Don't stop."

When she felt her climax hit, her breath caught with a sharp gasp and as he continued. She tensed up with a sharp cry while, behind her, Alaric's rhythm faltered, and he groaned roughly as he came.

When they were lying across the bed, Alaric's fingers tangled in Gemma's hair.

"Tell me about Evan," he requested, Ashlee's earlier words floating to the surface of his mind.

Battling the desire to drift in his arms, Gemma hummed a question. It took her a moment to realize he was referring to 'Ev,' her ex.

"Everett," she corrected. Now that they were officially dating, she supposed it was a topic that was bound to come up. Still, it seemed an odd time to discuss it. "Are you sure you want to talk about that?"

"He hurt you?"

Gemma's head popped up, stunned. "What? *No.* He would never."

"Emotionally abusive, then?"

A little startled and defensive, she asked, "Did you ask my friends about him?"

Alaric wasn't going to lie, but he also wanted to maintain her trust. "I didn't ask. Ashlee volunteered."

Gemma wished she would have been there to do damage control. "Ashlee never liked him," she explained. "He wasn't abusive."

It was clear that Alaric wasn't going to drop the subject, so she admitted a bit more about her reasons for ending their engagement. "He made me run all my plans by him and check in when I was out. It sounds stupid, I know. I would have done those things anyway, but he made it a requirement and would accuse me when I forgot. He was convinced I didn't love him enough. It wasn't healthy."

Alaric nodded. He agreed with her, wholeheartedly.

"I only have one requirement," he told her, his face grave.

Brow creased; Gemma waited. She wasn't sure what sort of rules long-distance dating required, but she suspected it might make him feel better to know what she was up to. Maybe not the same sort of 'keeping tabs' she was used to with Everett, but something to that effect.

"Weekly phone sex."

Exhaling a breath of disbelief, Gemma lightly tapped her hand against his cheek. "Idiot."

Chapter Twenty-Seven

♠

After a night of dancing and drinking in New York, Laurel awoke to the heavy hotel door snicking shut. It was around nine in the morning, and she was still tangled in the sheets. Meanwhile, Grayson had gone for a run and promised to return with doughnuts.

"Up!" he announced, already enjoying a mouthful of pastry.

Laurel groaned, opening one tired eye. "How are you functioning?" she complained.

Grayson pushed open the curtains, much to Laurel's chagrin. "Endorphins," he replied. "You're probably too young to understand."

Laurel pushed herself up to sit, squinting. His teasing remark caused her to realize with mild surprise that she didn't know his age.

"What're you, like thirty-nine? Forty?"

The disbelief crossing Grayson's face and rendering him silent had her laughing.

"You're hilarious," he grumbled.

"Oh, calm down," she chided. "You look great for an old man."

"I'm thirty-two," Grayson corrected, leaning over her for a good morning kiss. "Are you that much younger?"

"Twenty-six," she replied, patting his arm to soothe the sting of her teasing commentary. After a pause, she licked her lips and asked, "Ew, was that pistachio?"

A smile pulled at Grayson's lips, and he wiped the corner of his mouth, smirking. "And raspberry."

"Gross," she mumbled. "What else did you get?"

As Grayson opened the box, Laurel's jaw went slack over the quantity and assortment. "We're two people."

"Your point?"

Shaking her head, Laurel chose something smothered in chocolate.

"After this, I want to fuck in the shower," Grayson announced.

Laurel nearly choked on her doughnut. "Wow," she coughed, "How could a girl refuse an offer like that?" Still, she was smiling.

When Laurel crossed to the bathroom, Grayson pulled off his shirt and followed. He was almost to the door when his phone chimed. His face fell instantly at the text he'd received.

Slowly, Grayson stepped backwards until he could drop to the edge of the bed.

"Are you coming or what?" Laurel called over the hiss of the shower.

He barely registered her voice and quickly placed a call, passing a hand over his face. As soon as the line picked up, he accused, "You send that news in a text message, mom? Where are you? Does Delilah know?"

Laurel wasn't trying to eavesdrop, but Grayson wasn't keeping his voice down. It was clear he was on the phone, and she stilled under the spray of water, trying to deduce what had upset him so quickly.

"What's the doctor saying?" Grayson pressed impatiently.

After a long pause he replied, "New York. Yes, I know."

Grayson's sigh was resigned. "I'll try. No guarantees."

There was nothing further and Laurel got confirmation that the call had ended when he stepped into view.

"What was that?" she asked around the glass partition, looking concerned.

Grayson's attention was unfocused, his mind obviously working.

"Grayson?" Laurel asked, pushing damp hair from her face. "What's wrong?"

"It's my mom," Grayson said, finally making eye contact. "She's in the hospital."

The news hit Laurel like a cold slap. They hadn't talked much about Grayson's family. Laurel knew only that he had a sister. Her lips parted, taking a moment to absorb the news.

"Oh my God," she managed.

Grayson looked somewhat vacant as he gestured back into the bedroom. "I've got to call my sister."

"Delilah?" Laurel asked. She'd overheard that much, at least.

Nodding, Grayson was already looking at his phone, pulling up her contact information.

"Is your mom going to be okay?" Laurel asked. Something about Grayson's reaction to the news had her concerned about the prognosis. She watched as Grayson offered a noncommittal shrug, distracted as he began to close the bathroom door behind him.

"I'll be right out," Laurel offered. She was unsure what else to say or how to be supportive. Was it odd that he hadn't offered the reason his mother was being hospitalized? Was it odd that she didn't know anything about his family aside from his sister's location, and now her name? She supposed not, considering they'd only decided to exclusively date two days ago. However, she'd been spending most of her free time with him for the better part of two weeks.

Backtracking to the bedroom, Grayson dialed his sister three times before he eventually left a voicemail.

"Mom's in the hospital. Where the hell are you? I'm in New York. Call me."

Laurel quickly rinsed off and donned a robe. "Do you have to go?" she asked. "Is your mom still in Tennessee or is she here, with your sister?"

It nearly broke her heart when he didn't respond, his attention on his phone.

"Grayson?" Laurel attempted, her voice gentle. "Is it serious?" She feared it was bad news, and she put a comforting hand on his arm. "I'll make coffee."

Laurel couldn't help but think of her own mother, and how it might feel if the tables were reversed. She began to feel immense guilt over how she'd been handling things at home. Laurel had taken every opportunity to stay with Grayson or explore New York, anything that took her away from her current life. Meanwhile, her mom was still suffering from her addiction, her own life unchanged. When was the last time Laurel had even called to check in? She felt sick.

"My mom and I, we haven't been good in a long time," Grayson confessed.

Laurel turned as she prepared their drinks with the hotel's Nespresso. "I'm sorry."

"It's fine. I'm not—" He seemed to struggle, shaking his head in frustration. Grayson had all but written his mother out of his life. To some it might sound awful or unfortunate, but Grayson was a firm believer that it was best to cut out toxic people to increase your quality of life. However, now that he was faced with the decision to see her one last time, quite a few emotions were rising to the surface.

Ultimately, he confessed, "She had a massive stroke. They're not hopeful."

Laurel's face fell and she moved back to his side, looking pained. "Grayson, I'm so, so sorry."

He nodded because what else was he supposed to do? He felt trapped; wanting to stay and entertain Laurel while they were in Manhattan but obligated to react to this situation.

"I'm going to meet up with Parker for a few hours," he decided. "Can you explore on your own for a bit?"

"Yeah, of course," Laurel replied, taking his hand. "Whatever you need."

♥ ♠ ♦ ♣

That afternoon, Laurel felt useless. Grayson needed to be alone, or at least with a good friend of his, to sort out his feelings. She didn't fault him for it, but she also couldn't jump back into exploring New York while knowing he was in pain. Realizing their trip would need to end one way or another, Laurel got a head start on packing before going for a walk. She sat on a bench at Bryant Park and imagined the worst; Grayson going to his mother's funeral. Would he ask her to go with him? If he did, would she go? She liked to think so, but it would be a very different dimension to their relationship thus far.

Grayson was playful, flirtatious, funny, and juvenile. It unnerved her to see him so serious, dealing with a family crisis. This was a side of him she hadn't seen yet, and it reminded her of how angry he'd been that night Roman had cornered her. She shivered in disgust just thinking about it. Grayson had been drunk, but he'd been enraged, and Laurel had been surprised to see there was more to him than he let on.

At first, Grayson had just been someone who injected fun into her life. The new job and their secret relationship had been unexpected, but a shake-up to her monotonous routine. Now, she was starting to get a full picture of the man. He had plenty of emotions, most he masked with humor, but Laurel was catching glimpses.

As she sat at the park, people-watching and enjoying the sounds of the city, she wondered what it might be like to live there. Grayson had asked if the city had lived up to her expectations. She told him it had, and it had been mostly true; it was as massive and sprawling as she'd anticipated. It had been exciting to visit Times Square, walk across the Brooklyn Bridge, and peruse Central Park. However, Laurel was all too aware of the reason those excursions had been as memorable as they were. Grayson had been with her, and today as she ventured out solo to cross another tourist attraction off her list, it didn't hold the same enjoyment.

She felt the need to call and see how he was doing but trusted that he would check in when he was ready. The grief he felt must have been immense, and she wanted to give him the space he needed. Opting to deal with some of her own baggage instead, she called home.

♥ ♠ ♦ ♣

It was late that night by the time Laurel saw Grayson again. He was crossing the hotel lobby and she cupped her hands around her mouth, calling to him from the bar.

"Hey," she greeted as he approached, slipping from her stool to wrap her arms around him.

Grayson returned the affectionate squeeze, inhaling her scent deeply.

"Smelling me?" she teased, but it was gentle.

Grayson's smile was slight.

They settled down at the bar and Grayson ordered a drink, rolling his head on his neck.

Rubbing his back, Laurel cautiously asked, "Any more news?" She couldn't help but wonder if his mother had passed away already.

"No," he answered, clearing his throat. It was raw from some heated conversations earlier. Rather than seek out Parker, Grayson had ended up tracking his sister down. "But I found Delilah."

"Oh yeah?" she asked, "How'd she take it?"

Grayson's eyes swept the other drinkers at the bar, his defeated expression rather telling. "Not well. I mean, she lived with our mom up until two years ago. Ever since our dad left."

That was another nugget about Grayson's past that Laurel hadn't known. She remained politely silent, giving him the space to share at his pace.

As he was served his cocktail, Grayson took a sip and regarded the amber liquid. He appreciated Laurel's concern, and she was being nothing but supportive, but he didn't enjoy reliving his past. His entire personality and lifestyle revolved around living in the moment, on purpose.

"What'd you do?" he prompted. "Have you gotten to a Broadway show yet?"

Laurel shook her head, but smiled, nonetheless. "Just walked around. It was nice." She seemed to want to say more but stopped herself.

"I'm sorry I couldn't—" he began, hating how her first big New York experience had been dampened by the unexpected news.

"No, no, it's fine. Obviously, it's fine," Laurel rushed to ensure, putting her hand on his arm.

Grayson nodded, sipping his drink.

Laurel mimicked him, waiting a few long minutes before changing the subject. She sensed he might appreciate returning to a bit of normalcy after the day he'd had.

"I got a call from Alaric this morning," she informed, looking unexpectedly glad about it. "He has a few jobs for me."

Having spoken with her mother earlier, Laurel was feeling a renewed sense of duty and responsibility. It would be good for her to work, and with the new job she'd be earning more than before. Her mother worked too, but it was limited to off-the-books, word-of-mouth cleaning services. She hadn't been reliable or diligent enough for the service industry at local hotels, but she'd managed to gain a few long-term clients. Her downfall was drinking, along with some gambling, and Laurel was just glad she could hold down any job to help pay for a share of the utilities and groceries. It had always fallen to Laurel to cover what her mother could not.

Laurel felt that if she could finally get atop their overdue bills, her mother could handle new, daily costs. Laurel could move on, head to New York, and make a new life for herself. She had reasoned that if her mother needed help after Laurel relocated, Laurel could send her money as needed. Hopefully, even though

New York was expensive, she could spare a small amount monthly.

Grayson was glad to hear that Alaric was keeping to their agreement and offering more opportunities for Laurel to work. His hesitation was only due to his current situation, and he found himself unsure if he could agree to accompany her back to Atlantic City, if she were leaving soon.

"I think I need a few more days," he confessed. "I'm still trying to work things out with my sister, maybe fly her out to our mom."

"I figured," Laurel assured. "It's no problem. I looked up the bus schedules and I can take one at seven—"

Grayson turned to face Laurel fully, reaching out to slip his hand behind her neck. Carefully, he pulled her forward until their lips touched in a gentle kiss.

Surprise and warmth crossed Laurel's face and she held onto Grayson's wrist as he withdrew. "What was that for?" she smiled.

"You're pretty great," he told her, even though he hadn't managed much of a smile yet that evening.

She leaned back in to kiss him softly again, mumbling, "And don't you forget it."

"But I'll book a car for you," he assured, putting any argument to bed with a look. "Let me. Please."

Laurel sighed, resigned but thankful. Not having to navigate the New York bus depot would be very welcome.

"Are you thinking of going to Tennessee, too?" she inquired, wondering if he would join his sister.

Answering honestly, Grayson shook his head. "No, I think it'd do more harm than good."

She nodded, respecting his choice though it surprised her.

"When our dad took off," Grayson explained. "I took off not long after."

Laurel felt her chest clench. Their circumstances were vastly different, but she felt a clear parallel forming. Grayson had left, leaving his sister and mother to depend on one another. Laurel's situation seemed somewhat like his sister's; it had been Laurel and her mom against the world for as long as she could remember. However, she was envious of Grayson and the fact that he'd had the means to escape.

"My mom never really got over that. Deli, either."

Laurel couldn't help the small laugh. "You call your sister Deli?"

He hadn't even realized he had and cracked a small smile in response. "Yeah, a long time ago."

"Bet she hated that," Laurel teased, reaching out to run her fingers into Grayson's hair at the nape of his neck.

He nodded and added, "We found out our dad died two months later."

Laurel's features scrunched in sympathy at the news. "I'm sorry. I'm guessing you didn't get a chance to see him before it happened."

He shook his head. "Or after. No funeral, nothing."

Laurel kept scratching his scalp encouragingly, thankful that she could be here for him.

"Delilah claims I ruined her life. I told her it wasn't her job to become mom's caretaker at seventeen, but that's what she did."

Laurel nodded somberly, imagining the life he described. She was oddly fascinated that this sort of story lurked beneath Grayson's upbeat exterior. Since the day they'd met, Grayson had seemed unshakably confident and completely independent. She'd envisioned him stemming from a well-off family, but he was painting a very different picture.

Chapter Twenty-Eight

♥

The next day, Laurel enjoyed a comfortable ride back to New York. Grayson had walked her to the curb and kissed her goodbye, promising to call. She arrived at her mother's house a couple of hours later, only to find the place empty. Empty of life, that is. The place was full of plenty else, such as laundry, to-go containers, and depleted liquor bottles; it was almost comical that her mother cleaned houses.

Laurel got to work on the laundry first, adding her clothes from New York to the pile. She could understand not wanting to clean in your free time if that's how you earned a living, but she wasn't asking for spotlessness. Laurel would have been satisfied with an organized mess, which this was not. She bagged up the recycling and trash next, dragging them both out to the curb despite the pick-up dates being two and three days away. If she didn't do it now, she couldn't be sure it would get done at all.

Once the living area was tidy, Laurel started on the bathroom and the kitchen, bringing them back to a healthy level of sanitary. By the time she was finished she was covered in sweat. Although her eyes pricked with the onslaught of tears, she willed them away. This was nothing she couldn't handle, and nothing she hadn't faced before. Still, it brought to the surface all the feelings of her stagnancy in life.

Even if Laurel reached her savings goal, there were still problems unsolved by paying off their debt. Her mother would still need help. That was a thought Laurel had been avoiding for a long time. She had convinced herself that a certain amount of money would be the answer, but it was only one piece of an unsolvable puzzle.

The bills were a growing amount that seemed so far out of Laurel's reach that it didn't even matter what other complications existed. Now that she was due to bring home money more quickly, she had to consider those other complications. Even if her mom could keep up with new bills and solve all the problems money had created in their lives, she was still unable to care for herself.

Unwilling to dwell on it for fear of breaking down, Laurel sorted the mail. She opened the envelopes one at a time, noting with rising dread that there were a few unexpected charges.

"Oh, hi honey. When did you get in?"

Laurel's mother stood by the door, stowing her work totes in the front closet. "How was New York? Did you take pictures?"

"Hey, mom," Laurel greeted. "I'll show you later," she promised, reaching for the invoice she had just opened. "Did you go to an AtlantiCare last week?"

The mention of the local urgent care chain caused Laurel's mother to fall silent. She began to busy herself with the coffee pot before admitting, "I did. I hurt my leg."

Laurel noticed then that her mom was favoring one over the other. Concerned, she asked, "How? What happened?"

"I must've fallen, you know," she said, waving a hand to dismiss the topic. "You want some coffee? We're out of milk, but I've still got some sugar."

"Mom, what do you mean you must've fallen?" she pressed. "Where did you fall? How? Is it bad?"

"Laurel, really. It's not a big deal," she insisted, pulling down two mugs despite Laurel's lack of response. "I just got a hematoma, but it's practically back to normal."

Laurel wished she knew less than she did about injuries but growing up with a mother who got banged up more regularly than most, she'd learned about her fair share. In fact, this was starting to sound a little too familiar.

"Do you even remember falling?" Laurel asked, barely able to keep the accusation from her voice. She watched her mother's back as she added the coffee grounds to a filter, analyzing her stiff movements.

"Don't start with me."

"*Mom.* How did you fall?"

As the sound of brewing coffee began to fill the small kitchen, Ms. Price turned to face her daughter in defeat. "I'm tired, Laurel. Can we not do this right now?"

That seemed to confirm Laurel's suspicions; whatever had happened had involved alcohol.

Laurel tried to hold fast to her nerve, but she buckled. She always buckled. "I'm going to take a shower," she announced.

"I'm just home to eat lunch," her mother said. "I'm going over to clean the Hastings' place in a bit."

Laurel's steps slowed at that, her thoughts inexplicably returning to Grayson and his current situation with his own mother. It was enough to propel her back into the kitchen. She wrapped her arms around her mom in a tight hug, saying nothing, and just appreciating that she was alive. Things weren't perfect, but Laurel didn't need perfect.

Ms. Price seemed to accept the olive branch just as easily, and she patted Laurel's upper back gently. "Happy Fourth of July, by the way."

Laurel stilled, realizing the holiday had escaped her due to Grayson's family news. It was typically a massive holiday in Atlantic City, and Laurel was quietly glad she wasn't working.

♥ ♠ ♦ ♣

"I can't tell you how badly I've needed this," Laurel sighed, tipping her head back to let the sun shine directly onto her face. It was the following day, mid-morning, cloudless, and a perfect eighty-two degrees.

"Sunbathing is the literal cure to all ailments," Sadie replied easily.

Laurel laughed. "I'll keep that in mind."

The pair were laid out on towels, toes in the sand. They were enjoying the sound of crashing waves, seagulls, and families littering the beach. Both women had agreed it was a crime that they hadn't spent much time at the beach that summer and decided to take action to correct the issue.

Curious, Laurel rolled her head to look over at her friend. "How much longer are you planning on sticking around Atlantic City?"

"Not much," Sadie confessed with a sigh, turning over to expose her back to the sun's rays. "I've been here longer than usual. It's time to move on." She had won a decent amount of money between her time in Atlantic City, New York, and a brief stint in Connecticut, making her travels a success. She didn't want to push her luck.

"Any word from a certain Australian?"

Sadie's smile lifted against the towel at her cheek. "Maybe."

"That's a yes," Laurel laughed, pushing up to stare down at the shore and the bathers there. "When are you seeing him again?"

Sadie's reply was a wistful sigh. They hadn't made any promises to one another, and Sadie was looking for opportunities that would take her away from the east coast. It wouldn't be easy to continue the fun they'd been having, and she was depressed just thinking about it.

Laurel watched her friend, rolling her eyes. "Text him," she urged. "Like, right now."

"Now?" Sadie whined. "I'm busy. I'm working on my tan." However, when she heard rummaging beside her ear, she opened an eye to see Laurel digging around in her bag. "You wouldn't!" she accused, quick to push herself up.

Laughing, Laurel abandoned her search. "Text him," she repeated. "I'm sure he'd be thrilled to hear from you."

After a minute of hesitation, Sadie pulled out her phone. She made sure to act as if it were the most inconvenient action of her life, but she did as Laurel demanded. When words failed her, she opted for a photo instead.

"Here," she said, holding out her phone for Laurel to take. "We'll send him a picture."

Once Sadie was satisfied with Laurel's photography skills, which took four attempts, she sent the picture of her in a bikini off to Parker. His response was almost instant.

Parker: Where are you going to be on Saturday at 11:00AM?

Sadie's brows rose and Laurel reached out to shove her. "Was that him? See, I told you!"

The smile that graced Sadie's lips grew and lingered as she composed a reply.

Sadie: Depends.
Parker: East coast?
Sadie: Maybe NJ. Maybe not. Is there a reason I should stay?
Parker: Me.
Sadie: Compelling.
Parker: Saturday?
Sadie: Will you make it worth my while?
Parker: We both know the answer to that.
Sadie: To be determined?
Parker: You wound me, darling.
Sadie: Sue me.
Parker: I'd rather fuck you.
Sadie: Terms accepted. Saturday at 11.

"Oh my God," Laurel said, looking at Sadie in disbelief. "You're…*giggling*."

Sadie scoffed, putting her phone away. "I don't giggle," she assured. "You're mistaken."

"No, I'm pretty sure you—"

"Laurel," Sadie warned, lowering herself back down to the sand. "Be nice to me or I'll tell Grayson you said he's the best sex you ever had."

Defeated, Laurel dropped back down. "Ugh, you can't. Ever. He's insufferable enough already."

♥ ♠ ♦ ♣

That evening, when Laurel finally heard from Grayson, she braced for the worst.

"Hey," she greeted, her tone gentle. "How are you?"

A sharp blast of a car horn startled her, and she pulled the phone from her ear, laughing uncertainly. "Grayson?"

"Sorry," he sighed. "Just trying to cross the damn street. Hang on."

Laurel waited, setting the book she was reading down on her chest where she lay. She had a gig with Alaric later that night but was enjoying a few hours to herself alone at home.

"I have to say, Six, I miss waking up with you," Grayson said when he returned to the line.

Laurel smiled, appreciative of his words, but also glad to hear he was in a good mood. "Aw," she teased. "You dork."

Grayson laughed. "Remind me to never again try to be romantic with you."

"Oh, stop," she replied. "That was very sweet."

"Nope. Damage is done," he retorted. "I'm reverting to crass commentary in three…two…"

Laurel laughed, covering her face with a hand. "Grayson!"

"I miss banging you," he stated, his grin audible.

She groaned. "I shouldn't have said anything."

Though Laurel was glad to hear Grayson's laughter, she knew he was dealing with a tough situation beneath the humor. She wanted to ask about his mother or the decision to fly his sister out to her but felt guilty raining on his parade.

"It's your turn to say you miss me," he prompted expectantly.

That comment brought a smile to her lips and for a few moments, her end of the line was quiet.

"Six?" Grayson asked. He checked the phone to ensure the line hadn't dropped and then laughed. "Really? I don't even get an 'I miss you?'" he accused.

Laurel paused for effect and then stated, "I miss banging you."

Grayson hummed in agreement, laughing as his line went quieter. He'd reached his destination; a restaurant where Delilah worked.

Finally, Laurel felt she had to at least get an idea of what was happening in his life, as his girlfriend. Hopefully he'd understand she only meant to show she cared.

"How's your mom?" she asked. "Any word from the hospital?"

"She's stable," he replied. "For now. It's still touch and go. But I got Delilah to agree to head back tomorrow."

"Oh, that's great," Laurel replied, encouraged by the news.

"Yeah," he responded neutrally, easing into another topic. "So, how's it been, working with Al?"

Laurel offered a heavy sigh, pushing off the bed in search of something to eat. "Well, considering he's been his usual, grouchy self to me I'd say we're doing alright." She had expected him to blow up at her in person regarding her violation of his 'policies.' Oddly enough, he seemed to ignore the topic entirely. "He seemed pretty distracted," she added.

"Well, I told him I'd really start fixing games if he gave you shit," Grayson assured playfully.

"Yeah, okay," Laurel dismissed, trying to imagine Grayson cheating at cards. It was ludicrous. He didn't even need to cheat; he was that good. Not that she'd ever admit that to him, of course.

"I called him earlier, we talked about my mom," Grayson admitted. "But yeah, I got the same crap attitude. He said he took a few days off work, which is unlike him."

"Oh," Laurel said, surprised. "I mean, maybe he's sick. Did he say he wasn't feeling well?"

"No, he didn't really say anything."

"Huh."

"I've got to go, actually," Grayson offered. "I'm meeting up with Deli and my mood is about to turn to shit."

Laurel grimaced, understanding. "Okay. Go easy on her, alright? It's her mom, too."

"Yeah, I know," Grayson sighed. "Love you."

The words had been automatic, unhurried, and involuntary. Grayson hadn't meant to say them, but as they lingered, both stunned into silence, Grayson found he didn't necessarily want to make excuses. Instead, he decided to wait Laurel out, his grin growing silently. He could almost feel how uncomfortable his words had made her.

Eyes wide, Laurel stood in the center of her kitchen with her hand wrapped around a jar of peanut butter. She knew it was very likely that it had been an automatic response, something you said at the end of calls when you were on autopilot. Still, it felt huge after only two weeks of knowing one another.

Eventually, Grayson asked, "Is something wrong?" with a shit-eating grin that Laurel could literally picture.

"You—" she tried, but she was laughing through her embarrassment.

"I'm sorry," Grayson offered honestly, though his chest warmed at this rare genuine moment between them. "It just came out, but I don't not mean it."

Laurel's smile slipped, her eyes lowering into an unamused glare. "You don't *not* mean it," she echoed.

"Right," he grinned. "I don't not mean it, so I'm not taking it back."

Laurel sighed so heavily she was surprised she still had breath when she was done. "Goodbye, Grayson," she muttered.

"Wait, wait," he requested quickly. "I forgot to say I'm coming back tomorrow."

Willing herself to tolerate him for a few more minutes, she waited for the details.

"Early," he added. "Why don't you stay in my suite tonight? I'll wake you when I get in."

Laurel finished preparing her sandwich, cutting it into neat triangles. His idea was intriguing and would save her a trip home from Borgata's after her shift that evening.

"Okay, but I don't have a key to your room," she reminded.

"I'll call the hotel," he replied easily. "Right after we hang up."

"Deal," Laurel agreed.

Before they ended the call, Grayson offered a do-over of their farewell. "See you in the morning, Six."

♥ ♠ ♦ ♣

As predicted, Grayson found himself back in Atlantic City a little before nine o'clock the following morning. He had parted ways with his sister after booking her a flight back to Knoxville to see their mother. So far, she was still hanging on.

Standing in the doorway, Grayson removed his shoes as he watched Laurel sleeping. He had briefly wondered if she would opt to let him return to an empty room as payback for his playfulness around his "L" word slip. Thankfully, she hadn't chosen to be petty.

Quietly undressing, Grayson's gaze slid over Laurel's shapely legs and tumble of blond waves. She was covered by a loose sheet, and he lifted the edge to slip in beside her.

The movement caused by his weight had Laurel stirring, and she inhaled deeply with a groggy greeting of, "Welcome back."

Grinning, Grayson slid closer. "Thanks, baby." His hand went to her waist, easing her closer. "Thanks for being here."

She hummed quietly, nodding. Opening her eyes slowly, she watched him for a long minute. He seemed to be in the mood she'd come to know and appreciate as normal for him and deduced that there was likely no further news about his mother's condition.

Grayson's lips moved to her neck, and she wrapped an arm around him. It took only a minute for Grayson to slip his hand down between Laurel's legs, earning him a disbelieving gasp.

"One track mind much?" she accused playfully. Her blue eyes swept his features as he leaned back, lingering on the sexy curve of his lips. "I missed you," she confessed. Laurel hadn't meant to ruin Grayson's romantic commentary on the phone the day before, and she wanted to assure him she cared.

Her greeting seemed to satisfy him, and he leaned down to press his lips to hers in a kiss.

After a moment, Laurel's brows dipped. She pulled away. "Are you naked?"

Grinning, Grayson waggled his eyebrows at her. "I'm very efficient that way."

"Oh my God," Laurel groaned, rolling away from him. She yelped a moment later as he tugged her back, crawling over her with determination. "You knew what sleeping here would mean," he teased.

"You're ridiculous!" she whined.

In another couple of minutes, he'd stripped off the few articles of clothing she'd worn to bed and had her equally naked, bodies pressed close. Laurel reached between them to find him already sporting an erection and she closed her hand around him with a quiet moan. "That was quick," she breathed.

"I was hard for half the ride back," he grunted, running his hands over her as she settled above him. "It was hot as hell thinking of you waiting here for me."

Wordlessly echoing the excitement of having Grayson back, Laurel reached down and guided his length into her body, lowering her hips to slot him deep into place. Unprotected sex was not only unexpected, but new to him, and Grayson's next inhale was a little choked. He groaned, dropping his head back as his hands tightened on her hips.

"Shit, Six," he panted. He hadn't anticipated her skipping the precaution of a condom. With charged arousal, Grayson used his weight to roll with Laurel until her back hit the bed. He kept an arm beneath her thigh, staying inside her as they moved.

"You're incredible," he groaned.

"So talkative today," she mused, her own voice coming in shallow pants.

Grayson's hands slid beneath her shoulders, using the grip as leverage as his hips began to rhythmically thrust against her. The scent of him and his possessiveness threw Laurel's hormones into overdrive. Her arms came around him easily, her fingernails digging shallow crescents into his back. His cheek was peppered with stubble as it brushed hers, and her breaths mingled with quiet whimpers as her entire focus shifted down below, to how precise his movements were, to how every shift of his hips seemed to demand that her body respond.

After a few minutes, Laurel was shivering. The fingers of one hand threaded through his hair and she whimpered quietly, "So close."

Shifting to one side, Grayson propped his weight on an elbow and hooked his free hand beneath her thigh to hitch it higher. His eyes locked with hers as he asked, "Am I pulling out?"

Laurel quickly debated it. She was on birth control, which he knew, but there were other factors. Other factors, and the increased level of intimacy the action seemed to offer. Confident in the fact that their current sexual partners were limited to each other, Laurel decided in a breathless voice, "No."

Grayson crushed his lips to hers. "Oh, thank fuck," he groaned, bucking against her as he gave in to the orgasm he'd been holding at bay. He surrendered to the building pressure in his groin, feeling Laurel start to tighten up.

She gave a quiet cry, going rigid. She pushed at Grayson's chest until he made room and she tucked her hand down between them for added stimulation.

Slowing to a stop, Grayson watched with a heated stare as Laurel finished herself off, breathing hard, and looking fully satiated.

Minutes later, the bed shifted as Grayson stood, padding over to his bag, which he'd left at the door. "I got you something," he announced.

"Yeah, you did," Laurel mumbled, still dazed, and recovering. Their 'welcome home' sex had been well worth the wait.

"No, I bought you something," he clarified with a laugh, picking through his belongings for a recognizable blue box. "In New York."

She smiled but shook her head. "I don't care if you got me the keys to a Porsche, I can't move."

The bed shifted as he returned, looking rather pleased at her compliment. "Well, too bad for you, Tiffany's doesn't sell Porsches."

There was a pregnant pause before Laurel's eyes snapped open, landing on the square box he held. Try as she might to be unphased and collected in most situations, she couldn't stop from gasping at the sight. She was quick to scramble into a sitting position, grabbing it from him.

"Really?" she asked. "You went there?"

Grayson watched her regard the box, running her fingers over the printed lettering.

"Open it," he laughed. "I wanted to take you, but…" He left the rest unsaid; news about his mom had interrupted their explorations.

Carefully, Laurel removed the lid to find a soft suede pouch within, the same robin's egg blue as the box. She pinched her lips between her teeth as she poured its contents into her palm.

The weight of the sterling silver charm bracelet was significant, and she gently brushed a finger over the classic Tiffany closure. "Grayson…" she tried, words failing. Her eyes landed on one of the two charms, realizing it was a small dice padlock. She instantly laughed as she realized it was meant to signify Atlantic City, gambling, and Grayson. She looked up at him, shaking her head in wonder.

With a genuine smile, Grayson reached out to take the item and affix the piece of jewelry around her wrist. "I figured you needed something nice to wear when you work Al's games."

She held her wrist up, studying the other charm. "Is this—?"

"Yeah, it's a pretzel," he admitted, hooking a hand around his neck, and gauging her reaction. "They had a lot of ambiguous New York charms. If you want something else, I can—"

"It's perfect," she told him simply.

Looking a little more at ease, Grayson asked, "So, I did okay? You love it?"

Eyeing the bracelet and then eyeing him, she carefully replied, "I don't *not* love it."

Chapter Twenty-Nine

♣

Parker slung a packed bag over one shoulder and followed the side path around his Hamptons property to his waterfront yard. A Superhawk 48, a 50-foot yacht, was secured at the end of a long pier. He was looking forward to surprising Sadie with a day out on the water and wondered idly if she'd be impressed. She had a lifestyle that rivaled his own and although he was dazzled every time he saw her, he could only hope he was having the same effect on Ms. Bache.

It was overkill, but Parker loved a challenge, and he was happy to pull out all the stops. After she had treated him to a Yankees game, he was itching to reciprocate the gesture.

Having not made much use of his beloved powerboat since earlier that summer, Parker was happy to have the opportunity to get a solid weekend out of her. He checked the fuel levels, took stock of his emergency supplies, and set off for a four-hour ride to one of the Atlantic City marinas.

♥ ♠ ♦ ♣

Sadie had received a text from Parker confirming their meeting place and time. After clarifying the dress code, she had settled on a strapless one-piece bathing suit, sarong tied into a long skirt, and an oversized straw hat. She looked every bit prepared for a day on the water.

Her gaze was hidden behind shaded lenses as she watched the moored boats in the ocean beyond. When her phone rang, Sadie had to fight the smile at the sight of Parker on her caller ID. She'd updated his contact information with the photo taken of them at the ballpark and she did her best to ignore just how happy that made her.

"Did you dress up just for me, darling?" Parker asked.

Sadie glanced around the marina for any sign of him. "How big of a boat am I looking for?" she teased.

Watching her as she surveyed the area, he noted the direction of her gaze and encouraged, "Warmer…warmer…"

She laughed, shaking her head as she played along. "I don't see any dinghies," she smirked.

"Very cute. Right there, doll. On your— ah, yes."

Sadie spotted him where he stood, waving on the dock beside a rather impressive looking sport cruiser yacht. He hadn't provided details on whether they'd be sailing, cruising, or otherwise.

As she approached, she said into her phone, "I was starting to worry that we were going kayaking."

Parker laughed, removing his Ray Bans. They ended the call and Sadie made a point of eyeing his yacht as she closed the distance between them. "This a rental?"

"You're killing me," Parker teased, reaching for her hand to tug her the last few steps closer. "You're all mine today," he reminded her, catching her lips in a light kiss.

Humming in response, Sadie ran a palm down the front of his polo shirt. She tried not to think about how good it felt to be with him again, reminding herself for the umpteenth time that he was a temporary companion, and she ought to steer clear of catching feelings.

Parker's naturally sun-kissed skin made Sadie wonder if he was a yachting enthusiast, or if there were other outdoor hobbies up his sleeve that she had yet to uncover. She glanced aside to view their vessel for the day, eyes slowing on the script detailed along the hull.

Feelin' Nauti

"No," Sadie stated, stepping back. "Oh, no." She was equal parts amused and embarrassed. "I cannot possibly be seen on a boat called *Feelin' Nauti.*"

Parker's eyes narrowed at the description Sadie had used for his yacht, "I'm sorry, did you just call my baby a *boat*?"

Laughing, Sadie regarded him and then deliberately took in the splendor of his cruiser. "Oh my God," she deadpanned. "It's huge..."

"You dare to mock me?" he scoffed, aghast with playful offense.

Sadie pushed at his shoulder, nodding for him to get a move on. "Help me onto this thing already."

Parker stepped over first and Sadie tossed her straw clutch onto a padded bench while she awaited assistance. "Permission to come aboard, captain," she grinned.

"Granted," he quipped, holding her hand as she followed suit.

Sadie stepped out of her shoes and picked them up by the slingback straps, calmly watching Parker ready them to depart. She'd only been on yachts twice before, both as part of luxurious vacations. Both situations, she recalled, in which she'd been alone save for the crew.

The engine started and Parker's attention was split between guiding them from the no wake zone and watching Sadie where she'd taken a seat. She looked so perfectly at ease, and so comfortable with the elaborate idea for a date, that Parker was smitten. He could see her fitting into his lifestyle all too well.

It wasn't until he'd gotten them safely out to sea, with ten minutes of open water in their wake, that he cut the engine. The silence around them was deafening, only the caw of distant birds and the quiet sloshing of the waves accompanying Parker's words of, "You look beautiful."

Sadie turned, offering a soft smile. "Thank you."

She watched as he ducked into the companionway and returned with a bottle of chilled pinot grigio and two wine glasses, pinched by the stems.

"Holy…" Sadie breathed, struck by just how perfect this moment was. "I think I just came."

Parker laughed heartily, taking a seat at her hip. "Mission accomplished, then."

Sadie held the glasses while Parker poured, and soon they were toasting to a perfect day.

To keep things light, she teased, "Are you sure your wife doesn't mind?"

Nodding, amused, Parker replied, "Which one?"

Although they were teasing, Sadie still couldn't believe Parker was unattached. She could easily picture him with a trophy wife and a pack of children, attending fundraisers and soccer games. It was nauseatingly picturesque.

"Are you a horrible dancer?" Sadie asked suddenly.

Taken aback and laughing, Parker nearly choked on his wine. "Excuse me?"

"I mean," Sadie sighed. "I've slept with you. You're not lacking in that department. Also, you don't snore, you don't chew with your mouth open…I just don't understand it."

He smiled at the backhanded compliments. "Let me ask you, then," he countered. "Why are *you* single, Ms. Bache?"

She supposed she had that coming and she sighed, waving around them vaguely. "There are reasons."

"I'd love to hear them," he replied.

"I bet you would," she teased, sipping from her glass.

They sat in silence, neither answering, and Sadie felt that they were sharing a moment of rare understanding.

Parker stood, finishing off his wine. With a grin, he reached over his shoulders to pull his polo off his back, a hand slipping down next to pop the button of his khakis.

Sadie's breath caught and she felt herself oddly blushing. "Getting right down to it, are we?" she teased.

Beneath his pants Parker wore a tight pair of dark swim trunks. He dipped down to her eye level, sliding his fingers back through her dark curls. "I love how irresistible you think you are," he whispered, brushing his lips against hers.

Sadie's neck felt hot as he stepped away, scoffing at his back. "Aren't I?" she retorted with false bravado.

Following suit, Sadie set her hat aside, glasses too, and stood to slip off her sarong.

Parker's eyes did a lengthy once-over as he regarded her, whistling. "You most definitely are," he assured.

Stepping up to him, Sadie's hands curled around his biceps as he pulled her close. "Glad we're on the same page," she mumbled, eyeing his lips. Slowly, they kissed and moved towards the back of his powerboat and onto wooden slats, inches from the cold Atlantic below.

"Don't be mad," he whispered, giving Sadie just enough time for realization to sink in. As her eyes widened, he spun, pitching them both into water.

Sadie resurfaced with a whine, laughing. "You ass!" she accused, wiping water from her eyes.

Parker surfaced a mere two feet away, looking like the cat who caught the mouse. "I thought you liked it when I got you wet," he grinned.

She groaned at his sense of humor. "There's a 'down under' joke in there somewhere," she muttered.

Deeming it safe to return within arm's reach, Parker glided in front of her, latching an arm around her waist. Their legs brushed as they treaded water, his amusement clear. "Have you been?"

"To Australia?" she asked, shaking her head in response. "What's it like?"

"Beautiful, expensive…" he smirked. "Dangerous."

Sadie leaned closer to kiss him, tasting the brine of the water on his skin. "My type of place."

♥ ♠ ♦ ♣

It was difficult to return to reality after a near-perfect day on the water. It was some four hours later by the time Sadie and Parker finally docked together. He escorted her to the boathouse entrance, turning back to tip the marina attendant.

They'd decided to enjoy a drink at the oceanfront bar before finding a place to grab dinner and ultimately end up back at her suite. While she waited, she checked her reflection and waterproof makeup in a handheld mirror.

"Surprise, surprise."

Sadie tensed. It wasn't so much what was said as it was the tone in which it was delivered.

"Fancy meeting you here."

Sadie looked up to see a familiar man leering at her, having clearly just left the bar.

"Stew," she greeted politely, her smile tight. "Hi. Again."

With a fluctuating population of 39,000 and a high turnover rate, Sadie had hoped not to run into her ditched date. Alas, there he was, eyeing her with distaste.

"I'm willing to overlook the fact that you ghosted me," he told her. "If you—"

"Let me stop you right there," Sadie interrupted, returning her mirror to her clutch. She faced him, telling him what she should have told him that night they'd gone out. "You were very nice, but I was bored."

The look on his face was honest shock at her directness and he replied with a nasty laugh.

"And," she went on, "an opportunity to *not* be bored came along, and I took it."

Belatedly, Sadie had the good sense to think that she might have gone overboard in that moment, boat pun wildly underappreciated, as she watched his face morph into one of anger.

"You're a fucking tease," he bit out in a dangerously low voice.

It wasn't anything she hadn't heard before, but it didn't hurt any less. Her experience with men was that they felt entitled to her time and attention and got nasty when they didn't get what they wanted.

"Leave," she told him seriously, nodding her head in the direction of the parking lot. He had been on his way out of the boathouse, anyway.

He scoffed and turned, as if to gain sympathy from friends, but he was alone.

Sadie rolled her eyes, glancing away long enough for Stew to make a move. She inhaled sharply at the feel of a hand tightening around her wrist, keeping her rooted in place and forcing her to look at him as he bit out, "Bet you'll change your tune once I fuck you."

Sadie's lips parted, but she had no time to reply before he was yanked away.

A hand shot out, fingers curling tightly around the front of Stew's shirt and jerking him a few feet away. Stew had yelped, drawing the attention of a few people on the dock. Standing over him, Parker held fast to the material he clutched. There was enough fire burning in his eyes for the man, drunk or not, to rethink his actions.

But after a moment, Stew's vision seemed to clear, and his lip curled upon recognition. "For fuck's sake," he muttered, shoving at Parker's grip. "Not you again. Find your own whore."

Parker's fist flew across Stew's face in response, releasing the man so that he could stumble away. Typically, Parker was known for his level-headedness. But when he had seen Sadie grabbed, heard the venom in Stew's words, Parker saw red.

Stew failed to catch his balance and stumbled to the ground, stunned.

"Apologize," Parker instructed, advancing towards him.

Stew flinched away though he managed to scramble back to his feet. "Fuck you," he replied, spitting on the ground between them.

Sadie curled her hand around Parker's arm to draw him away. She put on a brave face, but the altercation stung.

"You can have her," Stew muttered, brushing himself off.

Parker had been willing to walk away; Sadie's behavior clearly suggested that she would prefer this be over. However, the entitled way Stew was acting grated on him, as if Stew was choosing to relinquish Sadie into his care.

"Just a minute, doll," Parker told Sadie, patting her hand. He stepped away and approached Stew. The drunk man had the good sense to back up, lifting his arms to protect his face. Unfortunately, that wasn't where Parker was aiming. He delivered a swift punch to the gut and told Stew as he buckled forward, "Next time you see us, walk the other way."

Sadie watched with a wince, but she was glad for Parker's parting words. If Stew would be around Atlantic City any longer, she would feel better knowing he would avoid them. She gathered her thick, air-dried hair over a shoulder and took Parker's hand when he returned to her side.

As a pair of staff members hurried over, faces hot, Parker was quick to form a narrative. "That man was touching this woman against her will. Please escort him from the premises."

It was the confidence in his voice that spurred the two into action. After they exchanged glances, they jogged away to remove the unwanted guest from the marina.

"You alright?" Parker asked, touching the back of his hand to Sadie's cheek.

Embarrassed, Sadie quickly nodded. "I'm fine," she assured, trying to laugh it off as her pulse calmed. "I could've managed without the rescue," she teased.

"I know you could've," he assured her seriously. "I was almost content to watch you destroy his self-esteem," he added, his left dimple winking into view.

Once Sadie understood that Parker's interference hadn't been because he thought she lacked the ability to stand up for herself, she relaxed.

"I wouldn't have landed as hard a punch," she conceded. "Thanks for that."

He kissed her then, cupping her face as he assured, "Anytime, Sadie."

She realized with a start that it was the first time she recalled hearing Parker use her name.

Chapter Thirty

♦

With two weeks until Jess and Kayla's wedding, Gemma was starting to feel the pressure. Thankfully, neither bride could be categorized as a Bridezilla, but there was still a lot to organize. In addition to Kayla's four bridesmaids, Jess had three of her own and her brother as best man. It seemed no matter how Gemma tried to avoid Everett, there was no escaping him.

"You're in the way."

Gemma whirled to find her ex-fiancé standing behind her, his arms straining around a large Amazon package. She quickly pressed herself to the wall to give him room to pass, rolling her eyes at how purposefully unfriendly he was acting. It was the morning of the bridal shower and the wedding party had been asked to haul all the pre-delivered gifts to the venue to be opened during Bridal Shower Bingo.

There were two large wicker chairs in the corner of the small restaurant, a growing pile of gifts behind them. Gemma looked up as she felt a tug, lifting her end of the garland that Ashlee was stringing around windows for the garden party theme.

"How does that look?" Ashlee called down, perched on a stool above Gemma.

"Really good," Gemma replied, giving her friend a thumbs up.

With half an hour before the guests were due to arrive, they were making good progress working through the checklist Hailey had prepared. Abandoning Ashlee to finish up, Gemma shuffled over to the door to greet a delivery man and offload the fresh doughnuts they'd pre-ordered as favors. As she turned away, a pile of bakery boxes in her arms, she nearly collided with Everett.

They spoke over each other, Everett criticizing Gemma for not looking where she was going and Gemma, frustrated with his constant hovering. She knew he was just trying to do what was being asked of him, but it seemed like they were constantly in each other's way.

"I've got it," he told her, tossing his flop of brown hair off his forehead. He began offloading the boxes from her arms, sighing. "Go find something else to do."

Gemma considered arguing with him, but she heard her phone ringing against a nearby table and abandoned the fight. She pushed the bakery boxes into his arms with more force than necessary, offered a tight smile, and hurried to ensure it wasn't Kayla or Jess calling. Her face lit up when she realized it was Alaric and she made a quick executive decision that she could sneak away, at least for a few minutes.

The couple had exchanged a few texts per day since parting ways in Atlantic City, squeezing in one FaceTime in the week they'd been apart. Three rings in, her voice filled his ear.

"I didn't think this would be so hard," she confessed, smiling.

"The shower?" Alaric asked, confused. "Don't you just have to decorate?"

Laughing, Gemma tucked herself into the small hallway leading to the bathroom. "No, I mean you and me. The long-distance."

"Sweetheart..." Alaric chuckled. "Please don't make me feel bad that I have a job."

The affection she heard in his voice was soothing and brought a rising blush to her cheeks. She'd been convinced that the butterflies would settle with distance and time, but they'd only worsened. "I can't help it," she whined.

"Gemma," Alaric stated, laughing despite his serious proclamation. "I will bring you back here in a heartbeat." He knew he couldn't ask that of her; she had her own life and responsibilities, but it would solve the problem at hand.

"I wish I could."

"So, how're things going? Did I pull you away from putting pacifiers around the place?"

"Pacifiers? This isn't a baby shower," she laughed.

"Well, I've been to neither," he defended, smiling. "It's going alright?"

Gemma glanced down the hall, watching the rest of the wedding party busy about the restaurant floor. Overall, the day was great. The venue had prepped everything to specification, there had been no catastrophes, and they even had good weather. The only hiccup, which she'd expected, was Everett.

"Yeah," she replied, but Alaric wasn't buying it. "Guessing he's there?" he asked knowingly.

"You would be correct," Gemma confirmed. "But it's fine, I'm ignoring him as much as I can. And Ashlee told him I have a new boyfriend," she shared proudly.

"Did she now?" Alaric mused. "Knew I liked her."

His eyes dropped to his desk calendar adorned with scribbled notes.

Untucking a corner to flip to the coming month, Alaric did a quick calculation.

"Gemma," he said, approaching the offer carefully. "What if you didn't have to go to the wedding alone?"

Gemma's lips parted and she struggled with an appropriate reaction that toed the line between begging him to join her and reassuring him it wasn't necessary. She settled on asking, "You'd want to come?"

"Do I want to come visit you?" he asked rhetorically. "Do I want to see you in that bridesmaid's dress? Do I want to show Ev—"

"Okay, okay, stop," Gemma laughed, covering her face with a hand. She was a goner for his kindness and his flirtation tactics. She sighed as a slow, reluctant smile formed, "I feel like I can't ask that. It's too…" she trailed off, unsure.

"Too serious?" Alaric finished, waiting.

"Kind of?"

Alaric gave her time, waiting in the silence to see what she'd ultimately decide. If she wanted him there, he'd take more of his unused vacation time. If she preferred to save a NY visit for a future date, he would just have to do his best to stop picturing her ex-fiancé bothering her.

"I own a suit," he offered. "In case it tips the scales."

She was smiling, but still unsure. If he attended the wedding, he would meet her parents and most of her close friends. It seemed like a monumental decision.

"Is this just because of Everett?" she asked.

Alaric wouldn't lie, but there was more to it. "He's one reason," he confirmed. "But he's not the only."

Gemma toyed with the fabric of her dress at her thigh, thinking. There was no denying she wanted him there, and she considered any reservations she had. It was fast, especially to meet her parents, but what was the point of turning down an opportunity to see him, especially when the distance complicated things?

"The wedding's on the twenty-seventh," she said at last. "I'd love it if you came."

Chapter Thirty-One

♠

Laurel groaned as Grayson's phone chimed obnoxiously on the nightstand. Since his return two days earlier, she'd been at his suite, only dipping out one afternoon to stock the fridge at home.

"Make it stop," Grayson groaned, tugging a pillow over his head.

"It's *your* phone," she grumbled. When he refused to move, she cursed and leaned across him to swipe his device from the charger. "It's Parker," she informed, dropping the phone to his chest.

Groaning, Grayson lifted the phone to his ear. "It's four in the morning," he complained.

"It's almost nine," Parker corrected. "And you need a job."

Grayson smirked, but his friend wasn't wrong. Ever since his agreement with Alaric, he hadn't had an opportunity to earn any income. He knew he needed to seek opportunities elsewhere, but he wasn't quite ready to leave Atlantic City again. Not now that Laurel had finally let her guard down around him.

"Listen," Parker said. "Are you still around? I want you guys to come out to the Hamptons this weekend."

Grayson rubbed his face. "I'm back in AC. Al agree yet?"

"I'm leaving that part to you."

Laughing, Grayson stretched and pushed up to a seated position. "Oh sure, like he ever listens to me."

Parker smirked, glancing up at his office door to see Hannah standing there with a file he'd requested. He waved her in and told Grayson, "Convince him. I'll text you a time to meet me and my date at the marina on Friday."

"Breaking out the yacht, huh? You must really be trying to impress this one,"

Grayson grinned, eyes quick to follow Laurel as she crossed to the coffee maker. She wore his t-shirt, the hem only just covering her backside, and his gaze roamed freely. He chucked a pillow at her, waiting until he had her attention to nod to her in appreciation, winking.

Laurel rolled her eyes, selecting a coffee pod from the hotel selection.

"Yeah, we'll go," Grayson confirmed, ending the call abruptly. He bounced off the bed, stark naked, and came up behind Laurel. "We've got plans next weekend," he told her, pressing his face into her hair to deeply inhale her scent.

"Smelling me?" she laughed.

"Yep."

"And were you going to ask me if I'm free this weekend before agreeing to plans?"

Grayson groaned, squeezing her. He reveled in the warmth and softness of her body, his morning arousal responding to the closeness. "Please?"

"Ask me," she insisted, casually adding sugar and creamer to her coffee.

"Six," he mused, "Would you please spend the weekend with me?"

"Depends. What are we doing?" she inquired.

"It's a surprise," he replied playfully as he plucked the coffee from her hand and set it back on the counter. He dragged her back to the bed, crawling over her.

Laurel was about to say she hated surprises, but the last time he'd surprised her had been with the charm bracelet still wrapped around her wrist. "Fine," she agreed, grinning as she lifted her knees against his sides.

Before he could so much as kiss her, his phone began to ring again. Rolling his eyes, he felt blindly across the sheets.

There was a clear shift in the air as Grayson noted the caller ID. He shifted his weight from Laurel, rolling over to sit up and accept the call.

Laurel could tell by the way he reacted that it was the call they'd been waiting on. In the suddenly quiet room, she realized she could hear a woman crying on the other end of the line. Delilah, she assumed.

Laurel set her hand on Grayson's back, rubbing slow circles to reassure him that she was there.

All Grayson said during the five-minute exchange was "okay," and Laurel watched him as he lowered the phone to his lap. She waited, but he only cleared his throat and moved to stand.

Catching his wrist lightly, Laurel's brows raised in silent question.

Grayson nodded in answer. His mother was gone.

Although he'd shared that they weren't close, Laurel knew the death of a parent was still a solemn occasion. She squeezed his hand, trying to convey her compassion.

Grayson stared aside, his thumb brushing her fingers as he processed the latest news. Sighing at last he asked, "Come for a ride with me?"

Laurel easily agreed and when she went to take a quick shower, Grayson pulled on some clothes. He ended up drinking Laurel's coffee as he placed another call.

"Hey," Grayson greeted when Alaric answered. "You got a sec? It's my mom."

Alaric sighed. That was all he needed to say; it was clear she had passed. "I'm sorry, Gray. What do you need?"

Grayson considered it a moment. He didn't need to go anywhere, didn't need to make any arrangements. He just needed his friends.

"Parker's Hamptons place this weekend. I want you there."

The next sigh was heavier. "Gray..." Alaric hedged. He didn't work typical Monday through Friday hours. Taking off for a weekend meant less time he could dedicate to going upstate in the coming weeks and months.

"You owe me," Grayson reminded, though his playful attempt to cash in on a favor for hosting the game in New York fell flat.

No favors were necessary. Grayson and Alaric were practically family.

"I'll be there," Alaric finally agreed.

"Thanks, I'm bringing Six," he added. "Parker said something about a date, too."

Alaric found himself with an unexpected opportunity to bring a date of his own, for once.

♥ ♠ ♦ ♣

The following night, Alaric still wasn't sure how he'd planned on convincing Gemma to join him for a weekend, but he was determined to ask. Requesting that she travel to see him only two weeks after she'd left seemed aggressive, but it would be nice to spend time together before the wedding, which would be another three weeks later.

Gemma: I have a room booked for the wedding night.
Alaric: OK. I'll find something close for the other nights.
Gemma: "nights"? how many?
Alaric: Four?
Gemma: Wow.
Gemma: Wow = yay!
Gemma: I'll take what I can get.

Moments later her phone buzzed, and Gemma answered with a smile as he appeared on-screen. "Really?" she teased, "FaceTime?"

Alaric had just pulled on a t-shirt and sweatpants. "Forgot what you looked like," he joked.

Gemma put a hand to her chest. "Well, we can't have that."

"Bad time?" he asked, mindful of the fact that he didn't quite know her typical schedule while she was home. He'd been careful in asking what she spent her days doing or inquiring about her plans. Ashlee had warned him about Everett's controlling behavior and Alaric wanted to be sure to respect her privacy.

"No, not at all. How was your day?"

It was such a normal, domestic question that it kept a smile on his lips.

"Not too bad," he replied, leaning back against the headboard of his bed. "I got a couple of hours in at the gym. Haven't been able to do that lately."

Gemma started grinning and Alaric smirked, "What's so funny?"

"Oh, nothing," she assured. "I'm just picturing you at the gym."

His brows popped at her confession. "Well, you'd better be picturing me being very sexy."

"Totally," she assured.

"Speaking of sexy, how's that tattoo healing?" he asked.

Gemma crossed to her bedroom mirror and lifted the side of her shirt to reveal the top of the perfectly healed feather design etched into her skin. "Great, actually." Switching the camera, she showed him her reflection in the mirror. She ran her fingertips over the exposed ink starting just below her ribs, pulling her shorts lower on her hip to reveal most of the design.

Alaric groaned as he took in her full-length appearance. Her tumble of brown hair, tight clothes, and exposed midsection. "Send me a picture," he requested.

"A picture?" she mused, checking to see if she could do so while still on the phone with him. "Do I get one, too?"

He dipped out of view and when he returned to the screen, he no longer wore a shirt. Her phone chimed just after, signaling the picture he'd sent.

Alaric checked as a picture arrived from Gemma in return and offered a playful whistle. "How far away is this wedding again?"

She smiled as she studied the picture he'd sent, which captured his sharp jawline and most of his tattooed chest. "I wish it was tomorrow," she sighed honestly.

"Let's say, for argument's sake, that it was," Alaric offered, lowering his voice. "Let's say I arrived today and I'm there right now."

Gemma took a seat on the edge of her bed, giving him a curious look. "Uh huh…" she said, letting him go on.

"I think the first thing I'd do is take that shirt off of you."

Gemma whined in embarrassment, glancing over towards her closed bedroom door. "Alaric, I don't think I can—"

"The shirt, sweetheart," he interrupted, looking expectant.

After a few long seconds of hesitation, Gemma set her phone down and peeled her shirt over her head. He hadn't known she was naked beneath it, but her bare shoulders when she returned to the screen confirmed it. Still, she kept the camera from dipping any lower than her collar bones.

Alaric's smile widened and he gave her an impressed nod. "Now we're talking."

He was already shirtless, so Gemma wasn't sure what to say next. She shifted back in bed to mimic his posture, catching her bottom lip between her teeth.

"Would it be at all possible for you to lower the phone?" Alaric requested politely.

Face hot, Gemma debated it. "You have to absolutely swear you won't take screenshots," she blurted.

Alaric raised a hand immediately. He knew that when a woman was willing to get naked, on video or otherwise, you played by her rules. "I swear."

With a deep breath, Gemma angled the camera lower. She had a bedside lamp on which provided just enough light as she revealed her bare breasts. She was rather pleased to be witnessing his reaction on FaceTime, laughing as he passed a frustrated hand over his face.

He spied the elastic of her shorts and asked, "Would you take off the rest?"

Gemma wasn't sure she was ready to get completely naked on camera. Alaric sensed her hesitation and offered instead, "Or maybe you could just slip your hand in?"

They'd sent one another suggestive texts, and Gemma had been thinking about him nightly, but this was something very different. This was phone sex, and Gemma was way out of her element. "I think I want to get off FaceTime," she told him.

Alaric's lips parted and he was quick to backtrack, "Gemma, I didn't mean to make you uncomfortable."

"No, no," she laughed, humiliated. "I mean, I think I'd rather do this on the phone. The regular phone. Like, just talking."

Alaric relaxed as she clarified. "Sure."

The moment it rang through with a normal call, he answered with a grin. "Are you touching yourself yet?"

Gemma whimpered at how easily he could reduce her to embarrassed laughter. "Oh my God, you're the worst."

"That a no?" he pressed.

Gemma battled the butterflies in her stomach as she admitted, "Not exactly."

Alaric's brows lifted, impressed. "Are you wet yet?" He made quick work of his sweats, pushing them lower to free himself from the confines of his clothing.

Gemma's fingers slowly dipped between her legs, running the pads of two fingers down against herself. "A little," she confessed, her voice quiet. She could hardly believe she was being this bold; her parents were downstairs, and her door didn't even have a lock.

In all her years with Everett they'd never done anything this salacious. Then again, they'd never had distance separating them. Gemma supposed this was something she was going to have to get used to.

Loosely, Alaric encircled himself, his hand began to lift and lower in his lap. "Do you have a good imagination, Gemma?"

The mild strain in his voice didn't escape her and she knew with certainty that his hand was equally occupied. The thought had her shivering.

"I can try."

Alaric felt that this was a good start for them; it wasn't dirty or desperate, just a display of affection in an intimate, if atypical, way.

"Imagine that's my hand, then," he encouraged. "And keep touching yourself."

Gemma's eyes fell shut and her fingers began to move in slow, concentrated circles, her breaths growing audible. She did her best to picture him there in bed with her, his hand wedged between her legs. "I really wish you were here," she confessed.

"I know, sweetheart," Alaric breathed, his hand pausing as he brushed his thumb around the head of his cock. "I wish this was you touching me, too."

He was being reserved with her, easing her into it. The last thing he wanted to do was scare her off with too much dirty talk. He heard her whimper and he instructed, "Can you fit a finger or two inside for me?"

A breathy moan filled her end of the line and Alaric pinched his phone between his cheek and his shoulder. With both hands free, he pumped his hand over his shaft with one and squeezed the heavy sack beneath with the other. He drew out his pleasure, forcing himself to wait. "Just tell me when," he requested, voice strained.

Gemma whimpered; was he already at that point? Dipping her fingers into her tight channel repeatedly, Gemma called to mind how good it had been on their final night together. Alaric had taken her once from behind and once with agonizing slowness, in missionary position like she envisioned now. It had been so intimate; it almost broke her heart to walk away from him the next morning.

She was nodding against her pillows, her fingers quickening. "Almost…" In another minute she offered an urgent moan. "Okay, now," she said weakly, shuddering. The phone nearly slipped from her hand as her head tipped back and her body tightened.

Alaric caved to the pleasure, grunting as he painted his lower abs with the result of his orgasm. He let out a heavy breath as his body calmed, beyond pleased with what he'd managed to hear on Gemma's end.

For a few seconds, Alaric listened to her labored breathing. "You good?" he asked.

"I— yeah..." she panted softly, flushed. "Did you—?"

"Yeah," he confirmed, smiling.

"Not a good enough substitute," she concluded.

Alaric smirked, appreciating the compliment. "But better than nothing," he offered.

"True," she agreed, humming happily as the exhaustion settled throughout her body.

As the pair fell into a lengthy, comfortable silence, Gemma let her eyes slip closed. She was all too close to falling asleep with Alaric on the phone when he proposed, "Come to the Hamptons and meet my friends."

Chapter Thirty-Two

♥

Grayson turned into an unfamiliar driveway on Friday afternoon, killing the engine of his bike. He was picking up Laurel at her and her mother's house for the surprise weekend trip he'd planned. It was his first time seeing her place, and she'd warned him that by coming by he may be required to meet her mother.

"You say that like it's a bad thing," Grayson had laughed.

Laurel had only grimaced. She often bypassed this step in relationships over the years: meeting the parents. Grayson, however, could not be deterred.

Knocking at the screen door, Grayson waited patiently with a small fruit basket tucked under an arm. He was prepared to make a good impression, and judging from the look Laurel gave him at the door, he'd surprised at least one of the Price women.

"Did you bring me a gift basket?" she asked.

"I did not," Grayson replied, looking rather pleased with himself. "I brought your *mom* a gift basket."

Laurel groaned, but it was mixed with defeated laughter. "You're ridiculous. Come in."

Grayson stepped inside, kissing Laurel's cheek as he went. "Where's mom?"

"At work," Laurel informed, giving him an apologetic shrug. "I told you she may or may not be here." It was almost comical how disappointed he looked. "I promise to tell her the fruit's from you."

Grayson set the basket on the kitchen table and was drawn to the refrigerator, smiling at the younger photos of Laurel.

She expected to be nervous with Grayson coming over for the first time, but she hadn't expected the self-consciousness. She had cleaned up, made the place look presentable, but there was no hiding the fact that they didn't come from much. Suddenly wanting to draw his attention away from the evidence, she asked, "Do you want to see my room?"

It had the desired effect; Grayson quickly looked her way, but his grin conveyed he was reading into the offer.

"I'm almost done packing," she explained with a roll of her eyes, turning to lead him down the hall. "I need a little more info. Are we going to be naked the whole time or do I need to bring a nice dress? I have no idea what I'm walking into."

Grayson was quick to confess, "I would very much like for you to be naked, but Al and Park will be there."

Laurel had known that much already. She stopped beside the half-filled bag on her bed and considered the outfits that were piled nearby. "Jeans? Dresses? Can you give me anything here?"

Distracted by the insight into a new part of Laurel's life, Grayson moved around the room. He studied the few prize ribbons from her youth, the photo booth strips tucked along a mirror's edge, and a larger framed photo of her with who could only be her father. She looked a lot like him, though she couldn't be more than ten in the picture.

"Grayson?"

He turned to find her holding up two different outfits, looking for guidance. "Yes," he confirmed. Considering her glare, he assumed his response was of no help.

"Pack a bathing suit, poolside gear, and casual clothes," he offered, holding up three fingers as he counted off the suggestions.

"Poolside gear?" she echoed curiously.

Grayson lifted his hands to outline a circle above his head. "Big floppy hat, sunglasses, all that."

Amused, Laurel nodded and began to weed her selection. A poolside weekend getaway sounded like an excellent trip, and she was thankful he wasn't planning anything too outside her comfort zone. Knowing Grayson, he could have been taking her wakeboarding or scuba diving. Then again, there was much that fell outside her comfort zone considering she hadn't had many opportunities to participate in those sorts of activities. If she had, she might have found she enjoyed them.

As they locked up the house and affixed their bags to the back of Grayson's bike, Laurel almost groaned to find her mother pulling their shared beater of a car into the driveway.

"Mom!" Grayson greeted, much to Laurel's chagrin.

Smiling uncertainly, Ms. Price closed the driver's side door and assessed Grayson and the motorcycle. She gave Laurel a curious look.

"This is Grayson, Mom," Laurel said, gesturing.

Laurel's mom took a breath, looking suddenly delighted. "The boy you're seeing."

"That's me," Grayson beamed happily, stepping forward to offer his hand. "It's lovely to finally meet you, Mrs. Price."

"It's Ms. Price, but you can call me Julia."

Breezing past the misstep, Grayson nodded. "Julia. I hope you don't mind me stealing Laurel away this weekend."

"This weekend?" They hadn't expressly spoken about Laurel's plans, though they rarely did.

"I left a note," Laurel offered lamely, nodding back over her shoulder.

Julia seemed unsure what to say. "Well, that's nice."

"Some of my friends are having a get-together," Grayson explained. He watched as Julia opened the car's rear door and extracted a few paper grocery bags. He stepped forward to help. "It'll only be for a couple of days."

"Oh, you don't have to do that," Julia assured, but Grayson was already shifting the groceries into his arms to take them off her hands.

Laurel visibly tensed at the knowing clink of glass bottles within the bags.

No one spoke for a minute.

"Laurel." Grayson was watching her. "Can you get the door?"

Inside, Grayson set the bags down. He sensed it was best to let Julia unbag her purchases once they'd gone. He didn't know the full extent of Ms. Price's vices, but he knew alcohol had been, or was, a problem for her.

"What's this?" Julia asked, setting her keys beside an arrangement of shrink-wrapped fruit.

Laurel set a hand on Grayson's shoulder. "That's from this guy."

"Flowers seemed impractical," Grayson joked. "Hope you like grapefruit."

"It's very nice. That was sweet of you."

Grayson couldn't tell if he was imagining it, but the air felt tense. Whether Laurel was uncomfortable with her worlds colliding or Ms. Price was surprised by the news that her daughter was leaving for a few days, Grayson couldn't tell. As politely as he could, he reminded Laurel, "We should get going."

It was hard not to look relieved as Laurel nodded. "See you in a few days, Mom."

♥ ♠ ♦ ♣

Parker walked the length of the dock to meet Sadie halfway, his brown hair tousled from the ocean wind.

"You look perfect, as usual," he greeted, giving her cheek a kiss as he took her bag. He gave a quiet laugh at the unexpected weight of it for only two nights, to which she smiled sweetly.

"You always know just what to say," she replied. "As usual."

"Sadie?"

Sadie turned at the sound of her name, curious.

Laurel slowed in honest surprise beside Grayson at the sight of her friend. Despite knowing that Parker was joining them that weekend, she hadn't considered this possibility.

"Laurel?" Sadie looked equally perplexed. Was she here by chance?

"Ten more minutes and we would've pushed off without you," Parker quipped, stepping forward to throw an arm around Grayson. "Sorry about your mom, mate."

Grayson took a breath, nodding in thanks. He was grateful for the timing of this weekend away, and thankful to have his friends and Laurel with him through the mixed emotions brought on by his mother's passing.

Sadie easily caught on to the fact that this was a group excursion. She experienced a twinge of disappointment that she wouldn't have Parker all to herself, but Laurel's smile made her laugh.

"Small world," she said, hugging the blond as she stepped closer.

Parker watched the girls hug, his brow dipping curiously. "You two know each other?"

Grayson laughed, clapping his friend on the back. "Wow. You know nothing, do you?" Tossing his and Laurel's bags onto the boat, Grayson hopped aboard.

It dawned on Parker slowly.

"You two play together," he realized, gesturing between Sadie and Grayson. "And you…" he looked between Laurel and Sadie, unsure.

"Are friends," Sadie concluded. "Well done."

Upon arrival at the marina, Grayson had confirmed that they were going out on the water with Parker. What he had neglected to inform Laurel of, however, was the type of cruising vessel they'd be taking.

Once Sadie had been helped aboard, Laurel stood looking dumbfounded at the luxurious watercraft. She could only guess, "Is this a yacht?"

Grayson's smile was genuine as he nodded. "Pretentious, isn't it?" he teased. "Park got it a couple of years ago. Paid full price. Idiot."

Dazed, Laurel nodded. She accepted Grayson's hand and joined him on the teak flooring. She settled beside Sadie on a cushion, shaking her head in disbelief.

"I guess things are going well for you two," Laurel prompted Sadie as Parker and Grayson went about stowing their belongings and untethering from the dock.

"This is a nice development," Sadie nodded, gesturing to Laurel and her unexpected presence. "This your first trip to the Hamptons?"

Laurel's eyes went wide. "I thought—" She'd thought the boat had been most of the surprise.

Grayson slowed as he passed them, giving Sadie an unappreciative glare. "Way to ruin it."

Laughing, Sadie threw up a hand. "I didn't realize you were kidnapping her, Grayson. Excuse me for thinking a woman should have the right to know where she was spending the weekend."

"Ludicrous," Grayson replied, smirking as Laurel turned her surprised expression his way.

Sadie rolled her eyes, asking, "Anyone else coming that I should know about?"

Grayson leaned down against the back of Parker's captain's chair and asked his friend, "Any news from Al?"

"He's coming straight to the house later tonight or early tomorrow," Parker replied.

Once they were free of the no wake zone, Parker eased the cruiser up to a decent speed and gave Grayson a pat on the back. "Be gentle with her."

Beaming, Grayson quickly slid into the white leather chair.

"Drinks?" Parker offered, taking note as Sadie's hand quickly lifted.

"Six!" Grayson called. "I need my first mate!"

Laurel carefully made her way over to him, offering an unconvinced laugh. "This isn't a motorcycle," she reminded, holding her hair back as it lashed at her face and neck. "You know how to drive this thing?"

Grayson made room and slid an arm around her as she took a seat. "Watch me." He waited about five full minutes before requesting, "Just let me know when you're impressed."

Rolling her eyes, Laurel fought a smile. In truth, all of this was impressive. The fact that they were taking a private yacht to the Hamptons was surreal.

"Never been on a boat," Laurel confessed.

"Yacht," Grayson corrected.

"Never been on either."

"You should have told me," he groaned, playful. "I would have made a much bigger deal about this."

Laurel spotted Parker joining Sadie for a drink and smiled. She felt bad about the drunken assumption she'd made the night they'd met in New York. Texting Sadie to rat Parker out for leaving a club with another woman hadn't been her proudest moment. Watching them now, and knowing how Sadie felt about the Australian, she had to admit they seemed happy. Laurel felt more comfortable with a committed relationship, but she couldn't fault Sadie and Parker for enjoying whatever they could have when they could have it.

Parker set a hand on Sadie's bare knee where her skirt parted, the two content to watch the scenery pass by. Sadie sipped her margarita in its stainless tumbler, fit with a lid to make it journey-proof. She turned over a question in her mind. She knew it would carry some hope, and she didn't want to be disappointed in the answer, but she had to know.

"So, you have a place in the city and one in the Hamptons. Anything further west?"

Parker briefly glanced over as Grayson shifted them into a faster gear. "Technically," he confirmed, but clarified, "In Melbourne."

Sadie nodded, her smile weak. So, she could see him on the east coast or on the other side of the world. Sarcastically, she thought that was just perfect.

She saw no reason to beat around the bush and decided to fess up.

"I'm leaving soon," she informed. She had checked out of Borgata's earlier that morning, the remainder of her luggage held with bell services. After the Hamptons she intended to move on, accepting the next opportunity. She would be gone in approximately forty-eight hours.

"Where?" Parker asked. Though his tone was neutral, his thumb slid over her skin affectionately.

"Black Hawk," she replied, finally meeting his stare. "Colorado."

Parker had been looking forward to this weekend; introducing Sadie to his friends and to the idea that what they had was more than casual. Now hearing that he had only two days until she relocated over fifteen hundred miles away was disheartening, to say the least.

At the helm, Grayson tangled his free hand in the ends of Laurel's wind-whipped hair.

"Your mom was nice to me," he mused.

Laurel was wondering how long he'd wait to debrief their introductory meeting. "She called you a boy," Laurel pointed out smugly.

"Because of my boyish charm."

"Sure," she laughed.

After a beat of silence, Grayson wondered aloud, "Does it bother you that I met her?"

"What?" Laurel looked surprised by the question. "I said you could come pick me up. I knew there was a chance."

"But it wasn't guaranteed," he pointed out.

Unsure what he was getting at, Laurel turned to him. "What do you mean?"

Grayson took a deep breath, retracting his arm. He could only hope he wasn't starting a fight by addressing Laurel's home life. She'd never been forthcoming about details, but he knew the gist.

"You let me come by, knowing there was a slim chance your mom would be there. You haven't invited me over for dinner or—"

"Grayson, we don't do 'family dinners,'" Laurel snapped.

Carefully, Grayson replied, "Okay. But you could. You *could* invite me over for dinner to meet your mom."

Laurel almost laughed. The thought of arranging a gathering at her house for Grayson and her mother to meet was wildly amusing. She opened her mouth to tell him as much, but she could see the odd discomfort tensing his brows. He was serious. Guilt seeped in as she realized that Grayson was talking about normal couple-like behaviors, and Laurel was acting outraged. Not to mention, Grayson had just lost his mom. It wasn't so outlandish to think he wanted to make a good impression on hers.

"I had no idea you wanted that," she confessed, sliding a hand over his leg.

Grayson shrugged. He wasn't trying to force anything, but it was an easy next step. Laurel's mom was nearby. It wasn't rocket science to think he'd want to meet her family.

"Anyway," he said, shifting the conversation to something else they needed to discuss. "I got an invite to a game out west."

Laurel gave a supportive smile, though she felt her pulse climbing. "Oh yeah?" They hadn't talked about what would happen when Grayson moved on from Atlantic City. She knew he wanted to try to make their relationship work despite his lifestyle, but she'd been too afraid to talk about long distance. Plus, the only residence he had was a few states away in North Carolina.

"It's in Vegas," he confirmed, glancing over at her. "Ever been?"

"Is that a serious question?"

He knew by now that she'd seen very little of the world.

"I've never even been on a plane."

"Well…" he smiled. "I was thinking you could join me. I'll be there for a few weeks, but you could come out for as long as you want."

Laurel's lips parted, seeming torn. Of course she wanted to see him and visit Las Vegas for the first time, but she had a new job and her mom to worry about. Grayson had seen Julia on a good day, thankfully, but it wasn't always like that. Cost was another factor, but she knew by now that his offer included covering the logistics.

"Can I think about it?"

Grayson lifted her hand and kissed her knuckles. "Only if you say yes."

Laurel rolled her eyes, laughing.

♥ ♠ ♦ ♣

Below deck, Laurel and Sadie fixed themselves drinks. They were about an hour away now, the trip taking longer than Laurel had expected. Still, it was a perfect day with cloudless skies. Laurel was also thrilled to find she didn't suffer from motion sickness. It was the first thing she had worried about when they'd arrived at the marina; being sick would have put a damper on the weekend.

"You two sure look cozy," Sadie commented, referring to Laurel and Grayson and how they'd been at the helm together.

"He's beyond impossible sometimes, but I can't deny it. He grew on me."

"Mr. Charming has charmed his way into your heart," Sadie laughed. "How apt."

As Laurel garnished her drink, Sadie lightly caught her arm. "What's this?" she asked, studying the jewelry on her wrist.

An uncharacteristic blush bloomed across Laurel's features. "It was a gift," she replied, her smile impossible to fight.

"It's a charm bracelet," Sadie noted expectantly.

Laurel gave her a curious look, retracting her arm. "Yeah?"

"Mr. *Charming* gave you a *charm* bracelet," Sadie laughed, her brows lifting in disbelief. "Wow, if that's not a sign from the universe…"

Wanting to escape any sort of otherworldly discussions, Laurel quickly pivoted the conversation to focus on Sadie and her blooming romance.

"What about you and Parker? What is this, your twentieth date?"

"Sixth," Sadie corrected, pausing to think. "Or something like that. Hard to count when they last more than twenty-four hours." It was more dates than she usually went on with men, anyway. "But all good things must come to an end, I'm afraid."

Laurel gave her a surprised look, dropping a lime wedge into her cocktail. "What? We're literally going to his house right now. Did you guys just break up?"

Sadie barked out an amused laugh. "Break up? Oh my God, you're cute. No, we didn't break up because we're not dating, hon. I'm hitting the road; Colorado-bound next week."

Laurel's face fell. She hadn't realized she was relying on Sadie to be around when Grayson flew off to Vegas. "You're leaving, too?"

"Too?" Sadie gave a sympathetic sigh. Frequent travel was the life of a full-time gambler, at least those who opted to partake in the face-to-face thrill as opposed to those that chose to sit behind the anonymity of an online handle. "Where's Gray going?"

"Las Vegas. He said I could come with, but…"

Sadie nodded in understanding. "He'll be back though," she offered with certainty. "He's obviously crazy about you."

Laurel shrugged, capping her drink. "You and me…we'll keep in touch, right?" Sadie had turned into a good friend; something she hadn't had in a while.

Sadie took a sip of her margarita, smiling genuinely. "I'd like that."

Chapter Thirty-Three

♣

As the group made their way along the private dock up to the main house, Parker slowed and checked his phone.

"Hold up," he announced, showing Grayson the picture on his phone. It was a live feed from his video doorbell, featuring an unfamiliar young woman. "This is here. Out front."

Grayson leaned in, inspecting the brunette and her rolling suitcase. "Who is it?"

"Yeah, that's the thing," Parker replied. "I've no clue, mate."

Intrigued, Grayson saluted their captain for the day. "Leave this to me." He dropped his and Laurel's bags at Parker's feet and jogged up and around the side of the house to greet their mystery guest.

Laurel would've called after him, but she was still recovering from shock at the size of Parker's home. Sadie snapped a pair of fingers at Laurel, playfully breaking the spell. "Don't give him the satisfaction of telling him how big it is, I beg you."

Beyond the sprawling green yard, there was a generous in-ground pool, firepit, and outdoor grill. Laurel had only seen comparable houses on *The Bachelor*.

Parker, weighed down by all four of their bags, laughed as he struggled to produce his keys for the back door.

"Sorry, can I help?" Laurel offered.

"You're a doll. Front pocket."

Sadie easily slid between the two to interrupt, smiling sweetly at Parker. "What was that?"

"Sadie, would you be a dear and grab my keys?" he asked, his smile broadening at the faint tinge of jealousy he sensed.

Moving around him, Sadie slipped a hand into his back left pocket, playfully humming in confusion when she found it empty. Her hand moved to his other rear pocket, giving his backside a firm squeeze. That earned a laugh from him as he clarified, "Front, darling."

Sadie gave Parker a thorough pat-down. By the time she came up with his keys, Laurel had turned away with a faint blush at the foreplay behind her.

Parker cleared his throat. "Thank you."

Inside, Parker deposited their bags on the tile floor. Hands now free, he checked his video feed. Grayson and the woman were talking, and his curiosity only grew as he noted his friend laughing. He turned up the volume, punching the speaker button even as he crossed through the house. "Gray?"

Grayson turned toward the sound of Parker's voice, gesturing to their visitor. "Bro, she's here for Al."

Looking embarrassed, Gemma gave a weak smile in the direction of the house. "I'm so sorry," she offered. "I thought he told you I was coming."

"Bloody hell," Parker laughed.

Unlatching the front door, Parker took in the sight of the young woman. "Alaric," Parker stated, as if clarifying that her Al was the same as theirs. "Alaric Nacario?"

Grayson grinned, wheeling her bag inside. "Trust me," he told Parker. "I already asked. Six-foot-something, brooding, snappy…she says it's him."

Looking sheepish, Gemma added with a gesture towards her chest and arms. "Tattoos all over."

Parker and Grayson exchanged a look, laughing even harder.

Movement just past the threshold had Gemma's eyes lighting up and she waved, relief washing over her. "Oh, hey…Six, right?"

The guys looked on in confusion as Gemma pointed out Laurel.

It took Laurel a few seconds, but she made the connection to the girl who'd been injured at Borgata's pool. "Oh, wow. Hi," she greeted. "Did I hear right? You're here for Alaric?"

Gemma lingered at the door, shuffling inside when Parker began to close it behind them. Grayson rolled her bag towards the stairs to drop it off with the others.

"Yeah, I live upstate. Flew into Islip about an hour ago."

Parker was still looking between the girls, unsure. "Why'd she call you Six?"

Laurel gave a bark of laughter, grabbing Gemma's wrist to pull her inside. "Grayson!" Laurel called, "Parker has a question for you!"

♥ ♠ ♦ ♣

An hour later, Grayson still couldn't believe it. Alaric had met Gemma Blake at Borgata Hotel about three weeks ago and was now in a long-distance relationship that neither he nor Parker knew anything about. Plus, he was planning to travel upstate to be her plus one to a wedding. Alaric still wasn't picking up his phone, either.

Parker: Al…Funny story…your GIRLFRIEND is here.
Grayson: YOUNG girlfriend*
Parker: I'm afraid to ask her age.
Grayson: Maybe I shouldn't have given her that beer
Parker: Where'd you pick her up? Borgata daycare?
Grayson: We don't have floaties…bring some on your way
Alaric: …
Grayson: There he is!!!!
Alaric: THIS IS WHY I DIDN'T TELL YOU
Parker: Aw calm down. We're glad you have a widdle girlfriend.
Alaric: I just switched trains. ETA 2 hrs.
Grayson: No worries
Grayson: I'll keep her company
Alaric: Please don't.

Gemma pulled her attention from the luxurious kitchen and glanced at her phone. Parker and Grayson were howling with laughter, and they were making it clear that Alaric was finally responding to their messages. She was nervous to be around his friends without him, but she was glad for Six, whom she now knew to be Laurel, and Sadie was nice enough, too.

When her phone rang, Gemma gave a relieved sigh and gestured, stepping out through the patio doors for a bit of privacy. "Hey," she greeted, uncomfortable. "Kind of awkward over here…"

"I thought I'd be there," Alaric apologized. "My train was delayed, and I was underground for forty minutes. Are you alright?"

Gemma smiled at the concern in his voice. "They're just really, really surprised I'm here."

Guilt had Alaric hanging his head. He'd meant to tell his friends, but he thought it might be easier in person.

"I haven't had as many girlfriends as those two. They give me a lot of shit when I'm into someone."

A beat of silence passed. Gemma suspected that was a compliment, and her face warmed at the fact that he was essentially telling her she was special.

Ultimately, Gemma declared, "I think my parents' house could fit inside Parker's kitchen."

Alaric laughed, finally cracking a more comfortable smile.

♥ ♠ ♦ ♣

When Parker's video doorbell alerted him to movement, he quickly ran for the door, outrun only by Grayson by seconds.

The door swung open and Grayson launched himself at Alaric, gripping his friend in a tight hug.

Although the embrace was playful, it faded into a sincere squeeze. "Hey, Gray. You okay?"

The brief acknowledgement of the recent loss of his mother had Grayson's grin losing some of its typical humor. Grayson appreciated that his friends knew how to be supportive without encouraging him to speak about his feelings on the matter. He nodded, clapping his friend on the back. "Glad you're here."

Alaric's attention lifted to the doorway. He spied Gemma lingering, lifting her hand in greeting. Walking past Parker, earning another clap on the back, he came to stand before Gemma. When she took a step closer, he dropped his duffle bag and caught her around the waist, lifting her in a tight hug.

Gemma slung her arms around Alaric's neck, held tight, and didn't pause to consider their audience. "I'm so, so happy to see you," she whispered.

"Same here, sweetheart," he replied, setting her back down and catching her lips in a lingering kiss.

When the two finally took their eyes from one another, Alaric wasn't surprised to find Grayson and Parker gawking at them. He rolled his eyes, face hot, and turned to head inside with his bag. His hand slipped into Gemma's, and he tried to ignore the disbelieving laughter echoing around the vaulted ceilings.

"Hey, Alaric," Laurel greeted, watching him and Gemma with amusement. She recalled their meeting at Borgata's pool and tried to imagine how that had led to anything romantic.

"Six, hey," he nodded. Grayson had told him he was bringing her, but it was still odd to spend time with her outside of work.

Laurel heaved a sigh. "Grayson!" she called, pointing to Alaric when Grayson popped into view. "Explain my name to him. I'm going to put a bathing suit on."

Parker clapped his hands, interrupting Alaric's confusion. "Great idea. Everyone go settle in. Bedrooms are upstairs. Poolside in thirty."

Alaric carried his and Gemma's luggage upstairs to the closest bedroom on the upstairs landing. "Does this work for you? It's where I usually stay," he explained.

Gemma looked around with mild awe, nodding. "It looks like a magazine cover." As soon as the words left her, Alaric's arms were around her middle. She smiled at him over her shoulder, noticing he'd closed the door.

"Wait," she laughed at his roaming hands, turning in his hold. She was glad to see him, and very eager for some time alone, but she would be more comfortable giving into that urge after nightfall.

Alaric smiled, hands sliding down her back to pull her against him by the backs of her thighs. He teased, "I thought you were so, so happy to see me."

She exhaled a heavy breath. He was far too good at distracting her. "I am, it's just…" Trailing off, she nodded toward the door. She could hear his friends moving around, seeking out bedrooms and laughing. There was no way she could loosen up enough to fool around with him and then walk back out with a straight face.

"Okay," he sighed, but his reluctance was playful. "Later," he decided. "And we turn in when I say."

Blushing, Gemma didn't argue.

CHAPTER THIRTY-FOUR

♦

As the sun inched its way beneath the horizon, the illuminated pool and garden uplighting fought the fading daylight. Two additional arrivals, a chef and server duo that Parker had sprung for, prepared dinner for the group. As they worked inside, Parker made sure his guests were having a good time outside.

Sadie curiously observed this new side of him as he interacted with his close friends. She was almost hoping to witness something unsavory; if she managed to spot even one red flag it might be easier to leave the east coast on Monday. So far, however, the biggest deal breaker she'd identified with Parker was his confidence; it rivaled hers. Unfortunately, it had the opposite effect as well; it was a major turn-on.

Parker tipped a beer to his lips and continued to press Alaric for details. While Gemma was out of sight, he needed the whole story.

"Come on, Al," he groaned.

Gemma had explained the basics; they'd met at Borgata Hotel & Casino during an unfortunate accident, and it had led to Alaric and Gemma flirting, spending time together, and deciding to try long-distance. Sweet, easy-going Gemma had made it seem so simple. Parker, however, couldn't quite picture how it had unfurled. The more he got to know Gemma, the more Parker couldn't think of a single soul more opposite to her than his best friend.

Alaric had expected the third-degree and had attempted to prepare on the train, but he hadn't come up with anything concrete. "It just works," he defended.

Parker held up a hand to assure Alaric he meant no harm. "I just can't remember the last time you were actually dating someone. You've been married to that fucking job since Columbia."

Alaric nodded, considering. When he and Parker had met at the graduate business program at Columbia University, Alaric had been dating someone. It had lasted seven months, which was his longest relationship to date. That was six years ago and despite dozens of dates since, Alaric hadn't put much effort into building a relationship or a family for himself. Instead, he'd thrown himself head-first into his career.

"Well, I like her," Alaric shrugged.

"I can see that," Parker smiled. "You know we're happy for you, right? I'm just not sure why you didn't say anything."

Arriving to find Gemma standing on his doorstep had been one hell of a slap in the face for Parker and Grayson. The trio was as close as family and realizing that such a key piece of Alaric's life had been hidden from them felt intentional.

Alaric didn't have a good response for that, either. "I knew you'd give me shit for it."

Sighing in amusement, Parker replied, "Because we love you, mate."

"Alright, alright," Alaric grumbled.

Slinging his arm around Alaric's shoulder, Grayson appeared with a look of disbelief. "Okay, we've got to know," he declared. "How in the hell did you land that girl?" Their obvious clash of personalities was startling and paired with the apparent age difference, Grayson was astonished.

"She's twenty-four," Alaric defended, hazel eyes cutting to Grayson seriously. "Can you please stop acting like I'm robbing the cradle?"

Across the pool, Laurel sat at the water's edge with a gin and tonic. Sadie drifted an arm's reach away on a foam lounge, a few tendrils of her dark hair brushing the water's surface.

"I could die happy," she declared.

Smiling, Laurel asked, "Would a certain Australian have anything to do with that?"

"Well, he is the owner of this property," Sadie replied matter-of-factly.

"You know what I mean," Laurel pressed, dipping down to wet her fingers and flick them in Sadie's direction. "It's obvious you really like him."

Sadie turned her head to ensure Parker was out of earshot. The last thing she needed to do was inflate his ego any further. She was willing to agree that she enjoyed her time with Parker, but she drew the line at silly professions of feelings.

"I've had a lot of fun with him," Sadie confirmed.

Laurel glared. "What a glowing review."

Sadie's painted lips turned up at the corner. "I'm sorry we can't all be in love like you and Mr. Charming over there."

Stiffening, Laurel quickly glanced towards Grayson. He was still wrapped up in conversation with Parker and Alaric, thankfully. She hadn't told Sadie about his slip of the "L" word and her pulse raced just thinking about it.

"I was teasing," Sadie assured, curious at Laurel's lack of response. "Unless…"

"Stop," Laurel pleaded, smiling pathetically.

"Oh, wow," Sadie laughed, nodding in realization. "Didn't realize you were there yet. Good for you."

"No, I'm not— I haven't—"

Laurel groaned, covering her face with a hand. She wasn't sure if she was in love with Grayson, and she certainly wasn't anywhere near saying it aloud.

Sadie guessed gently, "But he is?"

When Laurel dropped her hand and glanced towards her boyfriend again, she was surprised to see an unfamiliar woman standing with them. It wasn't the staff members she'd seen arrive earlier, either.

"Who's that?" Laurel asked Sadie, nodding in the direction of the guys around a petite blonde.

Sadie looked back, but couldn't see well from her position in the pool. Just before she turned forward again, however, she realized the woman was standing closest to Parker out of the group. And Parker, that handsome bastard, had his hand on her lower back.

Across the pool, Alaric said, "I haven't seen you since you started at Campbell's, Hannah. How've you been?"

"Good, good," she assured, her blond bob skimming her shoulders as she smiled up at Parker. "This guy's easy to work for."

Parker laughed. "You'll get better perks if you flatter my father."

"So, you were in the area or what?" Grayson asked, handing her a beer from the ice chest.

"Kind of," Hannah confirmed, accepting the drink. "I was visiting my parents in Riverhead when Parker said he was opening up the house this weekend."

"I'll be right back," Parker excused, stepping away to head for the house.

Sadie, patting herself dry, tracked his movements. She now recognized Hannah from her visit to Parker's office. Following him towards the back of the house, Sadie lingered at the door and continued to towel-off, watching him speak with the chef and server inside about their added guest.

When Parker turned, he smiled at the sight of Sadie scrunching the ends of her hair with a towel.

"Hello, gorgeous," he said, stepping closer to slide a hand around the curve of her waist.

"You sure know how to throw a party," Sadie complemented and draped her damp towel over his bare shoulder, looping her arms around his neck.

"Enjoying yourself?" he mused, brushing their lips together.

Sadie hummed in agreement, tipped her head, and pressed her mouth to his in a long, lingering kiss. Her fingers slid into his hair, her body arching forward into his embrace.

"When did Parker start seeing her?" Hannah asked, watching as her employer locked lips with the woman she had met once before.

Grayson scanned the area, smirking at the display of affection. He turned to find Laurel at the rolling ice chest behind him and snapped his fingers. "Six, when did that start?" he asked, pointing.

Laurel looked up, startled. "Did you just snap at me?"

Slowly, Grayson grinned, his dark brown eyes alight with mischief. "Depends. Did you like it?"

"No."

"Then no."

Shaking her head, Laurel glanced over towards Parker and Sadie. "Maybe three, four weeks ago?" She did the math in her head, nodding. She thought about the timing for herself and Grayson and tacked on an additional week. The fact that she'd only known him for five weeks was startling. He'd worked his way into her life, and maybe a little of her heart, as well.

Laurel joined the group and introduced herself to Hannah, taking Alaric's spot as he stepped away in search of Gemma.

Alaric knocked on their chosen bedroom door. "Gemma? It's me."

He heard movement in their connected bathroom and stepped over to knock. "Gemma?"

There was a muffled curse followed by her frustrated response. "Yeah, okay, come in."

Pushing open the door, Alaric found Gemma standing at a full-length mirror. "Everything okay?" he asked.

Gemma had a moment to appreciate his build, eyeing the dark ink twirling down his arms and across his chest. She whined, shifted on her feet, and kept hold of the cover-up against her chest. "I feel like my suit is really revealing," she confessed, her face reddening.

Alaric's brows went up and he opened his mouth to speak, but no words came to mind. This wasn't territory he'd navigated before. "Can I see?" he offered helpfully.

Rolling her eyes, Gemma obliged. She lowered the watercolor fabric to reveal a two-piece bathing suit she'd purchased for the trip. She had wanted to show off her tattoo, and maybe appear a little older, but was harshly questioning her choice now that she had an audience. The bottom piece was no more than a triangle of maroon at the junction of her thighs, the connecting strings across her hips floss-thin. The top was a little better, the matching material knotted between her breasts and tied behind her neck. Patches of red blossomed across her chest as Alaric scrutinized her appearance.

"Say something," she pleaded.

Alaric cleared his throat at last, reaching down to adjust himself in his swim trunks. "Christ, sweetheart. I'm not really sure what you want me to say."

Gemma dropped her face into her hands. "This was stupid."

"Uh," Alaric laughed, reduced to the most basic of thoughts and words at her near-naked state. "Not stupid," he assured, reaching for her wrist. "Just…effective."

Blushing madly, Gemma looked away. "You like it?"

"It's problematic," he countered. "I'm not going to be able to leave this room for a minute."

As Alaric pulled her flush against him, their hips connected, and Gemma's brows lifted. "Oh. Wow. That was fast."

Alaric laughed, a hand gliding over the panel of fabric tight across her backside. His other hand swept into her hair, and he leaned down to kiss her.

"Your friends," she mumbled, but her hands were already pulling him closer.

Their lips nudged and Gemma felt his fingers tangle in the knot behind her neck. It began to loosen, and she repeated through a quiet moan, "Your *friends*."

"They're all outside," he reassured, desperate for her. Still, his hands paused in undressing her as he waited for her agreement.

Gemma squeezed her eyes shut, her breath thickening. A few moments passed and she realized there was no sense in denying what they both wanted so badly. They'd been apart for almost two weeks and the anticipation of seeing him again had been foreplay enough. "Okay," she breathed.

Alaric groaned, quick to take action. It was easy to unknot the few strings and draw the shapes of fabric away from her skin. She was naked in no time and his hand went quickly between her thighs to the small patch of curls there. "God, I missed this."

An involuntary whimper left Gemma at his possessiveness, shivering at his touch. Her fingers hooked into the sides of his dry swim trunks, pushing them down hurriedly to even the score. "Need you," she panted.

Lips locked, Alaric picked Gemma up by her hips and seated her on the countertop. One eye open, he rummaged through the cabinet until he found a condom.

"This is going to be quick," he warned, tearing into the foil packet.

Gemma blushed, pushing her hair back as she watched him roll the latex into place. "We've got all night," she assured. It didn't bother her in the least to have a quickie to get their urges under control.

When Alaric reached for her again, Gemma gasped as he took his covered erection in hand to guide it between them. She hadn't expected they were going to have sex right there in the bathroom and a thrill went through her at the thought. She gasped, nodded, and wrapped her legs around him as she helped hold her weight on the counter.

Alaric fed himself into her slit, through the first ring of gentle resistance, and then deeper until their hips were flush. He took her weight, letting her wrap herself around him.

Gemma's breath caught, whimpering on an exhale at how satisfying it felt to be with him again. He began to pulse his hips upwards, Gemma feeling a deep aching soreness as her body relearned his size.

Groaning, Alaric tipped his head down to Gemma's shoulder, focused on the way the heat of her body yielded around his invading presence on each forward thrust.

As promised, his pace was quick and goal-oriented. Gemma felt shockwaves of pleasure as he struck deep, a mild curse leaving her lips. His thrusts grew rougher, his hands clinging to her back to keep her rooted to him as he grew closer to that peak of pleasure.

Gemma gasped suddenly, her thighs beginning to tremble.

Despite his best efforts to wait her out, Alaric's relentless pace had his pleasure and release spilling forth, his back arching as he climaxed against her. Shakily, he tucked a hand between them, thumb going straight for the swollen bundle of nerves between Gemma's thighs.

Whimpering his name, Gemma tensed for a long minute. When the force of her orgasm reached her, she shuddered and gasped, enjoying every torturous second of the pleasure as her hands clawed at his back.

As they recovered from their desperate coupling with panting breaths, Alaric grunted in satisfaction. "I don't know about you, sweetheart, but I needed that."

Gemma leaned back, gaze dazed and features flushed as she breathed, "Screw long distance."

CHAPTER THIRTY-FIVE

♠

Hours later, dressed and digesting dinner, Grayson stretched and announced, "We should get a game going."

Alaric, the voice of reason, gave his friend and his eighth-or-so beer a curious look. "You sure about that, Gray? I think you've had more than you realize."

"Count me out," Parker announced. "I'm bushed."

"Sadie?" Grayson prompted.

Sadie gave a tight smile as she declined. "I'd rather not."

Her eyes were still pinging between Parker and Hannah. She couldn't help but wonder at their history, and that wondering was ruining her night.

Laurel rotated her wine glass by its stem, asking Hannah, "How long is the drive to your parents' house from here?"

Hannah shrugged. "A half hour or so."

"But you've been drinking," Gemma pointed out the obvious.

Parker agreed. "You'll stay here." He gestured above them, indicating the multiple available bedrooms. "Plenty of space."

Hannah gave him a thankful smile, nodding. "Appreciate it."

He threw her a friendly wink. "My dad would have my ass otherwise."

Sadie rolled her eyes, sipping her seventh or so drink of the evening. The alcohol seemed to both feed and quell her rising anger. Knowing that she was leaving town soon left Sadie annoyed that Parker had chosen to fill their final weekend together with a bunch of people. Not that he knew about their expiration date before she'd told him, midway to the Hamptons.

Taking in her surroundings, Sadie noted that Grayson and Laurel were conversing with Gemma and Alaric. Still, the spotlight for her was on Parker and Hannah as the pair stood at the kitchen island, laughing over their quiet conversation.

Gritting her teeth, Sadie swiped her phone from the table and reread the Colorado invitation email to distract herself. She still had to book a flight, not that she could manage that currently. The room wasn't spinning, but it was most definitely slanted.

"Sadie?" Laurel's voice had the older woman looking up, brow tense. "You okay?" Laurel asked, cocking her head. "You're really quiet."

Sadie shook her head, putting her phone back down again. "Tired," she bit out.

Laurel nodded slowly, turning her attention back to the others. She spotted Parker and Hannah standing together and a pang of sympathy replaced her curiosity. Laurel could guess why Sadie was acting so standoffish; the two looked rather friendly, content to talk amongst themselves.

Sometime later, Alaric gave Gemma's hand a squeeze and suggested they turn in. Features warm, Gemma bid everyone goodnight and the two ascended the stairs with quiet laughter. Reduced to five, the group seemed content to converse, picking at a dessert tray the wait staff had left behind. Laurel had managed to engage Sadie in conversation, but the brunette was only half listening. Eventually, she could take it no more.

Parker and Hannah were far too cozy, and Sadie felt like an idiot standing by, watching them flirt. Sadie had considered this their final hoorah and yet Parker had specifically invited his attractive coworker to join them. Disbelieving laughter bubbled up and Sadie stood, fury radiating from her. Hannah's innocent touches all night made Sadie's stomach roll, and she couldn't tell if Parker was interested or just clueless.

Sadie was nearly shaking when she rose to her feet, watching Hannah lick chocolate from her thumb; the action was far too suggestive.

"Whoa," Grayson muttered, glancing over as Sadie's chair nearly fell over from the abrupt movement. He fixed his drunk gaze on Sadie's murderous glare, grimacing as she drew back her arm.

Then came a crash, which earned the rest of the room's attention.

All eyes turned to the base of the brick fireplace some twenty feet away, littered with glass. Slowly, all eyes slid over to Sadie where she stood, breathing hard.

"*Oops*," she stated loudly, despite the action having been entirely purposeful. It was her glass in shards on the floor and her eyes were locked on Parker.

Grayson and Laurel exchanged a panicked look, but neither seemed to know what to say.

Parker's easygoing smile faded as he made eye contact with Sadie, a bewildered expression crossing his face. He looked between the glass and Sadie, clearly deducing the intention behind her actions. Still, he struggled with processing the outburst.

"What...the fuck?" Parker asked, stilted.

"We should turn in..." Grayson slurred quickly, nudging Laurel to get up.

Sadie slammed her hand, causing Laurel to jump to her feet. She grabbed Grayson's hand and grimaced, mumbling a quick goodnight. This was not a fight she wanted to witness.

Grayson was hot on her heels, and he gave Hannah a quick grimace before they ducked out of view.

Hannah stood in stunned silence, unsure. She watched as Sadie muttered something unintelligible and disappeared into the backyard through the open french doors. Hannah turned to look at Parker, watching his profile as he stared after her.

It took him a long minute to spur into action, but then he was out the door, following without a word to excuse himself.

Sadie had decided that Parker, with his sweet words and charming accent, was no better than the many other men she'd let wine and dine her. He was no better than any of the many men she had never spent more than a couple of dates with, and certainly never taken to a baseball game.

Barefoot, she walked through his expansive backyard and marched along the sand, down to the shore. She'd embarrassed herself now, she knew, and she stumbled as she tried to clear her foggy head to think of a possible exit strategy.

Chasing her down to the beach, Parker muttered, "Jesus Christ."

Not only was he concerned over her behavior, but he worried over her intoxicated status as she grew closer to the water ahead.

"Sadie!" he called, cursing as he came down hard on a broken shell in the sand.

Realizing she wasn't alone and wanting to escape a humiliating confrontation, Sadie called over her shoulder, "Fuck you, Parker!"

She groaned in frustration as angry tears threatened her already blurred vision.

Parker closed in, catching Sadie's arm to turn and steady her. "What the hell just happened?" he demanded, forehead creasing as he noticed her tears. "What's wrong?"

Sadie would sooner scream than admit her jealousy. "Get off," she struggled, at war with herself. On the one hand, she wanted to be rid of him and put this entire chapter of her life behind her. On the other hand, he'd followed; he had left Hannah behind and chased after her.

Stumbling slightly, Sadie attempted to spin free. Parker's grip tightened to keep her from falling, locking her into place.

Sadie let out an exasperated sound. "Let go!"

"Sadie, talk to—"

Sadie spun again, this time her palm cracking loudly against Parker's cheek.

The slap seemed to sober them both and Sadie gasped, lifting her hand to her mouth.

Parker seemed to turn to stone. He'd experienced women's anger before; he'd been yelled at, threatened, even had a drink or two poured on him, but he'd never, ever been slapped. The side of his face stung lightly, but it was more the shock of it that had him unmoving.

Sadie took a half step back, shaking her head. "I didn't mean to do that," she breathed.

Once the spell was broken, Parker lunged, taking Sadie down to the sand.

She gasped and fought, but her heart wasn't in it. She was still staring at his cheek, guilt wracking her. She turned her wrists weakly as Parker pinned them in the sand.

"*Sadie*," he snapped.

Her terror abated when it was clear he didn't plan to retaliate, but Sadie couldn't hide her flinch.

That seemed to settle Parker's frustration and he sighed, hanging his head.

Sadie lay supine, a hot tear sliding down her face towards the sand. Finally, she confirmed his rising suspicions by asking, "Why did you invite her?"

Regardless of the vague pronoun, there was no need to clarify. It was clear that Sadie was referring to Hannah, and that jealousy was the emotion responsible for Sadie's tantrum.

Taking a deep breath, Parker lifted his head again. He smiled weakly at the sand sticking to her skin, brushing some away from her cheek with a thumb. His voice was low and serious when he spoke again.

"You're the only woman I want, Sadie."

Humiliated, Sadie closed her eyes as her tears continued to fall. She blamed the alcohol and the ticking clock related to her departure, but it was no excuse for her behavior.

"Look at me," Parker instructed gently, releasing one of her wrists to cup the side of her face with sandy fingers.

It was such a simple request, but it was more difficult than he knew; Sadie had never felt more vulnerable. She was adept at boxing up her life and her feelings each time she felt the need, moving onto a new location and new relation, but this time she struggled. Although she wished she could have held her ground, Sadie reluctantly obeyed.

Parker cracked a small, astonished smile as he ran his thumb across her damp cheek. "You're out of your fucking mind, I swear," he told her honestly.

A laugh bubbled up and Sadie relaxed at his teasing remark, not taking much offense considering the truth behind it. It wasn't as if she didn't know she was a handful.

"You know I'm crazy about you, yeah?" Parker asked, waiting expectantly until he earned a slow nod from Sadie.

"And that Hannah's a family friend?"

Again, Sadie reluctantly nodded.

"And that I've never been interested in her and never will be?"

He sensed Sadie relax beneath him and noted that that had been what she needed to hear most of all, oddly enough.

"Why?" Sadie pressed, as if needing a tangible reason to hold onto.

Parker thought it over, unsure what to offer. How did you explain a nonexistent spark? He wasn't sure he could. Ultimately, he teased, "I don't go for blondes."

Sadie rolled her eyes, but a weak smile played on her lips. "Make her leave."

Laughing, Parker knelt back and released his hold on her completely. "I can't just kick her out," he said, apologetic. "She'll be gone in the morning, okay?"

Sadie pushed up onto her elbows and blew her hair out of her face. She supposed Parker had cleared the air and she had nothing to be jealous over, either way. Not only was he uninterested in Hannah, but he'd also confessed Sadie was the one he was crazy about and the only one he wanted. She stared up at him where he straddled her, sighing. She supposed it was obvious by now that she had similar feelings on the matter.

"Don't go to Colorado," Parker requested.

Sadie's brows furrowed, surprised by the request. "I have to—"

"You don't and you know it," he countered. "You could push it back a week."

Declining the opportunity and rescheduling the opportunity were two very different things. Plus, Sadie couldn't deny the fact that she wanted more time with Parker. "A week?" she asked.

"Come back to the city with me," he encouraged. "Just for a week. Then we'll figure it out."

At long last, Sadie managed a nod. They did need to figure things out and establish what they wanted from one another. It would be hard with their transient lifestyles, but maybe it wasn't as impossible as she'd thought.

When the pair made it back to the house, Sadie was grateful that Hannah had made herself scarce. Sadie was confident in Parker's feelings, but Hannah's idle flirtations were another story, and she wasn't sure she would be able to keep herself in line if she had to tell the young woman to keep her hands to herself. Thankfully, Hannah had disappeared to her own room for the night.

As they entered the kitchen, Sadie reflected on the evening as much as her drunken state would allow. She had made a fool of herself, but instead of calling her on it, Parker had practically swooned over her. She flushed at that thought, just as Parker turned to her.

"Go on up," he encouraged. He gestured to the glass to indicate he wanted to clean up before joining her and Sadie felt her shame surge at the sight. "Don't worry about it," he assured, giving her a gentle push in the direction of the stairs. "Give me ten minutes."

Sadie obeyed and took a shower in the meantime, washing away the sand that stubbornly clung to her skin and was threaded through her hair. When she emerged, Parker slid around her to do the same.

Freshly washed, Parker smirked when he found Sadie naked in bed. "We're not having sex tonight," he stated seriously, surprising them both. He sensed

Sadie needed to feel her worth outside of being a sexual object, and it would probably be best not to reward that evening's behavior.

When Sadie moved to tease him, Parker kissed her to quiet her. "No sex," he repeated, laughing when she started to complain. "This isn't just physical," he said expectantly. Their interest in one another may have started that way, but Sadie was occupying his thoughts often. He was taken with her beauty, her confidence, her success, and, being honest with himself, her personal brand of crazy.

Chapter Thirty-Six

♥

Parker may have had his way the previous night, by punishing Sadie with no intimacy beyond sleeping curled together, but come morning Sadie was happy to regain control.

She smiled tiredly at the sight of Parker fast asleep beside her. He seemed perfectly content, dead to the world and gloriously naked. Sadie moved slowly so as not to wake him and slid lower, climbing over one of his bare thighs. She lowered her face to his stomach to run her cold nose parallel to the thin trail of hair leading down to his stiff, morning erection.

Just before he began to stir, Sadie cupped his heavy sack and pressed a trail of hot kisses across his abdomen.

Parker licked his lips and drew in a deep breath as he was dragged from sleep. Dreamily, he realized the sensations he felt were rooted in reality, and he blinked to clear his vision. He groaned all at once, hands fisting in the pillow beneath his head.

"Good God, woman," he muttered happily, voice groggy.

That seemed consent enough for Sadie and she offered a quiet hum in acknowledgement, taking the head of his cock past her lips.

Parker groaned as he gazed up at the ceiling, hyper focused on the warmth and smoothness of Sadie's tongue rubbing against the sensitive underside of his shaft. He chuckled, a little senseless, "I am so bloody lucky."

Smiling to herself at the thickness of his accent, she took more of his length into the heat of her mouth. She felt his hand slip around her head, gently fisting in her air-dried curls. She moaned in pleasure as he took to guiding her, his hips arching the faintest bit from the bed to slip a greedy inch further past her full lips.

He groaned, soft and low.

Sadie eased back a few moments later, breathing a little harder.

"Up here," he breathed, requesting, "Let me fuck you."

Sadie obeyed eagerly. She reached between them when she settled at his hips and wasted no time in guiding him between her thighs. Waking him with the attention had been plenty of a turn-on for her.

His shaft prodded her silky folds before sliding inside with ease. Both of his hands settled on her hips with a firm squeeze as their groins joined flush together. His knees lifted, one after the other, and he planted his feet to the mattress for leverage as he met the next roll of her hips.

Moaning softly, Sadie began to match his pace. "You like that, daddy?"

Parker's tired grin stretched wide at the term of endearment. She was the only woman who could get away with the nickname, since they both knew she was teasingly shortening the term 'sugar daddy'.

"You know I do, baby doll," he replied.

Parker slid a hand up her spine and caught a possessive fistful of her soft waves where they hung. As she tipped her head back and exposed her long neck, his eyes drifted lower to her glorious breasts and the ink beneath and between them.

He pushed up and rolled them aside, pounding between Sadie's thighs as he smothered her wrists into the mattress. Sadie writhed helplessly beneath him as a wave of pleasure crashed through her. The friction between them lessened at the result of their release and Sadie gasped, pressing a hand to Parker's chest as he attempted to continue.

"No, baby," he growled in response. "We're going again."

♥ ♠ ♦ ♣

Alaric awoke to find Gemma's side of the bed cold. He pulled on a pair of loose sweats and shuffled towards the bathroom as he heard the shower turn off.

The door was closed, but not locked, and he mumbled a sleepy, "Found you," as he pushed inside.

Laurel stiffened as Alaric leaned into the bathroom just as she was stepping out of the shower, a hand outstretched towards the towel rack. She managed to find her voice before he did, though she could see realization and panic dawning. Laurel jerked a towel towards herself, fumbling to wrap it around her body.

"Were you raised in a barn?!" she demanded; voice shrill.

Alaric winced and quickly backed away, banging into the door frame with a grunt. Pain flared and he fought embarrassment as he tugged the door closed. "I— I thought you were Gemma!" he defended unnecessarily. "This is our bathroom!"

"It's a Jack and Jill bathroom!" Laurel shrieked in return through the closed door.

Groaning, Alaric rubbed his face. Although he hadn't lingered, he'd gotten an eye full.

"Then you should have locked it!" Alaric protested.

"It's called knocking!" Laurel countered angrily.

"Well excuse me, *Laurel*," Alaric grumbled. Grayson had explained his ridiculous nickname for her, and Alaric was still annoyed by the situation.

Once sufficiently covered by a towel, she tugged the bathroom door open to glare at him in disbelief. "You honestly thought my name was Six? *Really*?"

Alaric seemed startled to be confronted. His expression hardened and said nothing, even when Grayson pulled the opposite door open to investigate the bathroom argument, fully naked.

"Christ," Alaric groaned, turning on his heels in search of another bathroom.

♥ ♠ ♦ ♣

Once the house came alive with activity, the couples split off to enjoy a day in the Hamptons. Laurel and Grayson were the first to head out, intending to visit Montauk Point to cross off another tourist attraction on Laurel's bucket list. As fun as the previous evening had been, Grayson was looking forward to a quiet day. Laurel encouraged him to open up more about his relationship with his mother, but there wasn't much to share.

Parker made sure Hannah cleared out before he let Sadie out of his sight. Then, the two departed to enjoy a few local wineries. That left Alaric and Gemma, and neither wanted to do much other than spend time together.

"This house is pretty amazing," Gemma had reasoned. "I mean, we could just stay here…"

As the others pursued their own interests, Alaric and Gemma were left to their own devices. By late afternoon they'd gone for a dip in the pool, taken a walk along the beach, and were looking for their second movie to watch.

"Is this boring?" Gemma wondered, mildly concerned their domestic Hamptons weekend was underwhelming for her older boyfriend.

Alaric passed her the popcorn bowl before chucking her beneath the chin. "Believe it or not, this is the best weekend I've had in a really long time," he assured, wincing as he amended, "Aside from this morning."

Gemma winced as well. She'd heard about his accidental run-in with Laurel in the bathroom and could only groan at how embarrassing that must've been for them both.

"I can't wait to have my own place," Gemma admitted. "Not like it'll be anything close to this, but it'll be nice to have my own space."

Alaric nodded. "Have you ever lived on your own?"

"No, I commuted to school, so I've always lived with my parents." After a beat, she asked, "Does that bother you? Is it another point against me?"

"There are no points against you, Gemma," he assured, reaching for a few pieces of popcorn. He knew she worried about their age gap, but it hadn't been an obstacle thus far.

Smiling, Alaric caught her hand and threaded their fingers. "I'm serious. You're practically perfect."

"Definitely not, but very sweet of you," she chided.

"Okay, hang on," he said, preparing another attempt at complimenting her. "I love almost everything about you."

Gemma went still, shocked at how casually he spoke. Her green eyes scanned his face, wondering if there was a 'but' coming. When she realized that he was finished speaking, she took a slow breath. She certainly hadn't expected that; it was kind of crazy, considering they'd only known one another for about a month. It had taken her almost a year to tell Everett she loved him, though they'd been so young she'd questioned what love felt like for a long time.

Processing Alaric's almost "L" word confession, Gemma found herself hung up on something he'd said. He hadn't actually told her he loved her; he'd said he loved almost everything *about* her. Also, what was that 'almost' about?

"Almost?" she echoed curiously.

Smiling, Alaric nodded. "I don't entirely love your choice in bathing suits."

"Oh, my God." Gemma laughed, rolled her eyes, and pulled her hand back from Alaric. "You are never going to let me live that down, are you?"

"Nope," Alaric reassured and found her hand to lace their fingers together. "Not ever."

Blushing, Gemma tipped her head down to his shoulder. She didn't feel pressured to tell Alaric she was feeling similarly; she knew her feelings were strongly carrying her in that direction, and she'd share them when the time was right.

"If you didn't live at the hotel," she posed curiously, "where would you live?"

"Not New Jersey," Alaric replied easily. "But other than that, I guess it doesn't really matter. I guess it would depend on work."

Gemma tried to picture Alaric in other professions, coming up blank. Still, she thought he deserved more of the relaxation she'd witnessed over the past twenty-four hours, as opposed to how tense he'd been when they'd first spent time together in Atlantic City. "Would you ever want to do something else?"

Alaric offered a casual shrug. "I've been thinking about it."

♥ ♠ ♦ ♣

Sadie and Parker stood outside at the vineyard; his arm looped around her waist as they watched the sunset. The winery's outdoor area was adorned in miniature lights, and Sadie leaned comfortably back against Parker's chest, smiling to herself.

Parker kissed the top of Sadie's head and gave her an affectionate squeeze. "This feels surreal, doesn't it?"

Sadie hummed in agreement. "Like a dream."

Being with Parker in the Hamptons, wine drunk and stupidly happy, Sadie could have cried. Again.

Thankfully, she'd gotten all her tears out the previous evening on the beach. Even considering her jealous meltdown, Sadie couldn't conjure up a weekend that rivaled this one.

"Makes you kind of wish every day was like this," Parker mumbled.

Nodding, Sadie sighed. "If only."

After a beat, Parker spoke again. "I mean, it could be."

Sadie blinked and tipped her head back to look up at him curiously.

"We could have every day," he told her honestly, loosening his hold as she slowly turned to face him.

Trying to focus through the pleasant buzz a day of drinking had brought, Sadie's features scrunched in thought. "What are you saying?" she asked. "I already said yes to New York. I said yes to doing this," she said, gesturing between the two of them, referencing the relationship they were both so obviously wanting.

Parker, however, wanted more.

"Then say yes to marrying me, too," he begged.

Sadie's lips spread in a wide smile, genuinely flattered that he'd even tease her about such a thing. "If only life were that simple," she mumbled, patting his cheek affectionately.

Parker clasped her wrist, leaning into her touch. "It is, baby. It really, really is. When you find something like this you don't let it go."

"I'm not—" she started, voice catching as she realized the seriousness behind his request. "I'm not letting anything go," she assured.

Willing all her courage, she confessed, "I'm falling in love with you."

As if that sealed the deal, Parker closed the few inches between them to press his lips to hers. He tightened his hold, sweeping her up in a kiss that left her breathless. When their lips parted, he repeated himself in earnest, "Then marry me, Sadie Bache."

Sadie felt a squeeze around her heart, her resolve weakening. "This is crazy," she whispered. Why would they jump into marriage before they'd done some work aligning their lives? Until they'd test-run their relationship? Her hands shook as she gripped Parker's arms and she searched his face, unsure.

"*Marry me*," he insisted stubbornly, tipping forward to press his face into her hair. "I love you. I think about you constantly. I want to know wherever you go you're coming back to me, always."

"Oh, Jesus," Sadie moaned, the sentiment nearly her undoing. She couldn't deny how much more comfortable she would feel, going off for weeks at a time at the invitation of casinos all over the country, to know Parker was that committed to her, too. Considering how she'd behaved merely from being in the same room as someone who was giving Parker lovesick puppy dog eyes, she supposed he knew it, too.

"Is this about Hannah?" she worried.

"Fuck Hannah," Parker laughed, drawing back with a furrowed brow. "I mean—"

"I know what you mean," Sadie laughed, shaking her head at him. She searched his face, struck by how genuinely sincere he seemed. "You're insane," she breathed.

He laughed. "You're pretty crazy, too. We're a perfect match."

At length, Sadie lifted a hand to rest against the side of his face. Sadie had thought they'd had their big revelation last night, but that was nothing in the face of what Parker presented her with, now. They were both tipsy and enjoying the high of a new and exciting relationship. All fears Sadie had had seemed to be put to bed; she was comfortable with what they'd established. She had gone to sleep the previous night ready to try a committed, sometimes long-distance relationship for the first time in her life. She hadn't expected him to throw another curve ball at her.

"You do realize that I slapped you last night and now you want to marry me, right?" she asked.

Parker grinned, nodding slowly. "You finally understand."

Quietly, with honest consideration, she asked, "Isn't this too fast?"

Watching her expectantly, hoping to convey that time wouldn't change his goal, he asked, "Would you rather I asked next week? Next month?"

"Maybe?" Sadie shrugged, squirming under the weight of his gaze.

Parker kissed her lightly and stood back, taking her hands in his. "I'm only going to ask once more," he warned, making it abundantly clear that she would have one final opportunity to dive headfirst into this moment.

"Sadie Bache, I want you. I want to lock this down before you bump into another man trying to steal your town car." He smiled as she laughed at his reference to the way they'd met. "We'll travel everywhere, and I'll give you everything you've ever wanted. Will you please marry me?"

There was a moment during Parker's short, epic speech that Sadie's smile cracked. Her heart was racing, and she wanted to tell him yes, that she wanted everything he promised; that she wanted him. The complication was in the final part of his promise. There was something he could never give her, no matter how much money or drive he possessed.

"Parker," she said, swallowing hard. "I can't—" she attempted, voice breaking. However, she pressed on, wanting to reassure him that she wasn't declining his offer of happiness together. "I can't have children," she whispered.

It took a moment for Parker to recall that bit of information she'd shared when they'd first had sex. He was quiet as he realized that this fact was holding her back from giving in. Parker gave her a soft kiss to calm her, reassuring, "I already knew, remember? It doesn't change a thing."

Her lashes were already wet as she began to cry anew. Relief slammed into her at his reassurance. Sadie's inability to have children was something she worried would prevent her from a happily ever after, but maybe she and Parker didn't need that final piece. Maybe they could find happiness in each other and take advantage of all that the world could offer them.

Against his lips, Sadie whispered her final answer.

"Yes."

Parker's relieved exhale was chased by laughter as he scooped her up, managing one spin before he feared plunging them both to the ground. After feverish kisses, he pulled back to marvel at her. It was as if they'd surpassed that final barrier or blockade that had kept them from the full extent of their feelings for one another. Knowing that there wasn't an ending around the corner gave them no reason to hold back.

"It was the accent, wasn't it?" Parker laughed, smoothing a hand down Sadie's dark hair.

"It didn't hurt your chances," Sadie admitted.

Chapter Thirty-Seven

♣

The next morning, the heavy scent of bacon and fresh coffee filled the Hamptons house, luring the guests to assemble in the kitchen. Sadie sat at the kitchen island, picking at a fruit platter as Parker cooked breakfast for his guests. The couple had agreed to keep their engagement news secret for a while. Sadie needed a ring, and both their parents needed a heads-up. Parker had agreed, but he'd had a further stipulation; he wanted to introduce his parents to their future daughter-in-law in person. Sadie could only imagine how that was going to go over.

Grayson and Laurel wandered down, Grayson dressed for a run. "Save me some of that," Grayson requested, pulling a bottle of water from the fridge as he walked out the back in the direction of the beach.

"Where does he get the energy?" Laurel murmured, dropping into the stool beside Sadie.

Smirking, Sadie teased, "You mean the stamina?"

"Morning," Gemma greeted, approaching the counter to prepare a couple of mugs of coffee.

"Where's Sleeping Beauty?" Parker quipped, moving a mountain of scrambled eggs around a pan.

Gemma laughed, shaking her head. "Sleeping in. I know he doesn't get to do that a lot, so I didn't want to wake him."

"Want to come have a spa day with me and Laurel?" Sadie offered.

Laurel's brow lifted. "First I've heard of it," she pointed out.

Sadie gave her a knowing look. "You're telling me you don't want to go get pampered on Parker's dime? Mani, pedi, facial, massage?"

Parker scoffed, amused. He was marrying this woman; he'd have to get used to it.

Nodding, Laurel waved Sadie on. "Continue."

"Gemma?" Sadie posed.

Gemma was carrying two mugs, trying to slip back upstairs. "I'm not sure," she confessed. She was there to spend the weekend with Alaric. As nice as his friends were, she was about to be separated from him for another two weeks. She'd hate to give up their final day together.

"What if I promised we'd be back before lunch?" Sadie offered; brows raised. Gemma seemed more interested with that stipulation and Sadie nodded. "Great. I'll call a car."

♥ ♠ ♦ ♣

When Grayson returned, he was surprised to find Laurel gone. "She said she wanted to do nothing today," he complained to Parker, finding a note on a napkin tucked beside a plate of food reserved for him.

"Sorry, mate," Parker sympathized over a mug of coffee and *The New York Times* on his tablet. "Pull up a stool. Eat your cold eggs. You can still do nothing without her."

"It's not the same," he muttered, chewing on a slice of bacon.

"You sound like a child," Parker noted.

Grayson rolled his eyes. He wanted a distraction; going for a run was usually a good way to clear his head and keep his energy up but being alone had brought about too many thoughts of his late mother.

"What's the name of the spa?" Grayson asked, pulling out his phone.

"Are you going to show up there and stalk your new girlfriend?"

"Yes, obviously."

Parker sighed, closing the cover of his tablet in a show of giving his friend his full attention. "Grayson, I love you, but I really think you ought to give that girl some space."

"She's literally on a weekend vacation with me. Why would I give her space?" Grayson countered.

"Do you give her space when you two are in AC?"

Grayson hesitated.

"Right," Parker continued. "So. Maybe you let her have a day with the ladies," he suggested, standing to refill his coffee. He rolled his head on his shoulders, muttering about Grayson's inability to get a clue.

"What's going on with you and the glass-thrower?" Grayson asked, turning the tables.

"First," Parker began calmly. "Never say that in her presence if you want to retain your testicles. Second, we might be getting serious," he confessed, willing to share that much for now, at least.

"Oooh," Grayson laughed, looking as if he'd uncovered some big secret. "Serious, huh?"

Parker turned to grin over at him. "She's my ultimate match, Gray. As if I'd ever let her get away."

♥ ♠ ♦ ♣

After a round of manicures, pedicures, and mini massages, the girls were on their way in just over two hours. As they stepped into the lobby area, the trio came to a stop at the sight of Grayson sitting on one of the tufted couches. He appeared to be flipping through a magazine provided for waiting customers.

"About time," he stated.

Grayson rose and dropped the issue back to the glass coffee table. "I cannot believe some of the articles in there."

"How long have you been out here reading Cosmo?" Laurel accused as she approached.

He gestured to the cover knowingly and replied, "Long enough to pick up seven new ways you can, and I quote, rock my world."

"Yeah, maybe on your birthday," she humored.

Sadie paid the hefty bill and Grayson produced his phone. "Let me get you guys a car," he said. "I was going to steal Six if that's cool."

Having no other plans, Laurel agreed. Since the group was due to depart according to their own schedules at some point that day, the girls bid one another farewell.

Laurel and Grayson walked hand-in-hand into the heart of the beach town. "Any news on Vegas?" she asked.

He nodded, adjusting his sunglasses. "I booked a redeye tonight. I can still get you a ticket," he offered. "If you want to come."

Laurel shook her head. "I can't right now, but I'll think about visiting." She needed to pick up some more jobs and be there to keep her mom on track. Only then could she consider making the trip to join him out west.

"Sure," he replied easily, pulling out his phone as it chimed. He skimmed an incoming email, a thoughtful sound escaping him.

"What's up?" Laurel asked.

"My landlord's selling," Grayson summarized, slowing to a stop to give it another quick read.

"Your landlord?" she asked.

"In North Carolina. He wants to give me the opportunity to buy before he lists," he explained.

Laurel couldn't help her surprise. She hadn't heard much about the beachfront condo and hadn't known that it was a rental. "Oh. Is that good or bad?"

Grayson scratched his head, considering. "Well, he's been discounting my rent in the off-season. It'd be a lot of upkeep to own."

Laurel nodded, wondering if that meant he was leaning towards letting it go. It seemed to be the only place he'd put down roots, though he'd admitted he wasn't there very often. She tried not to think about that fact; he lived such a transitory lifestyle, and she would have to cope. Though she wanted to offer some sort of advice or words of wisdom, she was far out of her depth. She understood the bare necessities of upkeep and amortization schedules, but no more.

"Want to get some Chinese?" Grayson asked, waggling his brows, and putting the decision-making aside for now.

Laurel laughed knowingly. "Your aphrodisiac of choice."

♥ ♠ ♦ ♣

Alaric: Taking Gemma to the airport in an hour. Will catch a train from there.
Parker: Thanks for coming out this weekend. We won't be back in time to see you off.
Grayson: WAIT AL! Take Six with you and I'll go with your girl since I'm Vegas-bound
Alaric: I'd rather not.
Grayson: My mom died
Alaric: That's low, Gray.
Grayson: :(
Alaric: Fine.

Laurel hadn't expected to be traveling six hours with Alaric back to Atlantic City, but train travel was the best method when you didn't have a yacht at your disposal.

Parker and Sadie had called a town car to drive them to Parker's city loft, and Grayson had taken a car with Gemma to the airport. Although it would be a long trip back home, Laurel was enjoying another first. The railroad was comfortable enough, the slight sway lulling her to nod off every now and again. Thankfully, Alaric wasn't big on talking. Almost as soon as he'd taken his seat, he'd donned Bluetooth earbuds and settled in for the ride.

By the time they made their transfers in the city and made it home, Laurel had calculated it would be close to ten at night. She hoped that before that time, Alaric would at least let her know about more work.

Gemma: Flight delayed by 1 hour.
Alaric: Sorry. Got something to keep you occupied?
Gemma: A book, but it's boring. Wish you were here. xo

Alaric: Me too. Wish I was going back with you.
Gemma: That would be hard to explain to my parents. They think I was visiting a girlfriend from college who moved…
Alaric: You lied? Have to say, I'm surprised.
Gemma: I just thought it'd be easier not to say anything yet…
Gemma: I'll be sure to tell them all about how amazing you are before you get here.
Alaric: That will require you to tell them I exist.
Gemma: Don't be mad. Timing hasn't been right yet.
Alaric: Not mad.
Gemma: OK

Chapter Thirty-Eight

♦

Gemma sat on her back porch, watching her parents work in tandem in the garden. It was a great day to tell them about her new boyfriend, or so she thought. Perfect weather, good moods, and less than a week until the wedding.

"Mom? Dad?" she called. "Can I talk to you guys for a sec?"

A loud bark sounded from the far end of the yard and a dog, a wolf-like Tamaskan, came bounding across the grass looking to play. He dutifully dropped a tennis ball at Gemma's feet, which she threw towards the back fence for him to retrieve.

"George! Come out of there for a second," Emily Blake called into the shed and pulled off her weeding gloves. She took a seat at the patio table and accepted a fresh glass of lemonade that Gemma offered.

Looking both miffed and grateful for a break, Gemma's father emerged with Max hot on his heels. "What's up, buttercup?"

Gemma couldn't help her slight fidgeting. She hadn't found a way to casually mention her new relationship status and now it seemed like she was making a formal announcement. Her darkening blush was unavoidable. "It's about the wedding."

Emily gasped suddenly, as if guessing the news. "Are they calling it off?"

"What? No," Gemma laughed. "Definitely not. They're solid, mom."

"Are they pregnant?" George asked, grinning at his own joke. It was a wedding for two women, after all.

"Hilarious," Emily deadpanned.

Gemma tossed the tennis ball again, watching Max bound after it. "I have a date to the wedding," she explained, hoping she was reaching that mix of casual and excited that she'd practiced. "His name's Alaric."

George took a long sip of lemonade, giving a slow nod. It wasn't all that shocking to him. His wife, on the other hand, seemed puzzled.

"Alaric?" she echoed. "That doesn't sound familiar."

"Right," Gemma nodded, taking a deep breath. "He doesn't live around here, actually. He's in Jersey."

"How'd you meet him if he's in Jersey?" George asked, grabbing a clementine and starting to peel the rind.

"Go wash your hands," Emily sighed, pulling the fruit from him to take over.

"I want to hear about Jersey, first."

Gemma shifted under the weight of her own discomfort as she confessed, "Well, I met him when I went to Atlantic City."

"Last week?" George asked, surprised.

"No," Emily clarified on behalf of her daughter. "Last week she was in Connecticut. The bachelorette party in Jersey was last month."

"Six weeks ago, actually," Gemma corrected, hoping the longer timeline would work in her favor. She decided not to clarify that she'd never gone to Connecticut, though. The Hamptons would remain her and Alaric's little secret, as far as she was concerned.

"And you've kept in touch?" Emily asked, surprised. "I thought something might be going on, but—"

"We thought you and Ev were patching things up," George confessed.

Emily shot her husband a quick look.

"Why would you think that?" Gemma asked, dumbfounded.

"You've seemed happy," Emily shrugged. "It's been great to see. We just didn't know that there was someone else in the picture, that's all."

Reassured, and calming from the sudden spike in blood pressure, Gemma nodded. "Okay, well, Alaric's coming up in a few days," she explained. "He's getting a hotel nearby and—"

"He's not a gambling addict or anything, is he?" George asked suddenly.

Gemma stared at her father, taken aback by the question. "What made you even ask that?"

"Well, why else would someone live in Atlantic City? Unless…was he vacationing there?"

"No, he works there," she clarified. "He's got a really great job, actually. He's got his MBA and he runs operations at a hotel." Gemma listed these qualifications as if they'd earn her parents' trust, but she realized her mistake when things got quiet.

Beneath the table, Max nudged her leg repeatedly with the tennis ball, waiting for her next throw.

Emily was the first to ask, easily doing the math. "How old is he, Gemmabean?"

There was simply no way to ease into the news. "He's thirty-three."

"Thirty—!" George laughed, but it wasn't kind.

Emily, at least, sounded concerned. "That's a lot older than you, honey. And you just got out of a very long relationship."

"This has nothing to do with Everett, mom. I've been trying to figure out a way to tell you guys for a while. He's really great and cares about me and we're dating long-distance for now."

"For now," Emily echoed, suddenly concerned for an entirely different reason. "Gemma Blake, you are not moving to New Jersey."

Gemma groaned, dropping her head to her hands.

"All right, knock it off," George interrupted. "No one's moving. Gemma's got a new boyfriend. We'll meet him in a week. Not the end of the world."

It sounded so simple when her father said it, but Gemma could feel the discontent between them as the conversation settled.

♥ ♠ ♦ ♣

After a few mornings of waking in Parker's loft together, Sadie had the startling realization that this was about to become hers, too. The lavish lifestyle Parker enjoyed rivaled that of her own, and it would soon be theirs to share together. She knew the luster would fade in time, but she was committed to soaking up every moment.

Joining Parker in the kitchen, Sadie found that he was already dressed in an impeccable suit. "Are you working today?" she asked, padding over for a kiss.

"Shopping," he corrected.

"You're going shopping?" she questioned skeptically.

"We," he clarified. "We're going shopping."

Humming curiously, Sadie reached out for a piece of fruit on Parker's breakfast plate. "How domestic. What are we shopping for?"

Clearly amused, he informed, "Your ring."

When they arrived in the diamond district, Sadie was buzzing with excitement. "I've dreamed of this my entire life," she confessed. Sadie was a flashy woman who appreciated the finer things in life, including jewelry. An engagement ring was the penultimate item, followed only by a wedding band.

At their destination, a well-dressed, friendly man stood with the couple at the end of a blinding display case. "Is there anything about your dream ring that I should know before we begin? Perhaps you favor a specific type of metal, setting, size, or shape?"

Parker had called in a favor, asking his parents for the name and number of their preferred jeweler. He still intended to break the news in person, but it wasn't too unusual for him to buy someone he was seeing a piece of jewelry.

Sadie cleared her throat, reigning in her elation. With an equally polite smile, she replied, "Platinum. Emerald and cushion cut D-grades with pave bands. Wide, if you have."

Silence followed her practiced statement, which caused her to flush. Clearing her throat she added, "Please."

"Excellent. And the weight, ma'am?"

Sadie glanced at Parker, for the first time wondering if they should have set a spending limit for themselves.

Parker gave her a knowing wink.

"Let's start with three carats," Sadie replied coolly. "Size seven, for reference."

When the consultant returned, the owner was in tow. "I had to see who had such magnificent taste," he complimented, shaking Sadie and Parker's hands.

A rectangular tray was set before them, featuring five rings that matched Sadie's specifications. The sparkling works of art rested atop black crushed velvet and had Sadie's full attention. Her hand caught Parker's and she took a deep breath, feeling the reality of their engagement fully hitting her once more.

Beside her, Parker asked quietly, "Want my opinion?"

Sadie nodded, not trusting herself to speak just yet.

Gently, Parker lifted the second ring and gave it a thoughtful inspection. Without a word, he lifted her left hand and slid the ring onto her finger. He brushed his thumb over the back of her hand, smiling.

Sadie lowered her attention, turning her hand slowly this way and that, studying the details. She had no criticisms; it was that perfect mix of what she wanted, and even more special that Parker had been the one to choose.

Clearing her throat, Sadie gave a firm nod. She wanted this ring, this man, and this life.

♥ ♠ ♦ ♣

Sadie called for Parker as she adjusted the screen of her laptop. She had arranged a Zoom call with her parents and had mentioned that she'd be introducing them to someone.

"I want you sitting here when they join!" she called to him anxiously.

Parker rounded the corner, running his hands through his hair. "I'm here, I'm here," he assured, dropping down and giving her cheek a peck. "Had to look good for the mum- and dad-in-law."

Sadie gave him a quick once-over, nodding. "You look great," she assured and shifted so that they were pressed closely together.

Parker took a long drink of his wine, setting it out of frame as he battled some unexpected nerves. Aside from his sweaty palms, he was sure he was pulling off calm and collected.

"My parents are going to be relieved," Sadie assured him. "You honestly have nothing to worry about. But let's do a recap."

Taking a deep breath, Parker summarized the basics from what he knew thus far. "Your dad's a retired psychology professor and loves fishing. Your mom organizes a book club and other programs at a few local libraries. Did I pass?"

Her brilliant smile confirmed as much.

The warbly tune of an incoming call drew their attention back to the screen and Sadie punched the key to accept.

"Pop!" she greeted, leaning forward. "Hey, Pop. Can you see me?"

A girthy man in his mid-to-late sixties with rimless glasses and a graying beard boomed a laugh. "There's my girl…" Melvin Bache turned his head to the side, to a spot off camera to shout, "Penny, you're missing it!"

Melvin seemed to be fiddling with the settings to get the audio to work better, and Parker's brows lifted when a brunette with softly graying hair joined the man in frame. Sadie looked so much like her mother it was startling.

"Hi, honey," Penelope greeted with obvious excitement. "We miss you so much. And who's this with you?" she asked.

Sadie felt warmth spread through her at her parents' knowing stares. She took a deep breath and turned to look at Parker beside her. "Well, this is Parker Campbell..."

Penelope mumbled to her husband. "He's so handsome, Mel."

"He can also hear you," Sadie added.

"It's great to finally meet you both," Parker interjected.

"Polite, too," Melvin mumbled back to his wife, winking at Sadie on screen.

Unsure of what else to say, and not certain she could stand the anticipation any longer, Sadie gave him an excited smile. "Well, we wanted to call you and tell you…" She lifted her hand out of Parker's to place it in view, showing off her engagement ring. "We're engaged!"

There was a beat of silence, but then Mr. Bache slapped a hand roughly against the top of the desk with a holler of surprise. "I'll be damned!"

"Honey!" her mother gasped, hands going to her mouth.

Parker glanced aside at Sadie, a disbelieving grin on his lips. "You certainly didn't waste any time," he accused, turning back to the camera with a guilty smile. "I'm sure this seems a little sudden."

"Parker," Penelope said, smiling warmly, "Sadie doesn't really do 'easing into things.' Surely, you've noticed."

He laughed, nodding as he captured Sadie's hand again. "I have. And I love that about her."

Melvin heaved a long sigh, shaking his head in disbelief. "I am so happy for you, honey. I wish I could give you a big hug right now."

"I offered to fly you out here," Parker confessed, shaking his head at Sadie and her decision to break the news over video.

"That was mighty kind, Parker. We don't travel much, but maybe you two can make the rounds and get out here one of these days."

"Of course, Pop," Sadie nodded quickly. "Soon."

"Do you exist on the thrill of high stakes like our daughter here?" Melvin asked.

"Sometimes, but I also work for my father's investment firm here in Manhattan, Campbell Holdings."

"Parker, dear, where is your accent from?" Sadie's mother inquired. "I'm detecting something, aren't I?"

Parker was immensely grateful for how conversation flowed and how accepting her parents seemed. "That's right, Mrs. Bache. I'm originally from Melbourne."

"Mrs. Bache," Penelope laughed, waving him off. "Obviously you should call me Penny, or mom!"

"So, Parker," Melvin began, curious. "Why is this the first we're hearing about you, son?"

"Well," he hedged, glancing at Sadie. How forthcoming did she want him to be about their timeline? She watched him with a calm smile, and he realized that she intended to be completely straightforward with them.

"We met about a month ago," he explained. He smiled at Sadie as he continued, "And from the moment I saw your daughter, I knew this was it for me."

The moment Parker had helped Sadie out of her town car outside Borgata Hotel, he'd never once stopped thinking about her.

Sadie fixed him with a look of surprise and stated, "Well, I didn't."

Booming laughter came from the computer and the couples fell into easy conversation. A few minutes later, from behind the lip of her glass, Sadie mumbled to Parker, "My parents love you."

Mumbling back, Parker squeezed her hand. "Two down, two to go."

Chapter Thirty-Nine

♠

Laurel: How's Vegas?
Grayson: Lonely without you
Laurel: Winning big?
Grayson: Not as much as I'd like
Grayson: How're things by you?
Grayson: How's your mom?
Laurel: All good here. Al's got me working 4 days a week. Mom's being mom.
Grayson: Meaning?
Laurel: Don't really want to talk about it.
Grayson: Call me later?
Laurel: I'm working.
Grayson: Call me now?
Laurel: I'm working.
Grayson: Is something wrong?
Laurel: No, why?
Grayson: Feels like there is. We haven't talked since the Hamptons.
Laurel: You haven't called.
Grayson: Sorry
Laurel: It's OK.
Grayson: Time difference and our work schedules
Laurel: I know.

♥ ♠ ♦ ♣

As Alaric touched down at Albany International Airport, he realized with rising anxiety that the next few days would make or break his and Gemma's new relationship. If meeting her parents didn't go well, or the travel was too problematic, there was a high chance they wouldn't last as a couple after this trip. Alaric was hopeful, so he planned to be on his best behavior; he didn't want to give her or her parents any reasons not to take a chance on him.

Gemma had wanted to meet him at the airport, but Alaric had insisted on finding his own way to his hotel and then to her parents' house. "I want to come to you," he'd said. "Anything I can do to show your parents I'm making the effort."

When his ride slowed at the curb, Alaric thanked the driver and spied Gemma, already stepping through the front door to greet him. Dashing out from behind her, a large dog made a beeline for him. "Is this guy friendly?" Alaric asked, bracing as Max plowed into him.

"Max!" Gemma laughed, jogging over. "Sorry, he's a jumper."

Alaric let the dog sniff him and offered a good scratching under the neck. "Hey there, Max."

Gemma's arms came around Alaric's neck in a tight hug. "My mom's probably watching," she admitted, pulling back to kiss his cheek. Alaric smiled warmly, nodding. "You look beautiful. Should we get this over with?" It was no secret that this meeting was dreaded on all sides.

As the pair stepped into the kitchen, Gemma called for her parents. She led Alaric inside with linked hands and offered her best reassuring smile. She was determined to ensure this went well, and even if it didn't, she was determined not to let it ruin what they had.

As Mrs. Blake appeared, she regarded Alaric openly. "Welcome," she greeted, pleasant enough. "Alaric, is it?"

Alaric nodded, releasing Gemma's hand to offer it to her mother. "Alaric Nacario. It's nice to meet you, Mrs. Blake. Thank you for letting me come by."

Emily gestured for him to take a seat and called up the stairs. "George, honey? Gemma's new boyfriend's here."

Biting back a groan, Gemma took the seat beside Alaric and flashed him an apologetic look.

"I hope you like pork chops," Emily offered, turning on the stovetop to start cooking the ingredients she'd prepped.

"That sounds great," Alaric replied genuinely. "I'm also happy to take us out to dinner, if you'd prefer."

Gemma watched her mother's response carefully. She seemed surprised by the offer, at least.

"That's not necessary, Alaric. Not like it's a special occasion."

The silence in the kitchen stretched and Emily realized she'd been a bit blunter than she intended. "Not that your visit isn't welcome," she clarified. "There's just no need to make a fuss is all."

"Who's making a fuss?" George asked, appearing at last.

Alaric stood and shook Mr. Blake's hand, offering a similar introduction and word of thanks for having him over.

"Oh, sure," George said, pulling out a chair for himself. "Glad to put a face to the name. Gemma here won't shut up about you."

"Dad!"

"He knows I'm kidding, Gemmabean," George laughed, loosening Alaric's nerves.

"Okay, well, let's not act like I'm some lovesick teenager," Gemma mumbled.

Alaric gave her hand a discrete squeeze beneath the table.

From her place at the stove, Emily asked, "So tell us about your job, Alaric. Gemma said you work at a hotel."

Alaric nodded, expecting this. Occupation chit-chat was a safe jumping off point for conversation. "Yes, that's right. Borgata Hotel & Casino, where Gemma stayed recently. I'm one of four operations leads." He did his best to toe the line between showing he was a hard worker, and not appearing too much Gemma's senior.

"How'd you get a job like that?" George asked, leaning aside just after to ask Gemma to set the table.

"I made some connections during my MBA," Alaric explained. "I put in a lot of applications and a good one panned out. I was very lucky."

"He works like crazy," Gemma added as she pulled plates from a nearby cabinet.

"Do you?" Emily asked over the sizzle of pork. "That must be hard. Not much free time."

Alaric wasn't sure if he was reading between the lines or looking for critique that wasn't there, but he hoped to convey he wasn't too busy for Mr. and Mrs. Blake's daughter. "I'm trying to find a healthier balance," he admitted. "I have vacation time, but it would be nice to have a more regular nine-to-five."

"Atlantic City's an interesting spot," George commented. "Only been down there once, myself."

"It's been good to me, but I've started to think about other opportunities. All on the east coast."

Gemma set the stack of dishes on the corner of the table, watching Alaric carefully. He hadn't mentioned anything concrete about changing jobs. She wondered if that was true, or if he was just trying to assure her parents that he was flexible.

Emily turned the chops in the pan, checking the scalloped potatoes warming in the oven. "Are you from New Jersey, originally?"

"Iowa, actually," Alaric answered. Both of Gemma's parents looked surprised to hear it.

"After my parents passed, I had no reason to head back."

Alaric continued to have Gemma's full, undivided attention. She was learning things about his past she'd yet to know, and she tried not to feel guilty over the fact that she hadn't asked these questions before. Then again, this was more of an interrogation than it was a casual conversation.

Mrs. Blake's neutral expression softened a bit. "I'm sorry to hear that. No other family out there?"

"Not much. Just an aunt, but I needed some distance after my mom died. They were identical and it was hard seeing her."

Equally fascinated and devastated, Gemma added silverware to the table.

"How'd they pass, if you don't mind?" George asked sympathetically.

Alaric cleared his throat. It wasn't so much that it was difficult to talk about, he just knew the topic was a mood-killer. He was hoping to focus on the excitement of his and Gemma's futures together, not his tragic past.

"My mom died of cancer and my dad had a heart attack less than a year later."

Gemma slipped her arms around Alaric's shoulders from behind in a hug. He set a hand on her arm, smiling up at her.

Emily was watching him with understanding. "My sister passed away from cancer two years ago."

"Aw, honey," George mumbled, and Alaric realized then that Gemma was wiping away tears behind him. He hadn't expected to see Gemma so emotional, but he realized they'd never spoken of his parents.

"I'm okay," Gemma assured, giving him a watery smile as she dabbed beneath her eyes. "I just didn't know."

"Well, let's eat," Emily suggested, waving for Gemma to help her. "This is just about ready."

Gemma waited until they'd finished dinner and were working through pie before dropping her next bomb. There was still one important fact she hadn't shared with them yet, and she was hoping that by stating it as fact in front of Alaric, they'd be more accepting.

"Alaric has a room in town, at The Stockade," Gemma mentioned during a lull in conversation. "We'll probably head there soon. I'll be back tomorrow to work on the favors with Jess, though."

Alaric's jaw slowed as he considered Gemma's comment. He glanced over at her, noting her nervous tells. His attention shifted to her parents, and he watched their quick exchange of glances. This was clearly the first they'd heard about Gemma's intention to stay with him overnight. Gemma, by her own admission, had grown up sheltered. Her parents might not respect the decision to shack up with her new boyfriend, but they weren't able to deny her; she was twenty-four. He hoped, for her sake at least, that they didn't undo all the progress of the evening by making their opinions known.

Thankfully, and to Gemma's delight, her announcement was met by silent acceptance.

As Gemma and Alaric bid her parents goodbye and thanked them for dinner, Alaric hefted the overnight bag Gemma produced. He stepped outside to give her some privacy for whatever thoughts and feelings her parents wanted to tell her in private, but he turned at the sound of George following him down the walkway.

"Gemma's all we got," he sighed, hoping it explained or excused his and his wife's behavior.

Alaric nodded in understanding. He hoped to convey his own behavior by explaining, "Your daughter's very special to me."

Melvin gave a small smile, turning as Gemma emerged behind them. "I know," he said. "I can tell."

♥ ♠ ♦ ♣

As soon as the pair had stepped past the threshold of Alaric's room at The Stockade, Gemma hopped up into his arms and rained kisses down on his face.

Alaric dropped her bag with a laugh and kicked the door shut behind them.

"Where was this energy all night?" he teased as his arms went around her back.

"Dinner was way too long," she complained, leaning closer to whisper, "I need you."

Alaric's hand fell from the wall, unsuccessful in locating the light switch. He decided it wasn't necessary and carried Gemma in the direction of the bed. He managed not to trip over his own luggage he'd dropped off earlier and lowered Gemma to her back. She clung to him, keeping him atop her as she nipped at his lips.

"Sweetheart," Alaric rumbled, amused. "You have to let go so I can take my clothes off."

His statement had the desired effect, and she retracted her limbs with a culpable smile.

Standing back, Alaric untucked his shirt. Mimicking him, Gemma echoed his actions where she lay, easing off her top. There was enough evening light coming through the sheer curtain panels to illuminate them, and Gemma watched with renewed attraction as his tattoos were revealed.

Once she was left in only her underwear, Gemma shifted to kneel on the bed. Alaric was gloriously naked, and she licked her lips in appreciation as he reached for her. Before he could climb back onto the bed, however, Gemma put a hand to his chest to keep him in place.

"Wait," she requested, nodding for him to step back.

Alaric watched with an ache as Gemma lowered herself to her knees between him and the bed. Watching him, she closed her hand around his thick shaft, bringing her warm lips closer to press along the side.

Groaning, Alaric's eyes grew heavy. He placed a hand in her hair, encouraging and affectionate. "You are—" he attempted.

"Sh," Gemma breathed, wetting her lips. She leaned back in with a cheeky grin, tongue caressing the underside of the plump tip.

Without a word, Alaric's hand slid from her hair to cup the side of her neck, applying gentle pressure to tip her head to the left. Gemma obeyed, eyes lifting to him curiously as his fingers trailed up her chin. At the feel of gentle pressure against the hollows of her cheeks, Gemma parted her lips. A spark of desire like she had never known gripped her as Alaric fed the tip of his erection past her parted lips and into the warm wetness of her mouth.

Gemma whimpered softly as he slid against her tongue and took it upon herself to lean closer. Alaric groaned quietly at her attentiveness, watching her pull back to move her hand over his length a few times. As moisture beaded at the tip, she leaned back in to lick him clean and slide her mouth back down over him.

"God," he muttered, his eyes falling fully shut. If there was an upside to long-distance dating, Alaric thought, this was it. Each time the pair was forced to separate, the sex was that much better when they reunited. Gemma seemed as desperate for him as he was for her, and it was that much more painful for Alaric to consider leaving her again in a few days' time.

The firm pushes of her tongue were heaven, quickly driving him towards his climax. "Open, sweetheart," he coaxed, watching as she welcomed him as far as she could. Alaric nodded, his breath coming harder, and he reached down to rub the pads of his fingers against the silken underside of his shaft that didn't fit within her mouth. With a satisfied groan, he came, his abdominals twitching in pleasure.

Gemma leaned back as Alaric straightened, swallowing. She was trembling lightly, more aroused than she remembered ever being before, and she was grateful for the assistance when Alaric hauled her to her feet. His hands slid beneath her arms, and she climbed back onto the bed beneath him, her hands raking over his inked arms.

Alaric reached for a condom he'd had at the ready, fitting it into place. "Legs up here, sweetheart," he coached, guiding her calves over his shoulders.

Gemma marveled at the fact that he was still hard, nodding weakly as she slotted her legs into the new position.

Alaric groaned as his hips came flush against hers, joining them.

With a soft cry, Gemma's head tipped back against the sheets. Her knees tightened on his shoulders, her body shivering in response to his shifts.

"So goddamned beautiful," he breathed, towering over her in the new position.

"I—" she started, but her words caught in her throat as her toes curled. With a keening whimper, Gemma grasped the covers beneath her and tensed. Alaric had her orgasm washing over her in a little over three minutes and she shuddered as his movements slowed to a more drawn-out, languid pace.

"That's one," he groaned, rolling his hips.

Gemma moaned, feeling far too sensitive. "O—one?"

"We're going for three, Gemmabean," he whispered conspiratorially, causing her to gasp.

Chapter Forty

♥

Laurel checked her phone as she finished catering a small business dinner for Alaric to find that she had four texts and one missed call from Grayson. His last message said to return his call when she was available, no matter the time. It was nine-thirty for her, which translated to six-thirty for him, in Vegas. As soon as she was on the bus headed home, she dialed.

"Hey, Six," Grayson greeted cheerily.

Laurel did her best to rally through her exhaustion. "Hey. I just finished."

"Nice. How was it?" he asked.

"Good, I guess. Made one to one-fifty almost every day this week. There's not a lot of those private games, but Alaric threw me some other stuff."

"Glad to hear it. I miss you."

"Yeah," Laurel smiled, covering a yawn. "Miss you, too."

"Sounds like it," he teased. He could tell she was tired, and he felt a nagging guilt for bothering her.

Laurel switched her phone between hands, waiting for him to go on. After a beat, they both spoke over one another.

"Was there something—"

"Are we okay or—"

They laughed softly and Grayson attempted once more, "I know you said nothing's wrong in your texts, but I can't be the only one feeling like something's off."

Laurel wasn't sure what to say. Nothing concrete was amiss between them; Grayson hadn't done or said anything wrong. They'd parted in the Hamptons on good terms, but it felt strained as more time passed.

"I'm just working and taking care of my mom," Laurel replied, repeating the only way she spent her time these days. If something was different, it wasn't on her end. "I mean, you're used to me being available twenty-four seven. This is a little more realistic, isn't it?" Her tone was calm, but her words had bite.

Grayson was quiet, trying to decipher her meaning. When they were together in Atlantic City, he would suggest they meet up at opportune times, but that's what people did when they were dating and wanted to spend time together. He hadn't expected Laurel to always make herself available, and he wasn't sure why she spoke as if he did.

"Laurel?" Grayson asked, the use of her name causing the conversation to turn serious. "Is everything okay with us?"

Laurel sighed. She knew why he was asking; they couldn't be their normal selves with playful banter over long-distance. She wasn't trying to punish him for being away, but she couldn't force what didn't come naturally.

"I guess I just don't have a lot to say," Laurel confessed. She sounded apologetic, accepting partial blame for falling out of the groove they'd had. "There's not much going on over here with me."

"Come out to Vegas," Grayson requested.

"It's only been five days," Laurel said with a soft laugh. "You can wait to see me," she assured.

"You don't miss me enough," Grayson playfully countered. He paused before confessing, "I'll be here for two more weeks, actually."

Going three full weeks without seeing one another wasn't ideal, but Laurel knew this would become routine in their relationship. This was only the start of awkward phone calls and feeling the distance between them. She hated the headache that ensued at the thought of feeling this way on an ongoing basis.

"I'd like to, but—" Laurel hesitated. She'd just gotten back in the habit of working and caring for her mom.

Defeated, Grayson admitted, "I already got you a ticket. I thought you'd want to come."

Closing her eyes, Laurel sighed. "It's not that I don't want to come," she clarified.

"I'll leave it up to you," he said. "I'll text you the details. You can even change the flight if you want."

She appreciated the offer, and his understanding.

♥ ♠ ♦ ♣

The following evening, Laurel had checked another first from her bucket list. She'd taken her first flight, a long one at that, and was arriving at Las Vegas International Airport. She'd considered her options, weighed the consequences, and reflected on the relationship she and Grayson were building. All guilt and needless thinking aside, the fact of the matter was that her boyfriend was offering her an all-expenses-paid trip to a city she'd not yet had a chance to visit. A quick jaunt wouldn't affect the longevity of her job, and her mother seemed to be in a decent place at the moment. Therefore, there really was no reason to decline Grayson's offer.

"I'll be damned."

Standing in the taxi line for hotel shuttles, Roman Hill tracked a familiar blonde as she wheeled a suitcase across the pick-up lanes. He watched as Laurel, who he knew as Six, jogged across the road and walked right into the arms of none other than Grayson Lee.

Roman's fingers tightened around the handle of his luggage, his blood instantly heating at the sight of the man who had humiliated him in New York almost a month ago. It obviously wasn't unheard of to cross paths with another card player in Vegas, but the universe had a sick sense of humor to deposit both Grayson and his cheap girlfriend in the same city as him.

Grayson's arms went around Laurel in a tight embrace, and he inhaled her scent.

"Smelling me?" she mused.

"Guilty."

He pressed his lips to hers and felt the tension melting away. It was as if any discomfort between them had never existed, and he was thankful she'd agreed to drop everything to join him.

"Good flight?" he asked.

"Nothing to compare it to," she reminded.

"Another first," he nodded and took the handle of her bag. He led her towards their rideshare and held her hand the entire way back as he clung to hope. Whatever discomfort or miscommunication the distance had caused felt nonexistent now, but he knew it would have to be addressed.

♥ ♠ ♦ ♣

At five to seven, Sadie was more nervous than she'd been in her entire life. She and Parker were having his parents over for dinner to announce their engagement and Sadie was ready to pray to any and every God for a peaceful outcome. Her parents had been thrilled upon meeting Parker, but for some reason she doubted her ability to equally woo the Campbells. Sadie wore a well-fitted, modest blue dress that she purchased especially for the occasion.

With Parker busy in the kitchen and the place spotless thanks to the cleaning staff, Sadie busied herself by worrying.

"Are your parents punctual?" she asked, adjusting the red wine breathing on the counter, white wine nearby in a chiller.

Parker grinned. "Calm down," he repeated for the third time that evening. He carefully turned over a perfectly browned cut of veal in the skillet he was handling. He wore an apron over a button-down shirt paired with charcoal slacks.

Sadie's heels clicked across the floor as she paced. "I should take my ring off, shouldn't I?" she asked, considering.

"If you'd like," Parker replied, holding out a hand. "Want me to put it in my pocket? I can put it right back on your finger the moment they know." He gave her a knowing smile, which seemed to have the desired effect. Sadie eased and handed over the ring with some playful difficulty.

There was a tone at the intercom and Parker lowered the burner's setting before jogging over to receive the update from his doorman about their guests' arrival.

"This is it," he told Sadie and paused to kiss her cheek.

All Parker had told his parents, to avoid an endless flood of questions from his mother, was that he had something important to discuss over dinner. There had been a bit of prodding as to the topic of conversation, but Parker had insisted on discussing the particulars in person.

As the elevator arrived with his parents, Parker greeted them with open arms at the door. "Mum," he smiled. "Love the short hair."

Pursed red lips pulled into a smile as Joyce Campbell scrutinized her son. "You might consider it yourself, Parker," she replied while eyeing his hairstyle.

Heart racing, Sadie lingered just out of sight. The sound of Parker's mother's thick Australian accent somehow made the unseen woman even more intimidating.

Jack Campbell gave an exaggerated roll of his eyes and helped his wife with her coat. Parker saw his father at the office on a regular basis, so dinner was not so much a special occasion for the men. "So, what's this about?" Jack prompted. "And what smells so good?"

"Veal scallopini," Parker replied. He hoped his next statement would sound like a significant announcement. "And there's someone I want you to meet."

Joyce, at least, seemed instantly curious. "Really?" There was no doubt in her mind that Parker meant to introduce them to someone he was seeing, romantically. She set her purse down, taking a couple of steps further inside. Parker very rarely introduced them to anyone one-on-one. He was known to show up to functions with beautiful women on his arm, but this seemed special.

Sadie took a deep breath, preparing to step into view, when Mr. Campbell spoke.

"I hope she's nothing like that Whitney girl," Jack said.

Clearly, it hadn't registered to his parents that their son's date was already present.

"I still haven't found my jade earrings," Joyce added, all but accusing one of Parker's previous girlfriends of stealing.

His parents were oblivious as they went straight to the bar area and Sadie froze in the middle of the living room. Panicked, she considered hiding to avoid an embarrassing moment of realization once they spotted her, but she couldn't bring herself to move.

Parker nearly choked as he realized how the misunderstanding had unfolded, and he groaned as he attempted to do damage control.

"No, mum—"

"I know, I know, you keep insisting she wouldn't have," Joyce sighed with a wave of her hand. "The fact of the matter is that they're gone."

"And replaced," Jack reminded. "I don't see the sense in harping on it."

"The woman I wanted to introduce you to," Parker rushed on to say, desperate to regain control. "Her name is Sadie Bache, and she—"

"Bache?" Jack asked with a thoughtful sound. "What kind of nationality is that?"

"Oh my God, please stop," Parker begged, laughing pathetically as he gestured to the living area. "She's *here*."

Joyce spun, gasping at the sight of another person present in Parker's loft. "Oh!" she offered, abashed. Looking remorseful, she approached and offered, "So sorry, dear."

"No, I— It's fine," Sadie assured, awkwardly coming forward to introduce herself. She attempted levity to steer the night back on track, joking, "I already have jade earrings, if it helps."

After a beat, Joyce erupted into laughter and clasped her hand. She seemed thankful for the icebreaker. "Aren't you a darling?"

Jack approached, offering his hand as well. "Sorry about that, love. Didn't see you there."

The handshakes seemed a little on the reserved side, but Sadie knew that so far, they only suspected her to be a new girlfriend, not a fiancé.

"If you don't mind me asking, how old are you, dear?" Joyce asked. Sadie seemed a good deal more mature and worldly than some of the other arm candy Parker was known to bring around.

Sadie hadn't expected to be grilled on demographics so soon, but she answered with a smile. "Thirty-three." She knew Parker was one year her junior from her internet sleuthing, but she was sure this was the first he'd heard of her age.

"An older woman," Jack laughed. "I like it."

Parker only winked over at Sadie, not phased in the least.

"So, what is it that drew you to our Parker?" Jack prompted.

"Getting right down to it, huh?" Parker smirked, turning away to ensure their dinner didn't burn.

Sadie smiled, feeling well prepared. She'd thought long and hard about the love she'd grown to have for the handsome playboy. For years, Sadie had run from any sort of real connection. She was committed to being an independent, free spirit. However, she'd also realized that her independence had turned into a solitary life.

Finally, in an even voice, Sadie replied. "He helped me face my fears."

That seemed to surprise them all, including Parker who regarded her curiously from the stove.

"I was running from the possibility of love for a long time," Sadie confessed.

Touched, Joyce put a hand on her husband's arm and mumbled imploringly, "Jack...how sweet is she?"

Jack seemed to consider Sadie's words for a time, smiling. It was quite the admission for a casual dinner party. The night was suddenly making a lot more sense to him and Jack was surprised it had taken him this long to read the room. He looked between Sadie and his son before prompting, "Well, go on. You have something else to tell us, I'm assuming."

Joyce, at least, seemed confused.

Parker turned off the stove and set his apron aside, crossing to stand with Sadie. His arm slid around her waist, and he leaned in to whisper, "Here goes nothing."

Joyce may not have been privy to Jack's hunch, but she wasn't slow to catch on. "What's going on?" she insisted, her smile growing to match her husband's.

Sadie's cheeks colored as she signaled for Parker to give her back the ring. As the magnificent piece of jewelry glinted in the light, Joyce instantly gasped. "Bloody hell!" she laughed, slapping Jack's chest expectantly. "You knew?" she accused.

"I suspected," he corrected.

Parker slipped the ring in place and kissed Sadie's cheek affectionately.

"So…" Parker began, as if an explanation still might be needed.

"You're engaged!" Joyce cried, stepping forward to throw her arms around Parker in a tight embrace.

Jack pulled Sadie into a hug as well, smirking. "I'm not sure you know what you've gotten yourself into, Sadie."

Patting her soon-to-be father-in-law's back, Sadie laughed. "He's worth it."

They switched just after, Joyce offering Sadie a more appropriate squeeze now that the news had broken. "When did this happen?" she asked, still stunned.

"A little over a week ago. Parker wanted to wait to tell you in person."

"You should've come over that day!" Joyce scolded, but she was clearly thrilled.

Keeping her own tears at bay, Sadie accepted the affection and happily showed off the diamond when Joyce lifted her hand for a closer look.

"Can we continue this over dinner?" Parker suggested hopefully. "I spent hours cooking for you."

"That's another reason," Sadie told Joyce, gesturing to the kitchen. "I can't cook worth a damn."

As the group settled around the table, Jack launched into the first of many questions that evening. "What is it you do, Sadie?"

Sadie began to pour wine around the table as she explained, "I'm a professional card player. Poker, mostly, though I'm coming around to blackjack."

"So, that's where you met Parker," Jack nodded, gesturing to the bottle of red.

"Actually," Parker began, but he wasn't sure how to explain their town car meet-cute and give it the justice it deserved.

Sadie jumped in easily. "It was at a blackjack table," she confirmed, filling Parker's glass next. After all, her fiancé had officially captured her attention the night she'd been gambling with Stew.

"Are you one of Grayson's friends?" Jack asked.

Before Sadie could answer, Parker quickly gave a flat, "No."

One time and one time only Parker had dated one of Grayson's 'friends,' and his father seemed insistent on never letting it go. She had, after all, drank an entire fundraiser under the table and bid ten thousand dollars of Parker's money on a jet ski lessons package.

"We did just spend a weekend with him," Sadie offered as she set the wine down upon filling Joyce's glass. She returned to her seat and spread a napkin across her lap just as Joyce asked, "None for you, dear?"

It might have been the first time in her adult life that Sadie had overlooked getting herself a glass of wine. That showed just how distracted she was, and she laughed, releasing some nervous tension.

"Oh, my God."

Sadie looked up to see Joyce covering her mouth.

"No wonder you sprung this on us!" Joyce accused, looking pointedly at Parker.

As Sadie realized what her lack of an alcoholic beverage had looked like to Mrs. Campbell, her face began to fall.

"Is there a baby?" Jack asked, picking up on Joyce's meaning. He looked between Sadie and Parker, waiting for confirmation, but even he looked hesitantly gleeful by the idea.

Parker quickly put the idea to bed, shaking his head. "No, no," he insisted, catching his mom's attention. "Mum, stop. No. There's no baby."

Parker reached out and set a hand atop Sadie's on the table, aware how the misunderstanding could upset her.

"Oh," Joyce offered, laughing off her exuberance. She didn't seem concerned by her overreaction. "Well, plenty of time for that," she concluded.

Sadie pushed her chair out slowly. Clearing her throat, she managed a polite smile. "Excuse me."

Parker passed his parents a dish as he stood. "Help yourselves. I'll be back in a minute." He followed Sadie into his office behind the living area to find her leaning against the edge of his mahogany desk.

"She's just excited," he excused his mother's presumptions, brushing Sadie's hair back from her face. "Everything's going great."

"I like your parents," Sadie assured. It had only been fifteen minutes since meeting them, but her fears of meeting her in-laws had dissipated. Now, she felt only defeat.

"They're going to ask us when we're having kids for the rest of our lives until we tell them," Sadie said.

"It's none of their business," Parker assured. "And we haven't talked about all our options, anyway."

Sadie looked up, unsure.

"Options, Sadie," he repeated. "There are other ways to have kids. If we want them."

Sadie fiddled with the band of her ring; her thumb pressed to her palm. "Do you want kids?" she asked.

Sadie had never thought to ask him because she couldn't conceive. When Parker had proposed he'd said her inability to have children didn't change his desire to marry her. Sadie believed him, but she realized there was still a discussion to be had.

"Can we talk about it later?" Parker asked.

The fact that he couldn't answer with certainty worried Sadie. He seemed to sense that and echoed, "Well, do *you* want kids?"

Deflating, Sadie lowered her gaze between them. "I can't—"

"I'm not asking if you want to get pregnant and give birth," Parker clarified. "I'm asking if you want to discuss our options to have kids someday."

Sadie worried that an answer that didn't align with Parker's vision of the future would be the end of them. Still, she couldn't deny that the idea of having children with Parker held her interest.

"I don't know," she admitted.

Parker nodded. "Then we should talk about it. And I *want* to talk about it," he added, finally offering an answer of his own. "Just so we have all the information, okay?"

"Okay."

♥ ♠ ♦ ♣

After dinner, once Parker's parents had left and the table was a mess of dirty dishes, Sadie lay with Parker on the couch. They were decompressing after a stressful evening and celebrating the positive outcome. All parents had been informed and all necessary introductions complete.

Sadie pressed her phone into Parker's hand, the camera already front-facing. She gestured for him to hold the device at arm's length and lifted her left hand into the frame. "Smile."

It wasn't the most glamorous of photo ops, but Sadie thought it was the perfect way to announce the news to their friends. Queuing up a group message, she sent it off.

Laurel: ARE YOU KIDDING ME?
Laurel: I'm with Grayson and he says "what the fuck, mate?" in a very, very bad accent.
Laurel: Congratulations!!!!
Sadie: Thank you! We're very happy.
Laurel: …is that ring real?
Sadie: What do you think?
Laurel: That's disgusting.
Sadie: Did you just call my ring disgusting?
Laurel: Lol no. That is a work of art. The amount of money it probably cost is disgusting.
Sadie: True.
Alaric: Some people are trying to sleep, you know.

The sound of Parker's phone ringing had him groaning, and he leaned forward to see Grayson's name on the screen. "Look what you started," he accused Sadie playfully as he accepted the call.

"Uh..." Grayson laughed. "You got something to tell me, man?"

"Nothing's really coming to mind," Parker replied, his grin growing.

"Is that shit for real?" Grayson pressed, shaking his head in disbelief. "Are you two really getting hitched?"

"It's for real," Parker confirmed with an affectionate squeeze to Sadie's side. "I couldn't let her get away."

Grayson sighed, mumbling, "Yeah, I know what you mean."

Parker looked over at Sadie's screen, noticing Alaric's response. "You think Al even saw the photo?"

"Oh, definitely not," Grayson confirmed. "He'll call tomorrow to tell you how stupid your life decisions are."

"Perfect," Parker grinned. "Wouldn't want to miss that."

Grayson nodded. "Well, I'm happy for you. I thought after she trashed your collection of whiskey glasses you'd bail, but I seem to have lost that bet."

Parker laughed. "Yeah, I guess I like them feisty."

Sadie turned in his arms as her brows lifted. "Excuse me?"

"I've got to go," Parker told Grayson. "The *fiancé* requires my attention."

♥ ♠ ♦ ♣

Alaric: Sorry, I obviously didn't see your announcement. Congratulations. I'll call soon.

CHAPTER FORTY-ONE

♣

"Let me help."

Alaric knelt in front of Gemma and lifted her foot onto his thigh. He slipped the silver strappy sandal into place, smiling as she held the bulk of her pale pink bridesmaid's dress out of the way.

"It's almost over," he reminded, hoping to calm her frantic energy. They'd spent the previous day handling last-minute checks and it was finally time for the official celebration.

"I know," Gemma agreed, though she requested, "Can we go through it once more? Do you mind?"

Alaric buckled the small strap at her ankle, calmly repeating what they'd agreed upon. "I'll drop you off at Kayla's and say hi to the girls. I'll head back here, get my suit on, and meet you at the venue at two. I'll bring your flats and the wedding card. At the end of the night, we'll get a ride back here."

Looking calmer, Gemma thanked him. "Perfect."

"I can put my suit on now, if you'd like," he offered. "If you'd rather I have it on when we see your friends."

"No," she assured. "That's okay. I'll look forward to seeing you in it later."

Alaric slid his palm up her calf, his lips curving. "Sounds good."

The chime of the bridal party group text spurred her into action, and she twisted, nearly falling over his shoulder as she reached for her phone. Alaric's arms came around her as he laughed. "You're going to break your neck, sweetheart."

Ashlee: ALERT. We have a run in K's stockings. Where are the spares?!

Gemma: Three pairs in the plastic bag hanging behind the dress.
Beth: Jess isn't wearing stockings. Do we care???
Hailey: It's not like they're going to photograph their legs…
Gemma: It's OK. They don't have to match.
Everett: Are you sure? How many lesbian weddings have you been to?
Ashlee: Shut up
Hailey: Ugh

♥ ♠ ♦ ♣

When Alaric and Gemma reached the house, it was abuzz with activity. Conversation and laughter permeated the walls, welcoming them as they climbed the driveway.

"Hello?" Gemma called inside as she pushed open the cracked door. Within, furniture had been rearranged to make room for a spread of bagels and fruit. The space was occupied by young women in various states of dress.

Alaric lingered behind Gemma as he waited for the all-clear.

"Gemma!" Kayla came sliding into view in a pair of white silken pajamas, proudly embroidered with 'One of the Brides.'

They hugged gently, to not ruin Kayla's hair or makeup.

Realizing Gemma wasn't alone, Kayla began to grin. "Mr. Borgata," she greeted. "What a pleasant surprise."

Of course, they all knew Alaric was attending. Seating charts had been reworked. Gemma had apologized thoroughly for the late accommodation for her plus one. However, Kayla and Jess were happy for their friend; it was amusing and exciting that Gemma's supposed one-night stand had turned into a long-distance relationship.

"Thanks for having me," Alaric replied. "And congratulations. Big day."

Kayla beamed. "Haven't even thrown up once."

Alaric's brows furrowed and he looked curiously to Gemma to silently inquire if that had been a joke.

"Why do I hear— oh!" Ashlee laughed, heading over to grab Alaric in a hug. "Look who it is."

Stiffening, Alaric gave her back a light pat. "Nice to see you."

"Girls, come meet Gemma's boyfriend!" Ashlee shouted.

Gemma grimaced, mouthing a quick apology in Alaric's direction.

More faces appeared, some Alaric recognized and some he didn't. He was introduced to them all, nodding politely. Once they'd had a chance to ogle him, he heard one remark, "Ev's gonna shit a brick."

♥ ♠ ♦ ♣

A little after two o'clock, everyone was in place. The bridal party was lined up behind a pair of double doors, prepared to walk the 'aisle' at the venue, ahead of the brides. Gemma and Everett were first in line, waiting for the attendant to give them a signal. The idle conversation they attempted was highly uncomfortable.

"I think I saw your date out there," Everett stated, unable to make eye contact.

"Yeah, probably," Gemma replied nonchalantly. Whether Everett believed it or not, she hadn't invited Alaric to upset him. She'd invited her boyfriend because she wanted him there; it was as simple as that.

"What is he, fifty?" Everett smirked.

Rolling her eyes, Gemma turned to fix an unamused look in his direction. "He's thirty-three, but I know it's hard for you to recognize maturity."

Everett fidgeted with his tie and pocket square. That seemed to quiet him, at least for a minute.

Taking pity, Gemma asked, "Are you nervous for Jess?"

Shrugging, he lowered his arms to his sides. "Not really. They've been dating forever."

Gemma swallowed hard. She and Everett had been dating 'forever,' and they had been planning to get married, as well. A long dating history didn't guarantee a happy future. Gemma didn't question her decision to end her relationship with Everett, but she knew he was still hurting.

"It'll be nice when this is all over," Gemma offered.

Everett scoffed, "So you never have to see me again?"

Taking a deep breath to temper her response, Gemma calmly explained, "I meant the stressful part. The planning."

"Right," he muttered.

"Jesus, Ev," Gemma breathed. "Can you please stop having a pity party for yourself and get excited for your sister's sake?"

Just then the doors were pulled open, and Gemma quickly plastered a smile on her face. Linking their arms, the two proceeded forward.

When Gemma found Alaric in the audience, she realized he'd sat with her parents. Any lingering frustration with Everett's behavior instantly melted away.

"Pay attention," Everett muttered under his breath, tightening his arm around Gemma's.

It took every ounce of willpower for Gemma not to shove him from her.

Alaric's brow dipped as he took in Everett for the first time. His eyes followed them to their assigned positions alongside the designated stage, lips lifting when Gemma smiled his way.

The ceremony was simple, complemented by personalized vows. Alaric thought the way in which the readings and statements made by the officiant were altered to be gender-neutral was a nice touch.

As the guests moved from one space to another for the celebration, a receiving line formed for the happy couple. As Alaric approached the brides, just after

Gemma's parents, he accepted a hug from Kayla.

"Congratulations," he told her. "That was beautiful."

His eyes slid to Jess, whom he had yet to meet, and Kayla was quick to explain, "This is him. Gemma's new guy."

Recognition dawned on Jess's face, and she gave him an unabashed once-over, laughing. "Oh, wow. Someone upgraded." Everett may have been her brother, but there was just no comparison.

Laughing good-naturedly, Alaric allowed the line to move him along. He located his seat and set Gemma's dancing shoes on her chair along with the wedding card. The room was full of flowers and soft lighting, high centerpieces topped with lavish floral arrangements. Alaric spotted Gemma at the bar and was very glad to join her there.

"Was that miserable for you?" she asked sympathetically, passing him a beer from the ice chest.

"Not at all," he assured and leaned down to kiss her. "I watched you most of the time, anyway."

Alaric turned at the sound of playful gagging behind him and saw Ashlee uncapping a beer. "Don't mind me," she smirked. "Continue the love fest."

He gave Gemma another lingering kiss.

When she withdrew, Gemma took a moment to appreciate him in his suit. He looked even better than he had in his work suits, and she bit her lip as she confessed, "I am really, really—"

"Gemmabean," George Blake said from behind the pair.

Gemma spun with a blush at what her father had almost overheard her admit.

"You look beautiful, honey," George told his daughter, accepting a hug and passing her off to her mom for a squeeze, as well.

"Gem, sorry, I need you for pictures," Hailey interrupted, pulling her friend away by the arm.

Alaric uncapped his beer and took a long sip, scanning the guests. A few people walked up and introduced themselves outright, wondering who he was. Each time, he was all too happy to point out Gemma. He enjoyed a few beers, picked at the platters of food, and made pointed eye contact with Everett on multiple occasions. Alaric was itching to approach him, but he thought it might make Gemma uncomfortable. He did his best to keep his distance but expected Everett would confront him at some point or another.

When Gemma returned to his side, Alaric asked, "Do I get a picture?"

All too happy to oblige, Gemma dragged Alaric in the direction of the photographer.

Across the room, Everett watched as Gemma cozied up to her new boyfriend for photos. Everett didn't sense the normal awkwardness new couples tended to put out, still getting used to one another. It infuriated him at how easy the pair seemed to fit together, Gemma happily smiling every time Alaric was in reach.

When the bridal party was called away for the formal introduction by the DJ,

Everett gave Gemma a pointed look as he crossed the dance floor.

"I'll be back," Gemma told Alaric, begrudgingly following.

When Gemma reached his side, Everett accused, "You know how this makes you look, don't you?"

Gemma fell to the back of the line to await instructions from the emcee. "I don't really care," she snapped. Everett seemed to think their friends and family would find her 'easy' for so quickly having a date to the wedding, but Gemma meant what she'd said; it didn't bother her.

Everett's jaw tightened. "You're all over him."

"So what?" she shot back, her voice louder than she'd intended. A couple of the bridesmaids turned, and she waved to reassure them everything was fine. No matter what Everett thought was or wasn't appropriate, Alaric was her boyfriend, and she had every right to be affectionate towards him in public.

As the line grew shorter and each person was called onto the dance floor by the DJ, Everett scoffed. "Yeah, well, I'm sure your parents are thrilled to know their daughter's a slut now."

Gemma stepped forward just as her name was called, pausing to deliver one final retort.

"I'm sorry I actually *want* to fuck *him*," she snapped, cheeks flushed.

She turned, pulse high, and forced a smile as she joined her friends in building an archway for the couple to run through. Everett stepped out next, blank faced, and walked to the opposite end of the archway.

After the DJ made a show of introducing "for the first time ever, the couple of the century," the guests gathered to witness the first dance. As the music changed and couples paired off, Alaric touched Gemma's back with a silent question.

Relieved, Gemma fell into his arms. They moved slowly together, and Alaric noticed quite a few stares lingering in their direction. The attention didn't bother him, but he knew many of these people had seen Gemma in a relationship with Everett for a very long time; it was obvious they were still processing seeing her with someone new.

"I need a drink," Gemma announced as the music and tempo changed.

"Allow me," Alaric offered, gesturing for her to enjoy herself on the dance floor.

When he reached the bar, he stepped up behind the figure he'd seen watching them, taking a deep breath to prepare him, finally, for the confrontation.

"Everett."

Casting an uninterested glance in Alaric's direction, Everett replied, "Yeah, can I help you?"

Alaric stood there for a moment, silent. It was as if everything he'd heard was validated in that one response from the young man. He was immature, defensive, and pathetic.

"Yeah, never mind," Alaric laughed, grabbing a pair of beers. He had every intention of leaving it at that, of heading back to the dance floor and dismissing the idea of having any words with Everett. However, Everett started speaking before Alaric could depart.

"What, she sent you to talk to me?" Everett smirked. "Because of what I called her?"

Alaric froze. He had no knowledge of what Everett had said to Gemma, but he could guess it wasn't kind. Either way, Alaric had no patience for baiting comments. He slowly uncapped each beer and moved them to one hand, leaving his other free in case Everett grew a pair.

Fixing him with a serious look, Alaric said, "Next time you're feeling sorry for yourself, remember that she used to love you."

After a beat, Alaric spoke again. "And then think about why she doesn't anymore."

They stared each other down in the resulting silence before Alaric turned away first, heading back to Gemma's side. He handed her a beer but wasn't fast enough in wiping the expression from his face. Gemma looked in the direction he'd come from and saw Everett glaring. She groaned, clutching his arm. "What happened? What'd he say?"

Alaric took a long sip of beer. In all seriousness, he asked, "Whatever was between the two of you is over, right?"

Startled, Gemma quickly nodded. She was suddenly worried Everett had lied to suggest otherwise.

Alaric continued, "He forfeited any right or claim to you. You're mine now. And I'm not going to let that asshole upset you. The next time he disrespects you, I'm not only going to talk to him. Hear me, Gemma. He gets this one and only pass. Understood?"

Gemma's lips parted, her breath coming quick. She wasn't sure she'd ever heard Alaric say so much at once, let alone get so riled up over anything outside of his work.

"Yeah, okay," she breathed. Oddly, she found herself aroused by his possessive proclamation. She pressed the cold sweat of the beer bottle to her neck. Of all the times for her hormones to get the better of her, now was one of the most inconvenient.

"Let's dance," Alaric stated, returning to a more collected version of himself.

♥ ♠ ♦ ♣

After dinner, long after Gemma had switched to flats, she led Alaric up to the bridal suite.

"Pretty sure I'm not supposed to be in here," Alaric smirked.

"Pretty sure I don't care," she retorted, grinning.

"You're drunk," he laughed, following her into the empty room of bridal party supplies, suit jackets, discarded shoes, and beer.

As if to confirm his suspicions, Gemma pulled him closer, falling into his lips.

Smiling, Alaric returned the kiss at length. They hadn't had much privacy that night and he was glad for the break from prying eyes. He drew a hand down the front of her dress, across her chest, drawing a sleepy moan from her lips.

Chuckling, Alaric withdrew. "You said you had something to tell me. Was that just a ruse?"

Gemma shook her head, beaming. "Nope," she assured. She waved him to lean down, going up on her tiptoes to meet him halfway. After a quiet laugh, she whispered, "I love you."

Alaric let out a quiet breath, smiling. It surprised him that she would use this moment to confess she felt what he felt, but it was touching. As much as it warmed him to hear her say it, however, he also knew she was intoxicated. Still, he gave her a soft kiss. "Thank you. I love you, too."

Come morning, he'd let her writhe in her own embarrassment.

"Got something for you, too," he stated.

Gemma watched curiously as he produced a small box from his pocket. Eagerly, she reached for the gift, causing it to tumble from his hands.

Laughing over her drunken behavior, Alaric crouched to retrieve the gift. He'd planned on giving her the earrings earlier in the evening, but he'd learned that the bridesmaids were wearing matching jewelry. The box was thin enough to slip into his pocket, and he wondered if there might be an opportunity to surprise her before the evening was over. He was glad to have them with him, now.

Cracking the lid, Alaric held up the box from where he crouched, showing her the pair of modest diamond earrings.

To their left, a voice filled the doorway.

"What the fuck?"

Everett stared wide-eyed at Alaric on one knee, a jewelry box in hand. It wasn't terribly difficult to draw conclusions. "Are you fucking kidding me?"

With a heavy sigh, the moment lost, Alaric snapped the box shut. He pushed up to stand, raking his fingers back through his brown hair to calm himself.

Playing peacekeeper, Gemma took a step between the two. There was still ten feet of distance, but she held out a hand in Everett's direction. It was obvious what he thought was happening, but she'd seen the earrings. They were beautiful, and she was frustrated by the interruption, but she could see how Everett's misunderstanding of a proposal was hurtful.

"Please go," Gemma requested and wished her head wasn't as foggy as it was. They had all been drinking; the last thing she wanted was for a fight to break out.

"Last I checked, you're not supposed to be in here," Everett told Alaric, never taking his eyes from the older man.

"Everett, get out!" Gemma shouted. A moment later, in a quieter voice, she added, "Honestly. You're embarrassing yourself."

Everett laughed, loud and exaggerated. "You embarrassed yourself when you showed up with this loser."

Alaric felt an unexpected flare of amusement at Everett's insult. "I'm a loser," Alaric repeated with a quiet chuckle, tightening his fist around the box he held. He turned, walking a few paces away towards the window.

Everett's childish behavior and remarks were laughable, but Alaric knew they pained Gemma. He couldn't imagine her spending six long years with someone so exasperating, but then again Alaric thought of Grayson and how much he put up with from his friend. Unlike Everett, however, Grayson was simply playful. And he would never, ever gaslight or emotionally abuse someone.

As if on cue, Everett smirked at Gemma, "You actually going through with it this time?" he taunted, reminding her yet again that she'd backed out of their engagement.

Alaric's attention turned toward Everett, but he stared past the younger man, into the hall. Certain there were no witnesses, Alaric crossed the distance in four quick steps. Gemma had just enough time to gasp before Alaric had grabbed Everett's dress shirt for leverage and buried his fist in Everett's stomach.

As the younger man crumpled, Alaric bent down to whisper an explanation. "That's for emotionally abusing her." Before Everett could regain his breath, Alaric shoved him to the ground. "And for whatever you called her earlier."

Gemma watched as Everett curled up, coughing out a curse. She wasn't a fan of confrontation or violence, but she didn't feel that bad for him.

"Let's go," Alaric suggested from the door, flexing his fist. He passed the cracked jewelry box to Gemma, saying loud enough for Everett to overhear, "Hope you like the earrings."

CHAPTER FORTY-TWO

♦

Across the country and three hours behind, Laurel and Grayson returned to their suite to find an envelope had been slipped beneath the door.

"This has your name on it," Laurel said as she passed it to him and kicked off her shoes. They'd walked a good portion of the strip and had enjoyed a brunch buffet. "I might take a nap," she admitted.

The envelope contained a simple, typewritten invitation to a private tournament on one of the upper floors of the resort. It promised discretion, required a large buy-in, and mentioned Alaric Nacario as a reference. It was scheduled for ten o'clock the following evening and was signed by hotel management.

"Sweet," he said, holding up the letter. "Two games tomorrow. Got something cooking around lunch and Al just threw me something after dinner."

"Nice," Laurel agreed. She dropped her clutch on the couch and trudged towards the bed, pulling back freshly made covers. She reached behind her to unclasp her bra and noticed Grayson had followed. He watched her, his hands immediately going to the fly of his jeans.

"Oh, my God. We're not having sex," she accused, laughing at his one-track mind.

"What, why?" Grayson half-demanded as his hands slowed.

"It's one in the afternoon," Laurel laughed. "I'm tired. I literally just said I wanted to take a nap."

Grayson, with his pants hanging open, crawled across the bed towards her and drew her forward into a kiss. His lips nudged hers softly, hands moving down her arms. "You'd sleep better if we fucked first," he mumbled knowingly against her mouth.

Even as she surrendered to his soft, manipulative kiss, she complained, "You're wearing me out."

His hands began to work on drawing her cotton dress over her head. "Yeah," he confirmed, as if that were his plan all along. "It keeps you from straying."

She hummed in consideration and allowed him to undress her.

In a more serious tone, he asked, "You okay being here?" It wasn't Atlantic City, and it wasn't New York, but he hoped she was happy.

Laurel's hands found the sides of his face and she brushed her thumbs over the light stubble he'd yet to shave that day. Everything about Grayson was as charming as it was frustrating, but she was coming to love that about him. She still believed New York would happen for her, but she wasn't disappointed taking time to be with him.

"I'm good anywhere with you."

Grayson looked almost impressed, nodding. "Good answer. In fact, I'm going to reward you for that," he announced.

"Is the reward sex?" she accused, her stare narrowing.

"Yes, but," Grayson hurried to say. "I'm going to let you have control."

Amused, Laurel slid her arms around his shoulders. "You think I don't always have control?"

Grayson was quiet for a moment. "I sense a trap."

Laurel laughed and shook her blond hair against the comforter where she lay beneath him. "What's this sex reward that gives me control?" she humored.

Grayson bounced off the bed, returned naked, and held up the terrycloth belts from their robes.

Surprised, Laurel pushed up onto her elbows. "Are you suggesting—"

"Tie me up," Grayson confirmed, his brows dancing. "Come on, I know you want to."

Laurel took the belts as Grayson handed them to her and she watched him with clear amusement. "You want me to restrain you?"

Quickly nodding, he pushed her to move so he could stretch out in her place.

Laurel considered it. Restraining Grayson would prevent him from getting what he wanted, and Laurel found she loved the idea. One at a time, she secured each wrist to the low headboard. He tested their strength and gave an approving nod.

"Okay, climb up," he encouraged, indicating his lap where he was already sporting a quickly growing erection.

Rounding the bed, Laurel scooped up her dress and gave him an apologetic look. "You gave me control, remember?"

Grayson watched, dumbfounded, as Laurel pulled a pillow off the bed and moved towards the doorway.

"Next time I say I'm tired, maybe you'll listen," she said with a sweet smile, just before shutting the door.

♥ ♠ ♦ ♣

The following night, Grayson made his way through the halls to his second game of the day. He was feeling pretty good after coming out on top that afternoon and was looking forward to riding that luck into another good game.

When Grayson knocked, a voice called for him to come inside.

Grayson found the suite was dark. His first thought was that he might have gotten the room number wrong. His second thought was that someone might have confused him with room service when they'd called him in. He didn't have time for a third thought.

Grayson took a couple of steps inside. Once he'd cleared the door, he was struck from behind. The breath was knocked from him, but he managed to reach out to catch himself on the edge of a marble counter. It didn't quite sink in that the action was purposeful, and he turned to see what had happened, such as something falling on him.

"Nice of you to join us, Lee."

The light came on then, and Grayson saw that the suite wasn't empty after all. One man stood behind him, cracking his knuckles. The blow had come from him, then. In front of Grayson, an unfamiliar bulky man stood beside a face Grayson would never forget.

"Roman."

Grayson noted that the man at his back was blocking his exit. His side ached fiercely where he'd been struck, but he suspected Roman's payback wasn't meant to end at a single blow. He squinted at Roman, putting the pieces together.

"There's no game," Grayson surmised; the invitation had been a ploy.

"So smart," Roman praised sarcastically. "Are you sure you never went to college?"

Grayson knew Roman was low, but an ambush? "You fucking coward," he muttered.

Roman was clearly unaffected. "Coward or not, I've got the upper hand."

Wincing, Grayson stood taller. "What do you want, money? Then you should fucking win it back from me."

A quick signal from Roman had the man behind repeating their earlier swing, Grayson going down to a knee.

"Fuck," Grayson muttered. Good sportsmanship had clearly gone out the window after their last encounter.

Roman moved closer, his polished shoes stopping right atop Grayson's hand and grounding down. "You shouldn't have fucked with me," he told Grayson simply. "You should have just let me have her."

At the mention of Laurel, Grayson made an angry grab for Roman with his free arm.

"Temper, temper," Roman scolded, easily stepping out of reach.

Seeing red, Grayson struggled to his feet. He was leaning, curling in on the side that had been repeatedly struck. His hand ached, too. "What do you want?!" Grayson yelled, as loudly as his failing breath would allow.

Roman planted an uppercut into Grayson's vulnerable ribs on the opposite side, watching the breath whoosh from him. It had hurt much more than Grayson was braced for, and he registered the glint on Roman's knuckles before he squeezed his eyes shut. He missed the wind-up as the older man threw another punch, this time the brass knuckles scraping across the left side of Grayson's face.

Light burst across his vision and Grayson wondered if the crack he heard was in his head or heard by all. Another blow landed at his ribs, and he coughed, vision darkening as he tried to cover his midsection with his forearms. There wasn't much maneuvering he could do, and the steel toe of a shoe hit him squarely in the back of a thigh, forcing him to buckle.

Grayson couldn't manage to throw a single retaliating blow; he was so focused on not passing out. His jaw throbbed and he spit a mixture of saliva and blood in the direction of Roman's voice, hoping for purchase.

His hair was grabbed, and Grayson winced, wheezing as his head was jerked back. "Thought you were a tough guy, Lee," Roman smirked coldly. "But I know your weakness. I know she's here. One wrong move and I'll make her scream again. Got that?"

Grayson was distantly aware of his arm being grabbed from behind and with a gasp, he felt it wrenched backwards. His raspy and short breaths turned to a gurgled scream as it was pulled from the socket. Then, mercifully, everything went dark.

♥ ♠ ♦ ♣

It was two hours later, when housekeeping made their rounds, that Grayson was found. When he was admitted to Sunrise Hospital and Medical Center, a chain of telephone tag began.

Grayson's next of kin was listed as his mother, but there was no answer at Mrs. Lee's residence. There was no way for the hospital staff to know of her recent passing.

It was Laurel who sensed something was amiss. Tournaments and private games were known to go on for hours, but Grayson had left at nine-thirty in the evening, and Laurel awoke to an empty bed. It was early, only six in the morning, but he still hadn't returned. There were no messages on her cell phone, and no sign that Grayson had been back and left again. Her calls were going unanswered, and unsure what else to do, she dialed Alaric.

"You know I'm on vacation, right?" Alaric sighed. Lucky for her, he rarely slept in, and it was already nine on the east coast.

"Sorry. Look, Grayson isn't back yet," she said, clearly concerned.

Alaric sighed, clueless. "From where? Vegas?"

Laurel's brow furrowed. "No, we're both in Vegas. I mean the game you set up last night. He isn't back yet."

Alaric looked to Gemma where she slept across the room, a cup of coffee balanced on his thigh. "I didn't set up anything last night," he informed. "Like I said, I'm on vacation."

Frustrated, Laurel rolled her eyes. "Referred him to, then," she corrected. "Did it run really long or something?"

"Laurel," Alaric said, not sure why she wasn't understanding him. "I don't know what you're talking about. I don't know Grayson's schedule or any games he's playing."

Sensing something was very, very wrong, Laurel took a picture of the invitation and texted it to Alaric. She waited as he looked it over. Ultimately, he admitted, "This is fishy. There's not even a contact. No phone number. Did you call the room?"

Laurel could have slapped herself upside the head. "I forgot you can do that. Hang on."

Putting Alaric on speaker, Laurel picked up the hotel's handset. She was momentarily distracted by the blinking amber light. The text beneath it read 'messages.'

A relieved sigh left Laurel as she punched the button, quickly telling Alaric, "Hang on, I think he left a message. Maybe his phone died or something, he can be such a—"

Slowly, Laurel's face fell, and her breathing picked up. She listened to the message in her ear, barely registering as Alaric asked, "All good? That him?"

Trembling, Laurel dropped the handset back to the receiver and grabbed her phone from the bed. "He's in the hospital," she breathed, shakily looking around for something to wear. "He's— they said he's—"

Alert now, Alaric asked, "The hospital? Did you just say Gray's in the hospital? What happened?"

"I— I don't know," she said, scatterbrained as she tried to quickly find her shoes and purse. "The hospital called the room…they weren't sure if he was traveling with anyone because he checked in alone."

"Laurel, listen to me. Tell me exactly what the message said."

Taking a deep breath, Laurel recited shakily, "Grayson Lee came in around midnight and any relatives traveling with him should come to Sunrise Hospital and Medical Center immediately."

Alaric felt as if the floor had dropped out from beneath him. "Shit."

Laurel felt the tears rising, an overwhelming panic settling in. "I have to go," she told Alaric. Grayson had been at the hospital for over six hours by then. "I have to go now."

"Call me the moment you get there," he instructed. "Leave your phone on."

Alaric ended the call and immediately pulled up the hospital's number. He explained he was looking for information on a patient and lied, saying he was Grayson's brother.

After an agonizing wait, he was given only the basics. "Grayson Lee was brought in late last night in critical condition," he was told. "The hotel called paramedics. They said they found Mr. Lee in a room that was supposed to be vacant but had a do not disturb tag on the door. They suspect a possible mugging."

When Alaric ended the call, he touched Gemma's shoulder to wake her, explaining the situation. They both packed and grabbed a ride to the airport to wait standby for any flights headed west. Gemma had insisted she accompany him upon seeing how distressed he was. It frightened her, honestly.

Once they were on their way, Alaric rang Parker.

"It's Gray," Alaric said. "He's in the hospital and it's not good. I don't have the details, but I'm trying to get a flight out."

Dread coiled as Parker imagined the worst possible scenarios. "Where are you?" he demanded.

"Upstate, New York."

"Fuck. Right. Find a private airport and charter a flight. Have Hannah do it if you have to. I'll be right behind you."

It went without saying that Parker would cover the cost and Alaric was momentarily thankful for having such good friends in his life. "Thank you," he said earnestly.

Parker packed as he relayed the news to Sadie. "They said 'critical,'" he admitted, feeling the edges of his composure start to fray. He couldn't imagine his future without one of his chosen brothers in it.

"He's the most stubborn man I've ever met," Sadie said confidently. "He'll live."

♥ ♠ ♦ ♣

At the hospital, Laurel received the same update Alaric had been given, and she was asked to wait for a doctor. It didn't take long, but every minute that passed had Laurel's desperation climbing. It was maddening to stay rooted in place for updates when traffic was flowing steadily around her. Patients and visitors continued to arrive, loved ones were called by doctors for updates, but Laurel stood, anxiously shifting her weight for any news.

Desperate for something to distract her, she pulled up a group text that Alaric had started earlier.

Alaric: Gemma and I are flying in soon. We'll have wifi. Keep us updated. Last I heard was possible mugging.

Parker: I'll be wheels up in 45.
Laurel: Still waiting to see him or speak to someone. I'm scared.

"Grayson Lee?"

Laurel turned quickly, lifting her arm on instinct.

"Hi, I'm Dr. Miller," the man introduced. "Grayson came to us in pretty rough shape. He's stable, but we're watching him very closely."

Laurel began nodding, latching onto the word 'stable'.

"He had surgery for internal bleeding, which went great," the doctor droned on. "He's on pain killers for a collapsed lung and dislocated shoulder, he's got two broken ribs, a fracture in his jaw, and…" he glanced down at the chart to see if he'd left anything out. "Oh, and a broken finger."

She managed to ask "how?," having a hard time wrapping her head around the list of injuries.

"I'm afraid I don't know. He's been pretty out of it with the pain meds since he woke up."

"He's awake?" she choked.

Chapter Forty-Three

A nurse stood beside Grayson's bed when Laurel arrived. She was holding up a pillow with a confused expression. "You want an extra pillow?" she clarified, nodding as she watched him try to focus on her. "I'm going to lean you forward, okay?"

Though Laurel wanted to rush to his side, she found herself hesitating at the door. Seeing him less than his arrogant, charismatic self was staggering. From the doorway she could see that half his face was deeply bruised, the skin at his cheek covered by a line of butterfly closures. He had a splint on one hand, and she knew there were many more injuries beneath the covers.

She heard his weak voice as he mumbled something to the nurse, causing the woman to laugh. "Only one, okay?"

Gently helping him forward, the nurse positioned the pillow. He spoke again and she shook her head. "Nope," she replied. "I don't even have six pillows to give you, hon."

Laurel's chest squeezed as she stepped inside, understanding what it was he was trying to say.

"Six," he mumbled again, rolling his head against the pillow as his eyes closed.

Quietly taking her purse off and setting it on the sterile chair in the corner, Laurel approached. She'd managed to throw on a bra, one of Grayson's t-shirts, and her jeans. She hadn't showered, hadn't even combed her hair, and looked worse for wear.

"Hey, hey, I'm here," she said softly, moving to his side.

The sound of her voice had Grayson turning, eyes snapping open. He tried to take a deep breath, a sign of relief, but it seemed to fail him. His eyes were glassy, pupils dilated.

"Grayson—" Laurel attempted weakly, wiping at her face as the tears kept falling. "Oh, my God…Grayson, what happened?"

His unbandaged hand gripped hers tightly, the rest of him relaxing against the bed as he took comfort in her presence. The pain killers had done wonders for his aches, but they also made him feel untethered. From the moment he'd regained consciousness he'd been panicked that Roman had gone after Laurel. He'd had no knowledge of whether she was safe, and seeing her here, crying but otherwise unharmed, was comfort enough.

After a few agonizing minutes, he licked his split lip and managed, "Roman."

Laurel felt a cold dread sweep over her, replaced by fury as his explanation sank in. This hadn't been some random mugging; this hadn't been random at all.

"Roman?" she breathed, shaking her head in confusion. "Roman did this?"

Grayson felt even more relief at her shock, confirming that Roman hadn't gone anywhere near her after leaving him in the hotel room the previous night.

"Do the police know?" she demanded.

With a creased brow, Grayson gave a short shake of his head.

"No?" she asked, obviously confused. "Have you talked to them yet?"

Grayson repeated the brief movement, signaling that he hadn't spoken to anyone and didn't intend to, either.

"But—"

"Six," he breathed, voice growing firm, "I can't—"

The attempt brought on a coughing fit, to Laurel's horror, but the nurse was quick to offer. "It's alright. It's a good sign, actually. It'll just take a while to go away."

Not wanting to worsen his condition or risk upsetting him, Laurel remained quiet on the matter. She would make sure Roman paid for this, after Grayson calmed down.

"You okay?" he eventually asked.

"Me?" Laurel cried, shaking her head. "Grayson, you're in the *hospital*."

"I am?" he tried to joke, but he couldn't quite muster his typical trademark grin.

"What can I do?" she asked, looking at the nurse who was just slipping Grayson's chart back into place at the foot of his bed. "Is it okay to touch him? Can I be here?"

"He's cleared for visitation," the nurse confirmed, giving Grayson a playful wink. "Hand-holding only, though."

He offered a raspy laugh, eyes slipping closed as he kept his grip on Laurel.

"Let me just—" Laurel attempted to pull her hand free, but Grayson's grip tightened and he looked at her.

"I'm just going to text the guys," she told him. "I'm not going anywhere, I promise."

Laurel: I'm with him! He's awake!
Alaric: How bad is it?
Parker: Is he out of ICU?
Laurel: He can have visitors. He looks awful but he's on pain meds. He doesn't seem like he's in pain, just drugged.
Alaric: Did he say what happened?

Laurel bit her tongue. She could sense that there was more to the story than Grayson could share at the moment, and she decided she would wait and let Alaric and Parker help her learn the full truth upon their arrival.

♥ ♠ ♦ ♣

Laurel stirred in the armchair some time later as a nurse checked on Grayson. Laurel's hand was still firmly in his, even as he slept and she repeatedly dozed. The sun was high in the sky and she expected his friends would be arriving soon. Nurses came often and Laurel had neither seen nor heard anything to suspect Grayson wasn't on the path to recovery, which soothed her.

Laurel noticed Grayson's eyes were open and she leaned forward to bring his hand to her lips, giving his fingers a firm kiss. "Good afternoon, sleepy head."

Grayson smiled, nodding. "Feel good."

She laughed quietly. "That's the drugs talking. Without them you'd feel like roadkill."

Grayson wrinkled his nose.

"Are you coherent right now?" Laurel asked, smiling weakly. "Are you going to remember this?"

He just looked at her, his stare glassy.

"I love you," she confessed despite knowing it wasn't fair to tell him now, when he may not remember the moment. Still, she couldn't keep it in anymore. When she had been on her way to the hospital, terrified to think he may have been dead, it was her biggest regret that she hadn't told him how much she cared for him.

A quiet groan left him, and Grayson lifted and dropped their clasped hands since that was really all he could do. "Timing," he complained. He attempted a warm, sincere smile. "Don't not?"

"No," she laughed. "I don't just 'don't not' love you."

His expression conveyed he wasn't in the headspace to handle triple negatives and so she stated, "I just love you. Got it?"

Grayson pulled her hand to his lips for a kiss. Thankfully, Laurel gasped and applied counter pressure just in time to prevent him from smacking himself in the jaw in the process.

"You have to be careful…" she admonished with a weak smile. "No kissing for a while."

Grayson groaned even louder.

♥ ♠ ♦ ♣

"Jesus Christ," Alaric breathed from the hospital doorway as he took in the sight of his damaged friend.

Grayson's heavy-lidded stare shifted towards the familiar voice, a smile spreading across his battered face. "Al?"

"Fuck," Alaric muttered, slowly stepping forward. Gemma trailed him with a small smile, unsure if she was intruding. It had been a long, emotional day. Alaric had been anxious the entire flight and it had worn off on Gemma; finally seeing Grayson alive and smiling offered some relief.

"Hey," Laurel greeted, rising from the chair she'd been occupying for hours. She accepted a hug from Gemma and patted Alaric on the arm. "I'm going to stretch my legs."

"I'll go with you," Gemma offered, wanting to give the guys a moment alone.

Alaric stood at the foot of Grayson's hospital bed. "You look like shit, Gray."

Grayson lifted his hand, smiling as he offered Alaric a splinted middle finger.

They laughed, which launched Grayson into a coughing fit.

"What the hell happened?" Alaric asked as he dropped into the available seat. "Laurel showed me that invitation you got. I didn't refer you."

Grayson held up a hand, nodding. Defeated, he explained with a single mumble of the attacker's name. "Roman."

Alaric looked bewildered for a moment, processing Grayson's meaning. "*Roman*? Roman Hill?"

"And two more," Grayson offered, knowing it was hard to believe Roman on his own could have done as much damage. "Much bigger," his ego added.

At length and with short sentences, Grayson explained the ambush. In the aftermath Grayson could see how it seemed unbelievable that he would have trusted the vague invitation. Alaric could hardly wrap his head around it, but he was seeing red. Grayson had been lucky to make it out alive, all over some stupid retaliation plan.

"You need a vacation," Alaric told him. "You need to lie low for a while, take care of yourself."

"I know," Grayson assured. He'd been thinking about it, at least a little, as he'd been in a drugged-up daze. "North Carolina," he said.

Alaric nodded. He knew it had been a while since Grayson had made use of his beachfront condo, and it sounded like the right move for recuperation.

They were interrupted by quick, heavy footsteps as Parker barged in. He seemed to relax at the sight of his friends, his hands going up into his hair. Slowly, he moved closer and grabbed Grayson's arm to steady himself. He'd been rocked, terrified for his friend, and needed a moment to find the words.

Sensing the questions Parker had, Alaric explained, "This asshole was lured to a fake card game. Three guys blindsided him."

Grayson gave a lopsided smile thanks to his swollen and bandaged cheek. "Don't forget…brass knuckles."

Parker's brows went up, his disbelief growing. "Only you, Gray. Bloody hell."

♥ ♠ ♦ ♣

Down the hall at a vending machine, Gemma and Laurel raided it for snacks. As Gemma bent down to retrieve her selection from the pick-up box, she set a hand on the front of the machine to fight a wave of dizziness.

"You okay?" Laurel offered.

Gemma slowly stood, an accomplished smile on her lips as she held up the bag of pretzel twists. "All good," she confirmed. "Long flight, emotional day…"

Laurel nodded, running a hand through her hair, and working out a few tangles. "I know what you mean. I've just been sitting in there, freaking out."

"Well, he was smiling," Gemma offered. "He's going to be fine, right?"

Punching a few buttons, Laurel watched as a paper cup dropped into view. "I think so, but the collapsed lung seems really bad."

"Is that what the doctor said? That it's really bad?"

Laurel's guilty smile preceded her confession. "WebMD."

"Laurel, don't do that to yourself," Gemma laughed sympathetically. "He's literally in a hospital. They're actively treating him. They will tell you anything you need to know."

"I just feel useless," Laurel groaned, eyes on the coffee as it began to brew and drip into the cup below. Her voice dropped as she said, "I should have waited up for him."

Gemma set a comforting hand on Laurel's arm. "Don't do that, either. That 'should have' and 'what if' thinking isn't going to help anyone. Grayson made it to the hospital, that's all that matters."

"But he was just lying there," Laurel said, her voice breaking as her tears returned. She wiped at her face, angry all over again. "They just left him there."

The mention of multiple attackers had Gemma's skin crawling.

"Here," she said, picking up the hot coffee and placing it in Laurel's hands. "Drink this and just take a minute to calm down."

As Laurel's change clinked down the machine, Gemma bent to retrieve it. Upon rising to stand, another wave of dizziness rushed in, and she stumbled. Before she could make sense of her fatigue, she hit the linoleum floor.

♥ ♠ ♦ ♣

"Excuse me, are any of you here with Gemma Blake?" a nurse asked.

Three heads swiveled in her direction and Alaric nodded, glancing into the hallway for any sign of his girlfriend. "I am," he confirmed.

The nurse leaned back out, calling down the hall. "Got him!" Turning forward again, she waved him forward with a reassuring smile. "Come with me, please."

Confused, Alaric moved to follow her. Considering the nurse's calm demeanor, he wondered idly if Gemma had forgotten the room number or dropped her ID somewhere. When they reached a room a few doors down, the nurse gestured for him to head inside. He found Gemma sitting on a cot with a bright strip of lab tape in the crook of her elbow. He faltered at the sight, brow dipping. "What—?"

Gemma looked bashful. "Sorry," she offered. "I'm fine, really. You can go back with Grayson."

"She fainted, but she's fine," Laurel explained, giving Gemma a quick smile. "You mind if I head back?"

Waving her on, Gemma nodded. "I'm fine," she echoed.

Alaric approached to slip his hand into Gemma's, still concerned. "Are you okay? Did you get hurt?" He eyed the colorful tape on her arm.

She was quick to shake her head. "I feel fine now, I promise. Just too much excitement and I'm really tired." She held up her arm. "They took my blood, though."

"Okay, maybe you should lie down," he encouraged.

At his insistence, Gemma stretched out. Alaric sat on the edge of the cot, holding her hand in silence. They listened to the constant hum of conversation and machinery and Alaric watched as Gemma's breathing evened out.

Gently setting her hand down so as not to disturb her, Alaric paced to the window. He considered the whirlwind of events over the past few days. There had been the anticipation of seeing one another again, the wedding that had finally come and gone, a last-minute flight across the country, and the stress of Grayson's condition. It was no wonder she was feeling out of sorts.

When Alaric heard movement, he turned to see a doctor at the door. Quickly crossing to meet him, Alaric stepped into the hallway. He wanted to give Gemma a few minutes of rest, if possible.

"Do you mind if we let her sleep? Did the blood test say anything?"

"Are you family? The husband?" the doctor asked, gesturing to Alaric.

He didn't even hesitate to nod.

"Well, nothing to worry about," the doctor assured, looking preoccupied. "She's dehydrated and anemic. She mentioned a flight today, so that probably tipped the scales."

"That—" Alaric paused, unsure. "That sounds bad. Why is she dehydrated? Does she know she's anemic?"

The doctor eyed him. "She's going to need extra fluids. I'll have a nurse bring over an IV, but she needs to get on prenatals to treat the low iron."

Alaric was silent. His first thought was that he had misheard.

"What?" he asked.

Alaric knew enough to know what prenatal vitamins were, but he was struggling to understand their relevance in the situation.

"Oh, I'm sorry," the doctor said, easily recognizing new-parent shock. "Were you not aware your wife was pregnant?"

Alaric had all but stopped breathing.

"Congrats," the doctor offered. "And her blood suggests multiples, so now you understand why she needs to focus more on hydration and start the vitamins."

The doctor seemed to be waiting for a response, so Alaric managed a stiff nod.

His mind, on the other hand, was chanting "multiples."

"I'll order an ultrasound, see if we can't get you two some more information."

♥ ♠ ♦ ♣

Alaric: Help. Room 8446.
Parker: Coming

When Parker stepped into the room, he found Alaric standing against one wall, Gemma sleeping on a cot on the opposite side. Before he could open his mouth to speak, Alaric was backing him up into the hall and down a few doors.

Parker's confusion was clear as he shook Alaric off. "What? What's going on?"

Alaric had regained the ability to breathe, but he was having difficulty with control. His chest rose and collapsed with the rising panic, struggling not to fall into hyperventilation.

"Al?" Parker asked, gripping his friend's shoulder. "I've never seen you like this, mate. What's wrong?"

Shakily, Alaric raked his hands down his face. "Gemma," he said, still processing what he'd just learned. He had a hard time voicing it, wringing his clammy hands together. Ultimately, he could only force out the single word, but he didn't have to say much more. "Pregnant."

Shock, though not nearly as deep as Alaric's, hit Parker squarely in the chest. After a moment of stunned silence, a brilliant smile broke out across the half-Australian's face, and he let out a joyous laugh. "Fuck off!"

A few stares turned in their direction, but Alaric and Parker were too absorbed in their conversation to care.

"Pregnant," Alaric repeated, looking desperately lost.

Since they'd known one another, they'd joked that if any of them were to knock someone up, it would be Grayson. Alaric was the last person Parker ever expected to be in an unexpected pregnancy situation and he was equal parts amused and concerned.

As a good friend invested in ensuring Alaric wasn't taken advantage of, he had to verify the facts.

"And you're sure it's yours?"

Alaric's expression morphed as anger rose to the surface. There was no questioning who the baby— babies—belonged to. Alaric knew they were his, despite always having worn protection. In his mind, there was no alternative to consider.

"Okay, okay," Parker was quick to assure, dismissing the line of questioning. "I had to ask."

They stood there, leaning against the wall side-by-side. Alaric, thinking of a new future, and Parker, imagining how this would never happen for him and Sadie. It didn't necessarily upset him, but he worried how she might react to the news. Throughout their lives together, he wondered if all pregnancy news would be hard for Sadie to hear. He suddenly wished he'd asked her to come with him. Grayson's accident had shaken him, and he'd spent the entire lonely flight terrified that he might arrive to find his friend hadn't survived. If that had happened, he would have needed Sadie, to hold him and pick up the pieces.

"Do you think she knows?" Parker asked finally, shaking Alaric back to the present.

Alaric hadn't considered that possibility and he took a moment to wonder. Gemma had been drinking heavily at the wedding, and they'd been inseparable in the few days after.

"She doesn't know," Alaric concluded.

"You've got to tell her."

"I know." Alaric sighed and rubbed the exhaustion from his face.

"No, mate, you have to tell her now," Parker insisted, gesturing down the hall.

Alaric watched, panic swelling once again, as a nurse pushed an ultrasound machine into Gemma's hospital room.

Gemma had roused and smiled sleepily as a nurse arrived. "Must have dozed off."

"Dr. Miller just wants us to have you checked out," the nurse explained, positioning the machine beside Gemma's bed, and pulling on a fresh pair of gloves.

Gemma gave a slow nod, but she was confused by the presence of machinery. "I honestly feel fine now," she assured.

Alaric stumbled in then and Gemma looked up, the sight of him causing her eyes to widen. He was looking between her and the machine, not speaking, looking unnerved and uncomfortable.

"Are you okay?" Gemma asked, concerned. She watched as Alaric struggled to nod, but she was distracted by the nurse at her side. She was still trying to understand why they needed an imaging machine.

"It's—" Alaric attempted, throat going dry as he pointed. First, to the machine, and then, to his own stomach.

Quiet, Gemma watched him repeat the movement. It took her a solid thirty seconds to connect the dots before it hit her. With a gasp, her hands lifted to cover her mouth even as she breathed, "No!"

The nurse glanced between the two, realization sinking in. "You didn't know?" she smiled.

Gemma's pulse skyrocketed, shaking her head quickly in response. Her first reaction was dread; this couldn't be happening.

"Let me give you two a minute," the nurse winked.

Lost, Gemma watched the nurse retreat. Her eyes fell to the ultrasound machine again, her breath coming short and fast.

"I should— I should pee on a stick," Gemma mumbled as Alaric approached, her panic clear. "I'm sure I'm not—"

"You are," he whispered.

"No—" she argued. "We always— we were careful—"

"You are," he repeated, reaching for her hand.

Gemma stared back at him, lost for words. They hadn't planned for this, she wasn't sure if they ever wanted this, and they definitely weren't ready for it.

"A baby?" she finally breathed. With the excitement of the wedding and traveling between New Jersey, New York, and Las Vegas, she hadn't been tracking her period. Now that she was forced to do the math, she realized it was a little over two weeks late. His smile was partially from nerves, but it was there.

Slowly, Alaric lifted his free hand and raised two fingers in correction.

Gemma stared in confusion, watching him point the two fingers towards her stomach. As realization hit her, she gave a quiet cry of disbelief. Two babies? She was certain she was going to faint again, and Alaric quickly took her face between his palms. "I'm right here."

"Is this really happening?" she whispered, panicked.

Tipping forward, Alaric lowered his forehead to hers. "Unless you don't want—"

A new emotion crashed into Gemma at the careful way he'd worded himself. He was giving her an out, reminding her this didn't have to be an eventuality. However, she felt a soft ache developing; a craving to have a baby that was a piece of them, and a future with Alaric.

"No," Gemma mumbled, pulling back to look at him. She was pro-choice, but she couldn't imagine choosing not to have Alaric's babies. Quietly, unsure, she echoed, "Unless *you* don't want—"

Alaric smiled, shaking his head. "We would have gotten here eventually."

♥ ♠ ♦ ♣

A short time later, Gemma and Alaric rejoined their friends with big news. Gemma was between six and seven weeks along, meaning they'd gotten pregnant one of their first times together, astonishing them both.

Parker was grinning, amused to high heaven at the latest development.

"Pregnant?" Laurel breathed in disbelief. "With *twins*?" The thought of Mr. No-work-all-play having children was startling to her.

"My mom was a twin," Alaric explained. "I just never thought…"

"My parents are going to disown me," Gemma laughed, a little queasy.

With a bit of effort, Grayson joked, "Name one…after me."

Alaric rolled his eyes. "Not happening, Gray. You didn't even die."

"Wow," he scoffed, coughing shortly. "Some friend."

Chapter Forty-Four

♥

That evening, Parker secured himself a room at a hotel nearby and crashed into bed. He hadn't felt so tired in years and wondered if his age of thirty-two was finally catching up to him. He couldn't drink like he could in his twenties, so why should he be able to handle stress the same way?

Parker rolled onto his back and kicked off his shoes, dialing Sadie for an update.

She picked up on the first ring.

"Hey, baby, how's Grayson?"

Parker smiled at the sound of her voice, feeling the unexpected prick of tears rising.

"Parker?" she pressed.

"Yeah," Parker replied, clearing his throat. "I'm here. Gray's gonna be okay."

Exhaling in relief, Sadie let that news settle. Laurel had been sending her a couple of texts as well, but it was good to hear Parker confirm his friend's prognosis.

"That's great. Are you okay?"

"I wish you were here," he confessed, lifting his free hand to press his fingers to his eyes and stave off the moisture welling.

"What's wrong?" she asked, concerned at the sound of his voice. "I'm worried about you."

"This is hard," he admitted. "Seeing Gray like that. Seeing Al—"

"Alaric? What's wrong with Alaric?"

Parker sighed, wishing she had been with him so she could already know.

"He's fine, but he and Gemma came out here," he explained. "She wasn't feeling well and…it turns out they're pregnant. With twins."

Surprise lengthened the silence between them before Sadie offered a quiet laugh. "Wow. Twins."

"I know," he laughed. "Hard to picture Al with kids, but it's happening."

"Is he okay? I'm sure that was a shock."

Parker thought back to the conversation he and Alaric had had in the hallway together, and Parker replied confidently, "Other than being terrified, he's thrilled."

"I'm happy for him," Sadie replied honestly. There would always be a moment when she thought of her inability to have children when children were mentioned, but it was an unavoidable part of life.

"Uncle Parker," Sadie added, musing over the title.

His laugh was more genuine, discomfort ebbing.

"I wish you were here," he repeated.

Sadie hadn't expressly said she would or wouldn't go to Vegas with him, but she'd helped him pack and then he was gone. Parker hadn't been thinking. If he had been, he would have asked her to accompany him. Thinking about it now, he knew she would have said yes.

"I can still come," Sadie assured. "If you need me."

It seemed silly considering he would only be in Las Vegas for a night or two, but Parker found he didn't care.

"I need you."

A knock at the door had Parker clearing his throat. "Sorry, I've got to go," he apologized.

"Sure," Sadie replied. "I'll get a flight out as soon as I can."

"Thank you."

Parker opened the door for Alaric, surprised to find him standing alone in the hallway. "Where's your baby mama?" he teased, but Alaric's smile was weak.

"We're down in three seventy-seven," Alaric offered, gesturing towards the elevators.

"Want to come in?" Parker asked.

Alaric shook his head. "I want to get back and make sure she's okay. I just wanted to check in with you."

Parker nodded, appreciative. "I'm alright. You're the one with the baby news."

"Don't remind me," Alaric sighed as he raked his hair back. He seemed to linger, but he wasn't sure what to say.

"You're going to be fine," Parker assured him. "Honestly. The two of you, you'll be okay."

"I know," Alaric sighed. "I've just got to figure out where we're moving first."

Parker shrugged, leaning in the doorway. "Gemma's from New York, right? I can help, in the city or on Long Island…"

Alaric scoffed. "I can't exactly afford either."

"I can help," Parker repeated seriously.

"I appreciate it, but I can do this. We can do this," he assured, taking a deep breath.

Parker studied his friend, feeling a pang of sorrow to know that Alaric and Gemma would be raising their children outside of New York. "I know we're not usually in the same place at the same time, but you're having kids, mate. I'd love to be a part of that."

Alaric was touched by Parker's genuine thoughts. He reached out to give his friend a hug, nodding. "You will, Park. Of course you will."

Clearing his throat, Parker nodded. He believed it.

"Uncle Parker," Alaric added, the tension easing as they both laughed.

♥ ♠ ♦ ♣

Alaric rejoined Gemma in their hotel room, thankful for Hannah's help with logistics. After the stress of the day and the life-altering news they'd received, they needed space to decompress.

Laurel had stayed behind with Grayson, though she'd gone back to the hotel for a shower and power nap while their friends had kept Grayson company.

Gemma carried their takeout to the bed, putting a towel down before she pulled out the containers. "Not very glamorous, but it'll do," she offered.

Alaric pulled the lid and straw from his soda, taking a long gulp from the cup.

"Thirsty?" she mused.

Aside from the brief time alone pre-ultrasound, they hadn't discussed next steps or future plans. It seemed far too soon to be talking about anything concrete, but Alaric knew that the remaining seven and a half months would pass in the blink of an eye. He needed to start looking for other work, something that gave him a healthier work-life balance.

"Alaric?"

"Sorry," he said, lowering himself to sit. "Just thinking."

"Yeah," she nodded. "I know what you mean."

"I need to get out of Jersey," he told her.

Gemma was surprised to hear him so committed to the idea and gave a slow nod. "If that's what you want."

"Is there somewhere specific you'd like to be?" he asked.

Looking uncomfortable with the power Alaric was offering, Gemma pulled a tomato off her grilled chicken sandwich. She didn't want to dictate where their future would unfold. They'd be starting a life together, and Gemma wasn't sure she wanted that life to be down the block from her parents.

"I'm open to ideas," she finally replied.

"There are one hundred ninety-five countries in the world," Alaric replied, cracking a smile. "Want to narrow it down for me?"

Rolling her eyes, Gemma stipulated, "America. East coast. Direct flights to

New York."

"I can do that," Alaric agreed easily.

♥ ♠ ♦ ♣

Grayson: Goooood morning Las Vegas!
Alaric: You're chipper.
Laurel: I caved…gave him his phone back.
Parker: Isn't he supposed to be resting?
Laurel: Grayson does what Grayson wants.
Parker: What's the latest?
Grayson: I've made a miraculous recovery and you should worship me as a modern-day miracle
Alaric: So, he's fine then.
Laurel: Lung is better. Discharging him tonight but he's got to rest for a few days before he can be cleared to fly.
Parker: Sadie and I will come by soon.
Laurel: Sadie?
Parker: She flew in this morning.
Grayson: Everyone bring sunglasses so mrs. Campbell's ring doesn't blind you
Laurel: He's got a point…that thing is MASSIVE.
Grayson: You know what else is massive??
Laurel: I'd say it's the drugs talking but you'd all know it's a lie.

♥ ♠ ♦ ♣

As soon as Sadie stepped into the hospital room Grayson threw up a hand as if to shield his eyes.

"He's been waiting all day to do this," Laurel said, unamused.

Sadie happily played into his teasing, waving her ring around the room as Laurel stood to greet her with a hug.

"Wow," Laurel laughed, getting a good look. "That's something, all right."

"Isn't it?" Sadie smiled. She moved closer to Grayson, her smile genuine. "You look awful."

"Thank you," Grayson grinned, wincing slightly. He was on less pain killers today, and the aching was only just tolerable.

"Glad you're alright," she said, patting his forearm. "Laurel was inconsolable."

Laurel only rolled her eyes in response.

"It was so, so sad," Sadie went on, playful. "She wasn't sure how she'd go on without you. She started looking up bridges to jump off. Unfortunately, there aren't any in Vegas. I recommended Hoover Dam."

"Oh my God, I hate you," Laurel grumbled, dropping back down into a chair. "He's going to be insufferable now."

"He's always been insufferable," Sadie assured.

"Right," Parker laughed. "Well, you seem much better today," he told Grayson, sitting on the edge of the cot.

"I feel better," Grayson paused. "Well, worse. But…they say that's good."

"If you say so," Parker sighed. He watched his friend, studying the shape he was in. He held Sadie's hand as he cleared his throat, broaching the subject of what had happened. "It's time to talk about Roman," he said.

All humor left the room and Grayson sighed, coughing for a few moments. He didn't doubt Alaric would have filled Parker in on the incident, but he also didn't look forward to arguing over his lack of interest in pressing charges.

"You haven't spoken to the police," Parker stated. "Why?"

Sadie squeezed Parker's hand supportively, the geode on her finger glinting in the fluorescence.

Grayson shifted in the bed, careful of his IV line. "Not worth it."

"What?" Laurel balked. "Of course, it's worth it. He needs to go to jail."

"Wasn't just Roman," Grayson argued. He'd had company that Grayson couldn't identify.

"Cameras," Parker reminded, bypassing the excuse. "Why aren't you ratting him out?"

It was obvious Grayson was reluctant to say, but he recognized he wasn't getting out of the conversation.

"He threatened Six."

All eyes shifted to Laurel who was staring at Grayson incredulously.

Parker and Sadie knew what had happened between Laurel and Roman in the first place, and how Grayson had retaliated with his fists. It made sense that Roman knew Laurel was his weakness, and that he'd hold it against him, but Parker thought it was likely an empty threat.

"He's not going to do anything to Laurel," he told his friend expectantly.

"And she wouldn't be stupid enough to follow a bogus invitation like that," Sadie added pointedly.

Grayson seemed undeterred. "Doesn't matter. He got his revenge. It's over."

"It's not over until he's behind bars," Laurel said, angry that Grayson was using the idea of protecting her as an excuse to not act. "And once he is, he can't come anywhere near me. Or you."

"It's my call."

Laurel rocked back as if slapped. It was the most juvenile thing she'd ever heard from Grayson. It equated to 'you can't make me' and Laurel couldn't believe his childish behavior. She found herself muttering an excuse to take a walk and cool off.

♥ ♠ ♦ ♣

Late afternoon, as they waited for news of Grayson's discharge paperwork, Laurel was still feeling the sting of his stubbornness.

"How's your mom?"

Laurel was surprised at the line of questioning, managing a small shrug. "I haven't really talked to her."

"Give her a call," Grayson suggested.

"Press charges against Roman," Laurel shot back.

They seemed to be at an impasse and Laurel sighed. "Sorry."

Grayson shrugged as much as his sling would allow. He was dressed with help from Laurel and seated atop the sheets, eager to be free of the confining hospital bed. Gemma and Alaric had stopped by briefly, but their focus was elsewhere. They wanted to return to Schenectady and share the news with Gemma's parents, as terrifying as it was. Grayson couldn't blame them; the unexpected pregnancy was enough to shake him, too.

"We've got the hotel room through Friday," he reminded. Per the doctor's instructions, he would need to give his lungs a few days of rest before he could board a flight. "Will you stay?" Grayson wasn't sure if Laurel felt obligated to get back to her mother.

"I can ask Alaric—" he began, but Laurel was shaking her head.

"I'll stay," she assured. Grayson was injured, and Laurel hadn't considered leaving him to fend for himself even once. "Of course, I'll stay."

"When I can travel, I'm going to head back to North Carolina," Grayson shared. They hadn't expressly discussed his destination post-Vegas, but he'd made mention to his friends about his potential plans. "Come with me," he requested.

Laurel was quiet for a long minute, picking at a loose thread. She'd allowed herself to become completely consumed by Grayson again, neglecting her responsibilities at home. Of course, he hadn't been in control of what had happened, and his injuries easily demanded her attention. However, she hadn't spoken to her mom since leaving town. She loved Grayson, but she didn't love herself when this happened.

"I can't," she told him finally, meeting his hopeful stare. Before he attempted to talk her into it, she stated firmly, "I need to go home."

Sensing the finality, Grayson nodded. "Of course." He couldn't hide his disappointment, but if Laurel wanted or needed to go home, then Grayson would respect her decision. "You'll come see me when you can?"

"Yeah," Laurel replied easily, but she worried it wouldn't be as easy as Grayson made it sound.

"Hello, hello," Sadie called into the hospital room, stepping through the door to reveal Parker right on her heels. Black patent leather pumps, to be exact.

"Hey," Laurel greeted, looking over Sadie's appearance. "Why are you all dressed up?"

"Big day," Sadie offered, waving towards Grayson. "Discharge day."

"National holiday," Grayson agreed, accepting a careful hug from Parker.

"Are you guys heading back to New York soon?" Laurel asked, looking between them.

Sadie hung on Parker's arm as she explained, "We're going to stick around a few days. Gamble a little. Forget all our troubles."

"Troubles," Grayson said with a failed attempt at scoffing. When he recovered from his coughing fit, he gestured between the pair as he pointed out, "You're engaged millionaires."

Parker smirked, mimicking the gesture. "What about you two?"

Laurel and Grayson exchanged glances, smiles tight between them. "I'm going home," Laurel confirmed. "In a few days, probably."

Grayson looked to Parker. "I'm thinking about North Carolina for a while."

Laurel glanced over at him.

A while?

CHAPTER FORTY-FIVE

♣

As the sun set and Vegas came alive, Sadie and Parker found themselves enjoying a few hours of gambling and drinks at The Venetian. He slid an arm around her waist as she stumbled a half step. "I can't carry you if you break an ankle in those heels," he warned, equally tipsy.

They strolled away from the hum of excitement on the casino floor, towards the popular Grand Canal Shoppes. Sadie tipped her head back, staring up at the famous faux sky. "I've always liked this," she admitted.

"Tourist charades?" Parker mused.

"The *dependability*," she countered, gesturing up towards the ceiling, painted blue with fluffy clouds.

Parker could only smile. "I never thought about it that way."

"Everyone's pictures look the same here," she continued. They slowed to a stop over a small stone bridge, watching the gondolas pass by. "Nothing changes."

Curious, Parker turned to watch her instead. "Isn't that sad?" he asked, brushing her hair off her shoulder. "Shouldn't things change? Evolve?"

Sadie didn't think so, or at least she didn't used to. "I like dependability," she replied.

"Am I dependable?" he asked with the quirk of a brow.

"So far, so good," she assured, leaning forward to catch his lips in a light kiss.

The topic still sat with Parker as a peculiar one. He couldn't help but ask, "Is there something in your life that's not dependable?"

Sadie held her tongue. Her go-to response of "men" still might apply to the world at large in her experience, but now that she was off the market the issue was less prevalent in her life. Shaking her head, Sadie dismissed the question. "I have you," she said with certainty, sliding a palm up Parker's chest.

Catching her hand, Parker leaned in to brush their lips together sweetly. She certainly did have him; his heart and his balls, wrapped around her little finger. He gave a low hum, withdrew, and nodded down the paved walkway. "Let's shop."

Sadie easily fell into step. "He knows the magic word…" she teased.

Mostly, they enjoyed window shopping. The Venetian featured plenty of high-end stores, but nothing New York didn't already offer. It was only when Parker spied a distinct white gown in a window display that he considered making a purchase.

They seemed to slow in unison, eyes drawn to a mannequin wearing a romantic, vintage lace dress. It had an open back and featured a figure-hugging trumpet silhouette.

"Did we just find my dress?" Sadie whispered.

Parker turned to her, overwhelmed at the mere idea of Sadie in something so stunning. "I can't wait to marry you," he confessed. A thrill went through him at a sudden idea, feeling reckless, but certain. "Let's do it. Right now."

Sadie pulled her attention from the gown, her lips parting in shock. "Now?" She had expected a long engagement, assuming they might need time to test the waters of their relationship. They'd jumped so fast into committing to one another, it seemed crazy to take another huge leap like this. However, that seemed to be their specialty.

"You're sure?" she asked around the lump in her throat. "You don't need trial and error before we tie the knot?"

Parker stared her down. "I don't."

"And you want to get married in Las Vegas?" she laughed, reaching up to wipe beneath an eye as emotion swelled.

"I do," he grinned.

"I do, too," Sadie whispered, a laugh bubbling past her lips.

Armed with the perfect gown, Sadie and Parker found the closest chapel with a one-hour-or-less guarantee. It was the opposite of the glamorous lifestyle they were used to, but that made it even more special. Sadie had only two requests; no Elvis impersonator, and they'd prepare handwritten vows.

The chapel had more neon on the exterior than Sadie had ever seen off the strip, and the gift shop was equal in size to the small church-like venue. They'd selected the Speedy Love Package, which included a handful of photos to document their life-altering decision.

When it was their turn, after two couples ahead of them, Sadie and Parker stood hand-in-hand. They faced each other, echoes of one another's' nerves. Hearing the previous couples swear to love and honor one another all the days of their lives had ratcheted up the anxiety, but neither had cold feet.

With a chime of bells, the overdramatic officiant began.

"Sadie Bache and Parker Campbell! Today is one of the happiest days of your lives. Your marriage is a promise to share one life together. Will you love and honor each other daily, remembering this promise to one another?"

In unison, they replied, "We will."

The attendant handed cheap gold-plated bands to the couple, a $59.99 add-on that Sadie intended to treasure.

"And now, the vows. Parker?"

Parker took Sadie's left hand, the ring poised. They hadn't had the time to lament over their wedding vows, but Parker had thought of a few choice things he wanted to convey to this woman who stole his breath. His voice was thick, accent more audible as he began.

"I'm so ready to begin a life with you, my love. I never knew what to look for in a partner until I met you. I see you as my equal and I want to be there for you however you need, always."

He gave a weak smile, stage-whispering, "How'd I do?"

Sadie sniffed, nodding quickly. She wiggled her fingers, laughing when he slipped the ring into place. As the cheap metal slotted against her splendid engagement ring, the pair laughed.

"Sadie?" the officiant prompted.

"Parker," she began, pausing to take a deep breath. "I never wanted to settle down. I saw it as defeat. It took me thirty-three years to understand that love doesn't mean sacrificing your independence. It's a choice to share your life, to build something new and wonderful you can't do alone. I want this with you. I'm sorry if I ever made you think differently."

Parker blinked back the threat of tears, nodding.

She began to move the ring onto his finger but paused. When he glanced up, she added one final piece to her vows.

"And I'll do anything to give you a family. We have so much. We can provide a child with an amazing life."

It took every bit of Parker's self-control to keep his distance and wait for permission to kiss her. He knew what it took Sadie to say such a thing, and he also knew that they would find a way to grow their family in time.

"Do you, Parker Campbell, take Sadie Bache for your lawful wedded wife, to have and to hold, from this day forward, for better, for worse, in sickness and in health, as long as you both shall live?"

"I do."

"Do you, Sadie Bache, take Parker Campbell for your lawful wedded husband, to have and to-"

"I do."

"Sadie..." Parker chastised, laughing in disbelief.

"Sorry," Sadie grimaced. "Sorry, can we go again?"

The officiant smiled, "To have and to hold, from this day forward, for better, for worse, in sickness and in health, as long as you both shall live?"

Sadie took a deep breath and stated easily, "I do."

♥ ♠ ♦ ♣

The newlyweds tripped over one another as they hurried to undress. The hotel door swung shut and Sadie abandoned her new ivory heels as they quickly crossed the room.

"Did you mean what you said?" Parker asked against her mouth, breathless as he pulled his crisp button-down free of his trousers. "About a family?"

Nodding, Sadie slid her hands into the collar of his shirt and pushed it free of his shoulders. Once he'd rid himself of the clothing on his top half, Sadie pulled him back into her chest.

"Because there's adoption," he offered, having clearly been considering options. "And surrogates."

"Can we talk about it after our honeymoon?"

With a soft laugh against her mouth, Parker mumbled, "Honeymooning in Vegas. How original."

"Oh, no," Sadie chuckled, humming in appreciation when his lips traveled down the column of her throat. "We are going somewhere glamorous as soon as possible."

"Anything you want," he assured. "Now, how do I get this off of you?" His hands traced her figure, hugged by vintage lace.

Turning, Sadie gathered her dark curls over a shoulder and revealed the clasp atop the open-back. Parker pressed his lips to her warm skin, drawing the material down her shoulders. Sadie let her eyes fall closed, savoring the moment. She wondered privately how she had never known someone like Parker could exist in the world. And, now that she did, she was happy to know she would never have to settle for less.

"We got married," Parker mumbled in awe, as if still reconciling the fact that they'd made good on their sudden plan.

"We did," Sadie replied, a soft smile playing on her lips.

Parker helped her to turn and gently swept the fabric from her body. Carefully, he laid the gown over an armchair and returned to pull Sadie closer.

"Mrs. Campbell," he grinned, walking her back towards the bed.

"Mr. Bache," she countered playfully, hands dropping to his fly.

As they lost the remainder of their clothes, Parker offered, "Should we hyphenate?"

Shaking her head, Sadie drew him down atop her. Her gaze was heated, body thrumming. "Let's talk about it later."

♥ ♠ ♦ ♣

Gemma sat crossed legged on another hotel bed, this time far from the excitement of Las Vegas. They'd flown back to Albany, with the intention of speaking with her parents, but she'd asked for a few more days to prepare. Alaric was in no rush either and had easily agreed. He was cashing in on more vacation days, but with new priorities and a decision to move on soon he was happy to make use of them.

Chewing on her thumbnail and listening to the quiet hiss of the shower, Gemma found her thoughts wandering. Since finding out about the pregnancy four days ago, they'd done little but think, worry, and stress. Gemma dropped her gaze to her still flat stomach. There was no faint curve, nor was there any nausea. If she hadn't felt faint at the hospital, how long would they have gone without knowing? Considering it was twins, she didn't think very long. Groaning, Gemma dropped onto her back. "I'm going to be huge," she complained.

Abandoning her spiraling thoughts, Gemma rolled off the bed and hurried for the bathroom. Without a word, she swept the curtain aside and climbed into the shower behind Alaric, clothing and all. Her arms went around his middle, hugging herself tightly to his back.

Blinking water from his eyes, Alaric laughed at Gemma's sudden presence. He reached back, feeling fabric atop her skin. "Are you in your clothes?"

Gemma whined, pressing her forehead between his damp shoulder blades. Inhaling his scent, taking comfort in his warmth, Gemma kept herself locked against him.

Alaric sighed, patting her where he could reach. "Loosen," he said, waiting until her arms slackened. He rotated and smiled weakly down at her. His tattooed body blocked most of the spray, but she wasn't staying dry. "Arms up," he instructed.

Gemma obeyed in silence and allowed him to peel away the shirt that had begun to cling to her skin.

"Do you want to know why I'm not scared?" Alaric offered as he slid his wet palms down her bare arms to catch her hands.

Gemma nodded quickly, already calming from the even tone he used.

"Because all we need is a house."

She echoed, "A house?"

"Somewhere to live," he explained. "I've boiled it down to the very next step, and that's what it is."

Gemma wasn't so convinced. "Telling my parents is next," she pointed out.

Alaric winced, shrugging. "Okay, fine. After that. Once they know, we just need to find a place to live."

"How do you figure?"

"If we have a place to live, then we have a place to raise the kids," he answered easily.

"I guess, but—"

"Just focus on incubating our babies," Alaric told her, hands guiding her pants off her hips and revealing her inked feather.

Heat rose in Gemma's face at his words, paired with his touch as he undressed her. She liked the sound of that. *Our babies.*

"Let me worry about everything else," he requested. The last few days had been intense; he'd barely slept at first, thinking through the drastic changes coming their way. He thought about getting a new job, relocating, finding a hospital for the birth, choosing schools, and by the time he was calculating how old he would be when he needed to afford two college tuitions at once, he'd realized there was no way he could survive doing this for the rest of his life.

The stress of micromanaging every step of his life was a burden he couldn't afford to take on, for his and his new family's sanity. He needed to identify milestones and commit to each one independently. He needed to clear the slate for Gemma to focus on herself and her health and reassure her that he was worth the commitment of a life together.

"This is just happening really fast," Gemma said, for the tenth time that week.

"I know," he assured, pressing his lips to her forehead. "Trust me, I know."

"I just don't want you to wake up one day and realize this wasn't what you wanted…"

Alaric lifted a pair of fingers to Gemma's lips to silence her, shaking his head. The look he offered conveyed just how ridiculous those words sounded to him.

With a breath, Alaric admitted, "I've been trying to figure out how to keep you in my life since Atlantic City." There was no part of him that wanted out of this situation. The idea of kids so soon had him nervous, but he'd never questioned wanting a life with her.

Gemma stretched up to kiss him, reassured by his certainty, and warmed by his devotion. "So, you got me pregnant on purpose?" she accused.

Alaric laughed, turning them so that Gemma was beneath the showerhead. As she squinted under the spray, he assured, "Getting pregnant was one hundred percent unplanned, but I wouldn't change a thing."

"That's a lie," she accused, handing him the shampoo.

As Alaric lathered her hair, he couldn't help but tease, "Would you have preferred marriage? Would that have been a better way to lock you down?"

Gemma's eyes were closed to prevent the suds from falling into her vision. She placed her hands on Alaric's bare sides, pinching playfully.

"Is that a no?" he laughed, mildly shocked. Did she not want to marry him?

Gemma leaned back to rinse out her hair as she explained, "I don't want to get married just because we have to."

This time, Alaric was quiet. He hadn't considered her wanting to delay tying the knot. Unfortunately, it was important for more reasons than his personal preference.

"We'll need you on my insurance," he explained, gaze dipping down her breasts, to her soft stomach. "And wouldn't you want us all to have the same last name?"

He was right, she realized. Marriage wasn't just about the vow of commitment, it had practical benefits that were equally important. Gemma felt a wave of shame over how naive she was, vowing to better herself. "Of course," she told him. "You're right, I'm sorry."

The apology had Alaric's brow furrowing. "We can look into other options if—"

"No," she assured, confessing, "I just didn't want you to think you had to marry me because I'm pregnant."

"First of all," Alaric smirked, turning Gemma at the shoulder so he could soap up her back. "*We're* pregnant." He dragged the lather around her sides, hands encasing her stomach affectionately.

"And second of all?" Gemma prompted, her hands going over the backs of his.

"I'd like to be your husband."

Tears crested her eyes and Gemma shook her head, turning again to face him. She was clearly enamored with him and so thankful that he seemed to return her feelings. She brought her hand to his abdomen, letting her fingers trail downward over his muscles to dip through the smattering of dark hair, teasing down his heavy length.

Alaric exhaled a heavy breath, watching her fingers as they trailed between them.

"I love you, you know," she said.

"I know," he smiled, leaning down to catch her lips in a soft, slow kiss.

Gemma's fingers curled around him, feeling him stiffen in her loose hand. Nudging her lips to his and feeling the warm water trickle across them, she offered a slow stroke of her hand from base to tip.

Alaric's hands slipped into her damp hair, cradling her head as he licked at her lips. "Your mouth," he requested.

Gemma nodded; at that moment she wasn't sure she could deny him anything.

Alaric rotated them once more so his back blocked her from the spray, giving her room as she lowered to her knees in the hotel tub. She reached for his length, leaning forward to take him into the heat of her mouth.

With a quiet breath, Alaric's eyelids grew heavy. He had a vision of her, belly round with their children, curled up together in bed. It was such a simple, innocent picture, but his arousal was spiking. He supposed it wasn't that odd for a man to be turned on by the thought of a woman carrying his baby, but he was rock hard as he imagined it with Gemma's lips around his cock.

Within minutes, Alaric's body tensed and his abs visibly clenched as he came. Gemma was quick to steady him, milking him of his release. With slow strokes and soft nudges, she helped him down from his climax.

After their long, hot shower, Alaric returned the favor happily on fresh sheets. As they settled down for one final night before breaking the news to her parents,

Alaric pulled his phone off the charger. He saw a thread had been active while they'd been fooling around, the first message including a photo of Parker and Sadie in a Vegas wedding chapel, lip locked.

At his slack-jawed expression, Gemma paused in turning down the bed. "What is it?"

Silently, he turned the phone around.

As she took in the obvious scene, Gemma gasped. "They got married!"

"I can't believe it," Alaric mumbled at the irony. "They beat us to the altar."

Exiting the conversation, he checked another string of messages, all from the same sender.

Laurel: Hey
Laurel: You there?
Laurel: I need to talk to you.
Laurel: You need to do something about what happened to Grayson.
Laurel: Roman can't get away with this.
Laurel: Hello?

Alaric sighed, feeling weight settle back onto his shoulders. Of course, he agreed; Roman shouldn't be allowed to escape prosecution, but Grayson had made his feelings known on the matter. Why would Laurel press Alaric to ignore his friend's wishes, and why was it fair to put the responsibility squarely on him? Considering recent events, Alaric had plenty to deal with without the burden of getting vengeance for Grayson.

CHAPTER FORTY-SIX

♦

Grayson's recovery over the next couple of days was rote; lots of sleep thanks to pain meds, showers with Laurel's help, and a soft-food diet. The hardest part was forcing himself to sleep on his back due to his rib injuries. That, and getting Laurel to loosen up with her policing of his pills.

"Two," Grayson requested, making a come-hither motion as Laurel approached. He lay supine, wincing a little at the discomfort in his side.

"One," Laurel countered, holding out a single pill.

"This is a level seven pain moment," he argued, pointing to his bare chest. "We agreed on two pills for anything over level five."

"You're just making up arbitrary numbers!"

"You came up with the system!"

Laurel added a second pill to his palm, sighing. "Whatever."

Grayson grinned as much as his bruised face would allow. "If I get addicted and start abusing my meds, you can have a big fat I-told-you-so moment," he assured. Thankfully, he'd gotten his breath back enough to return to his typical argumentative self.

Due to Grayson's lack of a sleep schedule, Laurel napped at odd times throughout the day as well. She awoke once to find Grayson sitting up, eating from a large container of egg drop soup. Confused, she'd asked, "Where did you even get Chinese food?" It hadn't been something she'd stocked up on from her grocery run. "Delivery," was his reply. "Any excuse," she'd mumbled.

Now, Grayson was propped up in bed, scrolling endlessly through his phone. He'd been able to cease wearing a sling and had retained a mild ache in his shoulder. His complexion had improved, too. He felt more alert finally and had started to look at flights. Laurel sensed the countdown as if it were an elephant in the room.

"Let me see your side?" she requested.

Grayson nodded, setting his phone down and folding the sheet back from his body. She'd been keeping an eye on his injuries a couple of times a day, and he seemed content to humor her. The fact that she thought she would be able to sense if something was amiss amused him.

"So?" he prompted. "How's it looking, Dr. Price?"

Laurel ran the pads of her fingertips across his skin. The bruising was changing, fading from reddish purple to an awful greenish yellow, but the coloration suggested he was healing on schedule. On his cheek, he'd graduated to being butterfly closure-free. The cuts were healing, the bruising following the same changes seen elsewhere on his body. Sensing she was ready to check his hand, Grayson proudly held up the middle finger splint.

"You're lucky you're cute," she grumbled, nodding to confirm her assessment was through. Laurel's attention was drawn away as her phone began to ring.

"Paging Dr. Price…" Grayson teased.

Smiling, Laurel retrieved her phone and grinned at the caller ID. "You crazy bitch," Laurel greeted Sadie as she answered.

"Hello to you, too," Sadie replied, laughing.

"You eloped!" Laurel accused, still beside herself over the photo she and Grayson had been sent a couple of days ago. Although she had only known Sadie for two months, the woman seemed to have a limitless supply of excitement in her life. Sadie had yet to return any of Laurel's texts or calls, but Laurel couldn't blame her. "Finally coming up for air? Did Parker survive the honeymoon sex-a-thon?"

"Well, that sounds amazing," Grayson mumbled, carefully getting to his feet. He gestured to the bathroom, assuring Laurel he could manage.

"You'll be pleased to know that my husband is alive and well, and fulfilling all marital duties," Sadie assured happily.

"I'm glad," Laurel laughed. "I'm so happy for you."

"Thank you. But tell me about you guys. How's Grayson healing? I'm sorry I haven't checked in."

Reassuring Sadie that she had other things on her mind and that Grayson was doing fine, she filled her in on their boring daily routine, the copious television they'd been watching, and their plans to take separate flights in a day or two.

"I'm sorry," Sadie offered. She understood that they each had things to take care of but could sympathize that splitting up for any length of time was less than ideal. "You'll go down and see him soon though, right?"

Laurel wished her gut reaction was different, but she felt instantly defensive by the question. She had been upending her life since meeting Grayson and wasn't sure how sustainable it was. Why was she expected to keep moving around to see him? Of course, there was a valid reason now; he was injured. Grayson was going to North Carolina to rest and flying back and forth to Atlantic City would be foolish. Still, it seemed like she was the only one making sacrifices. In addition to neglecting her mom, Laurel felt guilty for neglecting her ultimate goal: New York.

As the silence stretched, Sadie prompted with a twinge of concern, "Or not?"

Sighing, Laurel returned to the present. She wasn't going to vent to Sadie, especially when Grayson was only ten feet away. "We'll see," she replied neutrally, hoping to drop the topic.

Grayson reemerged, holding out his hand. "Let me congratulate the newlyweds."

As Laurel handed over her phone, she realized she hadn't heard the sink running. "Ew, did you not wash your hands?" she accused, looking crestfallen as he handled her cell.

"Is this the new Mrs. Campbell?" Grayson greeted Sadie, walking towards the window to stretch his legs.

"Indeed, it is," Sadie laughed happily. "How're you hanging in there?"

Grayson quickly lowered his voice, cupping his hand around the phone. "I will give you a thousand dollars to bust me out of here right now."

Laurel laughed in disbelief at Grayson's antics. "Unbelievable."

♥ ♠ ♦ ♣

The following week, over four hundred eighty miles separated Grayson and Laurel. He'd returned to accept the offer given to him, awaiting the paperwork process of becoming a homeowner. Laurel had returned to Atlantic City, back to accepting job offers from Alaric and growing her savings.

"Mom?" Laurel stood outside her mother's bedroom door, knocking for the third time. "Mom, you slept in," she called. "Don't you have to go clean the Ryans' place?"

Greeted by silence, Laurel let herself into the small bedroom. She approached the bed, reaching out to gently shake the sleeping woman. "Mom," she repeated. "You've got to get up."

Although not unresponsive, Julia Price only offered a low moan.

Concerned, Laurel shuffled closer and kicked aside a few articles of laundry. She shook harder. "Mom? *Mom.*"

Beneath the bed she heard a telltale clink and stooped to investigate. Empty liquor bottles.

"Goddamnit," Laurel breathed, fisting her hands in the shag carpet. "God*damnit.*"

Later, after Laurel had called to apologize to her mother's client and hidden the fact that she was blackout drunk, she dialed Grayson.

"Six," he greeted, sounding happy as ever to hear from her. "I was just going to call you."

"Lies," she challenged, but his voice brought a small smile to her lips. "How's beach life?"

"Getting colder," he replied. The temperatures were starting to dip below fifty at night now that summer was ending. "But it's nice out here even when it snows."

Laurel quirked a brow. "Have you ever been there when it snows?"

"I've heard," he amended, hopeful. "You'll like it."

The line grew quiet. Laurel wasn't against visiting Grayson, but he was now living in North Carolina, at least part-time. Grayson spoke as if he wanted her to live with him, too, but she had her sights set on New York. The snow wouldn't start for another two to three months, but he was already planting the seed.

"New York's nice in winter, too," she countered gently.

"Sure," Grayson smirked. "Zero sledding, hundred-dollar ice skating…"

She was quick to argue, "Christmas lights, Rockefeller Center, The Nutcracker…"

"That's just Christmas," he replied easily. "I'd love to take you there for Christmas."

She knew he meant well and that he was trying to give her some of what she wanted. Still, it wasn't enough.

"I want to live there, Grayson," she reminded, having avoided the flat-out argument for a while now.

Grayson respected Laurel, but he didn't always understand her motives. "But why?" he sighed, confused. "You don't have a dream job you're trying to land, your mom's not there, I'm not there…"

Laurel found it hard not to take offense when Grayson whittled down her dreams into practicalities. "Sometimes you just want something," she replied.

"Well, I want you," he sighed, clearly sad they hadn't made any progress on the discussion.

"It's not off the table," she offered honestly.

Grayson nodded. If he wanted to move to New York, they might be able to make it work. Unfortunately, he'd just put down roots in another state, and he had a family member in New York that stirred up emotions he had mastered suppressing. Sharing the same state as Delilah would grate on him over time, even if they never saw one another.

"How's your mom?" Grayson offered, hoping to change the subject. "Glad to have you back?"

It seemed everything they discussed that day was meant to compound Laurel's negativity.

"She's drinking too much again," she admitted. "Missed work today."

"Shit," he said, thinking. "Did something happen? Did something trigger it?"

Laurel didn't mean to snap at him, but he was asking questions she couldn't answer. "I'll be sure to ask her when she wakes up."

Silence stretched, neither knowing what to say. It seemed most of their conversations concluded in much the same way lately.

♥ ♠ ♦ ♣

When Alaric finally put his mind to it, he found that an answer came rather easily. Getting retribution for Grayson was possible, especially considering Alaric's position.

He started by making a perfect copy of the fake invitation Roman had used, referencing the photo Laurel had texted him. He changed the date to one in the near future, replaced the MGM Grand's logo with Borgata Hotel & Casino, and updated the room number to an available suite.

It was just as easy to update Borgata's hospitality system to reflect Roman as booking that suite in a few days' time. As a final touch, Alaric tucked the invitation into a Borgata embossed envelope. It looked official, even more official than what Grayson had been given.

Alaric sat back, marveling at his own handiwork. He sent a quick text to Laurel saying she owed him one, and then knocked on management's door. All he had to do was show them the invitation and suspicion followed.

"What's this?" his supervisor asked.

Alaric shook his head, feigning confusion. "No clue. I thought maybe you knew."

"It's got your name on it," the older man pointed out.

"Yeah, it's strange," Alaric replied. "I actually got a call three weeks ago from the MGM Grand out in Vegas. They said they found something like this with my name on it."

"Well, who's in this room?" the man asked, holding up the card.

"By that date? Roman Hill, actually."

There was a pause; they both recognized the name.

"Roman Hill?" Alaric's supervisor seemed surprised, but it was feasible considering Roman knew of Alaric's involvement in arranging tournaments.

"And the MGM confirmed Roman was staying with them when this turned up there."

That had his supervisor's attention hook, line, and sinker.

Taking a breath, Alaric added the final nail to Roman's coffin. "And a man was found in the room listed on that invitation, beaten badly."

"Jesus," the graying man murmured. "Did they question him? Was Roman behind it?"

Alaric shrugged. "I'm really not sure." His balancing act of providing just enough information without knowing the entire story produced the desired effect.

"That can't happen here," the man said. Alaric could imagine the PR nightmare for Borgata Hotel & Casino and knew it would be plenty motivating to spur the hotel into action.

Four and a Half Months Later

CHAPTER FORTY-SEVEN

♠

With Christmas around the corner, Sadie had suggested that she and Parker open their Hamptons house for a party. Most responses were immediate, but Laurel had taken some convincing. Since parting ways in Vegas, Laurel and Grayson hadn't visited one another. It had been a little over four months and the two existed on text messages and phone calls alone, the frequency of which had been dwindling. It was a mystery to Sadie; the two seemed crazy about one another, but something was keeping them apart. Distance was conquerable, so Sadie expected there were other reasons. Despite the awkwardness hanging between Grayson and Laurel, Sadie had eventually convinced her friend to put on a brave face and attend.

Meanwhile, Grayson was eager. Laurel hadn't visited him and his requests to fly up to see her had been denied. She said she was focusing on herself, that she was earning a lot, and that she was already looking at Manhattan apartments online. Grayson suspected she was scared; that physically being together again might sway her from her decision to go to New York. In all honesty he hoped that it would; he would try anything he could to have her join him in North Carolina. Laurel likely knew that, which was the problem.

Healed and back to his former glory, Grayson was itching for an opportunity to talk to Laurel face-to-face. When Parker had confirmed Laurel planned to attend his Christmas party, Grayson saw it as his final shot. He'd been close to showing up on her mother's doorstep but suspected it would only lead to a fight; Laurel wanted to be in control as to when she saw him again. Grayson could only hope that her decision to attend the holiday get-together was a sign that she was ready.

As an SUV rolled into the driveway, Parker jogged out to greet the trio. He watched Gemma easing herself from the passenger side and took her hand to help, marveling at how pregnant she appeared. "You sure you're okay to be traveling right now?" he teased.

Gemma gave a weak laugh. "I'm only twenty-four weeks."

Grayson emerged from the back, stretching overdramatically. "She only looks nine months pregnant."

Unamused, Gemma turned to glare at him. "If you weren't putting us up, I'd slap you for that."

"I've got it," Alaric assured, delivering a smack to Grayson upside the back of his head. He rounded him to get to Parker for a hug.

"This is new," Parker smirked, nodding towards Alaric's family vehicle.

Sadie waved from the doorway. "Hey, you three! Come on in where it's warm."

As Gemma handed over a bag of gifts and her coat, Sadie was quick to note the glint of the double bands she wore. "Married!" she exclaimed.

Laughing, Gemma nodded as if in defeat. "Surprise!"

"You bastard," Parker accused Alaric. "You gave me such shit when we eloped in Vegas."

"Yeah, well, we have two very good reasons," Alaric retorted, gesturing to Gemma's extended stomach.

"Thing One and Thing Two," Grayson agreed.

"Please stop calling them that," Gemma begged.

"And don't take it personally, Park," Grayson continued, "They didn't even let me go to the ceremony and we live together."

"What ceremony?" Alaric smirked. "We signed a piece of paper."

"And," Gemma added, "We're planning to have a celebration after we're moved into the house. And after the girls are born."

Mention of their house had Parker holding up a finger. He ducked from view, reemerging with a business card.

"What's this?" Alaric asked, accepting the ivory square.

Parker looped his arm around Sadie as he explained. "We called around your new neighborhood and found a custom home decor place."

Sadie finished excitedly, "They're going to furnish your nursery. Whatever you need."

"Our baby shower gift to you," Parker concluded.

Gemma's eyes watered, something that was becoming more and more frequent as the weeks passed. Alaric, too, felt choked up at the offer. "It's too much," he tried.

"Nonsense," Sadie assured. "This guy wanted to buy you two the whole house."

"You can buy me a house," Grayson interjected, shrugging out of his coat.

"You have a house," Sadie retorted.

After more hugs and appreciation, the four relocated to the kitchen to enjoy hors d'oeuvres.

"So, you're liking North Carolina?" Sadie ventured. "Grayson's not intolerable to live with?"

"We only want to kill him half the time," Alaric winked.

He and Gemma had started by visiting Grayson to research the area, surprised to find how much they'd liked it. Not only did North Carolina check off their must-haves, but it also had good school districts and a lifeline; Grayson. They'd looked at a dozen houses, found their starter home, and put in an offer.

The house needed a little work before they could move, so they'd accepted Grayson's offer to live with, and off of, him for a while. Alaric left his job, networking for other opportunities in the North Carolina area.

"He's been great," Gemma offered. His beachfront property only had one bedroom and Grayson had relocated to the couch without a word. She was thankful to him for how he went out of his way to make them feel welcome, but he wasn't perfect.

"When he's not commenting on how huge I am," Gemma amended.

"I don't do that," Grayson laughed, accepting a beer from Parker.

"You literally just did," Gemma pointed out, gesturing towards the front of the house.

Grayson tipped the neck of his bottle in her direction. "I stand corrected."

"Hello?"

Laurel's voice carried through the house as she stepped in from the cold. She was braced to see them all again, Grayson mostly. Part of her feared that this was the end for them. Although they'd never outright said that they were broken up, phone calls every other week were hardly enough. Laurel was scared to ask Grayson if he strayed because she knew it was a possibility; they hadn't been in the same place for almost five months. Plus, if he had been unfaithful, it would be even easier to end their failing relationship.

"Merry Christmas," Laurel continued, closing the door behind her.

Sadie came around the corner with a dazzling smile, encasing her friend in a tight hug. Laurel removed her heavy winter coat, eyes searching Sadie's. "Who's here?" she asked as casually as she could manage.

The small, sad smile she received confirmed her suspicions. Grayson had already arrived.

"Here," Laurel offered, passing a shopping bag over. "Just some sparkling wine."

Thanking her, Sadie took her hand and led her through the house. "Hey, everyone, look who's here."

Like magnets, Grayson and Laurel's attentions were drawn together the moment she came into view.

"So good to see you," Gemma greeted, waddling closer for a hug.

"Oh, wow," Laurel blurted, thankful for the distraction as her attention fell to

Gemma's round stomach. "You look amazing."

Gemma smiled, patting the thin sweater she wore, equally showing off her new rings.

"Did you guys…" Laurel trailed off, looking towards Alaric for confirmation about their marriage. It was strange to realize she'd missed him; she'd always butted heads with Alaric, but he'd been good to her. Before leaving his position, he'd recommended Laurel for a full-time job at one of the upscale restaurants in Borgata's, allowing her to keep working. It wouldn't be as high of a pay-off for short hours, but it was more than she would have made if she'd tried going back to Coastal Cafe.

Grayson was suddenly in front of her, and it took everything Laurel had not to let her emotions overwhelm her.

"Hey, Six."

The fact that he hesitated to touch her pulled at her heartstrings. "Hey," she greeted, nodding as she moved to hug him.

Behind them, their friends began to relocate. "Let me show you guys the tree," Sadie offered and soon the kitchen was empty save for Grayson and Laurel.

The hug was long, so much said with a simple touch.

"Merry Christmas," he finally offered, voice thick.

Laurel eased back, studying his face. He looked good, sun-kissed, and scruffy. Healed, with the faintest of scars across his cheek. "You, too."

"I miss you," Grayson said. He couldn't help but jump into attempts to patch up what they had. "Why don't I go back with you," he suggested, referring to Atlantic City. "I'm sure Al and Gem would like the privacy."

"Don't," Laurel requested quietly, putting a hand on Grayson's chest. It felt so good to touch him again. "Let's not talk about it now."

Tamping down his frustration, Grayson clasped her hand against him. They'd always done better in person than via long-distance and he wasn't going to pass up the opportunity to repair things. He intended to get their relationship back on track.

"It's been months," he reminded gently.

"I know," she sighed. "But I just got here."

Grayson had been hopeful. He'd imagined them running into each other's arms the moment they were reunited, laughing about their equal idiocy. He had expected things to fix themselves once they were together again.

"I just don't want to leave tomorrow and never see you again," he confessed his fear.

"I know," Laurel repeated, but she had nothing else to offer. She knew what Grayson wanted from her, and she still struggled to bend to his will.

It pained him to ask, but Grayson knew it was time. "Are we over?"

Laurel looked away, eyes stinging with the threat of tears. "I don't know."

"Look at me and tell me you don't love me, then," Grayson challenged. He hoped he wasn't gambling away their relationship by giving her an ultimatum.

"Tell me to move on. Because I can't do it otherwise, Laurel. I won't."

"Please," Laurel begged and wiped beneath her eye as he continued to clutch her hand between them. "Can't we talk about this later?" She looked aside, their friends' voices and laughter floating down the hall. She'd wanted to try and enjoy this visit, if possible.

Grayson felt mild relief that she hadn't confirmed the end of their relationship, but he wouldn't be satisfied without a response one way or the other. "Later," Grayson echoed.

Laurel nodded and leaned into his chest. She closed her eyes when his free arm encircled her, tangling his fingers in her blond hair.

"I love you," Grayson said earnestly. "Never stopped, never will."

"Sh," Laurel begged again.

Defeated, Grayson sighed. She couldn't avoid it forever, but if they only had one more day before Laurel popped the thin bubble that contained the remnants of their relationship, he was willing to hang onto a few more hours of hope.

♥ ♠ ♦ ♣

Later, as they settled around the table for dinner, Sadie turned to Grayson. "So, what's this about you helping with Alaric and Gemma's house?"

"Dormering the attic," Grayson confirmed, pouring himself and Laurel each a glass of wine. "I started doing some construction work for a friend. It turned into a part-time job."

"Do you miss poker?" Sadie wondered. She'd still been traveling on invitation, accepting opportunities that suited her and Parker's schedules.

"Not really," he replied honestly. "Even with Roman gone, my heart's just not in it."

Roman, as they had all learned, had been accused with much more than assault in the second degree. That charge had stuck, thankfully, but so had a dozen others the police had dug up. His assets had been seized and he'd received a five-year sentence.

Dinner conversation was mostly monopolized by the excitement in Gemma and Alaric's lives, but no one seemed to mind; the relocation and twins were big news. Gemma leaned closer to Alaric to whisper something in his ear, causing his smile to reappear.

"So, we've been thinking," Gemma announced, looking between Alaric and their friends. "About godparents."

Alaric nodded. "And while we sincerely doubt you guys will be prime examples, we agreed you'll spoil them." He looked between his best friends, brows lifting. "Parker? Grayson?"

Sadie could sense how much this meant to Parker. She slipped a hand onto his thigh, leaning over to coach playfully, "Say yes, baby."

"Yeah," Parker laughed, a little overwhelmed. "Yeah, of course."

"I get the firstborn," Grayson declared, winking in Gemma's direction. "Thank you."

Post-dinner, the group gathered in the living room for drinks and gifts. Sadie eagerly pulled Parker up to stand in front of their friends, nudging him expectantly.

"I guess I'm giving a speech," he muttered, kissing Sadie's temple. "Thank you all for coming," he told them. "I hope we can keep up with the tradition."

"Hear, hear," Grayson toasted.

"No, I'm not—" Parker sighed, shaking his head. "That wasn't the speech, Gray."

"My deepest apologies," Grayson replied and moved his hand in a flourish to return the floor to their host.

"Right. Well, Sadie and I have something to share," he explained, squeezing his wife against his side. "We've been thinking about our future." He gave her a dazzling smile, pure joy radiating between them. It had been surprisingly easy to agree and engaging with an agency had cemented their decision.

"We're adopting," Sadie announced. Among the gasps and mutters of disbelief, Parker took a deep breath to keep the waterworks at bay.

While they shared details, Gemma and Alaric passed around a few small gifts including copies of their birth announcement and new address cards.

"Hang on," Alaric said, reaching into the bottom of the bag they'd brought. As he pulled out an envelope with Laurel's name on it, he saw it was stuck to a small velvet box. Assuming it was meant to be given along with their other gifts, he dropped it into Laurel's palm. "Merry Christmas."

"Thank you," she replied, surprised. She popped the lid where she sat on the couch, going rigid as she revealed its contents.

Within the satin cushion was a white gold, diamond solitaire ring.

Laurel looked up quickly to find Gemma and Alaric caught up in conversation with Sadie. Laurel's eyes slid to Grayson where he leaned against the piano. Rising certainty doubled the pain in her chest. This was from Grayson, but he clearly hadn't seen that the box had been given to her. Breathing hard, she watched as Grayson's eyes found hers across the room.

Grayson showed a moment of concern over her expression, about to speak. Before he could utter a word, however, his eyes dropped to the jewelry box in her hand. He quickly pushed up, nearly dropping his beer in the process.

"Whoa," Parker said, grabbing it. "Drunk already, Lee?"

Laurel was already moving, running from the room. She left the ring on the couch, making a beeline for the back door. She couldn't believe that this was happening. Did Grayson honestly think the answer to their failing relationship was a proposal? Did he think that if they were engaged, it would be easier for her to give up her dreams?

Grayson was fast on her heels, calling, "Six, *wait.*"

Light snow blanketed the yard and Laurel was glad for the frosty temperature. She felt overheated, a mix between disbelief and anger on her face as she whipped around to find him following.

"What was that?" she accused.

"I'm not losing you," he said simply. He wouldn't apologize for loving her, but he recognized the timing hadn't been great. "I want to be with you. I love you."

"I don't want to get married!" she shouted. "How could you think I'd marry you?" she pressed, pushing aside the guilt she felt as his expression turned pained.

"We're good together!" he yelled back, pushing through the hurt he felt from her words.

"Tell that to the past five months," she argued.

Grayson sighed in frustration. "I should have gotten on a plane, is that what you're telling me? I should have ignored you and just showed up? Because I wanted to, Laurel. God help me, I wanted to, but you were very fucking clear."

Laurel sobbed and brought her hands up to cover her face. She didn't feel that she deserved all the blame; Grayson was painting a skewed picture.

"I'm sorry," Grayson said, approaching with caution. "I just don't know what to do. I can't lose you."

"So you propose?!" she exploded, turning her attention to him in disbelief.

"I didn't—" Grayson attempted, quickly biting his tongue. Technically, he hadn't proposed. He'd put the ring in the bag of things going to Parker's house. How was he supposed to know his temporary house guests would literally propose on his behalf?

"You were obviously planning to," she argued. "You bought a ring."

"I bought that ring the last time we were here," he countered honestly.

Laurel quieted at his confession. She hadn't considered that he'd been thinking about marriage before they'd even separated in Las Vegas.

Grayson paced in a wide circle, centering himself. If he had any hope of fixing things between them, he had to keep a clear head. "It was just something I was thinking about," he muttered.

Laurel crossed her arms and stared off towards the beach in contemplative silence.

"Are you cold? Do you want to go inside?" he offered.

"I think I should leave," Laurel confessed in a quiet voice. She couldn't imagine staying the night, even if she and Grayson had separate rooms.

"You can't," Grayson argued, pained. "Please, Laurel. *Talk to me.*"

Shivering from more than just the cold, Laurel turned her back to him to hide her tears.

"Laurel," he pressed, but he was met with silence.

Gritting his teeth, Grayson struggled to turn her to face him. The sight of her tears crushed him, but he held onto her wrist tightly. "Please—"

"Ow," Laurel hissed, pulling back her wrist.

Grayson's lips parted, quickly mumbling an apology. "I didn't mean—" He broke off, brows dipping. He'd felt something sharp beneath her sweater, against her pulse point. A glint of metal caught his attention. Suspicion raised, he reached for her sleeve.

Slowly, he drew back the wool to confirm that she wore the charm bracelet he'd gotten her on their trip to New York. Affection swelled and he lifted his attention to her face, hopeful. If he was looking for a sign to confirm her feelings for him, and a prompt from the universe on what to do next, he had it.

"I'll move to New York," he buckled. "I'll move to Atlantic City until you can move to New York."

Crying harder now, Laurel tried to slip from his hold. She tipped her head down, her hair falling forward.

"I'm moving," Grayson insisted seriously. "I should have moved the moment I was better." Brushing his thumbs across her cheeks, Grayson tipped his forehead to rest against Laurel's. "Just say okay," he pleaded.

Unfortunately, Laurel was still shaking her head. "I can't ask you to do that," she whispered, voice broken on a sob.

"You're not asking me," Grayson assured, his lips pulling up into a small smile. "I'm offering."

He struggled to understand her hesitation. Even now, when he was telling her he would do what she wanted and go where she wanted, she seemed to be unable to accept. With sinking dread, he breathed, "What aren't you telling me?"

Laurel lifted her stare to his dark brown eyes, a moment of sympathy crossing her face. She knew what he was asking, and she never wanted him to question her loyalty. "There's no one else, Grayson," she assured.

Relief washed through him, and Grayson pulled her into his body at last, embracing her with all the words he hadn't said over the past few months.

"I'll leave with you tomorrow," he decided, hoping he was getting through to her. He didn't want to separate, not even for a few days. He feared leaving her again and knew their relationship wouldn't survive if they found themselves in this place again.

"I'll think about it," Laurel told him, kissing his jaw. It was the best she could do.

Although it didn't fix everything, Grayson was content with his decision. He would follow Laurel back to Atlantic City the following day and woo her anew if necessary.

♥ ♠ ♦ ♣

The overnight party had been a lot to ask of his friends and Parker was appreciative that everyone had made the time. It had been worth it to share their exciting adoption news face-to-face, hear Gemma and Alaric's latest updates, and see Grayson and Laurel in each other's arms by the end of the night. On some level, they'd all needed the trip.

Breakfast the following morning had been a happy occasion, and the group spoke more about the exciting waiting game of adoption.

"It could take a year or two," Parker offered, tempering their expectations. "But we'll be ready."

"Sorry to make you do all that driving," Sadie told Gemma, giving her stomach an affectionate pat. Sadie knew she would never experience the miracle of childbirth herself, but she was finding happiness in the fact that she would be a mother regardless.

"It was good practice," Alaric replied. "I'm sure screaming kids aren't half as bad as Gray was on the drive up."

As Gemma and Alaric packed up and pulled away from the Hamptons house, Laurel made no protest over the fact that Grayson was left behind; she'd accepted that he intended to follow her back to Atlantic City.

As their rideshare pulled away, carrying them to the Long Island Railroad, Parker gave a long wave.

"You think they'll make it?" he asked of Sadie.

"Oh, yeah," Sadie assured. "She's been head over heels for Mr. Charming since they met."

At the station, Grayson held Laurel against him as they waited on their train. "Would you mind if we stopped off in the city?"

"What for?" she asked.

"My sister," Grayson admitted. "I think I should talk to her."

Surprised at his sudden interest in talking with his family, Laurel nodded. "Sure, we can do that."

Grayson nodded his thanks.

"There's just some stuff I've wanted to say to her for a long time."

Grayson had had a lot of time for reflection by himself on the beach before Alaric and Gemma had moved in. A regular part-time job and typical household chores had given him a lot to think about.

To warm herself, Laurel slipped her hands into Grayson's coat pockets. Her nose wrinkled at the feel of a familiar folded paper. "Do you have a Chinese food menu in your pocket?" she accused, not putting it past him.

Chuckling, Grayson's hand joined hers to check. His smile slipped a little and Laurel caught it.

"What is it?" she asked, starting to pull the menu free.

"No, don't," he attempted, but that only piqued her curiosity further. She turned her back on him and studied what she now held. It wasn't a menu, but a brochure.

"Asheville Recovery," she read quietly, swallowing a lump in her throat. "In-patient alcohol addiction treatment."

"It was just an idea," Grayson said gently, rounding to step in front of her again. "I didn't want to overstep."

Tears sprouted quickly and Laurel reached up to cover her mouth as a choked sob worked past her lips. The anxiety she'd felt over the past few months crashed into her. The thoughtfulness behind Grayson's actions as well as the reality of her mother's condition had Laurel unable to speak.

Grayson eased his arms around her, hating that he'd been the cause of her emotional distress.

"Laurel," he breathed. "I'm so sorry." He moved his hand in circles against her back, tucking his face into her hair.

Laurel had clearly needed the release that only a good cry could offer. She'd held it in for so long, tamping down her depression associated with Grayson's absence, pushing through her day-to-day responsibilities, and praying her mom had a good day every day. She knew it was no way to live and she wanted to hope that bringing Grayson back with her would make a difference, but she knew there was no changing things for her mother. Not in Atlantic City.

Laurel clutched the rehab pamphlet and took a few slow breaths. She knew she needed a fresh start, but maybe she was overselling New York to herself as the cure. Maybe with Grayson's support and a spark of hope for her mother's future she could be happy.

"I can ask," Laurel offered, swallowing hard. She wiped her face on her jacket, eyeing the happy faces of staff members staring up at her from the page. "I can't make her," Laurel said finally. "But I'll ask."

Grayson didn't want to get ahead of himself, but he had to clarify. "Rehab in general, or rehab in Asheville?"

Managing a watery smile, Laurel held up the brochure. "Let's go to North Carolina."

EPILOGUE

PARKER & SADIE

High above the busy streets of New York, Parker and Sadie set the table for four. Parker's parents were expected in an hour for their monthly dinner. Sadie selected the wine, the only job Parker had entrusted to his wife, while he handled the rest. Considering her attention was elsewhere, that suited Sadie just fine. She lingered nearby, scrolling properties recently sent by their agent.

"What about this one?" she suggested, holding out her phone. "Close enough to the water and about an hour drive to Alaric and Gemma."

Parker lifted the spoon he was using to stir a remoulade, see-sawing it in midair. "An hour seems far."

Sadie rolled her eyes. It seemed the distance was going to be the hill he died on, meanwhile Sadie had her own dealbreaker. "We can't move the ocean," she reminded. "So, unless they move, we can't do much better."

"Okay, okay," Parker acquiesced, gesturing. "Show me."

Swiping through the listing, Sadie talked him through the property details. Thirty-eight hundred square feet, six bedrooms, four bathrooms, and an outdoor entertainment space. "They'll come to us, anyway," she insisted. "We'll have the beach. And Grayson and Laurel are only thirty minutes away."

"I thought we said a *modest* condo," Parker laughed, turning his back on her. "That's as big as our Santa Monica place."

"And we love our Santa Monica place," Sadie replied easily. "You said you wanted a place that would fit everyone. That means six bedrooms."

He supposed he couldn't fault her for the math. They'd need a room for themselves, for Laurel and Grayson, for Alaric and Gemma, and for the twins. Plus, they were still waiting, both hopefully and patiently, for news of an opportunity to adopt. They'd been approved, but it was a torturous waiting game. The hope was that one of those six bedrooms would be for their own child, eventually.

"It's too far, doll," Parker concluded. "I'm sorry. And sure, I'd like everyone to come over often, but we don't need all those bedrooms if everyone lives nearby."

Sadie groaned. "But we wanted to be on the water…"

"We have the Atlantic in the Hamptons and the Pacific in Santa Monica," he reminded her. "The new place is so we can be closer to our friends."

Saying nothing, Sadie pursed her lips. He wasn't wrong.

"Let's try for twenty minutes from Al," Parker requested. "And then we only need a couple of bedrooms."

Resigned, she agreed.

As Sadie sent off a text to their agent to adjust the boundaries of their search, the phone began to ring in her hand. It surprised her at first, mostly because of the rare ringtone.

At the stove, Parker froze. Only the adoption agency was assigned that specific ringer, and it was very rare they received a direct call unless it was good or bad news. They never quite knew what to expect, but there was the expectation that one day that tune would bring them a family member.

Reaching for his arm, Sadie clutched Parker as she put the call on speaker. "Yes, hi, Manny?"

"Hi, Sadie, are you and Parker currently close to Stamford, Connecticut?"

Sadie's eyes shined with the threat of tears, nodding quickly.

"We are," Parker replied, peeling the phone out of Sadie's shaking hand. "I'm here too, Manny." He couldn't keep the hope from his voice as he asked, "Is this it?"

"This is it, Campbells," the answer was firm, and at ease. "Biological parents have terminated their parental rights and a baby boy needs a home."

Sinking to the floor, Sadie covered her mouth as the tears started. It was as if a dam had broken and a cascade of emotions poured through, rendering her mute. Overcome with joy and relief, Sadie was absently aware of Parker thanking their agent again and again, lowering himself to kneel in front of her.

"Sadie," Parker mumbled, gathering her into his arms. He hugged her tight, breathing her in. "This is it, baby. This is it."

A burst of a laugh left Sadie as she wiped at her face. She was elated, but also concerned for the thin trail of smoke in the air. "Dinner's burning."

Parker echoed her cheerful laughter as he smelled the truth behind her words. "I'll turn everything off and call my parents," he assured, pulling them to their feet. "We have to go."

"He's waiting for us," Sadie whispered in disbelief.

"Let's go be parents," Parker whispered in return.

Alaric & Gemma

With two six-month-old twin girls, Alaric and Gemma were getting the hang of constant feedings and diaper changes with little to no sleep. Alaric learned early on that once one of his precious angels got to crying, the other wasn't far behind. These days, it was the most predictable thing in his life. As a sharp wail roused him through a crackling monitor, Alaric rolled off the bed and stumbled over a pillow.

In the adjoining nursery, Alaric automatically went to the left of two identical cribs. His hands curled under the small body of Alexandra, who was notorious for being the fussier of the two. Unfortunately, he realized the baby now waking in his hands was not the instigator. Behind him, Tristan blared on. Now, thanks to his sleep-deprived mistake, he had two crying infants.

With a sigh of defeat, Alaric hefted Alex in her footed onesie. "Sorry, sweetheart," he whispered, kissing her soft downy hair. He set her on his shoulder and scooped up a kicking Tristan next, resting her in a mirrored position to her sister.

"Sh... Sh, girls..."

The chorus of cries roused Gemma. She contemplated the likelihood of them being nursing cries and shuffled across the hall with a wide yawn. She paused silently in the nursery doorway, spotting Alaric swaying gently on his feet between the cribs, his back to her. Matching pale cheeks were resting on his inked shoulders, making her heart squeeze. She watched in silence, amused with how he butchered a well-known lullaby.

"Hush little princesses, don't say a word. Daddy's gonna buy you whatever you want. And if that shit doesn't make you happy, daddy's gonna try something diff-er-ent."

Seeing Alaric coddling their two tiny surprises often rocked Gemma to her core. He'd made the entire process of marriage, moving, and motherhood as smooth as possible. At every turn he seemed to pull a five-step plan out of thin air. Alaric had literally operationalized their life, for a time, until they'd equally agreed they'd gotten through the hardest parts of it all. Every day presented challenges, but nothing was as scary as it had been that day at the hospital when Gemma found out she was six weeks pregnant. Except, perhaps, the day they'd told her parents. George Blake had looked as if he might actually murder the father of her children. Thankfully, in time, Alaric had won them over.

Gemma crossed to him, sliding fingers up his bare back to tangle in the hair at the nape of his neck.

"I have never found you sexier," she whispered.

Alaric turned with a sleepy smirk. In a low groggy voice, he muttered, "I think I'm offended."

Gemma smiled and reached out to place a knuckle at Tristan's lips to see if she'd latch. "She might go back down," she concluded.

On his other shoulder, Gemma found Alex's eyes were open. "Not so lucky over here," she sighed.

"Then you take Alexandra The Great," he muttered, passing off one daughter. "And I'll try to put Tristan The Magician back down."

Alaric eased his younger daughter by three minutes back to bed. Turning to Gemma with a victorious smile, he winked. To Alex, he asked, "Are you going to let daddy go back to sleep anytime soon, button?"

Alex gazed at him with wide eyes and kicked her legs, cheeks bunching in a smile, and she gurgled in response.

Groaning in defeat at how alert she seemed, Alaric asked his wife, "Any chance I'll still be sexy in about twenty to twenty-five minutes?"

Gemma handed Alexandra back, giving Alaric a light pat on the back. "I think you've got a good ten minutes at best," she confessed, heading back to bed.

Grayson & Laurel

It didn't take Laurel long to adjust to a simpler, more relaxed lifestyle. She had a reliable job as a manager at a nice local restaurant, her own dependable car, and no financial struggles. That last part was thanks to Grayson, who now made his living as a contractor. His foreman friend continued to make use of him, and Grayson found he liked the predictability and the ability to use his hands day in and day out. He and Laurel earned a respectable income and enjoyed the quaintness of his beachfront condo.

It was still strange to refer to North Carolina, and Grayson's place in particular, as home, but Laurel was settling in. Her mother was nearby, doing well in a private rehabilitation center. It hadn't taken much convincing; just one heart-to-heart conversation. Having agreed to start over, the opportunity to get her mother some help had been a welcome one.

Staying true to his word, Grayson had taken Laurel to New York twice already, and they had another trip planned for Christmas. He was careful to make her feel as though she hadn't sacrificed her dream to be with him and reassured her that they could make changes anytime she felt the need. However, Laurel found herself surprisingly satisfied with life as of late. Gemma, Alaric, and their twin girls were driving distance away and Sadie and Parker were closing on a house near to them. Half a year ago she never would have thought she'd be glad to be neighbors with Alaric, but he'd turned into a good friend.

Laurel pulled up her text thread from earlier that morning to see where Grayson had said he'd be working that day. When she wasn't on the clock, she'd taken to packing a lunch and stopping by his work sites. It gave her the ability to explore local areas and he seemed to sincerely appreciate her visits.

Tucking a pencil between his teeth, Grayson measured the one-by-fours he was sizing for trim. He was halfway through the bunch with his circular saw when he caught sight of Laurel pulling up along the curb behind his motorcycle.

As she approached, she heard classic rock coming from his workbench. Grayson whirled with a smile and pushed his safety glasses up into his hair, littered with wood shavings.

"This is a good look for you," she teased, stepping closer for a kiss.

"You know what a good look on you is," he began to retort, but Laurel was quick to roll her eyes.

"Don't say naked, Grayson," she muttered, but her glare was playful. She pushed the lunch into his hands, surveying the otherwise vacant garage and yard. "Just you today?"

Peeking into the bag, Grayson made an accomplished sound at the sight of leftover Chinese. "Just me. Want to take a look?" He led her over towards the interior garage door, sweeping his arm aside in a flourish. "M'lady."

The house was further along than Laurel was used to seeing at Grayson's job sites. The walls were being patched and painted, crown molding about halfway around the rooms she could see from the kitchen. "Nice place," she commented, running a hand along the marble countertop. "I love these sorts of open concept kitchens."

"I know," Grayson smiled, setting the paper bag on the countertop.

Laurel wandered over to the french doors at the rear of the house, taking in the yard. "Is that a hot tub?" she laughed.

"What do you have against hot tubs?" he accused, coming up behind her.

"The upkeep," she laughed, holding his arms as they went around her middle.

"Well…" Grayson began, swaying with her a little. "What if I promised to handle that part?"

Laurel leaned aside, eyeing him over her shoulder. "You want a hot tub? Since when?"

A smile pulled at the corner of his mouth. "Since it came with the house."

Laurel just kept looking at him, brow furrowing. "I'm not following."

"Jesus, Six," he laughed. "I'm trying to figure out if you're gonna kill me. I put an offer on the place."

A stretch of silence followed.

"Are you messing with me right now?" Laurel asked, her tone full of skepticism. Grayson was known to have an odd sense of humor at times.

She figured they'd talk about moving eventually, but she'd never expected Grayson to do something as sudden as put an offer on a house. It had come up before that they needed more space, and there were a few other towns more inland that they enjoyed, but Laurel hadn't expected those passing remarks to result in any concrete changes.

"Six?" He sounded worried. "If you don't start showing some excitement in about five seconds, I'm going to call the bank and forfeit my deposit."

"No!" Laurel shouted, her voice echoing in the empty house. A laugh bubbled out of her as she turned to face him, gripping his upper arms. "How did you do this without me knowing?"

Grayson was relieved at her reaction, but still guarded. "We were fixing the place to sell, and the buyer backed out. I saw an opportunity…"

"Oh, my God," she breathed, turning away to look around more closely. She pulled out of his hold, quickly moving down the hallway to inspect the rooms.

"Is that a good 'oh, my God?'" Grayson asked, trailing after her.

She called back from the first-floor bathroom, "Are you kidding me?"

Grayson winced, no closer to determining her mood. "I'm still debating if you're about to kill me," he confessed.

Laurel leaned out of the tiled bathroom, her wide smile making his dread dissipate. "Show me our bedroom."

"Now, that's what I'm talking about," he laughed, stepping forward to grab her around the middle and lift her from the floor. "No bed yet, but there's four fantastic walls to fuck against."

Wrapping her legs around him, Laurel echoed his laughter as they climbed the stairs.

♥ ♠ ♦ ♣

A few months into occupying their new home, Grayson had started his latest project: a treehouse for the twins. Alaric and Gemma were only ten minutes away and visited often. They weren't yet at tree-climbing age, but Grayson was determined. He entered the house through the back, his work clothes worn and splattered with paint. "Hey, hot stuff."

"Hey," Laurel replied, looking up from the mail she was sorting. "Gemma asked if we could take the girls this Friday."

Grayson nodded and stepped over to the sink to pour himself a glass of water and drain it steadily. With a heavy exhale, he turned and leaned against the counter. "Fine with me."

Laurel reached for her phone. "I figured as much. I'll let her know."

As she typed out a message, Grayson paused for a long minute. As if deciding something, he rapped his knuckles against the counter and pushed away. He crossed to the cookie jar, one that had been decorated and glazed with the twin girls' handprints.

When he returned to Laurel's side, Grayson slid into the adjacent chair. In silence, he set a ring box on the placemat in front of her. Then, he leaned back comfortably and bit into an oatmeal raisin cookie.

Laurel looked up from her phone, lips parting. It had been almost a year since she'd last seen that box. She'd never forgotten about it, but they'd also never discussed it. What they had was good, and it was working, and she hadn't wanted to overcomplicate things.

"Um," she offered, nervously laughing as her eyes shifted from the box to his face. "Gemma says thanks…"

Grayson nodded again, his grin growing as she read off the text reply. "I don't have anything else going on," he added regarding Friday's new plan.

Laurel's heart raced the longer they sat at the table, neither of them verbally acknowledging the ring box.

Leaning forward, Grayson reached for her phone and set it aside. He took her hand and pulled her from her seat, lowering her to sit across his lap.

"Are you about to do something stupid?" she accused; voice quiet. If anything other than that diamond ring occupied the box she'd never forgive him.

"Definitely," he confirmed, sliding the box closer. "Want to do it together?"

Laurel's blue eyes drifted back to the box, watching as he thumbed the corner of the lid. As the box opened and the ring sat staring back at them, Laurel felt all breath leave her.

"You're serious," she whispered.

"If you're ready," he agreed, giving her the space to ask for more time. He'd tried this once before and it hadn't been for the right reasons. This time felt appropriate, but he'd never force her.

Laurel nodded, cupping his face in her hands. "I'm ready," she assured, kissing him gently. Genuinely, she acknowledged, "I want to marry you."

Relief he hadn't known he'd been waiting to feel crashed into him. Grayson tightened his hold on her, the corners of his eyes dampening.

As the jewelry slid into place on Laurel's finger, she regarded it at length. Only after a few moments did she suddenly speak, laughing. "I'm going to have the stupidest name on the planet."

"Laurel Lee," Grayson voiced, laughing with sympathy. "You're right, that's awful."

"I could make you Grayson Price," she countered.

Grayson let out a disappointed groan. "Damn! That would have been a great gambler name," he admitted. "When people lost, I would have said 'It's time to pay the Price.'"

Laurel's face slowly fell until she sat glaring, as if disgusted with his sense of humor.

"Forget it," she declared, rising. "I changed my mind."

Grayson swiped for her, and she lunged away, the pair breaking out into laughter as he chased her through their house.

♥

About the Authors

Frederika Bradford and CL Marie have spent over fifteen years dreaming up a cast of characters and larger than life love stories. *Max Bet* was originally conceived and written by Frederika Bradford and CL Marie in 2014, edited in 2022 for publication by Frederika Bradford.

"Thank you for giving us an opportunity to share Grayson, Parker, and Alaric with you. We hope this trio has found a place in your hearts, as they have in ours. Please consider giving our work a review on your reading platform or online bookshelf of choice."

- Frederika Bradford & CL Marie

Connect with the authors and sign up for publication updates at www.frederikabradford.com.

Printed in the USA
CPSIA information can be obtained
at www.ICGtesting.com
LVHW040338100124
768594LV00037B/919

9 798985 933109